THE LAST VICTIM

The Last Victim

A Novel

Elaine Bossik

Portable Shopper, LLC

PORTABLE SHOPPER, LLC

Portable Shopper, LLC
Hypoluxo, Florida
www.scriptologist.com

Book cover painting by Eric Bossik
Book design by Glenn Bossik
Author photograph by Eric Bossik

ISBN 978-0-9842419-0-3
Library of Congress Control Number: 2009909883

Printed in the United States of America

For
Ray, Eric and Glenn,
my extraordinary husband and sons, who have always believed in me

Acknowledgments

Thank you to my husband, Ray, who read many drafts of this novel with the keen eye of an editor and never tired of it. Gratitude to my sons, Eric and Glenn, who made me believe this was possible, and whose exceptional talents helped to make it happen. Many thanks to the early readers of this book—Lee Newberg, Naomi Epstein, Eileen Herman, Aaron Herman and Arlene Hussey. Special thanks to Naomi Epstein for going the extra mile for me. I am indebted to those who inspired this novel—my mother and father, Pauline and Michael Hutt, my sister, Lee Newberg, and my brother, Arthur Hutt.

"While our eyes wait to see
the destined final day,
we must call no one happy
who is of mortal race,
until he hath crossed life's border,
free from pain."

—*SOPHOCLES*
Oedipus The King

Chapter 1

Blue, green and yellow lights hung precariously on wires strung over the doorways of the shops and across the tops of the pushcarts, transforming the otherwise drab Brooklyn marketplace into a mock carnival. Tonight was unusual. The marketplace was open late. By sundown tomorrow it would be Rosh Hashanah, the Jewish New Year, and the market would be empty and silent. The excitement of the coming holiday permeated the cool autumn evening as women hurried about pushing shopping carts, tugging heavy bags and pulling unruly children.

Makeshift wooden tables set up outside the shops were piled high with second-hand clothing. Peddlers shouted against the din, "Men's suits, slightly used! Like new! Two for five dollars!"

"Apples for the New Year, fresh from the trees! Five pounds for a dime!"

Sophie Rothman stopped at Hershel's pushcart to buy apples. She seemed like a large woman, yet she was only five feet one. She was broad, almost shapeless, except for her huge breasts, which strained against the buttons on her blouse. Sophie would complain about the burden of such large breasts, but she knew they were her greatest asset. She had brought three babies into the world and they never went hungry. And weren't her breasts what attracted her husband? She knew it was not her face. It was a plain face, not homely, but certainly not beautiful. She had an aristocratic nose and dark wavy hair that she wore short because she could never manage it. Life was too busy and hard for Sophie to waste time fussing over her hair.

Sophie fingered the apples in her chapped reddened hands. Jeanie stood close to her mother, her feet tapping restlessly as her mother selected apples. Though she was only five, she sensed the excitement vibrating through the marketplace.

Resting her heavy shopping bags on the sidewalk, Sophie examined an apple closely. "The apples have brown spots," she told the peddler. "I'll take six pounds for a dime."

"It's five pounds for a dime," Hershel insisted. "The apples are perfect."

"I'll give you ten cents for six pounds, or I'll go up the block to Moshe's." Sophie drove a hard bargain and usually won.

Hershel stuffed apples into a brown paper bag and placed the bag on a dented metal scale that hung from the top of the pushcart.

"Take out the paper wrappings," Sophie ordered. "I'm only paying for apples."

Hershel pulled several tissue wrappings out of the bag. "My children go hungry because of you," he complained.

"With all these apples, how could they starve?"

Sophie placed a coin in Hershel's callused hand and stuffed the bag of apples into her bulging shopping bag. Then she took the discarded tissue wrappings and tucked them in next to the apples. She would use the tissues for toilet paper. Sophie let nothing go to waste, especially now with the war dragging on. It was 1943 and there were shortages of everything. You never knew from one day to the next what would be scarce.

A cart with freshly made jelly apples glowed deliciously under the red light, catching Jeanie's eyes. "Momma, can I have a jelly apple?" She tugged Sophie's skirt.

"No," Sophie snapped. "It's bad for your teeth."

They walked on, passing the knish peddler who stood over his dented metal cart where knishes warmed inside. "Momma, can I have a knish?" The inviting smell of warm dough and potatoes made Jeanie's mouth water.

"No, you just ate dinner."

"But I'm still hungry."

Sophie ignored her daughter, hurrying to the pickle store, which was crowded with shoppers. The pungent smell of vinegar and freshly souring pickles mingled with the smell of knishes, sweet jelly apples and fresh oranges from the fruit stands. Huge barrels filled with vinegar, spices and pickles were lined up like obedient soldiers outside the store. Sophie put down her heavy shopping bags and reached for a wax paper bag and the pickle tongs. She sniffed out each barrel like a bloodhound stalking its prey. After selecting two choice pickles, Sophie paid the merchant and moved on, with Jeanie trailing close behind.

The sweet smell of freshly baked rolls and challah breads drifted into the street through the half-opened doorway of the tiny bakery. Sophie walked in to buy a fresh challah for the New Year. Trays of charlotte russes lined the case next to the challahs. Jeanie pressed her face against the glass. She could almost taste the soft mounds of whipped cream piled high on top of the delicate little cakes. She marveled at how each was wrapped so neatly in its own little white cardboard frame. Jeanie hardly ever got to have one. When she did, she slowly licked the sweet whipped cream off, letting it linger in her mouth and then finally nibbled the soft white spongy cake at the bottom. "Momma, can I have a charlotte russe?" Jeanie's small voice begged, her eyes pleaded.

"They're only five cents today for the holiday," said Mrs. Gerber, the baker's wife. "Buy one for the *shane maidel*, the sweet girl," she coaxed.

"I only came in for a challah," Sophie said sharply.

The baker's wife had four sons and longed for a daughter to pamper. "If I had such a *shane maidel*, a charlotte russe would be in her mouth every day," she said.

"She can live without it." Sophie picked up her bread and departed hastily from the bakery, dragging Jeanie from the case window.

"Momma, can't I have just one? I won't ask you for anything else ever again."

"No! And if you nag me again, this will be the last time I take you with me when I go shopping."

Jeanie trailed behind Sophie, her head down, hoping to find some lost pennies in the cracks on the sidewalk. They plodded slowly along the crowded streets. A sudden shrill scream pierced the air, falling like a shroud over the marketplace. All eyes sought out the source of such agony. Reva stood near the narrow doorway of the apartment building where she lived above a sweater shop. She pressed her three-month-old infant against her heaving breasts, her face twisted with grief. Animal cries choked out of her throat. "She's dead! She's dead! My baby's dead!" An empty carriage rocked beside her.

"Call an ambulance!" a peddler shouted.

Two women ran to comfort Reva, who held tighter to her dead baby.

Sophie set her shopping bags down on the sidewalk, her arms suddenly devoid of their former strength. Her breasts rose and fell under her tight blouse as her breath caught in short gasps. Her face paled as she asked a nearby peddler, "What happened?"

"Who knows?" he answered. "She was rocking the baby… One minute she was alive and the next minute she was dead."

Jeanie tugged Sophie's skirt. "Why's the baby dead, Momma?"

"God only knows." A distant frightened look clouded Sophie's face. Then she took Jeanie's small hand in hers and led her back to Gerber's bakery. "I'll take a charlotte russe for my *shane maidel*," she told the baker's wife, as she handed her the last five pennies in her purse.

Chapter 2

Jeanie and Sophie entered the three-story tenement building where they lived. The large building loomed above the stores in the heart of the busy street. Gray and unfriendly, it stood squashed between a dry goods store and a produce market. Sophie pushed open the heavy iron door that led to a long narrow hallway. It was lit by a bare light bulb that hung from the ceiling, casting tomb-like shadows on the walls.

Jeanie's heart quickened, as it always did, when she walked through the hallway, which held some unspeakable fear for her. It haunted her dreams long after she had grown up and left the place. There was a particularly dark cavernous spot beneath the first stairwell that led to a doorway and a dirty yard that terrified her. It was here, she feared, where a bogeyman with overpowering strength would one day grab her.

Sophie and Jeanie climbed the three flights of stairs to their third floor apartment, stopping at each landing so Sophie could put down her heavy bags and rest. Breathless and pale, Sophie brushed away beads of perspiration on her upper lip. Still shaken by the death of Reva's baby, she couldn't drive the scene from her mind. The screams still echoed in her ears. She would have to inform her relatives if they hadn't already learned of the tragedy. Bad news had a way of traveling with lightning speed. She would get the children to bed and then go down to the floor below where her younger sister, Ida, lived with her family. Then she would have to go upstairs where her brothers, Isaac and Leon, lived with their wives and children. Cousins, aunts and uncles occupied many of the other apartments in the building.

Though Sophie shared ownership of the building with Ida and her brothers, she didn't feel much like a landlord. Landlords were supposed to be rich. She hadn't seen a nickel from her inheritance yet and she probably wouldn't unless the property was sold. The meager rents that the tenants paid barely covered maintenance of the building. Then she had to listen to complaints from tenants, like Mr. Seline, who stopped her in the hallway every day. "Sophie, what's the matter? You can't give hot water? A cold bath I have to take all the time," he'd complain.

Sophie could hear Mitzi whining and scratching on the door as she fumbled with the key. She opened the heavy door and the puppy licked her legs affectionately and ran around in wild excited joy at seeing her again. Sophie was glad she had taken the puppy from a neighbor's litter. With Harry away in Newfoundland on a government job for the past three years, a woman alone with three children needed some protection. Mitzi would grow into a good watchdog, and the children had begged to keep her.

Jeanie ran through the five rooms of the apartment chasing the puppy. Mitzi jumped from the beds to the floor, to the kitchen table, and finally overturned a vase that stood on a mahogany hand-me-down table in the living room. Jeanie giggled with glee until the vase clattered to the floor. She quickly retrieved it, anticipating Sophie's anger. "It's not broken, Momma," she called out, hiding a large chip and carefully replacing the vase on the table.

"If you make the dog wild, I'll get rid of her," Sophie warned. If it wasn't Jeanie, it was Ruthie or Albert who over-excited the puppy. But the truth was that Sophie had grown attached to Mitzi, whose warm affection and blind devotion to her were very appealing. Unlike people, the dog demanded only Sophie's occasional attention, some food and a warm place to live.

Jeanie loved Mitzi. She stroked her black silky hair now and hugged her a little too hard, sending the puppy under the bed, yelping in pain. "I'm sorry, Mitzi," Jeanie apologized, trying to coax the puppy out from under Albert's bed. But Mitzi only whimpered, refusing to come out.

Sophie unpacked her purchases now, wondering how she would get all the holiday preparations completed by sundown tomorrow. All the golden honey cakes and Harry's favorite—apple cake fragrant with cinnamon—she would bake again. But for the third year, Harry would not be here to enjoy the holiday with them. She smiled, remembering how Harry would sit at the kitchen table eating one helping after another of her apple cake. "This is *some* apple cake," he'd praise between mouthfuls. "Sophie, I don't know how you do it." He'd smile, his even white teeth gleaming.

Sophie missed Harry's smile, his strong arms around her and his presence, which always made her feel safe. She knew it was her own anger that had driven him away, but why did he have to go so far? Newfoundland. He may as well have gone to another world.

Sophie removed apples from a paper bag, placed them next to the sink, and began washing them. The icy water ran through her fingers and her memory carried her back to a cold winter day when Harry returned from job hunting to tell her he was going away. He walked into the kitchen where she was drying dinner dishes.

"You're so late… I was worried. I kept your dinner warm." Sophie bent to open the oven door.

"I'm not hungry," Harry said, his arms hanging limply at his sides. His face was drawn, his dark eyes dulled by defeat. He sat listlessly in a kitchen chair, unbuttoning his coat.

"You look tired," Sophie said. "A warm dinner will do you good."

"I found a job today." Harry's voice was flat.

"That's wonderful." Sophie smiled, setting a dinner plate on the table, relieved by Harry's news. Harry had been out of work and she worried endlessly about money.

"It's in Newfoundland… I have to go away for a while."

"What? Where? Where's Newfoundland? Why are you going there?" Sophie stammered, her momentary joy turning to anxiety as she remembered Harry's absence only a few years ago when he had run off to Panama. She shuddered, recalling the devastating effect it had had on their marriage.

"It was the only job I could find," Harry explained. "It's a government job. I'll be part of a construction team building a military base."

"Where's Newfoundland? When will you come home?" Sophie twisted the dishtowel in her hands.

"It's off the coast of Canada. Not so far away."

"How could you take a job like that without asking me?" Sophie bristled.

Harry clenched his fists. "You want money! I'm going to make a lot of money there."

"You don't have to go away. There are plenty of factory jobs here if you're not so proud."

"I'm sick of listening to your complaints about money." Harry pushed his dinner plate away, untouched.

"I have a right to complain. It's my money you lost in that lousy service station business with your good-for-nothing brother," Sophie spat.

"There you go again. You'll get all your money back!" Harry's face reddened and his hands trembled.

"You don't have to go away. You want to. You… you like running away from your problems," Sophie shouted.

"You create the problems, Sophie. And then you tell me I'm running away from them."

"What did I do, Harry? You lost the business."

"How many times do I have to tell you it was nobody's fault. It was bad timing with a war on… Shortages of gasoline and car parts… I never asked you for your damned money! It was your idea. I know you well, Sophie. You'll never let me live in peace. Not until I pay you back every last cent. That's why I'm going to Newfoundland, so you can get your goddamned money back. It's settled," Harry told her with finality.

Sophie felt the muscles of her face tighten even now as she thought of her money lost in the business. The thousands of dollars she had carefully saved over the years before she even met Harry, by denying herself all the things a young girl wants. She had worked hard since she was fourteen, in millinery shops, in dry good stores, in dress shops, selling her heart out for a few pennies a day. But she had managed to save all that money, only to have Harry lose it. And the money Harry had sent her when he was away in Panama she thought of as hers, not theirs. She was the one who had sacrificed and saved it.

Sophie turned off the cold tap water and began drying apples with the dishtowel. Her face relaxed. She could forgive Harry now, she thought. He had more than repaid her with the money he sent home after his first year in Newfoundland. Why, she agonized, did he have to drag what was supposed to be a one year job into three? She had written and begged him to come home after the first year. *Please come home*, she wrote. *Albert and Ruthie miss you. Jeanie hardly remembers you.*

I'll be home as soon as I can, Harry wrote back. *I'm making a lot of money.*

Sophie couldn't deny that. Harry would be surprised at how much she had saved in three years. But she wondered if the job and the money were the only reasons Harry stayed away for so long. Surely he couldn't still be angry with her. She doubted that he had been faithful to her all these years. He was a handsome man and women were attracted to him. Well, she didn't condemn him for it. She couldn't. She had her own shame to bear. A pang of remorse swept over Sophie as her eyes rested on Jeanie, who sat on the floor now playing with clothespin dolls. She remembered with regret the two lonely years she had spent when Harry had gone off to Panama. Albert was six years old and Ruthie only three. Harry said he would only be gone for a year. But a year dragged into two and Sophie found the loneliness unbearable. She drew a deep breath, forcing herself to stop thinking about the past now. Surely Harry would be home soon, in time for Albert's Bar Mitzvah.

"Go downstairs to Aunt Ida and tell Ruthie and Albert to come home," Sophie told Jeanie. "It's time for bed."

Chapter 3

Harry pushed Lilly's slender arm off his chest. He wondered if all camp whores slept so soundly or just this one. She was beginning to bore him. He got out of bed and walked to the window, his strong lean body moving like a lynx. The floor was icy beneath his bare feet. Cold. It seeped into his bones and paralyzed his brain. He looked out through the grease-smudged window, past the weathered barracks and mess hall, across the barren land of Newfoundland. Shadows of dusk fell across the room. Harry lit a cigarette and looked at his hands, red and roughened from the insufferable cold, scarred from working with too many tools, building this infernal military base. Hands that should have been mixing medicines. A dying dream of his. His face, like his hands, bore the lines of hard living. He felt ten years older than his thirty-seven years and he wondered if cold and boredom could age you. Newfoundland… He was sorry he had ever heard about it. Three years ago it had seemed like a good idea. With the war on, the government was building a strategic base and construction workers were in demand. The pay was three times what he could have earned at home.

Sophie must be satisfied now, he reasoned. She was getting what she wanted most—money. Each month Harry sent her almost his entire paycheck, keeping only enough for some amusement… Lilly. A man has to have some distraction in this god-forsaken place, he rationalized. Three years had cooled his anger toward Sophie. She acted like he had lost her money on purpose, like he had made the business fail. It was always money they argued about.

Harry's toes grew numb now from standing on the bare floor. He walked back to the bed, where Lilly lay asleep, and groped for his slippers in the growing darkness. Then he returned to the window and watched men move like shadows from the dark barracks toward the mess hall.

Harry remembered the day he told Sophie the business was finished. When he walked into the apartment, Sophie was sitting at the kitchen table. Jeanie sat on her lap, eating soup from a bowl, making little puddles on the table with her spoon. "What are you doing home in the middle of the day?" Sophie asked, sitting Jeanie on the chair next to her.

"We're closing the garage this week. There aren't enough customers to feed one family. Jake's throwing in the towel and so am I."

"Just like that? What about my five thousand dollars?" Sophie demanded, her face flushed.

"We're not the only ones who lost money. Jake put up five thousand too."

"It was my five thousand, not yours. Not a nickel of it was yours!"

"Sophie, we're married. It's *our* money."

"No, it's my money, Harry! I brought my money into this marriage. You didn't have a nickel." Sophie clenched her teeth.

Jeanie covered her ears with her hands, but soon she began to cry. Sophie and Harry ignored her. Harry's voice rose with the color in his face. "Everything is yours. Nothing is ours. What's mine is yours and what's yours is yours. That's how you think. In a marriage you're supposed to share things… Anyway, I never asked you for the money. You offered it… Remember?"

"I didn't expect you to lose it. I want it back! It was a loan, not a gift," Sophie railed.

"You'll get it when I have it!" Harry slammed his fist on the table.

Jeanie's cries grew louder. "Shah," Sophie told her. "Go into the other room." Then turning to Harry, she asked, "What will you do now? You don't even have a job."

"I'll get one!" Harry stalked out of the apartment, slamming the door behind him.

Harry ground his cigarette angrily into a dirty ashtray now, remembering that argument. Wasn't that why he condemned himself to this lonely land? Well, he had repaid Sophie. She had nothing to complain about now. He had suffered, but so had she. Harry knew that somehow he could have found work at home, but he wanted to flee, to punish Sophie for making him feel like a failure, like he owed her everything. What was money for if not to enjoy life with? Sophie squirreled money away like a starving animal. She hadn't seemed like that when they first met.

Harry pulled an army blanket off the chair now and threw it around his shoulders. He plugged in a small electric heater that stood in a corner near the window. As he looked out at the desolate stretches of snow-covered plateaus surrounding the barracks, he remembered the warmth of the Brooklyn dance hall he and Sophie used to frequent when they first met, and he longed to be there again. Strings of gay lights, dance music, Sophie's face among their friends at the table they shared. Everyone laughing, joking. He hummed a tune he loved, "*I don't know why I love you like I do…*" Sophie was there smiling into his eyes. "Come on Harry, dance with me," she said, taking his hand. Harry's arms tightened around her as they waltzed around the dance floor, lost in the music. "You dance like Fred Astaire," Sophie joked.

"Let's get out of here. I want you all to myself," he whispered in her ear, breathing in the intoxicating scent of her perfume. Taking Sophie's arm, he guided her out of the dance hall into the warm spring air. He stopped at a flower stand and bought her a dozen yellow roses.

"You're so extravagant." Sophie smiled, gathering the bouquet in her arms.

Harry flagged a taxi and they drove from Brooklyn to Ratner's restaurant on the Lower East Side of Manhattan.

The brightly lit restaurant was crowded with late diners. They sat at a small table in the back. Voices and laughter from other diners filled the restaurant. A basket of freshly baked onion rolls sat on the table. Sophie picked one up and crumbled it in her hand, putting small pieces in her mouth as they waited for their order to arrive. The smell of pickled herring and fried onions hung in the air.

Their waiter arrived, carrying two large plates filled with blintzes. Sophie ate hungrily, piling globs of sour cream on her plate. "Aren't you going to finish your blintzes?" she asked Harry.

"No, would you like some more?" Harry asked.

"It's a shame to waste." Sophie helped herself to the food Harry had left on his plate, as he looked on amazed at her appetite. He hadn't realized then that Sophie's appetite for food was almost as large as her appetite for money.

The mournful howls of husky dogs outside shattered the silence in the room now. Harry's eyes wandered across the dimly lit room. How had he spent three years living in a room so devoid of all character? It was sparsely furnished with a bed, a nondescript dresser and a rickety wooden table. A torn window shade was the only covering on the window that looked out across the base. Heavy leather workboots and a pair of dirty socks lay in a corner on the floor along with yesterday's clothing. Empty cigarette packets, crumpled papers and a worn hairbrush littered the top of the dresser. Harry kept the room as a vagrant would, as though he expected to leave at any moment. He remembered suddenly that Lilly had once offered to make curtains for the window. "I have some chintz in my room, Harry. I could make you some real nice curtains," Lilly had offered.

"Don't do that, Lilly. I don't ever want to think of this place as home."

Harry's eyes rested on Lilly's hair, coarsened from the bleach she used to keep it the garish blonde color she thought was so beautiful. "You like my hair, Harry?" she asked every time they were together.

"It's beautiful, Lilly," Harry always told her. The truth was that Harry missed Sophie more when he touched Lilly's coarse hair and remembered Sophie's soft wavy hair and the healthy color in her cheeks. When Harry made love to Lilly, he turned the light out, pretending she was Sophie. Sophie was like a ripe peach, soft and juicy. She aroused him in a way no other woman had before. The curves of her hips, her magnificent breasts and full sensuous lips. He remembered the first time they had made love. He didn't think she would, they're not being married and all, but it wasn't as if they were strangers. And he had promised to marry her. Their passion seemed to grow and mount each time they were together until he almost couldn't bear to be apart from her. He would think about her all the time in those days. Her naked body would flash before his eyes. He found it difficult to concentrate in night school. The pharmacy school was demanding. He was tired after a day's work at the garage or a construction site, or at other odd jobs he did. But he didn't want to give up his dream of being something, of making something of his life. He didn't want to be a grease monkey or a laborer all his life.

If it weren't for his parents interfering, perhaps he could have convinced Sophie to wait until he finished school to marry. Harry remembered the blustery March day Sophie had come to his parents' apartment to confront him. She stood in the doorway, bundled in her brown wool coat, her dark hair blown into disarray by the wind. Her cheeks burned crimson and her eyes flashed with anger. "Harry, I wouldn't have you now if you were the last man on earth!"

"What? What are you talking about, Sophie? Come in!" He took her arms. She shook herself free of him as though she had been touched by a leper and stepped into the apartment.

"You know what I'm talking about. Don't pretend. Ask them." She pointed accusingly at Harry's parents, who sat silent and pale at the kitchen table, their evening meal forgotten by Sophie's intrusion.

Harry looked from Sophie to his parents and back to Sophie's flushed face.

"Don't tell me you don't know that your parents demanded money from my mother and father for your marriage to me. All you wanted was money.

My money. My parents' money. And I thought you were sincere. You're just like all the other men!"

"Sophie, wait. Listen... I didn't..." Harry stammered, a pained look on his face.

"And them!" Sophie pointed to the frail man and woman who sat silent and shaken. "Do they think I can be bought like a cow? And my parents gave them the money. They think I'll be an old maid if they don't buy me a husband."

A sickening feeling overwhelmed Harry. He loved Sophie and didn't want to lose her. How could he make her believe he had no part in this? He looked at the pathetic old people who sat at the kitchen table, totally dependent on him. His father's hands were gnarled from arthritis, unable to make a living any longer as a tailor. He couldn't blame them entirely for what they had done. They knew Sophie's parents had plenty of money and in desperation, they had done this terrible thing. What had once been acceptable in the Polish shtetl they had fled, was now insulting, even demeaning. Harry knew it was great need that had driven them to this act, yet he felt an all-consuming anger toward them now.

"Make them give back the money, Harry, because I don't want you." Angry tears coursed down Sophie's cheeks.

"Sophie, I love you more than anything. I didn't know about this. Please... please believe me," Harry pleaded.

"I don't believe you. I'll never believe you weren't part of this. And I don't want you." Sophie straightened her shoulders and walked proudly out of the apartment.

Harry was distraught. He returned the money the next day—one thousand dollars. He begged Sophie to forgive him and believe he had no part in it, but she would not even speak to him.

Weeks passed and Harry was obsessed with thoughts of Sophie. He could concentrate on nothing—pharmacy school, his dream, his job seemed like nothing next to losing Sophie. Finally she agreed to see him. "Sophie, how can I convince you that I love you?" Harry looked at her with longing and reached for her hand.

"You'll have to marry me, now. No waiting to finish school," Sophie said coldly.

They were married two weeks later. Harry had to drop out of school when Sophie became pregnant a few months later. Then she began to change. Harry didn't know if it was the baby or the marriage that changed her, or the fact that she always doubted his love for her. But she began to argue with him every time he spent money. Sophie no longer seemed pleased when he brought home flowers for her. "Why did you spend money on such a stupid thing? They'll be dead by tomorrow," Sophie complained. Harry never brought her flowers again.

Three years later, another baby was born. Another mouth to feed. Life went on, getting harder, more complicated. Harry felt trapped, angry. As his anger grew, his passion for Sophie cooled and he longed to escape. Then a job in Panama came along, offering a high salary and a chance to get away. It seemed like the answer to his prayers. Sophie couldn't object. He was doing it for the money, he told her.

Harry had liked Panama. It wasn't like Newfoundland. It was warm and green with lush vegetation. The women were warm too and voluptuous, the way he liked them. He had been there for two years and would have stayed longer if Sophie hadn't begged him to come home.

Sophie was different when he returned from Panama. They were like newlyweds again. She wasn't so tight with money and they began to have fun again. But it only lasted a few months and then Sophie was pregnant again. He didn't blame her. They just weren't careful. Sophie had seemed almost apologetic, acted like the baby was all her fault. That was when she offered him money to start a business, something he never expected from Sophie, who kept her private stockpile locked away in some bank. She'd never tell him how much she had. After all, she was twenty-five when he first met her, two years older than he, and working since she was fourteen. Things went well for a while until the business failed. But what was the use of dragging up dead fish now? It was more important to think of the future, Harry concluded.

Harry walked to the dresser now and looked in the mirror at the day's growth of stubble on his face. He picked up a brush and smoothed his tousled dark hair, receding at the temples. Tired eyes looked back at him from the mirror. "I'm beginning to look like a derelict," he spoke to his image. Then he moved to the bed and poked Lilly playfully in the ribs. "Wake up, Lilly! It's time for you to go. It's nearly six o'clock."

Lilly's eyelids opened reluctantly, revealing dull brown eyes behind thick black mascara. Red lipstick was smeared across one hollow cheek. Harry, looking down at her now, felt a sudden sadness for this woman he had used. He was sorry she had to be a whore. She looked cheap, pathetic. Thin women always reminded him of corpses. No one could ever accuse Sophie of being thin. Lilly's presence suddenly seemed like sacrilege against his thoughts of Sophie. "Come on Lilly, up and at 'em," Harry said, handing Lilly her clothes.

"So soon?" Lilly stretched. "Don't ya wanna to do it one more time?"

"Not tonight. Once is enough." Harry smiled, revealing even white teeth. "I have work to do."

"What kinda work at night?"

"I have to get my gear together. I'm leaving in a few days."

Lilly sat up suddenly. "Harry, you didn't tell me you were leaving!"

"I just decided. I've had enough of this cold to last me a lifetime."

"Jeez, I'm gonna miss you." Lilly reached out and touched Harry's cheek.

"Yeah, me too."

After Lilly dressed, Harry pulled a ten-dollar bill out of his wallet and pressed it into her hand.

"You already paid me." Lilly's eyes filled with tears.

"Buy yourself some perfume or a new dress." Harry kissed Lilly affectionately on her cheek and gently pushed her out the door. Then he opened the window a crack to let out the stale smell of cigarettes and cheap perfume. Tomorrow he'd go to headquarters and tell them he was leaving. Then he'd get on the first plane out of here and surprise Sophie.

Chapter 4

Albert and Ruthie charged into the apartment with Jeanie running close behind. "Last one in's a rotten egg," Albert yelled.

"You're the rotten egg," Ruthie teased, pointing an accusing finger at Jeanie.

"No, I'm not!" yelled Jeanie. "You didn't say it before, so I'm not."

"Okay, squirt," Albert said. "Be a sore loser."

"Stop fighting," ordered Sophie. "Drink your milk and get ready for bed." Sophie poured milk into three glasses she had set on the kitchen table.

"I get the sink first," shouted Albert, pushing Ruthie away so he could brush his teeth. The kitchen sink and the bathtub were the only sources of running water in the apartment.

"Momma, I was here first," Ruthie protested.

"Albert, wait till your father gets home. He'll fix your wagon!" Sophie warned. Sophie used this threat often, feeling helpless in dealing with the children's constant arguments and teasing. It usually worked with Ruthie and Albert. They remembered Harry. But Jeanie was too young when her father left to remember him. Maybe that was why she was the most defiant of her three children.

"Jeanie will use the sink first, then Ruthie, then you, Albert." Sophie's decision was final.

Jeanie pushed a kitchen chair over to the sink and stood on it. She wondered if she'd ever be as tall as Albert or Ruthie so she wouldn't have to stand on a chair. She turned the faucet on, wet her toothbrush, and sprinkled some coarse salt on it from a jar that was kept near the sink. Toothpaste was an extravagance that Sophie didn't allow. Jeanie quickly brushed and rinsed her mouth, grimacing at the salty taste. "How come we can't have toothpaste anymore, Momma?"

"There's a war on," Sophie said. "Toothpaste is only for the soldiers."

"What's a war like?"

"Stop talking and drink your milk," Sophie ordered, irritated by Jeanie's endless questions.

Albert took it upon himself to explain what war was like to Jeanie. "Our soldiers and the enemy soldiers, the Germans and the Japs, fight with guns, and bombs and planes. And whoever kills or captures the most people wins the war."

"Are we going to see the war?" Jeanie asked.

"Maybe next time there's an air raid, real Jap planes will fly over here and drop bombs on us."

"God forbid!" Sophie glared at Albert.

Jeanie's eyes widened as she sipped milk from the glass, mulling over Albert's words. She knew what an air raid was—loud sirens that hurt her ears; waiting in the darkened apartment for what seemed like an eternity while her stomach cramped with fear. The experience left her crying and trembling long after the air raid ended. "What's a bomb like?" Jeanie asked, wiping milk from her lips with her hand.

"It's like a big giant piece of dynamite that falls out of a plane and lands on you. It blows you to bits. And blood oozes all over," Albert explained.

Jeanie gagged and began coughing. Sophie, familiar with the sound, dragged Jeanie out of the chair and lifted her up to the sink, where she vomited. "I have no strength left from you," moaned Sophie, setting Jeanie down on the floor and wiping her mouth. She turned to reprimand Albert, who had slipped away quietly to his room and closed the door. "Go to sleep now," she ordered Jeanie.

Jeanie ran to her bedroom and crawled into bed beside Ruthie. "Why'd you vomit?" whispered Ruthie.

"I couldn't help it. I felt sick." Jeanie pulled the cover over her head and buried her face in the pillow, trying to shut out the vision of bombs falling and people being blown to bloody bits.

Sophie sat down at the kitchen table after the children were asleep and sipped a glass of hot tea. The sweet hot liquid was comforting after the busy late shopping and the tragic scene in the marketplace. She didn't need Jeanie vomiting to add to her misery. Of all of her children, she understood Jeanie the least, with her endless questions, wild imaginings, fears and stubbornness. She was so unlike her brother and sister in every way. Albert and Ruthie had dark wavy hair like hers, and the dark complexion of her family. Jeanie had a fair complexion and sandy-colored hair that turned blonde in the summer sun. Her eyes were blue and mesmerizing like those of Sophie's mother. When Sophie looked into Jeanie's eyes, she was reminded of her mother, who had died several years ago, never having seen Jeanie. She was grateful that her mother had never set eyes on Jeanie, for she knew with certainty that her mother would have known what no one else could guess. Sophie felt it was God's punishment that Jeanie's eyes were like her mother's, to look into hers, to accuse her 'till death.

Sophie pushed these disturbing thoughts out of her mind now as she began preparations for the holiday. She peeled apples methodically and placed them in a large wooden bowl. Then she chopped them into small pieces using the chopping knife that had been her mothers. She remembered how her mother's hands had held this same worn wooden handle hundreds of times. Her mother's hands—strong yet gentle. They could deftly braid her hair into two expertly woven creations that she'd wind and pin on top of Sophie's head in a queenly crown. "Sophila, you look like a little doll," Momma would say, admiring her own handiwork.

Sometimes Momma would plant a dry brief kiss on Sophie's forehead, but when Sophie tried to return the affection with an embrace, her mother would gently, but firmly push her away. Overt affection was frowned on by Anna Kerensky, who stood tall and proud, her head held high. Sophie could never look away from Anna's gaze, never lie to her or question what she asked.

Sophie mixed the ingredients for her cake now, kneading the soft dough between her fingers and humming a melody from her childhood: "*My sweetheart's the man in the moon…*" The music carried her back to a day she was proud of. She was twelve years old and Anna was in the kitchen baking a birthday cake for her and humming the same tune. Sophie carried a jar filled with pennies that she had saved all year, putting three of the five pennies Anna gave her each week into the jar. "Look Momma." Sophie held out the jar. "I saved a dollar fifty-six."

"Wonderful," Anna told her. "You should always save for a rainy day."

"I'm going to buy a pretty blouse I saw in Yetta Berlin's store," Sophie said.

"What do you need another blouse for?"

"But… but it's so pretty, Momma."

"Pretty isn't important. If you save your money, some day you'll be able to buy a hundred blouses."

Sophie jingled the pennies in the jar. All year she had walked everywhere she could so she could save the trolley fare, even when it was so cold that her fingers pained inside her gloves. Her mouth would water as she watched her friends enjoying treats from the bakery and penny candy from the corner store. She rarely allowed herself these small pleasures. "You're right, I don't need the blouse," Sophie told her mother.

Anna smiled approvingly at her daughter. "You won't be sorry. You could teach your brothers and your sister a thing or two about saving."

Sophie longed for an approving smile from her mother now as she floured the kitchen table and rolled out the dough for her apple cake. If Momma could only see how much she had saved from what Harry sent her each month, she would be so proud.

Sophie slid the heavy pan into the oven to bake now. She was proud of her apple cake. Her relatives would visit on Rosh Hashanah expecting tea with apple cake. Then Sophie prepared two loaves of golden honey cake. Honey for a sweet new year, she hoped. Maybe this year would be happier. Maybe Harry would come home for good.

Sophie left the cakes baking in the oven, took off her faded blue apron, stained with apples and flour, and hung it over a kitchen chair. Then she washed her hands in the kitchen sink and dried them on a dishtowel. It was getting late and she must visit her sister, Ida, and tell her the bad news.

Chapter 5

Sophie knocked on her sister's apartment door. "Who's there?" Ida's high-pitched voice sounded from behind the door.

"It's me. Open up!" Sophie said.

The door opened, revealing Ida, her stomach bulging beneath a brown chenille robe that she held together with bony fingers. Though she was only thirty-four years old, and five years Sophie's junior, she looked pale and haggard now from the strain of a bad pregnancy. The skin on her face stretched tightly across her cheekbones like that of a fragile china doll.

Ida scrutinized Sophie's face, sensing bad news. "Come in. I'm getting a draft from the hall," she said, clutching her robe tighter around her stomach. She padded into the kitchen where she sat down, exhausted, on a cushioned wooden chair and motioned for Sophie to join her.

Sophie, regarding her sister's pale face and listless eyes, wondered if she should tell Ida about Reva's baby. But she knew Ida would hear of it and she had a way of calming her. "Ida," she began, "a terrible thing happened today. You shouldn't know from it."

"What? What happened?" Ida's eyes widened in fear.

"Reva's baby died… right in the carriage… while she was rocking her."

Ida's hand swept to her lips to muffle a cry. "Oh God, no!" she wailed, rocking back and forth as if it were her own child who had died. It reminded Sophie of the way Ida had reacted when first Papa, and then Momma had died. It was Ida who had cared for their two aging parents in this apartment. Sophie hadn't been much help with two small children of her own.

"My Ida's a saint, a beautiful saint," Momma would whisper in an ever-weakening voice into Sophie's ear when she came to visit. A year after Papa's agonizing death from cancer, Momma had suffered a stroke that left her paralyzed and bedridden. She clung to life for a year after that, deteriorating from a strong proud woman into a fragile bird-like creature who finally succumbed to pneumonia. Ida rarely left their mother's bedside, tending to her every need. "Momma will get better," Ida would tell Sophie.

Sophie knew Ida was hoping Momma would recover so she could go ahead with her plans to marry Samuel. "Sam's been waiting for you for two years. Why don't you marry him now?" Sophie had asked Ida.

"I can't leave Momma now. Sam'll wait for me."

When Momma drew her last breath, Ida screamed and screamed. Sophie had to shake her hard by her shoulders to make her stop. "There's nothing more you can do," Sophie told her.

"But I loved her… I loved her," Ida cried, as though her love could have kept death away.

"She loved you too. More than anyone, she loved you best," Sophie had said, resigned and bitter over this truth. Sophie recalled Momma's words of praise for Ida. "My beautiful Ida gets the highest grades in her class… even helps Sophie with her school work. Imagine that!" Now that Momma was dead, Sophie could never prove she was worthier to be loved. Ida never saved as much money as she had. Ida was not shrewd, nor could she strike a bargain like Sophie.

After Momma was buried and the *shiva*—ritual mourning period—ended, Ida went to look for Sam, the only man she had ever loved. When Ida found Sam and his young bride living in a small apartment nearby, she returned home, blinded by bitter tears that flowed for months afterward as she sank into an ever deepening depression.

Ida turned to Sophie now. "How could Reva's healthy baby die… just like that?"

"Ida, calm down. You shouldn't get excited in your condition… I'll make some tea for you." Sophie rose and filled the teakettle with water. Sophie remembered how often she had filled this teakettle for Ida after the shock of Sam's marriage. She brought Ida food—roast chicken, blintzes, vegetable soup—but Ida refused to eat. "Ida, you must come and live upstairs with me and Harry and the children until you feel better," Sophie had begged, as her sister grew weaker and more despondent every day.

"I want to stay here," Ida insisted. "Leave me alone… I want to be alone."

"Ida, you should go back to your job… Such a good job. Most girls would be happy to have such a respected job."

Sophie had always envied the advantages Ida had. Ida finished high school and became a bookkeeper. Ida was pretty and always had boyfriends. "My Ida is so beautiful, so smart," Momma would brag to everyone. "She makes a wonderful salary as a bookkeeper." Convinced that Sophie was not a good student, Momma had asked her to quit school after eighth grade and get a job. While Sophie left the childish world of school at age fourteen to enter the working world, Ida stayed home to be pampered by Momma and encouraged to finish school.

In spite of Sophie's jealousy, she had compassion for Ida's suffering. "You must forget Sam," she had told her. "You're only twenty-five years old. A beautiful girl like you will find someone else to love."

"No, never." Ida sobbed at the mention of Sam's name. "I'll love Sam till I die."

It wasn't until a year later that Ida, pale and listless, was ready to face the world again. She found a job as a bookkeeper in a Seventh Avenue dress factory in Manhattan. It was there that she met Nathan, a lively energetic salesman, who asked Ida to marry him after her first week there. But it took Nathan two years to convince Ida.

"He's such a nice man," Sophie told Ida. "Anyone can see how much he loves you."

"I don't know. I… I'm not sure," Ida had said.

"You don't want to be an old maid, do you?" Sophie had warned.

Ida finally agreed, reluctantly, and she and Nathan were married. Ida insisted that Nathan move into the apartment she had lived in all her life. "Do you think it's a good idea?" Sophie had asked. "So many bad memories… Take a new apartment. Start out fresh."

"This is where I want to live," Ida insisted. So Nathan moved in and they began their married life together, sleeping in the tiny bedroom that had been Ida's. The large airy bedroom where Momma and Papa had made love, conceived their children and died, Ida kept locked and empty. Even after their first child was born, Ida refused to unlock that bedroom. Instead, she kept the child near her bed, ignoring Nathan's protests.

The teakettle whistled now, intruding on Sophie's thoughts. "It's ready," Sophie announced, turning off the burner.

A bed creaked now from the other room as Nathan was awakened by the whistling teakettle and the women's voices. He lumbered into the kitchen, a large man, powerfully built with thick arms and legs. His graying hair stuck out in disarray around a growing bald spot on top of his head. He rubbed his puffy eyes and squinted against the glare of the kitchen light, taking in the scene before him. "What's the commotion?" Nathan asked in a voice husky from sleep.

"Reva's baby died today," Sophie said.

"Oh, and you had to tell Ida?" He put a protective arm on Ida's shoulder, but she shrugged it off as though she were shooing away a fly.

"Better she should hear it from me than she should get upset if she hears it on the street." Sophie took three glasses from the closet and poured tea. She brought the glasses to the table. "Here, drink this," she told Ida. "You'll feel better."

Ida sipped the soothing tea, blinking nervously. Nathan still glared at Sophie for having brought bad news.

"How could God let Reva's baby die?" Ida continued to bemoan the tragedy.

Sophie finished her tea in silence and put the glass in the sink. "I have to go. I left cakes baking in the oven."

"Go! Go!" Nathan bellowed. "Bring cake next time instead of bad news."

Sophie left quietly, closing the door behind her, anxious to escape Nathan's condemning eyes.

Chapter 6

Harry stretched his long legs, trying to get comfortable in the military transport plane that carried him away from Newfoundland. Sunlight poured through the narrow windows and spots of blue peeked through the clouds like small puddles on a giant canvas. They would be flying over the ocean for many hours. Maybe he wouldn't get home until tomorrow. Home. He didn't want to wait till tomorrow to hold Sophie in his arms again, to see his son, almost ready for his Bar Mitzvah, his daughter Ruthie, who bore a striking resemblance to him, and Jeanie, only two years old when he had left.

Harry reached into his back pocket and pulled out his wallet, where he kept pictures of his family. He looked at a photograph of Jeanie, seated on a bench in Prospect Park, next to Albert and Ruthie. Jeanie's light hair and complexion were so different from her brother and sister. *If I didn't know better, I'd think she belonged to somebody else*, Harry thought as he studied the picture. Jeanie's eyes reminded him of his mother-in-law—Anna's eyes. He hoped it was the only resemblance to her. There was no doubt in his mind that Sophie had learned to be miserly from that old lady of hers. Anna had a strong hold on Sophie, even though she had been dead for years. Harry hadn't been able to change Sophie at all in the thirteen years they'd been married. She argued about every penny he wanted to spend. But he was not a man to give up easily.

Harry checked the duffel bag under his seat that was filled with presents for Sophie and the children. He had gone to the PX before he left the base and bought perfume for Sophie and dolls for the girls. And someone gave him a German helmet for Albert. There was also a big box of chocolates for everyone. If he had come home with gifts three years ago, Sophie would have started an argument over it. "It's thrown out money," she would have yelled.

But Harry knew she wouldn't argue now. He could tell from her letters that she missed him.

Harry took out the bottle of perfume and opened it, inhaling the light sweet scent. The smell brought back memories of Sophie when she was pregnant with Jeanie. Something about Sophie's last pregnancy always troubled him. She seemed somehow different than she had been during her first two pregnancies.

Sophie had become pregnant soon after Harry had returned from Panama. Panama… that hot exciting jungle he had escaped to six years after their marriage. It was because of Sophie's penny-pinching that he had fled there. He'd been working in Brooklyn ten and twelve hours a day to make a buck and Sophie was never satisfied, arguing over every penny he spent, and carrying her resentment into the bedroom.

Harry remembered the argument that finally drove him away to Panama. He had come home from work exhausted, his clothes grease-stained, his hands bruised from repairing cars all day. Sophie was in the kitchen stirring a pot of chicken soup, her face flushed from the steaming soup. "Chicken again?" Harry asked.

"We can't afford steak on the money you bring home," Sophie snapped.

"Other men make a lot less and they eat steak once in a while."

"If you saw their bankbooks, there would be nothing in them. Everything would be in their stomachs."

"At least their stomachs are satisfied."

"Someday you'll thank me for saving money. Someday we'll be able to enjoy everything."

"Sophie, let's enjoy something now… How about going to Ratner's restaurant with the kids on Sunday? Remember when we used to go… you and me?"

"Are you crazy! That's thrown-out money… And what do the kids need it for?"

"We can leave the kids with Ida and go alone. It'll be like old times."

"Absolutely not! We can't squander money in a restaurant! We can go to the Prospect Park Zoo. It's free."

"I'm sick of the zoo! I'm sick of chicken, and I'm sick of your penny-pinching!"

That was the last thing Harry had said to Sophie that day. When he got into bed that night, she had turned her back on him as she did for weeks afterward.

Soon after that argument, Harry had learned about a government construction job in Panama. He could get away from Sophie and the job he hated in the garage. Maybe Sophie would appreciate him more if he put some distance between them for a while.

Harry remembered the day he told Sophie he was leaving. "I signed up for a job in Panama. It pays $100 a week with room and board," Harry said.

"What did you say?" Sophie's hands trembled and she put aside a dress she was mending.

"I said I'm going to Panama."

"Why? What about your job here?"

"Sophie, the job in Panama pays $100 a week. I only earn thirty-five dollars a week here."

"But it's so far… I… I'll be here alone with the children. How will I manage all alone?"

"Your sister's downstairs. Your brothers are here. It's only for a couple of months."

"How many months?" Sophie bit her lower lip.

"Three… maybe four months," Harry had told her, though he knew it would be longer. He hadn't thought she would mind that much.

"That's four hundred dollars a month," Sophie quickly calculated. "I guess I can manage for a few months." Then as an afterthought, she had said, "Why did you take the job without talking to me first?"

"I figured you'd be glad to get rid of me for a while… You've hardly spoken to me for weeks, except to complain about money."

"Are you blaming me for that?" Sophie's face reddened.

"Yes, I'm blaming you. It's money you want, not me!"

Panama had turned out to be more than a few months. The months dragged into two years. Letters from Sophie told him she was miserable and lonely. Well, she was the one who had driven him away, he had rationalized. Though Harry missed Sophie and the kids, he was enjoying Panama. The work was hard, but the native women more than made up for it. Then a letter from Sophie summoned him home abruptly. She had had an accident, a fall down a flight of steps. She was badly bruised and had a mild concussion. Harry was worried and flew home immediately.

The plane dipped suddenly now, hitting an air pocket and shaking Harry out of his reverie. He rummaged through his pocket for a cigarette. He found a crumpled packet with one cigarette and lit it, inhaling deeply, exhilarated to be flying amidst the clouds. There was something serene and awesome about being in the sky… where angels must live, he thought. Angels. There had been something angelic about Sophie's poor bruised face when he returned from Panama. She looked pale and fragile lying on the bed beneath the blankets. She had lost weight. Her dark hair clung to her forehead in damp ringlets, and her eyes were sad. She cried when she saw him, clinging to him like a lost child.

Harry nursed Sophie back to health. Soon she was eating with her usual gusto and gaining weight. Her passion for him seemed as insatiable as her appetite. She wanted him all the time, as if she were trying to make up for the two years he had been away. They began to enjoy life again. They went out to restaurants with friends, entertained relatives, even went dancing. It was as if Sophie had turned back the clock to the time when they first met. "I saved most of the money you sent me from Panama, so we can spend a little now," Sophie had said.

An army sergeant nudged Harry, interrupting his thoughts. "There's chow up front if you're hungry."

"Thanks," Harry said, dropping his cigarette butt on the floor and grinding it out with his shoe. He stood up, stretched, and walked unsteadily to the front of the plane where someone was handing out sandwiches and beer. He returned to his seat and ate a tasteless roast beef sandwich, washing it down with warm beer. He hated warm beer. He closed his eyes, trying to remember Sophie when he had returned from Panama. He hoped she would be like that again. He felt excitement stirring within him when he remembered their lovemaking. A month after his return, Sophie had said, "Harry, I'm pregnant." He must have looked shocked, Harry thought now, because Sophie apologized, something she rarely did. "I'm so sorry, Harry. I didn't mean for this to happen."

"I don't blame you," he had said. "It was as much my fault as yours." He tried to reassure Sophie that everything would work out, but she was distraught. "It'll be all right… you'll see," he told her, but he worried because he didn't have a job.

"Maybe you could go into a business with your brother Jake," Sophie had suggested.

"You need a lot of money to start a business. What are you thinking, Sophie?"

"You and Jake are good mechanics. You could open a garage. I saved some money that you sent me, and I'll loan you some of my own. You can pay me back when the business gets going."

Harry couldn't believe Sophie was offering him her own money. He took it. He and Jake worked for months getting the garage ready to open, hustling for expensive equipment at bargain prices, as Sophie grew bigger with child.

She was listless, depressed, and still had another month to carry, though she looked as though she was already in her ninth month. Then Sophie shook him awake early one morning. "Wake up, Harry! I'm having pains. Take me to the hospital."

"It must be false labor," Harry groaned, rolling over in bed.

"It's real!" Sophie cried out, seized by a contraction.

They reached the hospital just in time. Half an hour later, a green-gowned doctor walked down the hospital corridor to shake Harry's hand. "You have a healthy baby girl," he said. "Six pounds, two ounces." Harry beamed, relieved that the baby was healthy and surprised she weighed as much as she did for a premature baby.

The baby thrived and Harry doted on her. He'd pick up Jeanie and hug her, throw her into the air, and listen to her giggle. Sophie fed and cared for the child, but something about the way she pried Jeanie's small hands from her skirt and sat her down abruptly, troubled Harry. There was unmistakable resentment in Sophie's voice when she spoke to Jeanie. "Finish your dinner! I'm not throwing out good food!" Sophie would scold. "And hurry up. I don't have all day to wait for you to finish!" Harry smiled, remembering how Jeanie would hold the food in her mouth defiantly, or swallow it and vomit, throwing Sophie into a rage.

Harry rose from the seat now, feeling light-headed from the warm beer, and walked unsteadily to the cockpit. "How much longer to New York?" he asked the pilot.

"At least seven hours, and we'll have to land for refueling… Relax."

"That's a joke," Harry said, walking back to his seat. He took out his duffel bag again and pulled out a magazine. He tried to concentrate, but found himself reading the same words again and again. Putting the magazine down on the seat, his thoughts turned to finding a job when he got home. If the war ended, maybe he could get a good job and go back to pharmacy school at night. Harry knew it was madness for him to entertain the idea of ever going back to school with a wife and three children to support. He knew it was a fool's dream, yet he nurtured it, hoping some day it would happen. Harry closed his eyes now, imagining how Sophie would look, what she would say when she opened the door and saw him after all this time.

Chapter 7

The plane landed at LaGuardia at 7:00 a.m. and it took Harry another hour by bus to get into Manhattan. He could scarcely believe he was here. Dazzling sunlight glinted off the tall buildings, warming the chill autumn air. It was a welcome change from Newfoundland. The only visible signs of war were the huge posters of Uncle Sam pointing at passing crowds and declaring, *I Want You*, in big bold letters. Horns honked and traffic crawled. Crowds spilled out of subway tunnels beneath the busy streets and people hurried to waiting jobs. The smell of morning coffee drifted out of coffee shops crowded with customers needing caffeine like cars needed oil.

Harry felt suddenly disoriented. He put his duffel bag down on the sidewalk and looked around, trying to remember which way to walk to the train station that would take him to Brooklyn. A passerby bumped into him.

"Watch where you're going, buddy."

"Sorry," Harry said, picking up his duffel bag and walking to a nearby coffee shop window to get his bearings. He stood transfixed for a few moments, watching a cook in a tall white chef's hat flip eggs on a hot griddle. He was suddenly overcome by hunger and couldn't remember when he had last eaten. He walked into the coffee shop, sat at the counter, and ordered eggs, home fries, toast and coffee. The red leather stools reminded him of the red cushions on the kitchen chairs at home. How many mornings had he sat in the kitchen watching Sophie frying eggs for him and stirring a steaming pot of oatmeal for the children? She always hummed as she cooked, as though there were some secret communion between her and the food. Then she'd place the plate of eggs before him as though it were a gift.

After the children left for school, Sophie would sit down at the kitchen table and finish the food that the children had left on their plates. Then she'd cook breakfast for herself and eat it slowly, savoring each mouthful. Harry wondered now if Sophie had changed or if she still considered the kitchen her private domain.

A waitress in a crisp black and white uniform placed a plate of steaming food in front of Harry now. He ate hungrily. The eggs were cooked to perfection and the toast dripped with butter. The coffee was hot and strong, the way he liked it. He downed two cups of coffee and finished his eggs, feeling less like an alien in a foreign country now. He peered across the counter at his reflection in the mirror, his hand moving over the dark stubble on his face, displeased with his unkempt image. He wondered what Sophie would say when she saw him and what he'd say to her after all this time. Would she be glad to see him? He worried.

"More coffee?" the waitress asked.

"No, that's all." Harry paid the bill and left the coffee shop, his duffel bag slung over his shoulder. He walked briskly, sure of where he was going now and determined to get there quickly. He found a subway station on the next corner and disappeared into the bowels of the city, emerging half an hour later on a sun-filled Brooklyn street. A bus took him a few blocks closer to home, and then his feet pounded the familiar pavement of the street where he lived.

The marketplace was crowded with morning shoppers carrying heavy bags and wheeling shopping carts. Harry recognized the familiar faces of the pushcart peddlers—Moshe Finkelstein weighing apples; Nathan Grubinsky arranging onions and potatoes as though they were rare gems.

Harry was glad nobody had recognized him. He didn't want to stop and talk to anyone now. He reached the building at last and stopped, looking up toward the third floor window of his apartment, hoping to catch a glimpse of Sophie or one of the children. The dull brick edifice loomed above him, unchanged by time. The same grimy windows concealed the faces of those who lived behind them, touched by happiness and sorrow through the cycles of their lives.

Harry bounded up the three flights of steps and stood frozen before the door that would open to the rest of his life, his heart pounding. He knocked on the door, hesitantly at first, then harder with certainty. The sweet soft sound of a child's voice reached his ears. "Momma, someone's knocking on the door."

Sophie turned off the water at the kitchen sink where she stood washing the breakfast dishes. It's probably the Fuller Brush salesman bothering me so early in the morning, she thought. "Who is it? Who's there?" Sophie called through the closed door.

"It's me, Harry. Open up!"

Sophie hesitated for a moment, not recognizing the unexpected but familiar voice. She opened the door and the two stood facing each other, Sophie with a look of disbelief on her face. "Harry… what are you doing here? You didn't tell me. I… I can't believe it's you." Her heart pounded as her eyes drank in the sight of her husband.

"I wanted to surprise you." Harry stepped over the threshold in one swift movement and kissed Sophie lightly on her lips.

Sophie wanted to throw herself into his arms, to cry, to laugh, to kiss his face, but instead she stood transfixed, staring into Harry's eyes in disbelief, tears ready to spill over, unable as ever to reveal affection. Gaining control, she said, "You… you surprised me all right." Her hand moved over her hair to smooth it. She looked down at her shabby dress and wished she looked better for Harry's homecoming. She welcomed the sight of him, but was flustered, unprepared.

Harry followed her into the kitchen and put down his duffel bag. They stood looking at each other for what seemed like a long time, like two strangers who had once been friends and now faced each other silently, wondering what each should say to the other after all this time. Sophie laughed nervously and smoothed her dress with her hands. "I can't believe you're really home. You're always full of surprises, Harry."

"I can't believe it myself." Harry's eyes fixed on Sophie, soft curls astray on her forehead, a faded housedress thrown carelessly on for her morning work, her large breasts straining against the thin fabric. "You haven't changed, Sophie. Well, maybe you put on a little weight."

"Nothing stays the same forever. You look good, Harry. A little tired."

"I just need a shave." Harry's hand glided over the bristles on his face. "I've been traveling for almost twenty-four hours."

"Come sit down. I'll make you a cup of coffee." Sophie busied herself at the stove, glad to be doing something with her trembling hands.

Harry sat down on the old wooden kitchen chair with the red leather seat. His fingers drummed nervously on the white metal tabletop as his eyes swept across the familiar kitchen. The same faded green linoleum covered the floor, a little more worn by the passage of time… the white stove, the old wooden ice box and the yellow kitchen curtains, transparent now from too many washings. His eyes rested on Sophie in her shabby dress. He remembered how Sophie had dressed before they were married, when he took her out dancing. She'd wear a stylish navy suit with a crisp white blouse and high-heeled shoes. Her hair was coiffed in neat ringlets around her face, and pink lipstick made her full lips moist and sensuous.

Sophie's lips were pale now and there were dark shadows beneath her eyes. She placed a steaming cup of coffee in front of Harry and sat across from him, studying his face, noting how gaunt and tired he looked. Harry sipped the coffee slowly, savoring the rich flavor and inhaling the aroma of the steaming brew. "You still make a great cup of coffee." Harry smiled.

"I didn't stop making coffee because you were away," Sophie joked. "How about a piece of my apple cake? I have some left from the holiday." She rose to get Harry the cake before waiting for his answer and placed a large piece before him. Then Sophie sat down and enjoyed watching Harry devour the cake. She thought, *it's good to have you home again, Harry*, but something kept her from saying it.

"How were the holidays?" Harry asked.

"It was hectic. Everyone came to visit. Aunt Rosie, Uncle Louis, the children. Even your communist sister!"

"I'd like to see the family, even my crazy sister."

"The Levines moved out from the upstairs apartment and a new tenant moved in, Mrs. Rivington… a widow, and her two children. Her husband died in a concentration camp." Sophie chattered on about other people, keeping herself from dwelling on her own feelings.

"Where are the children?" Harry asked, suddenly aware that all his attention had been focused on Sophie.

"Albert and Ruthie are in school. Where else would they be on a weekday? But Jeanie's here." She looked around for Jeanie, who had quietly disappeared. "Jeanie, come in here and say hello to your father. Come and give him a big hug!"

Albert's bedroom door, which led off from the kitchen, creaked softly. Jeanie stood shyly in the half-opened doorway, a battered rag doll hanging at her side as she studied the stranger whose voice she had been listening to. His face looked rough, covered with dark stubble.

Harry stood up, smiling down at his tiny daughter. His large calloused hands reached out for her, his body loomed above her, seeming giant-like to Jeanie, who now began to confuse him with the bogeyman, the man who Momma had always warned her about. Jeanie thought this man had come to get her at last for all the bad things she had done. Her heart pounded and she felt as though it would burst through her chest as she turned and fled from the doorway, away from Harry's outstretched arms, through the living room and the French doors, into her mother's bedroom. Harry's quick heavy footsteps followed her as she reached the far wall of the bedroom and crouched in the corner. Hot tears burned her cheeks as two rough hands reached out to embrace her. Jeanie's scream pierced the quiet of the bedroom. Then she coughed and vomited all over the bedroom floor.

Sophie followed Harry who now held the sobbing child in his arms. He looked down at her, confused, his face drained of color. He placed Jeanie gently on the bed, his hands trembling.

"She does this sometimes when she's frightened or upset," Sophie said.

"What's wrong with her?" Harry asked, finding his voice again, relieved that he hadn't frightened Jeanie to death.

"She doesn't remember you. I think she's afraid of you. Why don't you wait in the kitchen till she calms down?"

Jeanie lay on the bed, whimpering, while Sophie stroked her damp forehead. She couldn't blame Jeanie for being frightened of a man she hadn't seen since she was two years old, but she felt badly for Harry too. "Don't be afraid," she told Jeanie.

"He's the bogeyman," Jeanie sniffled.

"He's your father… You don't remember him. He would never hurt you."

Jeanie refused to leave the safety of Sophie's bed, and Sophie thought it better to let her stay there till she was ready to come out by herself. As Sophie walked out of the bedroom, she peered at her reflection in the mirror, wishing she had known Harry was coming home. She would have looked nicer for him, she thought. Maybe this wouldn't have happened.

Sophie returned to the kitchen, where Harry sat at the table, staring into his empty coffee cup. She sat down next to him and reached out to touch his hand. "Don't be upset. Jeanie can be a strange child sometimes. She'll outgrow it."

Harry was silent, exhausted now from the emotional scene. He felt like an intruder instead of a member of the family, like an enemy destroyer that had wrought havoc on a tranquil sea.

"Lie down on Albert's bed. You'll feel better after you sleep," Sophie soothed.

While Harry slept, Sophie busied herself in the apartment, wanting to make everything right for Harry. She'd cook some stuffed cabbage for dinner tonight. It was Harry's favorite. While Sophie swept the kitchen floor, Jeanie slowly advanced toward the kitchen, looking around for the strange man. Not seeing him, she bravely entered the kitchen and climbed up on a chair. "I'm hungry," she announced. "Where'd the bad man go?"

"He's not a bad man. I told you, he's your father… and he's sleeping now. Don't ever do that again… vomiting like that!" Sophie scolded.

Jeanie didn't answer, but she stared at Harry's sleeping figure through the half-opened bedroom door. Sophie placed a small bowl of bananas and sour cream in front of Jeanie, who ate some of it and then stood near the bedroom door studying Harry.

Sophie finished her housework, ignoring Jeanie now. Then she filled the bathtub with hot water. She settled into the tub, feeling the tension flow out of her body. Her eyes closed and memories flooded back… She and Harry were in Dubrow's Restaurant in Brooklyn, sitting around a table with a group of friends drinking coffee and laughing. Harry didn't look tired then. His eyes were bright and happy. He didn't look beaten. Well, being away for three years must have been hard on Harry too, Sophie concluded as she rose from the tub, dried herself and put on a freshly laundered dress. She combed her hair carefully and applied some lipstick, smiling at her image in the mirror. "I don't look too bad for a thirty-nine-year-old woman," she said aloud, startling herself with her own voice. Then she left a note for Harry and went out with Jeanie to do her marketing.

When Sophie returned, Harry was unpacking his duffel bag. He looked refreshed and calm. "You look better," Sophie said, setting the grocery bags on the table. Jeanie stood near the door studying Harry, reluctant to move closer.

"Don't be afraid. I'm not going to hurt you," Harry told her. Jeanie remained silent, watching the now clean-shaven stranger pull things from a large bag. "This is for you." Harry touched Sophie's hand lightly as he held out a bottle of perfume.

"For me?" Sophie sounded surprised that Harry would bring something for her.

Then Harry took out two dolls with pretty painted faces and blue eyes that opened under dark eyelashes. "This is for you," he said, holding one of the dolls out toward Jeanie, who looked longingly at the doll, but kept her distance from Harry. "I'll leave it on the table for you next to the doll for Ruthie," he told Jeanie. "And this is for Albert." He pulled a helmet from his bag.

Jeanie edged cautiously toward the table, her small hands aching to hold the doll. She picked up the doll slowly and Harry smiled at her.

"What do you say?" Sophie prodded.

"Thank you," Jeanie said in a barely audible voice, and then retreated into the living room to play with the unexpected treasure.

"You spent a lot of money on all these things," Sophie said.

"A man's allowed to buy presents for his family."

"Thank you for the perfume." Sophie smiled, pleased with the gift in spite of her practiced self-denial. She remembered the last time Harry had given her a present. It was several days after Jeanie was born. Harry came home with a small package wrapped in powder blue paper and tied with silver ribbon. "For the new mother." Harry presented the gift with a flourish. Sophie opened the box silently, her hands caressing a delicate white silk scarf. "It's a stupid waste of money. I don't need a scarf." She pushed the gift away.

"I want you to have it," Harry insisted.

"I don't want it! Take it back." Sophie closed the box and walked out of the room to hide her tears. Why did Harry have to be so nice to her when she didn't deserve it? Why was he making such a fuss over this baby? It wasn't her first baby. She had looked down at the tiny infant sleeping in the cradle near her bed and hated her for being born, for making her feel guilty. That was a long time ago. Now she thought she deserved a present after three years of being alone.

Harry was glad that Sophie liked the perfume. Maybe she has changed, he hoped, but his thoughts were interrupted by the sound of children's voices in the hallway. The door flew open and Ruthie stumbled in, pushed from behind by Albert. "Don't push me! Momma, he's pushing," Ruthie complained and then stopped in mid-sentence when she recognized the unexpected figure of her father. "Daddy!" she shouted and flew into his welcoming arms.

Albert stood back, shyly at first, then offered his hand for a formal handshake. Harry shook his son's hand and then embraced him. Grinning at each other in pleasure, father and son looked searchingly into each other's eyes. "You got so tall." Harry rumpled Albert's hair. Then, holding out the helmet for Albert, he said, "I brought you a German helmet."

Albert held the helmet in his hands gingerly. "A real German helmet! Dad, this is so great! The kids at school won't believe it. Is it from a dead German?"

"I don't know. One of the guys on the base gave it to me. I knew you'd want it."

"Gee thanks, Dad. It's the greatest thing I ever got."

Harry picked up the doll with the pretty painted cheeks and red cupid lips for Ruthie. He wondered now if ten-year-old girls still played with dolls. "She's beautiful, Daddy. I'll keep her on my dresser." Ruthie held the doll carefully as though it might break at any moment and she'd never get another.

The news of Harry's homecoming spread quickly. An endless parade of neighbors and family stopped in to welcome Harry home, studying him closely for any change, then leaving with apologies for invading the family's privacy.

Children ran through the apartment in a steady stream, alternating between staring at Harry, who had become a legend for having ventured out of Brooklyn, and gaping at the treasured German helmet and the new dolls. When the tumult had at last died down and the last ogler had departed, the family settled down to a quiet dinner, each one eager to fill Harry in on the events he had missed over the years and to hear Harry's tales of Newfoundland. Even Jeanie vied for his attention now. "I'm going to school next year, and I know how to read already," she told Harry, proudly.

When the excitement of the day had passed and the children were finally asleep, Sophie and Harry faced each other alone. They stood in the familiar kitchen, the hush of evening blanketing the air. Only the muffled sound of a voice from a distant radio, and the steady drip of ice melting into the pan beneath the icebox shattered the silence. "I missed you." Harry brushed Sophie's cheek lightly with his hand.

Sophie felt her body stir with longing. "I missed you too," she said breathlessly.

Harry's arms reached out, enfolding Sophie in an urgent embrace. He bent to kiss her and his strong lean body pressed against her. Sophie felt suddenly weak with desire. Together they walked into the familiar bedroom where they had made love so many times before. They undressed quickly, eager to explore each other's body again. They made love with fierce urgency, like newly proclaimed lovers discovering each other for the first time. Then they lay back, their bodies damp with exhaustion, their arms still intertwined, afraid to let go lest the other slip away and shatter the fragile new foundation they had begun to build.

Chapter 8

The weeks following Harry's homecoming were fraught with a frenzy of activity. People to see and places to visit again. The Rothmans celebrated Harry's first Sunday in Brooklyn with a trip to the Prospect Park Zoo.

The zoo was crowded with families when the Rothmans walked down the narrow steps to the animal cages. Albert climbed on the railing outside the lion's cage to get a better view. The lion's mangy hair hung in clumps around his face and he roared menacingly at Albert, who fell backward, startled, into Harry's arms. "Let's go see the seals." Jeanie tugged Harry's hand.

They marched across a wide square to the seal pool. Harry lifted Jeanie onto his shoulders so she could have a better view. She laughed as she watched the sleek black seals swimming playfully and barking at each other. She liked sitting on Harry's shoulders, and affection for him began to grow despite her initial mistrust.

The seals reminded Harry of the icy waters off the coast of Newfoundland and the cold gray mornings when he awoke next to Lilly. He wondered whose bed Lilly slept in now. Standing next to Sophie now, he could almost feel the heat from her body that had enveloped him in bed the night before. When he had reached for her beneath the blanket, she came willingly into his arms and they clung feverishly to each other in their lovemaking. He smiled warmly at Sophie as she pulled the collar of her coat up. "It's getting cold," she said, shivering. "We should get home early."

"I want to see all the animals," Albert protested.

"Let's go see the elephants," Ruthie said.

"Good idea," Harry agreed. "First we'll buy some peanuts to feed them." They marched off to a concession stand that sold small bags of peanuts, boxes of crackerjacks, balloons and banners printed with *Prospect Park Zoo.*

"The children don't need peanuts," Sophie protested. Harry bought three bags of peanuts despite Sophie's protests and gave them to the children, who ran off excitedly to the elephant house. Harry followed slowly behind with Sophie.

"Sophie, you haven't changed much," Harry said, taking her hand in his. "You still can't part with a nickel."

Offended, Sophie pulled her hand away. "And you still spend money like a drunken sailor."

"I made a lot of money in Newfoundland. You must have saved most of the money I sent home."

"I saved a lot of it."

"How much?"

"I don't know exactly."

"Come on, Sophie. I can always count on you to know how much you have down to the penny."

"Well, I don't remember. I… I'll have to check the bankbook," Sophie lied.

"I'm sure there's plenty for us to live on for a while."

"Why? Aren't you going to look for a job?" Sophie's voice rang with alarm.

"I… I thought we could live on what you saved for a while and I could go back to pharmacy school."

Sophie stopped walking and glared at Harry. "You must be crazy. How can you even think of doing that?"

"If I finish pharmacy school, I can open a drugstore and then we'd be comfortable for life."

"The money I saved is not to spend now. We wouldn't have anything left if you did that."

"What'd I work my guts out for in Newfoundland?" Harry felt his stomach tighten.

"So we can have some savings for later… when we need it."

"I need it now! I want to be something. A pharmacist, not a laborer."

Sophie's lips set in a hard line. "You're not a kid any more. You have a family to support. I won't let you touch that money," she said sharply, and a passersby stopped to stare.

Harry felt the old familiar anger fomenting inside him. Sophie hadn't changed. She was glad he was home so she could have a man around the house, but she still wanted everything her way. "You keep talking like the money is all yours," he said.

"I saved it," Sophie snapped. "If it wasn't for me, we'd have nothing."

"If I can't spend it, it's as good as having nothing. Can't you see how important it is to me to go back to school, to make something of my life?"

"You have made something of your life. You have a family. You need a good job now, that's all."

"It's what you want, Sophie, not what I want."

"You ran off to Newfoundland. You left me alone for three years with three children. You had your fun!" The resentment in her tone struck Harry.

"You think Newfoundland was fun?" Harry shouted, as a woman standing near the llama cage turned to stare. "I worked like an animal. I sweated for every nickel I earned. I deserve to use some of that money the way I want to," Harry hissed between clenched teeth.

"You're behaving like a schoolboy…. a dreamer. Look at you. You're thirty-seven years old and talking about going to school."

Sophie's words shamed Harry and he felt suddenly dispirited as they walked to the elephant house in silence.

"Did the elephants like the peanuts?" Sophie asked the children.

"Yes," Jeanie said. "I ate some too."

"Can we see the monkeys again?" Ruthie asked.

"It's getting late. We'd better go," Sophie said.

Jeanie walked over to Harry, who stood silently against the railing, and she put her small hand in his, sensing a change in his mood. He reached out and patted her head, her soft hair like silk between his fingers. The growing trust of a child was small compensation for a dream beyond reach now. Sophie has a special talent for shattering dreams, Harry thought. It means no more to her than snuffing out the life of an insect with the heel of her shoe. Why can't she understand that dreams give life dimension and promise? Maybe that's why she never shows real feelings. She's incapable of dreaming. *I'll never give up my dream*, Harry thought defiantly. *Without it, there is no hope.*

Chapter 9

Winter arrived early that year. It was as if Newfoundland had followed Harry like a shadow, haunting him with its cold breath, spreading bleakness everywhere.

Harry soon found a construction job at the Brooklyn Navy Yard. Sophie was happy that he was back at work, earning money. Harry no longer cared if his hands got bruised and calloused. He knew they would never mix medicines. He was tired of running away, tired of arguing with Sophie. So he resigned himself to life as it was for him. He enjoyed his children, and he focused with renewed interest on Albert, whose 13th birthday and Bar Mitzvah were only two months away. He listened each night as Albert practiced his *Haftorah*, a portion of the sacred Torah he was studying, chanting the ancient Hebrew words in a new deep voice. "He's a smart boy," Harry remarked to Sophie. "Maybe he'll be a doctor."

"Maybe." Sophie smiled. "Our son… a doctor." She liked the sound of it.

Sophie had arranged for a large celebration in honor of Albert's Bar Mitzvah. It was the most money Sophie had ever allowed herself to spend on a celebration. "For our only son, we should make a big party," Sophie said. "We have to invite all the relatives and the apartment is too small."

They rented a basement room used for meetings and parties on Eastern Parkway. A caterer was hired to bring in roasted chickens, chopped liver, stuffed derma and a Bar Mitzvah cake.

The day of Albert's Bar Mitzvah arrived, a sun-drenched day early in March 1944, with warm breezes and a promise of spring. The small neighborhood synagogue was crowded with family members who had come from all over Brooklyn and the Bronx. The men separated from the women as they entered the sanctuary, the men sitting downstairs and the women banished to the upper level.

Sophie's eyes settled proudly on Albert in his new blue-serge suit, blue velvet *yarmulka*, and a white prayer shawl draped around his shoulders. He stood confidently next to the rabbi, his eyes bright and his voice strong as he chanted Hebrew prayers. The words were a comfort to Sophie, yet she did not understand them. She was proud that her son could communicate with God with mysterious words, though she could not.

Harry had a seat of honor on the bema where Albert now read from the *Torah*. His son's strong voice and confidence filled Harry with profound happiness. Looking at Albert's broad shoulders bent in prayer, Harry pictured his son in a white jacket with a stethoscope draped around his neck. He imagined Albert walking along a hospital corridor after a successful operation, meeting with a family and explaining the complicated surgery he performed. Harry beamed, content with his thoughts, confident that his son would fulfill his dream.

The service ended and guests emerged from the dimly-lit sanctuary, squinting in the bright light that bathed the corridor, eager to congratulate Albert on becoming a man. A table covered with a white damask cloth was laden with trays of golden sponge cake and small glasses of sweet red wine. A respectful silence settled over the group as Albert chanted the *kiddush* prayer, thanking God for the fruit of the vine. Everyone drank and voices shouted, "*Mazel tov*! Congratulations!" Relatives and friends planted wet kisses on Albert's smooth cheeks, which he brushed away with his hand, grimacing after the assault on him subsided. Then the celebrants walked noisily to the reception party several blocks from the synagogue.

Sophie reveled in playing hostess. Guests were seated at long tables set with white linen cloths. Golden brown rolls sat next to each place setting and trays of roasted chickens and stuffed derma steamed in the center of the tables. A huge *challah* bread sat waiting for the traditional prayer and slicing. Sophie stopped to talk to each guest, confident that she looked her best for the occasion in her new, royal-blue taffeta dress trimmed with white lace collar and cuffs and new shoes. It was the first time since Harry had been away that she had bought herself a new dress. Everyone had new outfits, except for Jeanie, who wore a pale-yellow party dress that Ruthie had outgrown. "I want a new dress too," Jeanie had protested, but Sophie refused adamantly. "There's nothing wrong with this dress," Sophie told her. "You'll wear it."

The party continued for hours, until most of the food was consumed. An accordionist played *Hava Nagila* and the celebrants joined hands in a great circle for a traditional hora dance. Albert was raised up on a chair by four strong uncles while the guests danced around him, rejoicing in Albert's achievement.

Soon the cake was cut and passed out. The guests kissed Albert once more before departing and stuffed envelopes with money gifts or new fountain pens into his hands. After the last guest had left, Sophie and Harry sat down at a nearby table, cluttered now with the remains of the feast. Exhausted and happy, they smiled at each other. Empty trays and half-filled glasses, bits of food on grease-smudged dishes, paper doilies and soiled napkins were all that remained as evidence of their great celebration. The music still rang in Sophie's ears. "Albert's a fine boy… a fine boy. He made me very proud today," Harry said.

"It was a beautiful party," Sophie said, smiling. "The family will be talking about it for years." Then Sophie took out the shopping bags she had brought along and wrapped the uneaten food left on the trays for the trip home.

"Albert, give me all the envelopes in your pockets. I'll count the money when we get home," Sophie said. "And look around before we leave. Make sure you didn't drop anything on the floor."

"I want to hold the envelopes," Albert said.

"Give them to me. I'll take care of them," Sophie demanded.

Albert handed her the stack of envelopes obediently. Sophie let him hold the new fountain pens.

When they arrived home, Sophie sat down at the kitchen table, the stack of envelopes in front of her. She methodically opened each one, reading the notes aloud and counting the cash enclosed. "Five dollars from Aunt Minna. Imagine the nerve. Such a cheap gift."

"Sophie, that's all you gave her son for his Bar Mitzvah," Harry reminded her.

"I'm sure I gave him more."

"You never want to give more than that."

"I don't remember. You were probably out of work. She should understand… Oh look, ten dollars from Uncle Izzy! Now he's a *mench*."

After all the envelopes were opened and the money counted, Sophie announced, "Three hundred thirty-five dollars! Very nice!"

"Momma, what are you and Dad going to give me?" Albert asked.

"Well, I think…" Harry began, but was interrupted by Sophie.

"We gave you a party. You wouldn't have three hundred thirty-five dollars now if we didn't give you the party. You're a very lucky boy."

"Can I have my money?" Albert held out his hand.

"Of course you can, when you're old enough. I'll put it in the bank for you and you'll get interest. Then you'll have even more."

Albert's hand dropped to his side. "But I'm old enough now. I'm a man, aren't I?"

"Well, you are and you aren't. You're not old enough to take care of your money."

"Can't I have some of it to buy some things I want?"

"No. We'll put it in the bank. Some day you'll thank me for saving it for you."

Albert knew it was no use arguing with his mother when she had made up her mind. So he went to bed, exhilarated by his accomplishment that day and richer than he had ever been before. Harry and the girls went to bed. Sophie stayed up for a while. She unwrapped each parcel of food that she had salvaged from the feast, examined it with pleasure and rewrapped it. Then she stacked the parcels in the icebox, satisfied that there would be enough food for several days. She undressed finally and slipped into bed beside Harry. "That was *some* beautiful Bar Mitzvah," she whispered. "Everyone will be talking about it for years."

Harry barely heard her. He was lost in a dream where a shingle on a polished black door read, *Dr. Albert Rothman.* A smile crossed Harry's lips and Sophie moved closer to him, but he turned away. His dream was enough.

Chapter 10

The summer of 1944 suffocated Brooklyn with its oppressive humidity and relentless heat. The pushcart peddlers maintained their loyal vigil in the marketplace. They rolled up their shirtsleeves and donned hats to protect themselves from the scorching sun. The smell of rotting garbage from the marketplace drifted through the open windows of the Rothmans' apartment and lingered there, a blanket of hot stinking air.

It was the combination of the heat, the humidity and the smell of garbage that drove Sophie and the children away from Brooklyn for the summer to the Catskill Mountains, where they could fill their lungs with fresh cool air and their eyes with tall trees, wild flowers and freshwater streams. Harry would visit them on weekends, enduring Brooklyn from Monday to Friday so he could earn a living.

On the last Friday in June, Sophie packed feverishly, anxious to escape the stink of Brooklyn as quickly as possible. Her hair clung damply to her neck and rings of perspiration stained her dress as she packed clothing, blankets, linens, pots and dishes. Harry tied the cartons and suitcases with heavy cord to secure them for the long journey. The trip, though only 120 miles away, would take six or seven hours. It seemed to Harry that all of Brooklyn poured onto Route 17, like a gypsy caravan, clogging the northbound highway with its cargo of humanity and all its litter.

For years the Rothmans had spent summers in the Catskills, renting one room where they crammed themselves and their belongings for the entire summer, sharing a community kitchen and bathroom. They always returned to the same place, renting the same room from Solly Aaronheim, who offered rooms for rent in a large, gray clapboard country house, or an entire bungalow if you could afford it. Ida and her family came too, renting the room next door to Sophie. "Maybe we should rent a bungalow this summer," Ida had said. "How will I manage in the kitchen with my baby and other families?"

"Mothers with younger babies than yours manage. You can too," Sophie told her.

"We could share a bungalow… Maybe it wouldn't cost so much."

"One room is all I need," Sophie insisted. And she returned to the small room crammed with three beds, a dresser, a tiny closet hidden behind a tattered curtain and barely enough floor space to open the door. Ida rented a small bungalow with her brother and sister-in-law.

"It's a pleasure to share a kitchen with only one family," Ida told Sophie.

"It's nice if you can afford it," Sophie said.

"If I can afford it, so can you," Ida had said.

"That's what you think. When you have three children like me and a husband who's never sure of his job, you have to watch every penny. And don't forget, we just bought a car." Sophie was very proud of their first car, though it was eight years old and leaked exhaust fumes into the passenger seats. Now Sophie could travel to the Catskills in the luxury of her brown, wood-paneled station wagon. "At least I don't have to travel by hack this summer like a sardine," Sophie told Ida. "And Nathan can come on weekends with Harry in the car. He doesn't have to take a bus anymore."

"Nathan didn't mind taking the bus," Ida said, apprehensive about the old car whose back doors had to be secured with ropes.

It took the Rothmans seven hours to reach their destination in Monticello that summer. The back of the station wagon was stuffed with bedding, pots and pans, shopping bags and cartons. The children sat atop the bedding, singing songs and playing word games for hours until they reached the halfway mark—*The Red Apple Rest*—a landmark stopover for weary city refugees. Harry parked the station wagon, and the Rothmans joined the throngs of people streaming out of cars, taxis and buses to use the urine-soaked bathrooms and eat hot dogs and French fries at the greasy outdoor counters. After a brief rest, the family had to endure three more hours of snail-paced travel and a flat tire before arriving at Aaronheim's bungalow colony in Monticello.

"Ah, smell that fresh air." Sophie inhaled deeply as she emerged from the car in her perspiration-soaked dress.

The children ran off in search of old friends who they hoped had returned this summer. Ida, seeing the car from her bungalow window, came out to greet them. She had arrived earlier that day by hack—a hired taxi. "I was getting worried," Ida said. "What took you so long?"

"When you have your own car, you can take your time. What's my hurry? The meter isn't running."

"I thought, God forbid, you had an accident."

"The car broke down," Harry said.

"What did you need a car for? Another headache." Ida's brow furrowed.

"How's your bungalow?" Sophie asked, ignoring Ida's comment.

"It's beautiful! Come in later. You'll see."

Mr. Aaronheim lumbered toward them, his dark bushy beard concealing fleshy jowels. "*Nu*, what took you so long?" He held out his thick hand to Harry.

"My new car," Harry said.

"Oh." Aaronheim eyed the car approvingly. "Very nice." He handed Harry the key to their room. Then turning to Sophie, he warned, "Remember the rules. No cooking in the room, only in the kitchen!"

Harry and Sophie unpacked the car now, and Sophie arranged things as best she could in the small room. "Aaronheim has a lot of nerve talking to me like that," Sophie told Harry as she placed the children's hairbrushes on the dresser.

"He has a big place to take care of. He doesn't need extra work if people break his rules," Harry said, recalling the mess Sophie had made last summer when she splattered the walls with blackberries she was canning.

"He can afford to hire help… I wonder how much money he makes. It's not a bad idea. He only works in the summer."

"A big place like this is hard work," Harry said.

"Harry, maybe when you come back for vacation, we could look around for a place in the Catskills."

"What are you thinking of?"

"A small house, or a bungalow or two we could buy. We could rent out rooms… We have a little money. It would be an investment."

The idea of owning property in the Catskills excited Harry. He thought about it during the entire drive back to Brooklyn on Sunday night.

Chapter 11

Sophie enjoyed the country. She spent long lazy days watching the children swim in a nearby creek and evenings in the community room playing cards or talking to Ida and the other women. When Harry came on weekends, they went on picnics. Harry fished in a nearby stream with Albert, catching trout that Sophie would cook for dinner. She loved food that she didn't have to buy.

The voices and laughter of the children broke the stillness of the night as Sophie sat on the steps one weekday evening, watching the sun fade into darkness. The children toasted marshmallows over a bonfire, their faces aglow in the firelight. Sophie's eyes rested on Jeanie, who was one of the youngest there. The sun had tanned Jeanie's skin to a rich bronze and turned her sandy-colored hair blonde. She had a fine straight nose and high delicate cheekbones. She'll be a beautiful woman one day, Sophie thought now. She looks more like Lev Kramer every day.

Sophie closed her eyes, trying to push Lev's face from her memory. She didn't want him invading her consciousness after all these years. It was seven years since she had last seen Lev, when he had lived in the apartment across the hall from her in their house in Brooklyn. He had moved in with his wife, Minna, and two young sons a few months after Harry had left for Panama. Five months later, Lev's wife died of pneumonia.

Sophie would watch Lev's seven-year-old boy, Joel, till Lev returned from work in the evening. Joel went to school with Albert every day. "It's no trouble to watch Joel after school," she had assured Lev. Lev's younger son, David, only three years old, had to be deposited with a different relative every day. "Poor David," Sophie had told Ida. "A baby losing his mother is the worst thing."

"Mr. Kramer will find another wife," Ida predicted.

"It's not so easy to find a woman who wants a ready-made family."

"Such a good-looking man… someone will grab him fast," Ida said.

"He makes a good living too," Sophie added. "To come from Europe only a few years ago and be a foreman in a dress factory already is nothing to sneeze at."

Lev's handsome face sprung alive in Sophie's mind now. He was taller than Harry, muscular and slim. His hair was sandy colored as was his short well-trimmed beard. The beard made him look older than his thirty-five years, and his gray eyes were intense and sad. Sophie wondered what Lev had ever seen in his wife, Minna. She doubted that Harry would ever grieve for her the way Lev had grieved for his wife. Harry wouldn't have gone off to Panama and left me if he really loved me, Sophie had thought then. He married me because I pushed him into it. He must be sleeping with a different woman every night in his jungle paradise, she concluded.

The year after Lev's wife died was a difficult one for him. Sophie would bring chicken soup to his apartment on Friday nights. She'd knock on the door softly. "Mr. Kramer, I had a little extra chicken soup for you and the children. It's still warm."

"Thank you, Mrs. Rothman." He would take the pot of soup from her. "Good *Shabbes*."

"Good *Shabbes*," Sophie answered, satisfied that she had somehow lightened his burden and made the Sabbath more peaceful for him.

Later in the evening, when the children were asleep, Lev would knock on Sophie's apartment door. When Sophie opened it, he would hold out the pot for her, scrubbed clean of any trace of chicken soup. "It was delicious, Mrs. Rothman. Thank you for your kindness."

One night, noticing that Lev's gray eyes looked especially sad, Sophie said, "Come in, Mr. Kramer. I'll make you a cup of tea… And you can call me Sophie. After all, we're neighbors now for almost a year."

"Thank you," he said, entering the apartment reluctantly. "You can call me Lev."

Albert and Ruthie were asleep and the stillness of the Sabbath evening settled around them as they sipped tea in the quiet of the warm kitchen, watching the Sabbath candles flicker. Lev talked mostly of his dead wife and how much he missed her. "Minna loved to read. She wanted to be a teacher one day. She took care of everything in the house and still found time for her books… I liked to watch her read in the evening," he told Sophie, his eyes misty.

"One day it will not hurt as much," Sophie soothed. But even as she said those words to Lev, the pain of Harry's absence grew stronger and her loneliness harder to bear.

Sophie's thoughts were interrupted by Jeanie, who stood before her now, melted marshmallow clinging to her lips and fingers. "Albert took the last marshmallow off my stick and ate it!" Jeanie was irate.

"Tomorrow he'll give you one of his," Sophie told her.

"I want it back now!" She stamped her foot.

"It's time to go to bed."

"I want my marshmallow!" Jeanie clenched her small fists.

"Albert, why did you take Jeanie's marshmallow?" Sophie called out.

"I didn't take it," Albert shouted. "She gave it to me."

"He's a liar. Liar! Liar!" Jeanie shouted angrily.

"It's time to get ready for bed." Sophie rose from the steps. "Don't touch anything with your sticky hands," she told Jeanie, opening the door to their room and taking a towel from a hook behind the door. Then they waited in the hallway outside the community bathroom until it was free.

After Jeanie was tucked into bed, Sophie went outside again to find Albert and Ruthie. She called into the darkness, where she knew they were playing hide and seek with the other children. The bonfire had burned itself out and all she could see were tiny flickering lights made by the fireflies. Albert and Ruthie appeared as suddenly as they had disappeared and agreed to go to bed after many protests.

Sophie sat down on the steps in front of the house again. The air had grown chill and damp as the evening dew settled around her, and she pulled a sweater around her shoulders. Soft laughter and the murmur of voices drifted out of the community room where women had gathered for evening card games. Sophie felt suddenly lonely for the company of a man, the way she had felt when Harry was away in Panama. Lev had come into her life then, filling the emptiness and tempering her anger at Harry.

After that first night years ago, when Sophie had invited Lev in for tea, his visits became a ritual that she awaited eagerly. Lev would sit in her kitchen talking to her for an hour, sometimes longer. One night, several months after Lev had been coming to visit, he said, "Sophie, I want to thank you for listening to my complaints for so long."

"I'm glad to help… But you still look sad," she had said.

"I'm not so sad any more. You make me happy." He reached across the kitchen table and covered her hand with his. Sophie felt her skin burn under his touch, kindling desire deep within her. She drew her hand away and they both rose. "I must go." Lev's voice was suddenly hoarse.

"Yes," she answered and walked with him to the door.

In the dim light of the entryway, they both reached for the doorknob and Lev's warm hand was upon hers again. Sophie laughed nervously as Lev brushed passed her and said, "Good night." After getting into bed that night, Sophie had tossed and turned for hours, feeling restless and uneasy.

Sophie shivered now, the cool dampness seeping through her summer dress. She pulled the sweater tighter around her shoulders and listened to the comforting chirping of the crickets, trying not to think about Lev. But memories flooded back to haunt her.

Sophie remembered her agitation as the next Friday approached so long ago. She had sensed a change in Lev and in herself that week. She opened the door to his soft knock that night with eagerness to see him and apprehension about what might happen. Lev slipped into a kitchen chair, and Sophie felt his eyes on her as she set two cups of tea on the table. His fingers drummed nervously on the table as they drank the tea. "Some more tea?" Sophie asked, setting her cup in the saucer with trembling hands.

"No." Lev's voice was low.

Sophie walked to the stove to replace the teapot, and suddenly Lev was behind her, his hands on her shoulders, turning her gently around to face him and then drawing her against him. She felt the heat from his body, his male hardness against her thigh, as his soft beard brushed her face and his lips found hers. She clung to him, feeling her legs weaken. He guided her to the bedroom and she followed, drawn to him, unable to stop herself as the door closed behind them.

Lev undressed her in silence, never taking his eyes from her body. Then he undressed quickly and took her in his arms again, kissing her neck, her breasts, her stomach. "You're beautiful," Lev murmured, as his beard brushed the inside of her thigh and he kissed her soft flesh. Sophie breathed in the clean soapy smell of his body and she clung to him as they lost themselves in lovemaking.

They lay back exhausted afterward, the sheet damp beneath them. Sophie's body throbbed from Lev's touch and a deep satisfaction filled her. Lev turned to her, looking into her eyes in the dim lamplight. "Are you sorry?" he asked.

"No… No, not at all." She hadn't felt sorry then. Why should she? Harry was probably having himself a good time in Panama. How would Harry ever find out? She was lonely and Lev was lonely. They were just two lonely people looking for a little happiness. They weren't hurting anyone.

"Sophie, are you out there?" Ida called into the darkness now, interrupting Sophie's reverie.

"Yes, I'm here."

"I saved you a seat at the card table. Everyone's waiting," Ida said.

Sophie rose from the steps and walked across the damp grass to the recreation room, anxious to flee her haunting memories.

Chapter 12

Harry left the Navy Yard early on the last Friday in July, eager to begin his weeklong vacation with Sophie and the children. He didn't mind the crawling traffic along Route 17 this Friday, happy with the prospect of spending an entire week away from Brooklyn.

When he arrived at Aaronheim's bungalow colony, the station wagon sputtering and banging, the children ran out to greet him. "Daddy's here!" Jeanie shouted excitedly, running into Harry's outstretched arms. He lifted her high above his head and she giggled. Unlike Sophie, Harry was always pleased to see Jeanie. "You're getting too heavy for me," he teased, setting her down and then kissing Ruthie on her cheek.

Albert ran toward him, clutching a jar with a fat green frog in his hands. "Look what I found, Dad." He thrust the jar in front of Harry's eyes.

"Don't keep him in there too long," Harry warned as he watched Sophie approach.

"You're early," Sophie said. "Did you remember to bring the bagels?"

Harry handed Sophie a brown paper bag filled with bagels, and she inhaled the delicious yeasty smell that escaped from the bag. "They rob you for everything in the country, even bagels," Sophie complained.

Harry took his suitcase and a new fishing pole from the car. "That's a nice fishing pole, Dad," Albert said. "I'll carry it for you. Can I fish with it too?"

"You can have my old rod," Harry told him.

"Gee thanks, Dad." Albert said, grateful to discard the fishing pole he had fashioned from a tree branch, a string and an old hook.

"What did you need a new pole for?" Sophie asked.

"It was time for a new one. And Albert needs a fishing pole too."

"You'll catch the same fish with the old pole," Sophie said, frowning.

Ruthie and Jeanie ran up the steps of the community house and held the door open for Harry. They walked down the dim corridor to their room and Sophie unlocked the door. The room smelled damp and musty like the hallway. The smell of too many people crammed into too small a space. Harry threw his suitcase on one of the beds. The three beds took up most of the room. Only a narrow aisle separated the children's beds from the bed that Harry and Sophie shared.

The children jumped on the lumpy beds, excited by the prospect of their father's vacation. Sophie helped Harry unpack his bag. His hand lightly brushed hers as she pulled a shirt from the suitcase. "We should have taken a bungalow this year," he told Sophie, resenting his forced celibacy in the summer. He would have to scheme to arrange even half an hour alone with Sophie.

"Maybe we can go to Beaverkill Campsite tomorrow," Sophie said.

"Can we, Daddy?" Ruthie asked excitedly.

"Sure." Harry smiled. "Why not?"

"Yay!" the children cried in unison, bouncing on the beds.

The family rose early the next morning for their outing to Beaverkill Campsite. The children piled into the back of the station wagon with the fishing poles, picnic bags and blankets. "Do we have everything?" Sophie checked the back of the car, and they took off in a cloud of black smoke that spewed from the car's exhaust pipe. The children sang, "*When the lights go on again all over the world,*" and it made Harry and Sophie share thoughts of the war still raging on the other side of the world. Sophie hoped the war would end soon so prices would go down and things wouldn't be so scarce. Harry thought how strange it was that he could gaze at miles of sun-drenched peaceful countryside while millions of men, women and children met agonizing deaths and cities were reduced to rubble. He looked through the rearview mirror at Albert now, relieved that his son was too young to go to war. *I'll never let him go to war*, Harry thought. *Never.*

"Look!" Sophie pointed. "Over there, a 'For Sale' sign. Let's take a look."

Black hand-painted letters—*FOR SALE*—stood out boldly on a weathered wooden sign planted in the ground in front of a white clapboard farmhouse. Acres of grass and wild flowers surrounded it. A large red barn, empty now except for scattered mounds of dried hay, stood near the roadside, and a small cottage lay hidden in the distance as though it was painted on a canvas.

Harry pulled off the road onto a dirt path in front of the house and they all piled out of the car. "Look, a swing!" Jeanie shouted, delighted with her discovery of a handmade swing strung from clotheslines between two trees at the side of the house.

"I go first!" Albert shouted, racing ahead of Jeanie and Ruthie.

"Be careful!" Sophie cautioned them, as she and Harry stood gazing at the property like two children eyeing icing on a cake. They watched a gaunt figure in blue overalls and a striped shirt approaching from a house on the adjoining property. "Can I help ya? I'm Mr. Carswell," he drawled, extending a bony suntanned hand.

"Mr. and Mrs. Rothman," Harry said, surprised by the man's strong handshake.

"We noticed your sign. Could we see the property?" Sophie asked.

"Be happy to show ya... You folks lookin' to buy?" He bit on his corncob pipe.

Mr. Carswell led them through the house, the barn and the cottage. The house was large. A kitchen with a coal stove, a large parlor and a sunroom were downstairs. There were five bedrooms upstairs and no bathroom. Sophie's mind whirled as their footsteps echoed through the empty rooms. Harry's eyes met Sophie's and silently they shared the same thought—there was more space here than they had ever seen.

Outside the house, Mr. Carswell pointed to a weathered wooden shed behind the house. "That there's the outhouse."

Wouldn't it be wonderful if... Harry mused, but his thoughts were interrupted by Mr. Carswell. "You folks want to buy? It'll cost you eight thousand dollars."

"The price is too high for us now. Maybe in a few years," Sophie said.

Sophie noticed the smile fade from Mr. Carswell's thin lips. "Well, maybe I could see my way clear to lettin' you folks have it for a little less. Have to talk to the Missus... Ya'll come around again." He shook Harry's hand.

The Rothmans arrived at Beaverkill Campsite an hour later. Ruthie helped Sophie spread the blankets on a grassy spot near the lake. Other families were already clustered around the lake. The children stripped to their bathing suits and splashed into the icy water. They took turns drifting on an old inner tube Harry had filled with air. "Watch your sister," Sophie ordered Ruthie and Albert, concerned that Jeanie might drift out too far.

"What do you think about the property, Harry?" Sophie munched on a sandwich.

"It's very nice, but it's too much money."

Sophie knew there was enough money in her bank account. An account book she kept hidden in a drawer beneath her nightgowns, she considered hers. Some of the money she had started out with before they were married. Most of it she had saved when Harry was in Newfoundland. She wouldn't let them use that money. She kept another account, with four thousand dollars that she had saved when Harry was in Newfoundland. That was the money she would allow them to use now. "Mr. Carswell will lower the price. Times are bad. We'll offer him four thousand dollars," Sophie said with finality.

Harry laughed. "You think he's going to take four thousand when he wants eight?"

"I don't see people standing on line to buy his property. He'll take four thousand." Sophie was already making plans as if Mr. Carswell had accepted their offer. "We can rent the cottage to one family and we can have boarders in the house. There are five bedrooms. We can rent three. It will bring in money to pay for other things."

"I could build two bungalows out of the barn." Harry's ideas rushed ahead. "And there's plenty of property… Every summer I could build another bungalow. Soon we'd have a whole bungalow colony."

"We'll put up a sign—*ROTHMAN'S BUNGALOWS*." Sophie smiled.

One by one, Jeanie, Ruthie and Albert emerged from the lake, shivering and hungry. They wrapped themselves in towels and sat on the blanket, munching sandwiches.

After lunch and a game of catch with the children, Harry went off to fish with Albert and Ruthie. Ruthie took along a jar to catch minnows, and Albert proudly carried the old fishing pole Harry had given him.

Sophie stretched out on a blanket under the warm sun. Jeanie lay down next to her, reaching out to touch her mother's arm, which lay motionless and unresponsive. She watched Sophie doze as leaves on a nearby oak tree cast dappled shadows across her mother's face. She wished her mother would hug her sometimes, the way Aunt Ida hugged her children. Sophie always pried Jeanie's arms away when she hugged her and said, "Not now." Jeanie's need for Sophie's touch diminished as she grew older. Anger now replaced her need for Sophie's affection. It was an undirected anger that she did not understand, that would always cloud her feelings for her mother.

"Look Momma! They caught a fish!" Jeanie shouted in Sophie's ear as she lay in a half-sleep under the soothing sun. Sophie rubbed her eyes and sat up, watching Albert running toward them with a large trout that he waved wildly through the air. Harry and Ruthie followed close behind.

"I caught a fish!" Albert shouted, holding the fish up proudly.

"That's *some* fish." Sophie squeezed the fish's fat belly. "It'll make a good dinner for us tonight."

Jeanie reached out to touch the fish that still wriggled and slipped through her fingers.

"He's a good fisherman." Harry patted Albert's back.

"We'd better pack up. It's getting late and we have a long trip back," Sophie said.

The children slept in the back of the station wagon on the trip home. Harry felt relaxed and happy, his thoughts wandering back to the house in Livingston Manor. "Should we stop and make Mr. Carswell an offer?" Harry asked Sophie.

"Wait a few days," Sophie reasoned. "We don't want to seem too anxious." It was settled then, Harry thought happily. They would arrive at some bargain.

***

Before the end of the week, Sophie and Harry returned to speak to Mr. Carswell. "We can't pay more than four thousand dollars for the property," Sophie told him

"Can't sell it for that little," Mr. Carswell said, his Adam's apple bobbing nervously in his throat.

"Well, it was nice meeting you, Mr. Carswell," Sophie said, knowing that her refusal to bargain at all would insure the sale. "Let's go, Harry." Harry looked puzzled. They had come to strike a bargain and Sophie had agreed to go higher. He wondered what kind of game Sophie was playing now as she walked toward the car. He hated when she acted like this.

Sophie opened the car door and got in. Harry followed her. Mr. Carswell waved, calling, "Hold on there just a minute. I'll go talk to the Missus." Sophie and Harry waited in the car, each lost in thought while Mr. Carswell conferred with his wife. Sophie's mind was busy furnishing the empty rooms of the house. She had barely finished the downstairs when Mr. Carswell returned. "We have a deal, Mr. Rothman." He extended his hand to Harry, ignoring Sophie as if he knew intuitively that it was she who had conned him. "Come and meet the Missus, and I'll write everything down on paper… to make it all legal."

They followed Mr. Carswell, across what Sophie already considered her property, to a spotless white house bordered by rows of yellow mums and multi-colored portulaca. The door opened, revealing gleaming floors and polished furniture. The house smelled faintly of lemon oil, berries and dried rosemary.

A small woman with a wrinkled sun-baked face and luminous blue eyes emerged from the kitchen. Clad in a pale green dress, a starched white apron and ankle-high leather boots, Mrs. Carswell looked as scrubbed and polished as her furniture and floors. "Welcome," Mrs. Carswell drawled in an accent peculiar to the region. "So pleased to meet ya." She herded them into her kitchen, where she bustled around, serving them home-baked muffins with blackberry preserves she had just canned and steaming cups of tea.

"Wonderful preserves." Sophie licked her lips, savoring the tang and natural sweetness. The words had barely left her lips when Mrs. Carswell disappeared into her pantry and returned with a jar of preserves for Sophie to take home.

"Thank you," Sophie said, sipping the tea and marveling at how this frail-looking woman kept her home so immaculate and managed to cook, bake and can food while she herself had trouble keeping her kitchen floor clean for more than a day.

Harry drummed nervously on the table as he waited for Mr. Carswell to record their agreement, marveling at the gleaming pots and pans that hung above the coal stove.

"It's ready." Mr. Carswell placed a hand-written document before them and handed Harry a fountain pen. They all signed and shook hands, sealing their bargain. "I'll send you a deposit next week," Harry promised, standing to leave.

"Welcome to Livingston Manor," Mrs. Carswell said, her eyes twinkling as if she knew a secret she wouldn't share with them.

Sophie and Harry got into their car for the trip back to Aaronheim's, where they had left the children in Ida's charge. They shared the excited anticipation of new property owners. "I can't wait till next summer when I can start building. We're going to own a country place." Harry beamed and patted Sophie's knee affectionately.

"Yes, we're going to build a bungalow colony." Sophie smiled, delighted with the venture that would change their lives.

Chapter 13

The first boarders to occupy the Rothman's new country house lived there rent free. Harry needed help building bungalows the following summer. He needed a carpenter to help him construct the buildings, a plumber to install the pipes, and an electrician to do the wiring. His cousin, Murray Landau, who was a plumber by trade, occupied one room in the farmhouse with his wife, Gertie, and their three children. Irving Kaplan, an electrician who Harry knew from Brooklyn, and his young wife, Eva, and their baby occupied another room in the house. Harry also invited Norman Lasnik, a skilled carpenter who worked beside Harry every day at the Brooklyn Navy Yard. Norman was delighted to spend the summer in the Catskills with his wife, Molly, and their twin daughters.

When the three wives complained that their rooms were too small, Sophie silenced them. "Wait till you see how wonderful your children will look at the end of the summer. There's nothing like country air. And it's all free for you this summer. Next summer you'll be begging me to rent you a bungalow."

The summer flew by. Six bungalows were built and sparsely furnished from a Sears Roebuck catalog and country auctions. Everyone was surprised at the speed with which the bungalows took shape. With the war over in Europe and building materials available again, there were no obstacles in their path.

Harry and the men took a rare afternoon off at the end of the summer to go fishing. The women dutifully packed lunches for them, and the happy foursome went off to a nearby trout stream. Sophie watched through the kitchen window as they disappeared down the winding road, their fishing poles and tackle boxes bobbing in their hands. Sophie had never seen Harry so happy. He was pleased with the development of the new bungalows and excited to be a landowner. She was glad he no longer spoke of pharmacy school. It was a childish idea. She knew what was right for them. He was a stubborn man, but she had always been able to make him see things her way. Though she had to admit, when he had gone off to Panama so many years ago, she felt more like a loser than a winner. How different their lives might have been if Harry had never gone to Panama. Lev Kramer would just have been a neighbor, and Jeanie never would have… The chatter of children's voices drew Sophie away from the window and her thoughts. "Momma, we're going swimming now," Ruthie announced, dressed in a blue bathing suit and canvas sneakers, an inner tube from an old tire slung over her shoulder.

"Momma, tell Ruthie she has to share the tube with me," Jeanie said.

"Don't worry, she'll share it." Sophie handed them a bag of sandwiches.

Albert opened the screen door and stuck his head into the kitchen. "Come on squirts, let's go!"

Molly's twins, dressed in identical red bathing suits and sandals, raced down the steps. "Now you be careful, girls," Molly cautioned. "I'm walking into town with Eva and the baby."

Gertie's boys followed down the steps, stomping and pushing each other as they always did. Gertie, clad in a black swimsuit, her plump figure straining against the seams, trailed behind them. Gertie, who usually stayed in the house, complaining that the sun was bad for her delicate complexion, was accompanying the children today. "Don't work too hard at home," Gertie called to Sophie as they left.

Eva strapped her baby into a stroller, and Molly held the screen door open for her. "You sure you don't need anything in town?" Molly asked Sophie.

"No, nothing today. Have a nice time." Sophie watched the last of her boarders disappear down the road. She was glad to be rid of them for a few hours along with their chatter. A rare silence settled over the house. Sophie picked up a wooden bowl of peas that needed shelling and went out to the front porch to sit on the rocker. The air was still and warm. The only sounds were the late summer cicadas and an occasional car passing in the distance. Even Mitzi was asleep under the large shade tree on the front lawn, her tail slapping now and then at an annoying fly. Harry had cut the grass earlier that week with a scythe, and the boys had raked it into little mountains of hay that sat baking in the sun, filling the air with a rich sweet scent.

Sophie's thoughts turned to Lev Kramer again, just as they had last night when she and Harry had made love quickly and silently, trying not to be heard by any of the boarders in the adjacent rooms. She had tried to conjure up Lev's face so she could somehow rekindle the excitement she had felt long ago, excitement that lately seemed missing from her lovemaking with Harry. Sophie's affair with Lev had gone on for months. They had started meeting more than once a week. Sophie had given Lev a key, and sometimes late in the evening, he would slip quietly into her apartment, taking care not to be seen in the hallway by any neighbors. In the darkened apartment, Lev would take her hand and guide her to the bedroom, where they would lock the door and undress quickly, eager to satisfy their lust. "I missed you," Lev would say, holding her in his arms, caressing her.

Each time they were together, their lovemaking reached a higher pitch. It was as if they knew intuitively that each night could be the last. The futility of their affair and its inevitable end was never far from their thoughts. The affair in itself was enough for Sophie. She felt fulfilled. Her life took on a new dimension. The days no longer seemed lonely and difficult with Harry away. She had the nights to look forward to. Harry did not deserve her virtue, she rationalized. But Sophie did not want to complicate her life with any thoughts beyond her affair. She did not want to leave Harry or marry Lev and be saddled with his two children. She knew she could never face her family and friends if her infidelity were exposed. Besides, she loved Harry as much as she could love any man, and she wanted him back. He belonged to her, like her apartment, her furniture, her bankbooks. Did she love Lev too, she wondered? Well, she supposed she did in a way, yet she would not change her life for him. She was content to have things go on the way they were.

Lev found it more and more difficult to be away from Sophie. She was more sexually fulfilling than his wife had been. His wife had made love timidly, passively accepting his body as though it were her duty and obligation. He had loved his wife, but with Sophie he had discovered what lovemaking should be. Sophie abandoned all inhibitions along with the clothing she shed and left in a heap on the floor. He wanted to marry Sophie so he could have her as a love object always.

After their lovemaking one night, Lev sat up, his elbow propped against the pillow, his fingers curling playfully in Sophie's hair. "Sophie, I was thinking, maybe we could go to Palestine."

"Palestine? What do you mean?"

"I want to marry you. We could make a new life in Palestine. It's far enough away so that…"

Sophie put her finger to his lips to silence him. "Don't, Lev. Don't even think it. I could never leave Harry. No one must ever know about us."

"I… I don't understand." Lev's voice grew husky and his gray eyes held hers with a piercing intensity. "I thought you loved me."

"It has nothing to do with love. Harry's my husband. My life is here with him and my children."

"He left you. What kind of husband is he?"

"He's coming back and…"

"Then you don't love me… You never did," he said, realizing for the first time the truth of his words. Lev rose from the bed and dressed silently, the muscles in his face tense. "You used me," he said then, his eyes burning with anger and humiliation.

Sophie got out of bed, the starkness of her naked body softened in the dim light. She moved toward Lev, reached out and touched his arm. "I didn't use you. That's not true. We needed each other. We were both lonely. Try to understand. For you it's different… your wife isn't coming back. You had nothing to lose."

Lev pulled away from Sophie's touch. He couldn't bear to touch her and not possess her entirely. He realized that what Sophie left unsaid was more important—she never told him she loved him. If she did, she would leave Harry. He had loved Sophie completely, but she had used him. He felt betrayed, humiliated and insanely jealous of Harry.

"Please don't go like this." Sophie reached for Lev's hand. She was not ready to give him up. But he pushed her away and left hurriedly. Sophie felt abandoned then and profoundly empty, though they had just made love, for she knew it was over. She could not run off to Palestine with Lev like some irresponsible schoolgirl. And there was an unspoken truce now between her and Harry that she sensed from his letters. She knew Harry would be coming home soon. It was best that her affair with Lev was ending now.

In the weeks that followed, Lev passed Sophie in the hallway many times. They took pains to avoid each other's eyes. One afternoon, there was a note from him in her mailbox.

> *Dear Sophie,*
>
> *I'm leaving for Palestine with my boys next week to join my brother and his family. I'm not angry with you any longer. It is probably all for the best. I cannot stay here and be so close to you every day if you cannot be mine. I must make a new life for myself in Palestine.*
>
> *Lev*

The night before his departure, Lev knocked softly on Sophie's apartment door.

"I couldn't leave without saying goodbye," he said softly, pressing the key she had given him into her hand.

"I'll miss you," she started to say, but his lips were on hers in an instant and he pulled her against him.

"I want you one last time so I'll never forget you," he murmured in her ear. Lev came to her with a fierce passion she was not prepared for, but which she welcomed, surrendering to him and her lust in this final act. They clung to each other for a long time afterward, each unwilling to release the other. Then silently Lev rose to dress, bent to kiss Sophie's damp forehead, and was gone.

A month later, a new refugee family occupied Lev's apartment, and Sophie knew with certainty that she was pregnant.

Chapter 14

Sophie put down the bowl of peas she had been shelling. She rose from the rocker where she had been sitting on the porch and walked down the path in front of the house to view the freshly painted sign Harry had put up that day. The sign stood firmly planted in the ground, facing the roadway—ROTHMAN'S BUNGALOWS—FOR RENT. Sophie surveyed all that was hers—six new bungalows, the farmhouse, the cottage, the land. She was pleased with it all. Next summer it would begin to pay off. Maybe they would buy more land if they made a good profit, her thoughts raced ahead. Now she must get back to the house and start dinner so her boarders could have their turn in the kitchen.

Everyone returned at once. Suddenly the house, whose rare silence Sophie had briefly enjoyed, was filled with children's laughter and women's chatter. The screen door banged constantly as the children chased each other in and out of the house.

Soon the men returned with a bucketful of trout that the women fried for dinner. They took turns in the kitchen, one family eating while the other cooked.

The finishing touches were put on the bungalows during the last two weeks of the summer. Windows were set in place and a fresh coat of paint was applied inside and out. Labor Day weekend was spent celebrating their achievements. The Rothmans gave a party for their boarders. Sophie baked apple cakes and pies with blackberries the children had picked in the woods behind the house.

Sophie went into town, accompanied by Jeanie, to purchase several chickens for the party at the local poultry market. The poultry farm was on the outskirts of town, where the smell of chicken droppings, feathers and dried blood was less offensive.

Sophie walked to the back of the market where the chickens were crowded into wire cages. Jeanie watched the chickens pace back and forth nervously in the small space inside the cages, stepping on their own droppings and pecking at their food and each other. Their small beady eyes peered out at her, and Jeanie wondered how it would feel to be a chicken in a wire cage waiting for death.

Sophie selected six plump chickens, which a butcher in a bloodstained apron promptly removed from the cage. He quickly and expertly slit the chickens' throats. Jeanie covered her eyes as the headless chickens did a ghastly dance of death in the blood-splattered courtyard and fell silent. The butcher carried the headless still-warm chickens back into the store where the air was thick with feathers and the smell of dried chicken blood. Jeanie watched kerchiefed women sitting on wooden stools plucking feathers from the dead birds. Feathers floated through the hot air, falling in clotted mounds on the sawdust-covered floor.

The butcher wrapped the freshly plucked chickens in brown paper and loaded them into Sophie's shopping cart. Jeanie was glad they were leaving. The sharp cries of the slaughtered chickens still rang in her ears as she walked beside her mother into the small town. They passed a grocery store, a produce market, a hardware store, a movie theater, a drugstore that also served as a luncheonette, a barbershop and a funeral chapel. There were also several bars that Sophie disapproved of. "Imagine people drinking in the afternoon when they should be working," Sophie told Harry only last night. "Ignorant hicks, that's what they are."

"What's a hick?" Jeanie had asked.

"Those are the people who live here all the time, dummy," Albert had informed her.

Sophie knew her prospective tenants would not be coming from the local gentile population, but from Brooklyn or maybe even the Bronx and Queens.

"Can I buy a comic?" Jeanie asked now as they passed the drugstore. "I have a dime."

"Go ahead, I'll wait out here." Sophie watched through the doorway as Jeanie thumbed through the comics on the display stand. Her daughter had grown taller during the summer, and her features were more sharply defined, less babyish. A ray of sunlight from the window illuminated Jeanie's hair and Sophie had an impulse to stroke her hair. But something stopped her. Something always did. She could embrace Ruthie and Albert, though she rarely did, not feeling the need to show affection when she felt any. But she did not want any physical contact with Jeanie, always haunted by resentment and guilt. She knew it was not fair to the child, and occasionally she tried to make amends.

"Can I have an ice cream cone?" Jeanie called out, expecting Sophie to say no. But Sophie surprised her today and bought her a chocolate ice cream cone that she held in one hand while she helped Sophie push the shopping cart.

The chickens were roasted the next day, along with potato puddings, and the kitchen was filled with the smell of garlic, potatoes, onions and spices. The girls helped set the long table in the dining room. The celebration began in the late afternoon. Albert brought the radio into the dining room and tuned it to a local station that played country music. The children danced about, laughing and chasing each other. Sophie was complimented for the delicious meal. Jeanie pushed a drumstick back and forth across her plate with a fork, unable to eat it. "You should have seen the chickens running around without their heads," Jeanie told everyone, but Sophie cut her short.

"No one wants to hear about that when they're eating."

After dinner, Harry brought out a bottle of brandy that he poured into small glasses for the adults. "A toast," he said, and they all lifted their glasses. "To all of you for helping to build Rothman's bungalows. We thank you and wish you well. *L'cha-yim*… to life."

"*L'cha-yim*," the group sang out in unison.

"And to peace, thank God, and the end of the war and Hitler's tyranny," Norman Lasnick added.

Only a few short weeks ago, newspaper headlines proclaimed, "*PEACE*," after four years. The war in the Pacific was finally over. Harry recalled with horror *The Daily News* headline on August 8th—*Atom Bomb Hit - A City Vanished.*

"To peace!" They all agreed, each having been touched in some way by the tragedy of war and Hitler's monstrous evil. Norman's parents had never seen his twin daughters and they never would. They had been trapped in Poland when the war broke out, and perished later in the Treblinka concentration camp. Gertie's nephew had died fighting in the Pacific. Eva Kaplan still clung to hope that cousins, who had fled Russia during the German invasion, would turn up as displaced persons somewhere.

The boarders left early the next morning, each in a hired hack whose roof and trunk were piled with their belongings. The children said their goodbyes, promising to visit each other in Brooklyn. Sophie and Harry waved goodbye from the porch. "Remember," Sophie called, "you have first choice of any bungalow next summer."

The Rothmans left early that afternoon, after packing their belongings into the car and locking up the house and bungalows for the winter. Then they joined the caravan of cars returning to life in Brooklyn. Armed with glossy black and white photos of Rothman's bungalows that Albert had taken with his Brownie camera, Sophie would spend the winter in quest of tenants for the following summer. She already worried about the success of their venture.

Chapter 15

Albert was awake by 6:00 a.m. on his graduation day in June 1949. Today was both an end and a beginning for him. He viewed it as the end of his childhood. The awesomeness of the task that lay before him excited and frightened him. He was among the intellectual elite—graduating from the Bronx High School of Science—a school for academically superior students. Albert earned admittance to the school without any effort and breezed through the courses of study in mathematics and the sciences. But it was not mathematics or the sciences that interested him. It was the literature and drama classes that excited him. He would start his pre-med studies in the fall at City College.

Harry already thought of Albert as a doctor. "I'll pay the first year's rent for your office. I promise you that," Harry had said.

Albert had never said he wanted to be a doctor. Why did Harry make him feel that he had to achieve this for him, he agonized? There was never any discussion. Even Sophie would say, "One day when you're a doctor…" Not if, but when. Albert didn't think Sophie cared much either way, but Harry was so obsessed with it that Sophie had come to accept it. Sophie wanted him to be a doctor because doctors made a lot of money, but she'd be just as satisfied if he became a lawyer or a big-time gambler, Albert reasoned.

Time and again Albert had tried to tell Harry that he was not interested in medicine. "Dad, I'm in a play at school—*Our Town*. I really love acting."

"Good, good," Harry had said. "A little recreation is important, but don't let it interfere with your studies."

Albert was glad summer was almost here and his parents were not forcing him to spend another boring vacation at the bungalow colony in Livingston Manor. Four years of summers there were enough. It was fun if you were thirteen years old and could amuse yourself with frogs and snakes all day, but he had outgrown that. He would stay in Brooklyn. He already had a summer job as a stock clerk at Macy's department store. It wasn't far from Broadway and the theaters where he could go to shows when he got paid, or wait backstage to see the stars when he had no money to see them act. Even if he couldn't live it, he could pretend that he was part of it. Albert learned a lot about acting from watching the stars. At home he would practice in front of a mirror, reading from books of plays he collected and stored in his room.

This was going to be the first summer Albert would be on his own. He promised his parents he would join them on weekends, but he figured he'd think of a way out of that after a few weeks. Sophie and Harry would be too busy managing the bungalow colony to give much thought to him. After buying the adjacent property two years ago and building ten more bungalows, which were rented well in advance of the season, Sophie and Harry had more than enough to keep them busy. While other bungalow colonies were sometimes difficult to rent, the Rothman's bungalows were never vacant. "It's better business to charge a little less than everyone else for the bungalows and rent everything than charge more and have empty bungalows," Sophie reasoned. Even in her eagerness to make money, Sophie did not lose sight of human nature. And her shrewd business sense had enabled them to pay off their first mortgage, purchase new land, build more bungalows and earn a large profit.

Harry had left the Navy Yard job three years ago. He spent winters on short-term construction jobs so he could quit early in the spring and devote his time to getting the bungalows ready for the summer occupants.

Albert wondered why, with all the money they were making, they still lived in the dreary apartment on Prospect Place. He had seen many of his friends move to better neighborhoods. Even the pushcart peddlers were leaving one by one, forced out by the growing number of supermarkets. Aunt Ida and Uncle Nathan and the children had moved out of the building last winter. All their relatives had moved on to something better. "Right now this is good enough," Sophie had said. "Besides, who will take care of the property if I leave? After all, it hasn't been sold yet."

"Did Ida care about who would take care of it? Did your brothers care?" Harry reasoned. "They left. We should move out too. It's not a good environment for the children."

"It was good enough for me all these years. It's good enough for our children. Are they royalty or something?" Sophie argued.

Albert knew the real reason Sophie stayed on here. The rent was free. It didn't matter to him now because he was already grown up, but he worried about his sisters. It wasn't safe for them. He even saw an occasional drunkard loitering in the downstairs hallway. And you could always tell it was Saturday night from the frequency of the police sirens or the flashing lights of the ambulances collecting knifing victims.

The neighborhood black people, who lived around the periphery of the Jewish neighborhood, gave vent to all their frustrations on Saturday nights. Whisky bottles were emptied, knives flashed and furniture was heaved out of windows onto the littered streets. Although there was an unspoken peace between the black and white people who lived side by side here, gangs of marauding black teenagers often attacked their white neighbors.

Albert fingered a thin white scar on his forehead now, recalling the incident that caused that scar and all the racial overtones of irrational hatred. It had happened a week after his fifteenth birthday. He had emerged from the subway station, returning from school late in the afternoon. He wore a navy pea jacket that his parents had bought him for his birthday and carried a stack of heavy books under his arm as he walked up the subway steps. Suddenly, a gang of black boys attacked him from behind. They shredded his books and pushed him roughly. "I'm goin' to git me a new coat," one of the black boys announced, as he tugged Albert's new pea jacket off. He quickly donned the new jacket, strutting in front of Albert defiantly on the deserted street as Albert shivered under the late December sky.

"Don't you go tellin' on us now," another boy warned, digging his fingers into Albert's fleshy arm. Then, just to be certain that Albert wouldn't tell anyone, two of the boys tackled him onto the cold cement sidewalk, where they smashed his head against the edge of the curb, leaving him stunned and bleeding.

Albert stumbled home, clutching his ruined books. Blood trickled down his forehead into his eye and he stifled a sob as he stepped into the safety of his home. Sophie gasped when she saw him. "What happened?" Her voice trembled as she guided Albert to a kitchen chair and took his torn books from him. Then she washed his wound and dressed it as she listened to his story. "No good *shvartses*," Sophie said. "All they know how to do is fight. If they went to school like you, they wouldn't have time to fight."

When Harry came home from work, he was furious. "Imagine the nerve of those goddamned niggers attacking my boy like that! We'll find them, Albert. And I'll kill them. I swear I'll kill them."

"You'll never find them," Albert said. "It was a whole gang. I couldn't even identify them."

"Sophie, this is no place for the children to grow up. We're going to look for a new place to live," Harry said adamantly.

Sophie didn't argue then. She knew it was futile to argue with Harry when he was this angry.

Albert traced the scar on his forehead now, an indelible reminder of hatred he did not understand.

After that incident, Ida had warned Sophie. "We have to move away from here. I'm afraid for my children."

"It could happen anywhere," Sophie argued. "It's just one of those things." Sophie was not afraid. But Ida rented an apartment on East 95th Street in the East Flatbush section of Brooklyn, not far from their brothers' homes on Kings Highway.

Early the following September, Albert had watched as a moving truck was loaded with Ida's piano, her treasured cherry wood secretary, an over-stuffed sofa and barrels of dishes. Ida and Sophie had kissed goodbye then. Jeanie and cousin Helen said a teary farewell as though they were parting for distant lands rather than another part of Brooklyn. Albert remembered feeling a pang of envy because he was not leaving for some place new and better. He promised himself then that he would work for his dream. He would go to California and Hollywood somehow… one day soon.

Albert rose from bed now, too restless to lie there any longer. He washed and shaved at the kitchen sink, using a small hand mirror. Then he closed the door to his room and dressed in a freshly laundered white shirt, a tan suit and brown shoes shined to a mirror finish. He knotted his tie carefully and stared at his reflection in a mirror that hung above his dresser. He smoothed his thick brown hair with a brush and patted his face with lime-scented aftershave. He was not at all displeased with the reflection that stared back at him. Albert knew he was good looking, with broad shoulders and a muscular frame that made him look taller than five feet eleven inches. His nose was straight like Sophie's, and his strong angular jaw bore a striking resemblance to Harry's. His face, one might say, was nearly perfect except for the small scar that marred his smooth forehead.

Albert heard the alarm clock ring in his parents' bedroom now. A few minutes later, Sophie came into the kitchen with a robe thrown carelessly around her. Her hair was uncombed and stuck out in disarray around her face. She had grown too plump in the past four years, and it seemed to Albert, as he sat at the kitchen table eating, that his mother no longer had a waistline. She looks forty-five years old, he thought, not like some of his school friends' mothers who took care of themselves and wore stylish clothes. He hoped

Sophie wouldn't embarrass him today by wearing one of her cheap garish dresses and shoes with worn-down heels. Hadn't she heard the war was over?

"Well, today's the big day," Sophie said.

"It is," Albert answered, through a mouthful of corn flakes.

Sophie went to wake Ruthie and Jeanie, who would be going to school today while she and Harry attended Albert's graduation. Harry came into the kitchen now to shave at the sink. His chest was bare and his pants were held up loosely with a belt. "Good morning, graduate." He smiled at Albert. Harry's hair had grown thinner on his head and grayer on his chest. He had grown quieter and more introverted over the past four years, and his face bore a look of resignation. The old spark that had once shone in his eyes was gone. His parents didn't argue very often now, and Harry was given to long silences. Albert loved Harry. He did not know if he loved Sophie or if he ever could. But Harry disappointed him because he had given up on himself and allowed Sophie to mold their lives. Albert sensed a change in the relationship between his parents, but he didn't understand it. It seemed to Albert that Sophie made all the decisions about spending money and Harry gave silent approval, no longer fighting for his convictions. Albert felt a mixture of disgust and anger for Harry, yet he loved him. He felt a pang of guilt because he did not want to be a doctor. He didn't want to bring another disappointment into Harry's life. But Harry's regrets were his own making, Albert reasoned. The bungalows were bringing in plenty of money. Harry could do whatever he wanted and he could stand up to Sophie, who had become a fat forty-five-year-old tyrant.

Albert's stomach knotted in anger now as he watched Sophie put the coffee pot on the stove to brew. He thought of the little he had asked for over the years and all that Sophie had said no to. "You want something, get a job," she had said. "I worked when I was fourteen years old, so can you." Sophie seemed to be punishing everyone her whole life for the hardships she had endured. Even though life could be easier now, she'd see to it that it wasn't, Albert thought.

Albert had worked at odd jobs—selling newspapers on the corner, shining shoes, sweeping the poolroom floor, stocking the corner grocer's shelves. That was how he earned money to buy all the extras he wanted—dates with girls, movies, books, ball games and ice cream sodas. He often bought things for his sisters when he had a little extra—a story book for Jeanie who loved to read, a bracelet for Ruthie who was always grateful to have something new. He promised himself he'd take care of his sisters one day when he became a famous actor and was rich. He'd give them all the things they never had and would never get from Sophie.

Albert put his empty cereal bowl in the sink now. "I'll see you after the ceremony," he told Harry and Sophie. "I have to get to school early."

***

The large auditorium at the Bronx High School of Science was already crowded when Sophie and Harry arrived. "Why couldn't we get here earlier so we could get good seats? We're always late for everything because of you," Harry complained. "We won't be able to see Albert from here."

"I can see fine," Sophie hissed, looking at the graduates seated in the front rows as they waited impatiently for the ceremony to begin. "They all look alike from behind," Sophie said.

The bandleader tapped lightly with a baton and suddenly the band played *America*. Everyone rose and heavy velvet curtains parted across the stage, revealing the American flag and a row of dignified men whose boring speeches they would undoubtedly all have to endure. They saluted the flag and the audience joined in singing the national anthem. Sophie's voice was loud. She liked to sing and was proud of her voice. Harry cast a threatening look in her direction, which she ignored. Albert thought he recognized Sophie's voice above all the others. His face flushed and he wished the singing would end.

The speeches went on for nearly an hour. Each of the men seated on the stage was introduced in turn and spoke endlessly of the road ahead for the graduates. The air grew stifling in the auditorium as the June sun beat overhead and the hour drew closer to noon. Sophie dozed as she usually did during ceremonies, and Harry nudged her. The principal called the graduates by name now, and they walked across the stage to receive their diplomas and congratulatory handshakes.

Sophie pulled a handkerchief from her frayed purse and dabbed at the perspiration on her face. People fanned their faces with the graduation programs that had been given out at the door. "Albert Rothman," the principal called out. Harry's face broke into a smile as he watched his son walk across the stage to accept his diploma. He remembered the moment in time long ago when he too had received his high school diploma and was full of hope and dreams for the future. Now his son would fulfill his dream.

Though Sophie had never earned a high school diploma, having left school after eighth grade, she was nevertheless proud of Albert's achievement and in awe of his knowledge of so many things that were a mystery to her.

The ceremony ended with special awards for outstanding achievements.

Albert could only imagine the look of surprise on his parents' faces when his name was called again. "Albert Rothman… for outstanding achievement in drama and theater," the principal's voice boomed. Enthusiastic applause followed as Albert once more walked across the stage.

"Well, I'll be…" Sophie's mouth opened in surprise.

"*Some* boy we have!" Harry stood and applauded. "That's my son," he said, turning to the stranger seated next to him. If only it could have been a science award, he couldn't help thinking.

Parents and relatives found their graduates in the melee that followed the final march of the graduates into the front lobby. There was a warm exchange of wet kisses, back slaps and hearty handshakes. Albert had no trouble finding his parents. Sophie's red and yellow flowered dress distinguished her from the rest of the women dressed in tailored pastel suits. "Albert! Albert, over here!" Sophie shouted, waving to him from across the lobby. Standing next to a classmate, Albert felt his cheeks grow hot.

"Are those your folks over there?" Kenny Gerber, his classmate, asked.

"Yeah, I have to go, Ken."

"I never met them."

"It's kind of crowded now. Maybe you can come over some time."

Ken lived with his parents and grandmother in a fine apartment building on the Grand Concourse in the Bronx. Albert was impressed each time he had been invited there. Thick blue carpeting covered the floors, and there was a large formal dining room. The bathroom had a sink with a mirror over it. No one had to wash at the kitchen sink.

"We'd like to meet your folks too," Kenny's father said, joining them.

"Yes… maybe soon, Mr. Gerber. They're in a hurry to get home now." Albert watched Sophie and Harry moving toward him across the crowded lobby. "I… I really have to go," he said.

"Good luck, Albert," Mr. Gerber said, shaking his hand firmly. Mrs. Gerber moved beside him, placing her cool hand in his, the smell of fine perfume lingering around her. "Come visit us when you start college, Albert. We'll be lonely with Kenny away at Princeton."

"Take it easy, Al," Ken said, slapping Albert's back affectionately.

"You too, Ken." Albert raced across the lobby and hurried his parents out the door.

"What's the rush?" Harry asked. "We never met your school friends."

"It's hot in here, Dad. I want to get out."

"I didn't even congratulate you," Sophie said, planting a kiss on Albert's cheek, which he involuntarily brushed off with the back of his hand. Harry put his arm around his son's shoulder. "We're proud of you, Albert. Imagine winning a special award. What a nice surprise!"

Sophie and Harry took Albert to Horn and Hardart's Automat for lunch afterward. The self-service cafeteria was crowded with lunch hour regulars who came for the large portions of food at small prices. It was one of Sophie's favorite places, and she didn't have to leave a tip. "What'll it be, graduate? Anything you want?" Harry asked.

"A roast beef sandwich will be fine. And a coke."

Harry put the required number of nickels in the sandwich machine and the glass door encasing the sandwiches opened for him. He filled a tray with the rest of their order and silverware.

Albert wished they had gone to a quieter place. The clatter of dishes and noisy chatter disturbed him now. "Eat!" Harry said, placing the tray on their table. "Doctors need their strength."

"I'm not a doctor yet."

"But you will be. I know you will."

Sophie nodded her agreement, more interested now in eating a chicken potpie than in giving Albert's career any more thought.

"That award you won was very nice," Harry went on.

"Thanks, Dad."

"Very nice," Sophie added through a mouthful of chicken.

"People might get the idea that you want to be an actor instead of a doctor," Harry said.

Albert sighed. He knew he would be the greatest disappointment in Harry's life.

Chapter 16

Albert spent the last day of August cleaning the apartment before his family arrived from Livingston Manor. He didn't want any evidence around pointing to his summer escapades. He smiled now, sweeping a stray cigarette butt into the dustpan and remembering last night and his good fortune. He had gone to Coney Island Amusement Park with his friends, Stanley and Harold. They picked up three girls near the Ferris wheel. Liz had smiled at Albert through nicotine-stained teeth and lips glossed with thick red lipstick. "I'm taking this one," Liz announced to her two girlfriends, claiming Albert for herself.

Liz wore a tight black skirt and a red satin blouse that clung to her generous breasts. Her coarse black hair was piled atop her head and clipped with a rhinestone comb. Albert's eyes were riveted on a large silver crucifix that dangled from a chain around Liz's neck, resting between her breasts. He found himself attracted and repelled by her at the same time. "Got a cigarette, honey?" Liz asked Albert, who didn't smoke but obligingly bought her a pack of Chesterfields.

Albert's friend, Stanley, who was with Liz's blonde friend, whispered in Albert's ear, "This is it. We're going to get it tonight."

Harold, who was with the homeliest of the three girls, complained to Albert, "How'd I get stuck with this one?"

They went on the Cyclone roller coaster, where Liz screamed and let her hand fall on Albert's thigh. Then they joked around in the fun house, where they made grotesque faces in the warped mirrors. After eating foot-long frankfurters at Nathan's, they headed back to Albert's empty apartment. "What did I tell you, *shiksas* always do it," Stanley whispered to Albert on the bus.

"Shh," Albert cautioned them when they arrived at his apartment building. "I don't want my neighbors to hear us."

"What's the matter, honey? Is momma gonna spank ya?" Liz teased, smacking her lips on a wad of chewing gum.

Albert locked the apartment door and each couple headed for an empty bedroom. Albert heard muffled squeals from the other rooms as he fumbled for a condom in his wallet. He put a new condom there every few months since he was sixteen, but this was the first time he was going to use it.

Albert took the mop out of the kitchen closet now and decided he'd better wash the kitchen floor. It was sticky from the soda and beer they had been drinking last night. He wondered now if Stanley was right—Did *shiksas* always do it? Albert could testify to the fact that the Jewish girls he went out with never had sex. Maybe it was just the girls he knew, he reasoned.

***

The Rothmans arrived in Brooklyn on Labor Day evening, tanned and tired from their summer in the country. Albert ran down the three flights of steps when he saw their new green Studebaker pull up in front of the house. The old station wagon had been junked last winter and Harry, after much arguing, had convinced Sophie to let them buy a new car. "We'll get another used car," Sophie had said.

"Old junk is nothing but trouble," Harry had told her. "It will cost you more in the end."

"Okay," Sophie finally agreed after days of arguing. "We'll get a new car. I don't want to listen to you blaming me every time we get stuck."

Mitzi jumped out of the car and onto the sidewalk now, barking excitedly and licking Albert. He patted her head and stuck his face through the open car window. "Hi, squirts," he teased his sisters. They smiled back at him. He knew they weren't squirts any longer. Ruthie was fifteen, a young lady now and a very pretty one, with curves in all the right places. Jeanie was nearly a young lady herself, twelve years old already and becoming a beauty too. He kissed Ruthie, squeezing her shoulders. "I'm glad you're home."

"I am too. Boy was this summer boring. I saw every movie in that hick town three times," Ruthie said.

Jeanie stepped out of the car and ran into Albert's arms, hugging him tightly. She had grown taller over the summer, her head reaching the top of his chest now. "Albert, I missed you so much."

Sophie smiled a tired smile at Albert through the open car window. "How are you, Albert? You look good."

"I'm fine, Mom." He did not kiss her. A distance had grown between them that widened with each passing year.

"Hello, Albert. Come help me with the suitcases in the trunk," Harry said. He had been the only one who had seen Albert during the summer, returning to Brooklyn several times to make sure everything was in order and to deposit rent money in their bank accounts.

Harry opened the car trunk. A drunken black man staggered toward the car, his hand outstretched. "Get away from here! Go home!" Harry hissed, angry that the man had crossed the invisible line that separated the black and white neighborhoods. The man stumbled down the street that was littered with dirty papers and rotting vegetables from the pushcarts. The smell of putrefied garbage hung in the night air like the stench from a gangrenous wound. "Take one of the suitcases and go into the house," Harry told the girls. "Don't come down again!"

In the apartment, Sophie busied herself getting everyone settled. Harry sat down on the living room sofa and lit a cigar. He had taken to smoking cigars lately.

"Dad, it's been really bad here this summer," Albert said. "You can hear police sirens almost every night now. I've chased drunkards out of our own hallway… A house was burned to the ground on the next block by an arsonist."

"I know, I know! I have eyes… I can see what's happening here." He ran his fingers through his thinning hair. "We have to get out of here."

"Albert, you kept the apartment nice and clean," Sophie called from the kitchen.

"Clean, yes," Albert said. "Nice, it will never be." He was glad he had cleaned the mess from last night.

"Listen to the big shot," Sophie answered. "He's going to college so he thinks he should live in a mansion now."

"Sophie, can't you see how bad it's gotten here?" Harry asked.

"It looks the same to me."

Albert went into his sisters' room. He wanted to spend some time with them before they started back to school the next day, and he didn't want to hang around listening to his parents arguing.

"Sophie, I want us to look for another place to live this winter," Harry went on.

"We'll see. We just got home."

Ruthie and Jeanie giggled from the other room. A vision of the drunken man and the dirty street passed before Harry's eyes again. "No, don't tell me 'we'll see.' No more waiting. You can stall for another year and another year. Let's get out of here now."

"Maybe I shouldn't even unpack the suitcases."

"It's not a joke, Sophie. Didn't you see that drunkard?"

"I've always seen that here. So what? They're harmless enough. No one's ever bothered us." Sophie turned and walked out of the room, something she did when she felt she could not win an argument. Harry, red-faced, rose from the sofa and went into the bedroom, slamming the door behind him.

He's just tired from the long trip and the long summer, Sophie thought now. He always picks a fight when he's tired. She sat down on a kitchen chair, slipped her shoes off and stretched her legs. They had worked hard this past summer. Managing sixteen bungalows and keeping everyone happy was no easy task. But it paid off. Sophie took her two bankbooks out of her purse and examined them. They had deposited $5000 this past summer just from the rentals and another $1500 from refreshments and supplies she sold to the tenants at the canteen she operated. Added to their other savings, there was quite a sizable sum now. Sophie was pleased with their profits, but she wasn't going to spend it all on a new place to live, not right now when they were living here rent free. Maybe when the property was sold and she and Ida and her brothers divided the money. Harry would have to be patient. They would all have to learn to be patient. If it wasn't for her, they wouldn't have twenty-five thousand dollars now, she reasoned. Some day they would be rich. That was her dream. She never lost sight of it. Then, and only then, could they have everything they wanted.

Chapter 17

The Rothmans didn't see much of Albert once he started college. He left the apartment early each morning for his classes, studied at the college library in the afternoon and stayed late for evening drama club rehearsals. Albert played a part in every play that was produced at City College.

Ruthie was attending Jefferson High School. She met her girlfriends each morning at the bus stop and returned with them in the afternoon. She was a good student. She wanted to go to college like Albert, but Sophie had other ideas. "Learn typing and bookkeeping. Then you'll be able to get a good job when you graduate," Sophie told her.

Jeanie attended the junior high school on Dean Street. She walked three quarters of a mile to school each morning, linked arm-in-arm with her girlfriends, and returned home at 3:30 in the afternoon. They all raced home at lunch hour too, unwilling to eat in the school cafeteria where the black students were hostile to them. Jeanie was in a class with mostly white children, totally segregated from the rest of the school. It seemed to her that she moved about there like a prisoner, locked into one ghetto and locked out of the other. Each group feared and resented the other. Neither understood why.

Returning home from school one day, Jeanie and her friends were challenged by a group of black girls. Approaching from behind, their leader called out, "Git outa my way, whitey!" Jeanie and her friends unlinked their arms, making a path for the black girls in an attempt to avoid a confrontation. The black girls pushed them, knocking Jeanie's friend, Fran, to the ground. Jeanie helped her stunned friend while her other friends fled in terror. The black girls circled them, silent and threatening, awaiting a signal from their leader.

Jeanie's heart pounded. "Let's try to walk away slowly," she whispered to Fran. But the black girls were upon them, pinning them to the cold sidewalk and punching them mercilessly. A stinging pain shot through Jeanie's eye. Her fear suddenly turned to rage and her fists shot out in retaliation before an approaching passerby broke up the fight. The man helped Fran and Jeanie to their feet. "You girls shouldn't be wandering around here alone," he advised. The girls fled to the safety of their homes to nurse their bruises and wounded feelings.

Sophie gasped when she opened the door. Blood oozed from Jeanie's lower lip and her right eye was purple and swollen. She fell sobbing into Sophie's arms. "What happened? Tell me what happened!" Sophie guided Jeanie to the kitchen sink and washed the dried blood from her lip.

"They beat me… They… they beat me." Her words came in short gasps.

"Who? Who did this?"

"Black girls… from school. I thought they were going to kill us."

"Who was with you?"

"Fran. They beat her too. A whole gang of them."

Sophie led her daughter, now three inches taller than she, to a kitchen chair and pressed an ice-filled washcloth over her swollen eye. "Okay, calm down," Sophie soothed, her hands trembling slightly as she patted Jeanie's head.

Jeanie's tears soon changed to dry hiccupping sobs as she recounted the humiliating attack. A threat from one of the attackers still rang in her ears, "I'm gonna git you, you motherfucker!"

Jeanie spent the rest of the afternoon in bed. Ruthie was horrified when she saw her sister. "You poor kid," she murmured as she sat at her side, reading to her from a book of jokes. Ruthie even went to the candy store and bought Jeanie a vanilla Mello Roll, but Jeanie's lip was too swollen to bite into the ice cream sandwich, which only made her cry again.

By early evening, Jeanie's eye looked worse. It was painfully swollen and discolored. Sophie knew Harry would go wild when he saw her. She tried to prepare Harry when he walked through the door. "Don't get upset when you see Jeanie," she began. "There was a little accident. Some nasty girls pushed her down and her eye is black and blue."

"What? How?" He pushed past Sophie to find Jeanie. His face paled when Jeanie looked up from the book she was hunched over as she sat on the living room sofa. A grotesque, half-closed purple eye and bulbous lip now marred the delicate features of his daughter's face. "How did this happen?" Harry's voice trembled. When he heard the whole story, he flung the metal lunch box he was still holding onto to the floor. "Niggers… Goddamned niggers! I told you we have to get out of here." He turned to Sophie. "You see!" He pointed to the proof. "Next time they'll kill her. First Albert, now Jeanie. What are you waiting for, Sophie? Are you waiting for us all to move into the cemetery?"

"It's not my fault," Sophie protested. "You have no right to blame me. Those lousy *schvartses* did this, not me."

"Ida moved out. Your brothers moved out. If we had left when they did, this wouldn't have happened."

"We'll move soon." Sophie tried to soothe.

Harry did not speak to Sophie for the rest of that evening or the following day. Sophie called the school principal at the junior high school the next day and reported the incident. "I'm afraid there's nothing I can do, Mrs. Rothman. It happened outside the school. The police should be notified," he advised. But the girls feared reprisal if the police were called, and the whole matter was dropped.

Jeanie's face and eye healed in a few weeks. Her friend, Fran, moved to Brighton Beach with her family soon after that. The Rothmans stayed on. Sophie waited for a buyer who showed interest in their property to make a decision. "I know this man, Mr. Schneider, is interested in buying. He has a lot of money to invest. As soon as the deal is settled, we'll move," Sophie promised Harry.

In March, Mr. Schneider had still not made up his mind. "So sell for a few thousand less," Harry advised. "Your brothers don't care about a few thousand dollars. And Ida just wants to sell."

"I'm not giving it away. Mr. Schneider will pay a higher price. You'll see."

"Sophie, it's not worth waiting for any longer."

"Money is always worth waiting for."

She always has to have the last word, Harry thought with disgust, walking out of the room.

***

Jeanie was awakened at dawn the next morning when a harsh acrid smell of smoke filled the bedroom. She coughed and sat up in bed, her heart pounding with sudden fear. She shook Ruthie, who slept soundly beside her. "Wake up! Wake up! I think the house is on fire!" Ruthie sat up, startled, and coughed. The girls jumped out of bed and opened the bedroom door. The strong smoky smell was everywhere. "I'll wake Albert," Ruthie coughed. "Go wake Mom and Dad."

When Jeanie reached her parents' bedroom, she discovered the source of the fire. Through the bedroom window she could see the wood-framed house across the street enveloped in orange flames. Billowing clouds of black smoke, fanned by the March winds, blew in their direction. The Rothmans gathered in front of the window and watched the horror scene that unfolded in the street below as though it were a scene in a play. They had seen it before, many times. Mitzi barked and paced nervously around the bedroom, frightened by the smoke and the crackling sounds of the fire. Fire engines arrived noisily and firemen emerged, unwinding long hoses and hooking them up to the street hydrants. Too late to save the building, they tried to stop the fire from spreading to adjacent wood-framed houses.

Women clad in nightgowns and thin robes shivered in the street below, some holding babies in their arms. A barefoot man in workpants and an undershirt held firmly to the hands of his pajama-clad children. A woman who managed to salvage her coat, which was thrown over her thin nightgown, wept on her husband's shoulder as flames consumed everything.

Jeanie watched firemen in yellow slickers run across the rooftops of adjacent buildings with long hoses, wetting the roofs as angry orange flames licked at them. She shivered in spite of the heat she felt through the window. Harry put his arm around her shoulder and watched, silent and grim. People led out of the adjacent building by firemen joined others already in the street. Sleepy children rubbed their eyes and watched in confusion.

The Rothmans did not go back to sleep. The flames finally subsided in the early morning hours, leaving only a charred and smoldering shell, the remains of what were once the homes of sixteen families. Harry left for work earlier than usual, brooding and silent. Albert left for City College without eating breakfast. Ruthie drank only a small glass of orange juice. Jeanie nibbled on a slice of toast, which reminded her of the charred remains of the building, and she gagged and spit it out. Sophie was glad they had all left early, before the firemen carried out three bodies wrapped in blankets, one very tiny, from the smoldering rubble.

The blackened frame of the building remained as a grim reminder of what had been and what could be again. Sophie kept the bedroom shades lowered after that. "It was a wooden building," Sophie told Harry. "Those buildings were always fire traps. Our house is brick. We don't have to worry about a fire here."

"What do you worry about?" Harry had asked.

The following week Sophie called the prospective buyer. "Mr. Schneider, you have till the end of the month to make up your mind. We've had another offer for the property. Think it over… You'll never get a deal like this again. Real estate is going up."

"I'll let you know," Mr. Schneider said, stalling.

Sophie worried that she wouldn't get her price, that Mr. Schneider would know she was bluffing.

Chapter 18

Ruthie dressed excitedly for the party at her friend Sandy's house on the last Saturday in March. Should she wear her red high-heeled shoes or her black? She agonized over the decision. "Are you finished ironing my skirt?" Ruthie called to Jeanie in the kitchen.

"Almost."

"Careful, don't burn it," Ruthie said, as she brushed her hair behind her ears, grimaced at her image in the mirror, and brushed the dark waves back over her ears again. She had just turned sixteen, but the boys Sandy had invited to the party were eighteen, maybe even nineteen. They were expecting older girls and Ruthie wanted desperately to look more sophisticated. Sandy had met a boy in the balcony of Loew's Pitkin Theater last week, and he had agreed to bring his friends to their party tonight. "He's gorgeous," Sandy had said. "I can imagine what his friends are like."

Ruthie applied pink lipstick with slightly trembling fingers. She smiled at her image in the mirror. She was proud of her creamy complexion, not like the angry red pimples that many girls her age tried to hide under layers of pancake makeup.

Jeanie came into the bedroom with Ruthie's freshly-ironed, black taffeta skirt. "Here it is." She held up the skirt for Ruthie's scrutiny.

"Thanks, you're a doll." She brushed Jeanie's cheek with a soft kiss. Jeanie sat down on the edge of the bed to watch her sister finish dressing and dream about the parties she might one day go to with older boys. Ruthie lifted the skirt over her head, which still ached from the tight curlers she had wound her hair in all day. The skirt billowed out over two crinolines. She clasped a red cinch belt around her waist. Her slender arms gleamed through a sheer nylon blouse. "My God, you look like Scarlet O'Hara," Jeanie gasped dramatically.

Ruthie left the room in a flurry of rustling taffeta and crinolines. "I'm leaving now," Ruthie called to her parents who sat on the living room sofa.

"Have a nice time," Sophie called back, catching a glimpse of Ruthie hurrying out and marveling at how lovely her daughter looked.

"Make sure someone walks you home," Harry cautioned. "And don't come home too late." He stood and watched her leave, already worrying that she might come home alone in the dark, though she was only walking a few blocks. He sat down on the sofa again, glancing at the darkening sky through the window.

Ruthie hummed to herself and stepped lightly, her high heels clicking on the stone steps. She passed the second landing, her gaze falling on the door that once led to Aunt Ida's apartment, where a strange family now lived. She missed her aunt and uncle. Maybe they'd live near them again soon, she hoped.

Ruthie reached the ground floor landing and glanced nervously at the closed doors of the two apartments there. The recluses who lived behind those doors had lived there ever since she could remember. Behind one door lived ancient Mr. Cohen, who left milk bottles filled with fresh urine in front of his door each morning to ward off evil spirits.

Mrs. Meltzer, a widow who adopted stray cats, lived next door to Mr. Cohen. She dressed the cats in her husband's old ties, and they paraded boldly around the apartment and the marketplace dressed in their flowered, dotted and striped ties for all to admire. The neighbors came to accept the bizarrely-dressed cats. Only strangers thought them strange now. "A *meshugener*," Sophie had said often. "Mrs. Meltzer is crazy, a *meshugener*."

Ruthie heard the cats meowing now from behind the door. A strong feline odor filtered into the hallway, mingling with the acrid smell from Mr. Cohen's bottles of urine. Ruthie coughed and quickened her steps. She passed the dark alcove that led to the outside courtyard. Jeanie always grasped her hand firmly when they walked past this dark alcove, always fearful of some imagined horror. "Don't be a baby," she had told Jeanie so many times. Now she too felt uneasy as she hurried toward the front door where she longed to fill her lungs with fresh air.

A large grimy hand reached out now, suddenly, without warning, clasping Ruthie tightly around her waist, driving the breath from her lungs and pulling her onto the stone floor, into the dark abyss behind the stairwell. She tried to scream, but the attacker clamped his other hand against her mouth so that her teeth bit into her lip and she tasted her own blood. He breathed heavily and lifted her carefully-ironed taffeta skirt and two crinolines. He clawed at her underwear. She squirmed beneath him, trying to free herself from the huge assailant she could not even see. Her nostrils filled with the smell of him. Whiskey and stale food. Rotten teeth and unwashed skin. A muffled cry sprang from her throat. He smashed her head against the stone floor and slapped her across her mouth. Her head whirled and tiny lights flashed behind her eyelids. She felt dizzy and nauseous. Then a sharp painful thrust and Ruthie lost consciousness.

Harry looked up from the newspaper he was reading. He heard noises in the hallway, many people talking at once. A loud insistent knock at the door. "What's that commotion?" Sophie asked, putting aside her sewing.

Harry went to the door, the newspaper still in his hand. Mrs. Meltzer's grief-stricken face greeted him. A brown cat in a blue and white polka dot tie stood incongruously at her side. "Come down quick!" she said. "Hurry, hurry!"

"What's the matter?" Harry thought she'd gone quite mad.

"Come, come! It's Ruthie!"

Harry pushed passed her and raced down the steps two at a time. Sophie and Jeanie followed close behind. Mr. Cohen had brought a flashlight to light the alcove. Mrs. Seline had covered Ruthie with a blanket. Apartment doors opened and worried neighbors gathered around the helpless victim. They parted now to make way for Harry. He lifted his daughter's limp shoulders and head onto his lap with trembling hands. His pale face matched the color of his daughter's cheeks. He bent his head close to hers and felt her shallow breathing against his face. Thank God she's still alive, he thought. "Call an ambulance!" he ordered a neighbor.

Sophie fell to her knees beside Ruthie. "What happened? My God, who would do this?" Her hands trembled. The courtyard door banged open and shut in the wind.

"I heard some noises, some shuffling, so I ran out to see," Mr. Cohen said. "A man… a tall man ran through that door." He pointed to the courtyard door.

Mr. Rabinowitz ran out into the courtyard. "No one's there now," he called to them. "The *gonif* is gone."

"I didn't see nothing," Mrs. Meltzer said. "Otherwise I would have sent my cats out to kill him… the anti-Semite!"

Jeanie could not stop trembling, nor could she control the sobs that sprang from her lips as though they had a will of their own. It seemed to her that her worst fear had become a reality. And she had become a victim along with her sister. She would always remember the mournful wail of the ambulance, the running feet, the white-uniformed men lifting Ruthie onto a stretcher and whisking her away.

Inside the ambulance, Jeanie held her sister's limp hand in hers. Harry held Ruthie's other hand, a dazed look in his eyes. Sophie was aghast at her ashen-faced, unconscious daughter, trying to grasp what had happened and refusing to accept the reality. The ambulance sped them to the emergency room at Kings County Hospital.

They waited. Harry sat on a cold wooden bench in the corridor outside the hospital examining room. He held his head in his hands as though it would tumble off his body if he dared let go. He stared intently at a fixed spot on the floor as though the answer to his misery lay on the cold stones. Sophie sat next to him, unmoving except for a handkerchief she twisted between her fingers. Jeanie stood near the window, alone in her own private hell, her shoulders moving in rhythm with dry hiccoughing sobs.

Albert, unknowing, was walking across the stage of City College's auditorium, dressed as Polonius in a Hamlet production, bowing to the applause of the audience.

They waited. A green-gowned doctor walked out of the examining room. "Mr. and Mrs. Rothman?" he spoke softly, trying to ease their pain. Sophie and Harry rose from the bench and waited apprehensively for his words. "Your daughter's been badly bruised. She has a concussion." He hesitated for a moment with the worst news. "And we've confirmed the rape."

"No!" Harry said, as though his words of denial would negate the brutal crime. He sat down on the bench again, and covered his face with his hands. Jeanie watched her father weep through the blur of her own tears.

"It's a mistake maybe?" Sophie asked. "How… how can you be sure?"

The doctor put his hand on Sophie's shoulder. "We're sure, Mrs. Rothman."

"Will she be alright?" Sophie asked.

"She needs a few days in the hospital… some treatment. We want to watch her. I gave her a mild sedative. Why don't you come back in the morning?"

Sophie took Jeanie home. Harry sat by Ruthie's hospital bed through the long night, watching her fitful sleep, making certain no harm would befall her again.

***

By the second week in April, Mr. Schneider made his final offer to Sophie to buy the marketplace property. He raised his bid three thousand dollars. That brought the price to $60,000 for all the property. "You're getting *some* bargain, Mr. Schneider," Sophie told him. "Come to my apartment Wednesday evening at 7:30 with your lawyer. My brothers and sister will be here and we'll sign all the papers."

Chapter 19

The Rothmans moved into their new house on East 96th Street, just one block from where Ida and Nathan lived, late in the month of May. It was a quiet tree-lined street in the East Flatbush area of Brooklyn where each four-family brick house was distinguished from the others by the flowers planted in the small front gardens and the numbers on the front doors.

"Look, there's a tree outside our bedroom window… and birds, and our own garden," Jeanie said to Ruthie as they unpacked boxes in their new bedroom. "I'm going to plant zinnias and mums. Won't it be fun to plant things? Will you help me?"

"Sure," Ruthie said in the monotone in which she had lately begun to speak.

"Which bed do you want, Ruthie, the one near the window or the one near the wall?" The girls still shared a room, but now each had her own bed.

"The one near the wall will do." Ruthie looked vacantly around the room where the new furniture had been arranged—a white Formica dresser with brass knobs, two matching bedside tables, lamps with white shades trimmed in gold braid. And turquoise wall-to-wall carpeting covered the floor.

"Why don't you take the bed near the window?" Jeanie offered. "It'll be nice to wake up and look at the sky through the trees."

"Who cares." Ruthie sat listlessly at the edge of the bed.

"You have to care about something." Jeanie turned worried eyes toward Ruthie.

"Why? Why should I care?"

"Look at the beautiful room we have. Carpeting in the living room and the bedrooms, a tiled bathroom with a sink." Jeanie's voice trailed on, but Ruthie wasn't listening. She was lost somewhere in the twisted wreckage of her mind.

Jeanie unpacked her sister's things and arranged them neatly in the dresser drawers, fighting back tears as she set a pink and white stuffed rabbit on top of the dresser. She had hoped the stuffed rabbit gift would make her sister smile. When Ruthie had opened the box and seen the rabbit, she kissed Jeanie and then she cried. It was as though the small kindness caused her greater pain.

Sophie's voice trailed in from the other room now. "Over there... Put that box over there," she directed the movers.

Harry stuck his head in the bedroom doorway. "How're you doing, girls?" he asked, smiling.

"Great, Dad!" Jeanie answered for them.

"When the moving men leave, I'm going over to the deli on Rutland Road to pick up some lunch for us. How about a nice, fat corned beef sandwich?" He tried to interest Ruthie, who grew thinner each day and whose complexion had changed from peaches to paste.

"That sounds yummy," Jeanie said.

"I'm not hungry," Ruthie said.

"I'll bring back a sandwich for you anyway. Wait till you smell it! Instant hunger," he joked, but his eyes betrayed the smile on his lips.

When all of the family's belongings had been deposited in the small apartment, Sophie sat down on her new turquoise sectional sofa. She sighed with exhaustion. "What a job this moving has been," she said half to herself, half to Mitzi, who wagged her tail and stood loyally at her feet. In less than two months the Rothmans had bought this four-family house, sold their old furniture, purchased new furniture and carpeting and moved into their new home.

"Why can't we have a house all for ourselves instead of a four-family house?" Jeanie had asked.

"We're not rich," Sophie had told her. "We need the income from the other apartments. We're going to buy all new furniture and carpeting," she promised. "Ruthie, you'll help pick out the furniture and colors." But Ruthie had lost all interest after she returned from the hospital.

During the last month that the Rothmans had lived on Prospect Place, Sophie had watched her thin pale daughter return to Jefferson High School. She worried about her. Ruthie will be alright as soon as we move and she's in a new environment, Sophie thought then. She'll make new friends. She'll forget. Sophie worried about people knowing the truth, about her daughter's chances for marriage in the future. She knew how people judged you when something like that happened. People were not understanding, she reasoned. She had cautioned Ruthie when she returned to school. "You don't have to tell anyone what happened. The less they know, the better off you'll be. You don't have to ever talk about it again… Don't think about it either. Make believe it didn't happen."

Ruthie had nodded in silent agreement, feeling more like a criminal than a victim. She tried to forget, but memories forced their way back into her consciousness. She trembled in terror each time she saw a man with large rough hands. The smell of whiskey brought on overwhelming nausea. And dreams of falling and being suffocated haunted her nightly.

Jeanie too had become a victim. Even the new light Harry had installed behind the lower stairwell in the building was insufficient to quell her fears. She began to have a recurring dream of a shadowy figure pursuing her to the front door while she tried in vain to open it.

Sophie had warned Jeanie too not to speak about Ruthie's misfortune. "Why not?" Jeanie wanted to know. "It wasn't her fault."

"People don't understand. Just don't tell anyone," Sophie insisted.

Ida and Nathan had come to the hospital to see Ruthie as soon as they had heard, but Sophie hid the truth from her own sister.

"What really happened? Tell me the truth," Ida had asked Jeanie in the corridor outside the hospital room.

"She was raped."

"Oh God, no!" Ida moaned and dabbed at her eyes with a handkerchief.

Harry had sat in silent vigil at his daughter's bedside. Nathan put an arm on Harry's shoulder to comfort him, also a victim. "The police will catch the S.O.B. Such an animal. He's not fit to live," Nathan told Harry.

But the police never caught the rapist. Ruthie could not give a description. She had never seen him. No one had seen him. Harry had to be satisfied with fantasies of catching the rapist and strangling him until his neck snapped.

Sophie rose from the new sofa now. Harry would be back with sandwiches from the deli any minute. "Girls, come help me unpack the dishes," she called.

Sophie and the girls worked side by side now in the small kitchen, removing newspapers that the dishes had been wrapped in and setting them in the closet that still smelled faintly of fresh paint. "I love the new furniture, Momma. It's so beautiful," Jeanie said.

"It's the nicest furniture we ever had," Sophie agreed. She was right to have chosen the less expensive furniture, though Harry tried to persuade her to buy a better sofa. "It will last longer and it looks better," he had said.

"This is good enough." Sophie had insisted on the two hundred dollar turquoise sectional. "After all, we have to buy furniture for a whole house."

"I wonder if there are any girls my age on the block," Jeanie said now. "I hope they're friendly… Well, I'm glad Helen lives so close now. At least I have one friend."

"There are lots of nice people here. You're both going to meet new friends," Sophie assured them. "Mrs. Goodman, the tenant across the hall, told me there's a girl named Sheila who lives in the next house and she's just your age, Ruthie. I'll ask her to introduce you later." Ruthie nodded silently and continued methodically crumpling the newspapers she removed from each dish.

The apartment door swung open. "I'm back," Harry said, smiling. And the kitchen was at once filled with the smell of corned beef and mustard, sour pickles, rye bread and Dr. Brown's celery tonic. "Our first meal in our new house." Harry put his arms around Ruthie's bony shoulders and squeezed gently. "Eat! Eat! It's good food."

"It smells great," Jeanie agreed.

Sophie cleared the table of unwrapped dishes and they sat down to eat their sandwiches. "Umm… Now this is *some* sandwich," Harry said through a mouthful of corned beef.

Jeanie bit into a crisp sour pickle. "The best pickle I've ever tasted." She licked pickle juice from her lips.

Ruthie nibbled at her sandwich. Her mouth felt dry, the sandwich tasteless. Sophie pushed a pickle toward her. "Have a pickle. They're delicious," she coaxed.

"Maybe later. I'm really not hungry now." Ruthie pushed her sandwich away and rose from the chair.

"I'll put your sandwich in the refrigerator. You can eat it later, when you're hungry." Sophie rewrapped the sandwich she knew her daughter would not eat, and her worried gaze followed Ruthie as she left the kitchen.

Jeanie looked up from her sandwich and her eyes met Harry's, sharing the same helpless despair. An uncomfortable silence settled over their midday meal. Jeanie finished eating quickly. She gulped down the rest of her celery tonic and wiped her lips on a paper napkin. Then she left Sophie and Harry alone in the kitchen.

"I told you we should have listened to the doctor in the hospital," Harry said. "Ruthie needs a psychiatrist."

"My daughter doesn't need a psychiatrist. She's not crazy. She's just upset. She'll get over it," Sophie said.

"She's my daughter too and she's not getting over it. Look at her. She looks like a scarecrow. Her eyes are red from crying all day and…"

"We just moved in," Sophie said. "Give her a chance… She'll come out of it. She'll be alright."

"She's not alright. I don't know if she ever will be."

"And you think a psychiatrist will make things better? It's bad enough already… People will find out if she goes to a psychiatrist and that'll finish all her chances." Sophie's face flushed.

"I don't care about people. I care about Ruthie." Harry's fingers curled tightly around Sophie's arm. She pulled her arm away, but Harry's fingers left angry red impressions on her skin.

"Shh! She'll hear you… We'll talk about it later."

"Two more weeks," Harry hissed. "Then I'm going to do what I think is right. If I hadn't waited for you to make up your mind about moving…"

"You have no right to blame me," Sophie shot back at him, angry that his words expressed the guilt she struggled with.

Sophie rose from the chair and gathered the empty sandwich wrappings. Harry's eyes followed her as she returned to unpacking dishes. *Sophie's right*, Harry thought. *I have no right to blame her. It was my fault. I should have moved out with the girls and Sophie would have followed.* But even as he thought this, he knew that he would never have done that, and that realization intensified his own self-hatred. He watched in silence now as Sophie bent over a carton of dishes, and he wondered when his love for her had turned to contempt, his desire to revulsion.

Harry went into the living room and began unpacking cartons of dusty books that had been accumulated over the years. He stacked shelf after shelf of books, his energy fired by anger. Chemistry and mathematics books that belonged to Albert… Eugene O'Neil, Shakespeare's tragedies, books that he never had time to read. *Organic Chemistry* slipped from his fingers onto the floor. He picked it up reverently and his eyes rested on a page of formulas whose letters and numbers remained a teasing mystery to him. He knew Albert could understand all of this. He dusted the book cover with his shirtsleeve as though it were a treasured religious object and placed it carefully on a shelf next to Albert's other books.

Albert would be here tonight to see their new apartment and have dinner with them. Albert had decided to move in with a friend who had an apartment in Manhattan. It was closer to City College, he had convinced them, and since he spent long hours in the library studying, it would be less trouble if he lived there. "I'll come home on weekends," Albert had promised. The Rothmans had bought a large overstuffed chair that opened into a bed, and Albert could sleep in the living room on weekends. Sophie had opposed the arrangement from the start. "An apartment! You're not even working. Who's going to pay for it?" she had asked.

"Well, I'm only paying half the rent. It's only $30 a month for me... I'm still working part time at Macy's and I can pay $15," Albert had argued.

"We only have to give him $15 a month for the apartment," Harry had said.

"No! It's out of the question. It's not just $15. What about his books that we pay for, and food, and everything else?"

"Sophie, it's for a few more years. When Albert graduates, he'll make a fortune."

"No. Albert can take the train and come home every night."

But Harry had finally convinced Sophie. "We can take the two-bedroom apartment in the house instead of the three-bedroom one. We won't need a room for Albert. Then we'll get a higher rent for the three-bedroom apartment." The prospect of earning more rent money finally convinced Sophie to let Albert live in the city.

Harry stacked the empty book cartons against the wall and sat down on the new peach-colored chair, overcome by sudden weariness. He looked around the room at the tweed carpeting, the new furniture, the freshly painted walls. His nostrils filled with the smell of newness. Bright afternoon sunlight spread across the room from the wide windows behind the sofa. The smells of spring filtered in through the half-opened windows—elm trees in full bloom, tender shoots of young grass and fragrant flowers in gardens that lined the street. A distant car and the soft laughter of children playing in the street below were the only sounds that reached Harry's ears from outside. It stood out in sharp contrast to what they had left behind—the dreary apartment on Prospect Place, shabby furniture, cracked linoleum, cockroaches, grit-smeared windows that let in only gray light, the smell of garbage and the noise of too many people struggling too hard to live.

Why did he not feel happy now when he had all these things he had waited so long for and worked so hard for, Harry wondered? He rested his head against the chair and drifted into a fitful doze.

Harry was still dozing when the doorbell rang half an hour later. "It's only me." Mrs. Goodman's singsong voice trailed into the apartment.

"Come in, come in," Harry heard Sophie tell her.

Mrs. Goodman stepped through the doorway, pulling Sheila after her. "This is Sheila," she announced. "She just got home from school and I caught her outside. I wanted her to meet your Ruthie. *Nu*, so isn't she as beautiful as

I said she was?"

Sheila blushed, still holding a stack of school books. She was indeed a beautiful girl—tall with shapely curves and sleek black hair that framed her perfect features. "Nice to meet you, Mrs. Rothman." She smiled brightly.

"It's nice to meet you. Mrs. Goodman should be your agent. She'll get you into movies… Ruthie, come in here! Come meet Sheila, the beautiful girl from next door," Sophie called.

Ruthie and Jeanie emerged from their bedroom. "Hi," Jeanie said. "I'm Jeanie. And this is Ruthie." She pointed to her sister who stood shyly in the doorway.

"Hi," Ruthie said quietly.

"Gee, I'm real glad to meet you." Sheila held out her hand, smiling warmly.

Ruthie managed a weak smile. "Would you like to see our room?" Jeanie asked.

"I'd love to," Sheila said, as Jeanie led the way.

"This is my father." Ruthie introduced Sheila as they passed through the living room en route to the bedroom. Sheila was ready with her disarming smile. "Hello, Mr. Rothman."

"Hello, Sheila." Harry smiled, his heart lightening at Ruthie's interest in someone.

"A cup of coffee, Mrs. Goodman?" Harry heard Sophie ask from the kitchen.

"Don't trouble yourself. But if you're making it, I wouldn't mind a cup." She arranged her small round body on a kitchen chair and smoothed the blue cotton dress that she had carefully ironed to make a good impression on her new landlady.

Sophie filled the coffee pot with water, measured out coffee and placed the pot on the stove. Then she sat down opposite Mrs. Goodman and waited for the coffee to brew. "I want to thank you for bringing Sheila over to meet Ruthie. My daughter's a little shy. It's hard for a girl her age to move to a new neighborhood and make friends."

"She's a pretty girl, your Ruthie, but so thin. She doesn't eat?"

"She's on a diet," Sophie lied. "You know how young girls get crazy ideas sometimes and think they're too fat… Maybe Sheila will talk some sense into her."

"Sheila can do anything."

Sophie poured hot coffee into two cups, hoping that Mrs. Goodman was right about Sheila. Light laughter drifted out of the bedroom. Sophie recognized Ruthie's restrained laughter. It was the first time she had heard her laugh since that awful day when she had been carried into the ambulance. Sophie was surprised at the sudden tears that filled her eyes now.

Harry rose from the living room chair, the sound of his daughter's laughter giving him new energy. He walked into the kitchen. "How are you, Mrs. Goodman?"

"I can't complain," she said, offering him philosophy along with her answer. "You can call me Goldie. After all, we're neighbors now. We don't have to be so formal."

Ruthie, Jeanie and Sheila suddenly appeared at the kitchen doorway. Ruthie had put on some pink lipstick. "We're going next door to Sheila's house," Ruthie said, her voice still echoing a dull monotone. "She invited us."

"Go! Go!" Harry said. "Have a good time." He held the door open for them.

"I have to go myself," Mrs. Goodman said, finishing her coffee. "You two come over and visit Murray and me. Don't be strangers."

"Thank you, Goldie. We will," Harry said.

"And thank you for bringing Sheila here," Sophie said.

The door closed quietly behind her. Harry and Sophie faced each other now, their anger and guilt abated by their daughter's quiet laughter and the possibility of hope.

Chapter 20

By mid-June the Rothmans had settled into their new apartment in East Flatbush. Ruthie was attending Tilden High School during the last few weeks of the school year and Jeanie was registered at Winthrop Junior High School. Ruthie was welcomed into Sheila's circle of friends. She showed renewed interest in socializing with new friends, but she declined dates with boys, which Sophie fretted over. Sophie was certain that Ruthie was on her way to recovery, but Harry still worried, especially when Ruthie lapsed into long melancholy silences. "I'm not convinced that she doesn't need a doctor," Harry said.

"Look at her," Sophie said. "She gained some weight. She's going out with friends… You want miracles overnight? Even doctors aren't miracle workers."

So Harry waited for everything to right itself, to develop as it would without his intervention, just as he had waited and watched other things happen in his life. He felt more and more like a distant observer, watching his life unfold as he moved about like a disjointed marionette while Sophie pulled the strings.

Jeanie had come home from her first day at the junior high school and announced, "I hate it! I hate the school! I hate the kids! I hate everything!" She struggled to fit into her new school environment and longed for her old friends.

Sophie dismissed Jeanie's sullen moods now as she dressed for a visit to Ida. They would be in the country at the bungalow colony in another two weeks and, after the summer vacation, the new school year would be better for Jeanie, she reasoned.

Sophie looked at her reflection in the mirror now. She thought about getting her hair cut as she brushed a few unruly curls from her face and wondered if Harry would notice if she did. Maybe she should buy a new dress and new shoes too. Many weeks had passed since Harry had made love to her or shown any interest in her at all. Since that awful day when Ruthie had been attacked, Harry had turned away from her in bed. Last night she had casually let her arm slide across Harry's back. He pretended to be asleep, but she could tell from the way he breathed that he was awake.

Sophie had a momentary vision of Lev Kramer holding her in his arms. He had never turned away from her. Sophie applied lipstick now, using her pinky finger to scoop the remaining lipstick out of the tube. She made a mental note to buy a new lipstick. She would have to hurry now if she wanted to spend some time with her sister.

Sophie was still thinking about Lev Kramer when she rang the bell to Ida's apartment. "Come in." Ida opened the door. "You're late and lunch is on the table." She motioned for Sophie to sit down. "Take some cold chicken," Ida offered. "And fresh rye bread. I went to the bakery this morning."

"You shouldn't have made a fuss, Ida."

"Where do you see a fuss? So tell me, you're all settled in the apartment? Everything's unpacked?"

"Almost. What's my rush? I'm going to be there for a long time."

"How's Ruthie?"

"She's fine."

"She didn't look so fine to me when I saw her last week. So thin. I'm worried about her."

"You don't have to worry. Ruthie's alright. We'll be going away for the summer soon. The country air will do her good… give her an appetite."

"What does the doctor say?"

"He said the county is a good idea," Sophie lied, avoiding her sister's eyes. She wished Ida would stop questioning her so she could stop lying. She had to remember all her lies so she wouldn't get caught in them. Sophie put another piece of chicken on her plate. She wasn't hungry anymore, but it gave her something to do while her sister probed.

Though Ida knew the truth, she nevertheless wanted to hear it from her sister's lips, but Sophie never used the word, rape. And yet Ida understood how hard it was for Sophie. She herself had struggled to hide behind lies and pretensions. She pretended to love Nathan and to be happily married. So the two sisters remained, as always, separated by lies, never achieving the closeness that comes with complete honesty. And Sophie suspected that Ida knew the truth, but she chose to go on evading.

"Coffee?" Ida asked.

"Yes, I'll have a cup of coffee."

Ida poured the coffee, recalling another truth she had never confronted Sophie with. She had suspected that Sophie and Lev Kramer were having an affair years ago. She had seen the way Lev had looked at Sophie when they were together, talking in muffled tones in the hallway, meeting on the street. Ida hadn't thought much about it then, but Jeanie's resemblance to Lev Kramer was undeniable. Ida would have been a sympathetic ear for Sophie's confessions, but Sophie trusted no one completely, so her secrets would remain buried, simmering into guilt and anger.

"Ida, I heard the house next door to mine is for sale," Sophie said, changing the subject.

"So someone will buy it."

"That someone could be you and Nathan."

"Me! What kind of business would I have buying a four-family house?"

"It's a good investment. You collect rent. What are you going to do with the money you inherited?"

"It's not a fortune… Anyway, I got enough headaches. I don't need tenants. I'll keep my money in the bank where it's safe."

Sophie looked at the kitchen clock that hung above the table. It was nearly 3:00 o'clock. "I have to go." Sophie rose. "The girls'll be home soon. Thank's for lunch, Ida."

"We'll have to start packing for the summer before you know it," Ida said, walking Sophie to the door.

"Yes, another two weeks and we'll be breathing country air."

"I hope the shower in my bungalow is fixed."

"Don't worry, Ida. You worry too much about everything. Harry'll fix it as soon as we get there."

Ida closed the door behind Sophie, her forehead furrowed with permanent worry lines.

Sophie hurried home to prepare dinner. Albert was coming tonight and she would make stuffed cabbage. It was one of Albert's favorite dishes.

Sophie heard Mitzi whining as she put the key in the lock and opened the apartment door. The old dog did not get up. She had been sick for the past two weeks and barely had the strength to wag her tail now. Sophie patted Mitzi's head. "How're you doing, Mitzi?" She brought her some fresh water. "You haven't touched your food. How will you get well if you don't eat?" She knew even as she scolded that the dog she had grown so attached to over the years would probably not get well.

Sophie stuffed cabbage leaves with a mixture of chopped meat, rice and spices. Then she set them in a large dented pot on the stove to simmer slowly in an aromatic gravy of tomatoes, vinegar and brown sugar.

Two hours later, everyone arrived at once. The girls were home from visiting friends and Harry returned from work. Albert raced up the stairs, inhaling the smell of the spicy sauce that filled the hallway. "How did you know I was in the mood for stuffed cabbage?" Albert smiled, stepping through the doorway.

"I knew because you're always in the mood for it." Sophie smiled, happy to see her son, whom she saw less and less lately.

"Albert's here!" Jeanie came running from the bedroom and they embraced.

Harry slapped his son affectionately on his back. "So how's it going, college boy?"

"Great, Dad," Albert lied, hoping he would have the courage to tell Harry the truth tonight.

"Where's Ruthie?" Albert whispered to Jeanie. "Is she okay?" He worried endlessly about Ruthie and could not fully accept the tragedy that had befallen her. He had promised himself he would somehow get her out of Brooklyn. When he got to California and made some money, he would send for her.

"She's okay," Jeanie told him, looking into his worried eyes. "Honest, she's much better."

Ruthie came out of her bedroom to greet Albert, her hair combed neatly in a pageboy style and her lips pink with fresh lipstick. "Ruthie, you look great!" Albert's arms encircled her and a smile of relief spread across his face. He would never forgive his parents for what had happened to Ruthie. He blamed Sophie for her greed, for valuing money above her children's safety, and he blamed Harry for not having the courage to fight her. He gazed at the freshly painted walls and the new furniture. At last they lived in a decent place, but it was too late for Ruthie.

The family gathered around the kitchen table for dinner. Mitzi lay listlessly in a corner of the kitchen near the stove, where she trembled every few minutes in spite of the warmth from the oven. "What's wrong with Mitzi?" Albert asked.

"She's very sick." Jeanie's eyes filled with quick hot tears.

"We took her to the vet," Harry said, shaking his head hopelessly.

"It's her kidneys," Sophie said. "She's very old and… well it's not good to grow old… for dogs or for people."

Sophie set a plate piled high with stuffed cabbage and mashed potatoes in front of Albert. "Is this for me or for all of us?" Albert asked.

"Albert with the jokes," Sophie said.

"You look like you lost weight," Harry said. "What's the matter, you don't have time to eat?"

"I'm very busy studying and acting."

"So stop acting and concentrate on studying," Harry advised.

"I love acting."

"And he's so good at it," Ruthie said, smiling.

"Some day he'll be a famous star," Jeanie said.

"Star, schmar… He'll be a doctor!" Harry said.

"You know, Dad, medicine isn't for everyone," Albert said.

"I know, I know. Not everybody's as smart as you."

"Being smart isn't everything. Your heart has to be in it. And… well I'm not sure my heart's in it." Albert felt a sudden rush of relief telling Harry how he really felt.

Harry looked up from his plate into his son's eyes. "You're young. Follow your head, not your heart. When you're a doctor, you'll appreciate what I'm saying now. People will look up to you like you're a miracle worker. You'll make a lot of money, maybe even be famous."

Albert realized his words had tumbled off Harry's ears. It was going to be harder than he thought. Albert finished his dinner in silence. They sat in the living room for a while after dinner, but Albert was restless. By 9:00 o'clock he insisted that he had to leave. "Will we see you again before we leave for the country?" Sophie asked.

"I don't think so. I forgot to tell you. I'm going to Connecticut next week. I got a job for the summer."

"In Connecticut? What kind of a job?" Harry asked.

"In summer stock."

"Albert, that's so exciting!" Ruthie said.

"What's summer stock?" Sophie wanted to know.

"It's an acting job in a summer theater. I'll write and tell you all about it." He kissed his sisters goodbye and hurried from the apartment, eager to escape the disappointment in Harry's eyes. He had not told his parents of his plans to change his course of study at City College next semester from pre-med to literature and drama. He would give them time to digest his summer job.

It's only a summer job, Harry thought to himself as he undressed later that night. But he sensed a change in Albert, which disturbed him and left him feeling uneasy for days afterward.

Chapter 21

Early the following week Sophie began packing household things for the family's summer home in Livingston Manor. She opened the closet Harry had built in the living room where she stored extra blankets. She would need warm blankets for the chilly country evenings. Sophie pulled a small carton from the floor of the closet, trying to recall what she had stored in it.

The mid-day sun poured in through the living room windows, heating the room to a stifling temperature. Sophie wiped her damp forehead with the back of her hand. She snipped the cord on the carton with an old pair of scissors. Photograph albums, envelopes with old pictures and yellowed papers filled the box. She sat down on the plastic-covered sofa, the carton at her feet, lifted a photo album and placed it on her lap. Pictures of Momma and Poppa posing stiffly for the photographer. Momma in a dark gray dress with a high collar and a row of tiny buttons cascading from her long neck to her waist. Her thick dark hair was coiled in a smooth chignon, her head held high, her piercing eyes staring at Sophie now from the photograph.

Sophie looked into her mother's eyes in the photograph. Momma would be proud of me if she could see me now, a proprietor of a bungalow colony and a four-family house. Ida has nothing. Momma loved the wrong daughter, she thought.

Sophie sighed. Her memories carried her back to a day when she was twelve years old and had saved pennies all year to buy something special for herself. She still remembered the beautiful blouse she longed to buy. Her mother had been so proud of her then, but Momma had shown her that the blouse was not as important as saving money. And Momma had been right. The blouse would not have lasted long.

"Momma, I have twenty-five thousand dollars now and so much property," Sophie spoke aloud to the photograph, startling herself with her own voice. Momma would have smiled approvingly and patted her head. Momma might even have planted a kiss on her forehead as she had often done with Ida. *It wasn't so hard to save,* Sophie thought. *I gave up nothing. I simply postponed things.* Sophie had done without things for so long that she no longer wanted them. It pained her now to spend money on new furniture for the house, on clothing, on entertainment of any kind. There were, in fact, only two things that Sophie valued in life—food and money. She was willing to spend money on food because eating gave her enormous pleasure. The refrigerator and pantry were always well stocked, usually overstocked to the point of bursting, for fear that she might run out of something she craved. She got the same satisfaction from her growing wealth. Knowing it was there was far more important than spending it. Possession of it had long ago replaced the goal of collecting it to spend later. But she told herself that one day they would all be able to spend it, when there was enough. And she would decide when there was enough.

Sophie closed the old photo album, recalling Momma's words: "You'll never be sorry you saved." She quickly flipped through the rest of the things in the carton—pictures from Albert's Bar Mitzvah, their first summer in Livingston Manor, old receipts. She didn't want to look through all these old things now. The temperature in the room had grown oppressive and Sophie's thin cotton housedress, damp with perspiration, clung to the plastic cover on the sofa. She would put everything back in the box until September when she'd have more time to look through it. Sophie picked up the photographs and papers piled on the sofa and put them back in the box. A yellowed envelope drifted to the floor. She stooped to pick it up. It had a foreign stamp and unfamiliar handwriting. She opened the envelope and a flood of memories poured out.

Haifa, Israel
11 July, 1948
Dear Mrs. Rothman,

I am sorry to be the bearer of sad news, but your letter to my brother, Lev, could not be delivered. He died last week, bravely defending our kibbutz against an Arab attack. He often spoke of you and his other good friends in America. He looked forward to your letters. His wife, Hannah, and sons, David and Joel, are well. Joel speaks of you as the kind lady in America. We hope that you will be consoled as we are, knowing that Lev has given his life so that Jews can at last come home.
Yaakov Kramer

Sophie pressed the letter against her breasts. Old tears had left small stains on the yellowed paper. Its edges crumbled between her fingers now. Why had she saved this letter when she had destroyed all the others? She and Lev had corresponded often during the nine years Lev had lived in Palestine. His letters were always warm, friendly, filled with details of life on his kibbutz. She would read them with eager anticipation and feel the flames of old desire stir again. Then she'd destroy each letter, wanting no evidence around to spark Harry's suspicion. As soon as she destroyed a letter, she would wait impatiently for the next. She never discouraged Lev from writing to her, even after he married Hannah, a survivor of Dachau, in 1946. Even before his marriage to Hannah, Lev never declared his love for Sophie in his letters or tried to persuade her again to join him in Palestine. Yet Sophie always sensed his love.

Lev was a fervent advocate of Zionism. Sophie recalled his agitated arguments to persuade her to go to Palestine with him. They would sit in her kitchen on Prospect Place with steaming glasses of tea in front of them. "The only hope for Jews is a Jewish homeland," Lev argued. "There's only one place where we can be safe from pogroms, from restrictions—Palestine."

"Jews are safe in America. I lived here all my life. There's no persecution here," Sophie said, sipping her tea.

"Sophie, are you blind?" Lev's face flushed. "There are unspoken restrictions and prejudice. There are jobs a Jew can never hope to get. There's always a line that separates the gentile world from the Jew, even in America."

"You've lived in America for a few years. Haven't you been happy here?"

"Yes, I have. It's been better than Poland. Minna and I were lucky to get out of Poland, but we would have gone to Palestine if we could have. It was easier to get into America, and that was only because we had relatives here already. But I promised Minna. It was our dream to go to Palestine. I always thought of America as a stopover on the way to Palestine."

"Be practical. What's in Palestine for you? It's a desert with Arabs who want to kill you. It's no better than Poland." Sophie brushed grains of sugar off the table.

"My brother, Yaakov, writes to me, begging me to come and live on his kibbutz, help farm the land, make a new life for my boys."

"What do you know about farming?"

"What did my brother, a Talmud student, know about farming in 1918 when he immigrated to Palestine?" Lev said, pulling a worn picture from his wallet. "This is Palestine... green and beautiful."

Sophie recalled that picture now. She had stared at a tall bearded man who bore a striking resemblance to Lev, though he was ten years his senior. His feet were planted firmly like the rows of trees in the olive grove where he stood. And his eyes were bright with hope and determination.

"Maybe it's okay for you to take a chance, but how can you think of taking your children to a place that's so dangerous?" Sophie asked Lev.

"It's safer than Europe and probably safer than America… It was their mother's dream." Lev's eyes misted.

"Their mother's dead. They need someone to care for them, not foolish dreams."

"Then come with me to Palestine." Lev took Sophie's hands in his. "Be my wife. My children love you and we would be happy."

"It's not the kind of life I want for me or my children. And we're Americans." Sophie slipped her hands from Lev's grip.

"You're also Jews." Lev's voice rose and his eyes flashed. "One day you'll realize that Palestine is the only place for Jews. Try to understand what we lived through in Poland. We were always afraid, always running away. I don't want to run anymore. That's why I'm going to live on the kibbutz with my brother and his family."

"You'll never be happy on a kibbutz, Lev. You'll work hard and get nothing in return. No money. No property. Nothing."

"I don't need money or property to be happy." Lev looked at Sophie longingly.

Sophie had realized then that Lev meant what he had said and that their goals in life were too far apart to ever find a common ground. If she had ever given any thought to leaving Harry and running off with Lev, it was quickly squelched by the socialist philosophy of kibbutz life.

Lev had fulfilled his promise to himself and his dead wife. He had gone to Palestine with his sons. He wrote to Sophie and told her how happy he was there and how well the boys had adjusted. Yagur was a well-established kibbutz, and its women cared for his boys. He felt useful and young again, he wrote. He was learning to farm and to use a rifle.

Sophie remembered the jubilant letter Lev had written after Palestine declared independence and became the new state of Israel. His dream of a Jewish homeland had become a reality. He described the joy, the dancing in the streets on that day. But the joy of independence was soon drowned in the blood of Israel's first war. Sophie had listened to news bulletins on the radio and she worried. Two months later, this letter she held in her hand had arrived, and Lev's dream was buried with him in a dusty desert grave.

So much for dreams. Where would she be now, Sophie reflected, if she had listened to Lev? Probably rotting next to him in a dry grave instead of on her way to becoming a wealthy woman. The whole idea of collective living and sharing conflicted with her need to acquire money. Time had proven her right. She crumpled the old letter now and walked into the kitchen where she tossed it in the trashcan. It was too risky to save letters like this for the sake of sentimentality.

Sophie opened the refrigerator and took out a bottle of seltzer. She filled a clean glass with the cold liquid and drank thirstily. She wondered what had become of Lev's sons. She remembered how David, only three when his mother had died, had sat on her lap and buried his head against her breasts, searching for the love that had been prematurely robbed from him. Like a puppy weaned too soon, he cried often, not knowing why. Sophie would rock him in her arms then and sing to him till he smiled at her. They had grown fond of each other, and David came to her apartment often and was always reluctant to leave. She wondered if David even remembered her now. She doubted that a fourteen-year-old boy would remember a woman who had shown him some kindness so long ago.

Sophie walked back into the living room to return the photo albums to the carton. There was a picture of Jeanie when she was two years old that had come loose from the album. Sophie stared at the photo of the small child with delicate features and sandy hair. She remembered how Harry fawned over Jeanie, showering unnecessary attention on her. Why did he have to love this child born of desire, never wanted, even hated by her at times? There was too much suffering attached to her birth—a birth she had tried to prevent.

After Lev left for Palestine with his sons, Sophie had known with certainty that she was pregnant. With Harry away in Panama, she had to keep her secret. She had planned to have an abortion. She even went as far as finding an abortionist, and she remembered traveling on the subway to a dingy street in lower Manhattan where she had the address of an abortionist. When Sophie reached the wood-framed building on a dirt-littered street and saw an ambulance parked in front and a woman's blood-soaked body being lifted into it, she had fled in terror.

Frantically, Sophie had tried to abort the baby herself the following day by throwing herself down the flight of stone steps next to her apartment door. Her sister and several neighbors had found her huddled unconscious at the foot of the steps. She spent several days in the hospital, where a fractured rib and numerous bruises were treated, while the fetus clung to life within her, growing stronger each day. Sophie returned from the hospital, despondent and anxious about her progressing pregnancy. Then she telegrammed Harry to come home immediately.

All these years she had kept her secret. Lev had never known he had a daughter, and Harry never suspected Jeanie was not his child. Maybe it was for the best that Lev was dead, Sophie thought now. Harry would never know. No one would ever know. She would carry this secret with her to her grave. No one could possibly be hurt if it remained her secret, she reasoned.

Sophie tucked the picture of Jeanie back in the album. There was a faded picture of Harry with his arm around her shoulder, her pregnant stomach bulging beneath her coat. Harry stood straight and proud, tanned from the Panama sun and deceived into thinking that the child growing in her womb was his.

Sophie remembered vividly the day Harry had returned from Panama. She lay listlessly in bed, recovering from her bruises and waiting anxiously for his return. Harry let himself quietly into the apartment with his key. He stood in the bedroom doorway, tall, lean, his skin bronzed and leathery from the sun, looking more handsome than she had remembered. All her anxieties were over now. "Harry, Harry," she sobbed, as tears spilled down her cheeks.

He was at her side, holding her in his arms, brushing away her tears, kissing her eyes, her cheeks, her lips. "Don't cry. Everything will be alright." He gently touched her bruised cheek with his fingertips.

Sophie recovered quickly after Harry's return. She clung to him desperately each night when they lay in bed together, lost in their renewed love. The old anger was forgotten. The reason for his running off to Panama was buried in their lovemaking.

"I'm pregnant," Sophie told Harry a few weeks after his return. His face broke into a broad smile. He was pleased though they had not planned on having any more children. "I'm sorry," Sophie had said. "We should have been more careful. We don't need another mouth to feed right now."

"Don't apologize." He pressed his lips against the palm of her hand. "I had something to do with it too… A child born of love can only bring happiness."

Why did Harry have to be so happy about it? Sophie felt a pang of guilt for deceiving Harry, even now after all these years. She tore the picture of herself into little pieces now, trying to blot out the memory of that pregnancy. But here were other pictures in the album, pictures of Harry holding the new baby in his arms, smiling lovingly at her. Sophie couldn't destroy all the pictures. And she couldn't destroy Harry's love for the child. Why did he have to show Jeanie so much attention? Sophie remembered taking the baby from his arms many times and putting her back in the crib. "Don't hold her so much. You'll spoil her," she would tell him.

"How can love spoil a child?" Harry had asked.

Sophie had tried to love Jeanie, but she couldn't. She waited for the love to come, but it never did. She remembered the tender feelings she had had when Albert and Ruthie were born. When each new baby swaddled in soft blankets was placed in her arms, she was overwhelmed with joy and awe at the child she had produced. But the sight of Jeanie, who even then resembled Lev, filled her with guilt and revulsion. "Here, take the baby back to the nursery." She had thrust the baby back into the nurse's arms at the hospital. "I'm too tired to hold her." And the milk, which had flowed from her breasts so profusely for Albert and Ruthie, dried up a few short weeks after Jeanie's birth and Sophie had to resort to formula.

As an infant, Jeanie cried endlessly and only Harry and her sister could soothe her. Sophie sometimes felt tempted to put a blanket over Jeanie's face to silence her cries, to smother her life, which was an ever-present reminder of her guilt and deception.

Well, Sophie thought now, *I made it up to Harry. I loaned him money to start a business. It wasn't my fault that the business failed. And he's on his way to becoming a rich man now because of me.* Sophie closed the carton and pushed it into the back of the closet. She closed the closet door on the box filled with memories that she had no wish to keep alive.

Chapter 22

The front door swung open and Jeanie walked in. "No more school! What a relief." She flung her loose-leaf book on the hall table and kicked off her shoes.

"Till September," Sophie said from the kitchen.

Jeanie walked into the kitchen and opened the refrigerator. She took out a bottle of milk. Sophie handed her a clean glass and she poured cold milk into it. "I hope I never have to go back."

"After the summer, you'll feel different."

"No, I won't!"

Jeanie sipped milk and watched Sophie peel potatoes for dinner. She tried hard not to listen to Mitzi's labored breathing as she lay in a corner of the kitchen close to Sophie. Last week they had taken Mitzi to the vet again. Sophie didn't want to and refused to pay for the vet, but she and Ruthie had pooled their money and Harry had slipped a few bills into her hand. "I can put her to sleep quietly," the vet had suggested. "She won't be in any pain."

"No!" Jeanie refused, and she took Mitzi home, carrying her up the stairs to the apartment and laying her down gently in her corner spot in the kitchen. Listening to her dog's labored breathing now, Jeanie thought she had been selfish. She watched Mitzi's stomach rise and fall with each painful breath, hoping it would not be the last. Mitzi's large sad eyes were half closed now, and the old dog drew one final breath. An oppressive silence filled the kitchen.

"She's gone!" Sophie dropped the paring knife.

Jeanie ran to Mitzi's side. She bent over the still warm body of her friend and gently touched her silky hair with her fingertips. Tears spilled from her eyes, her face masked in grief. "Who will listen and understand me now?" she whispered. But her friend did not answer.

Sophie wiped her eyes with the back of her hand. She too would miss the dog. She covered Mitzi with an old blanket and waited for Harry to return from work.

***

Jeanie was still crying when Harry came home and took Mitzi away. "Where are you taking her?" Jeanie screamed.

"We can't have a dead dog in the house. I have to take her away."

"No, I want to bury her."

"There's no place to bury her." Harry lifted the bulging blanket and went quickly from the apartment with his burden, feeling like a kidnapper. He returned a few moments later, the empty blanket draped over his arm. Jeanie knew with certainty that Harry had left Mitzi to be collected with the morning garbage. She would never forgive him for that.

Ruthie shared Jeanie's grief. The girls still mourned three days later when they left for Livingston Manor. They did not sing their usual medley of songs during the car trip, but gazed aimlessly out of the car window at acres of meadowland spotted with small farms and country houses, barns and grazing cattle.

The Rothmans settled quickly into their summer routines. The demands of maintaining sixteen bungalows and keeping all the tenants happy kept Sophie and Harry busy from early morning till late in the evening. There was the lawn to be maintained, a small playground that the mothers demanded to have in working order all the time, and the bungalows. Sophie pacified tenants while Harry raced to make repairs. Leaky faucets, broken door locks, windows that stuck, showers that didn't work and scores of other complaints kept Harry on the move all day with his tool box in hand. "You should hire someone to help Harry," Ida had suggested.

"What else does he have to do all day?" Sophie asked. "He doesn't need help."

"Mrs. Rothman, my mattress is so lumpy," Mrs. Goldberg complained to Sophie one day. "Maybe you have another mattress for me."

"I'd give you my own mattress if I thought it was better than yours," Sophie told her. "After all, you have to rough it a little in the country. Breathe that fresh air! Isn't it wonderful? With air like this, who cares about a few lumps in a mattress?"

Jeanie and Ruthie took turns running a small concession stand near the playground when Sophie was busy. They sold ice cream in small cups, fudgicles, creamsicles, nuts, candy, soda and popcorn. "Stop eating all the profits!" Sophie scolded when she caught Jeanie eating a creamsicle or crumpling a candy wrapper.

"Sophie, why do you have to charge so much for ice cream?" Mrs. Adler wanted to know.

"Do you want to walk a mile into town to get it for less? I have to get paid for my work. You'd think I was making a fortune from a Dixie cup… It's only a few cents more," Sophie said.

Sophie raised the prices at the concession stand each summer, knowing that the tenants would pay rather than walk into town. Profits from the concession were substantial. Every Wednesday afternoon Sophie and Harry drove into town to replenish their supplies. On one such Wednesday late in July, they met Morris Solomon, a former bungalow tenant who had bought a small hotel in South Fallsburg. "So how's the hotel business, Morris?" Harry shook his hand.

"I can't complain." Morris patted his round belly, which hung over his pants, and he wiped his balding head with a handkerchief. "Business is so good, I have waiting lists for my rooms."

"What are you doing here in Livingston Manor, Morris?" Sophie asked.

Morris and Bertha Solomon and their three children had rented the Rothman's best bungalow every summer until last summer, when they went into the hotel business in South Fallsburg. South Fallsburg was closer to New York City and more desirable as a summer resort than Livingston Manor, Sophie knew, but she failed to understand why. South Fallsburg had become densely populated, and rows of hotels and bungalow colonies dotted the landscape. She herself preferred Livingston Manor, where life was quieter and there was more space. But she had to admit that the hotels attracted a steady clientele with the swimming pools, entertainment and three meals a day they offered. People were willing to pay for all the luxuries of hotel life in the Catskills, and the Solomons were probably making a fortune, Sophie surmised.

"I'll tell you the truth, Sophie. I'm here because I went to see the owner of the Waldemere," Morris said.

The Waldemere was a nearby luxury hotel built alongside a lake. Sophie and Harry had been there on several occasions when guests they knew had invited them to spend an evening. On those rare outings, Harry dressed in a suit and tie and polished his good brown shoes. They'd drive up to the guard at the hotel gate and announce that they were invited guests. They always enjoyed the show, which included a dance act, a singer and a comedian. After the show they danced to the big band music in the large ballroom. Harry always felt nostalgic at those times, remembering the old days when he and Sophie had gone dancing at Roseland in Manhattan. He'd hold Sophie close, pretending it was long ago when life was less complicated and he was filled with love for her and hope for his future. Sophie was delighted to see the show at the Waldemere and dance to the wonderful music, especially since it was free.

"Are you buying the Waldemere?" Sophie asked Morris.

Morris laughed, his belly rolling beneath his thin summer shirt. "I make a nice living, but I'm not a millionaire. I went there to make Mr. Waldemere a proposition. I know he has money to invest and I have money to invest. A new hotel is going up just down the road from mine and they're short of cash. Right in the middle of building… and you should see it. It's going to be a beauty. Anyway, Mr. Waldemere isn't interested. He said he had enough headaches with one hotel."

"So you're investing in this new hotel, Morris?" Harry asked.

"Sure I am. I know a good thing when I see it."

"Don't they have enough hotels in South Fallsburg already?" Sophie asked.

"There's always room for more. You should see… people stand on line to get into them. It's *some* business." Morris mopped perspiration from his forehead with a damp handkerchief.

Sophie turned to Harry. "Maybe we should look into it."

"You're interested?" Morris asked.

"Maybe," Sophie said.

"Why don't you come over to my hotel tomorrow afternoon, about 3:00 o'clock. We'll talk. I'll show you the new hotel."

"We will," Sophie said.

Harry shook Morris's hand. He turned to Sophie after Morris left, a puzzled look on his face. "What are you planning now? Are you going into the hotel business?"

"Maybe we will."

"We? It sounds like you decided already before asking me."

"Harry, you know we always decide these things together."

Harry knew too well that Sophie thought of everything as hers—her bungalows, her house, her bank accounts. Ever since Sophie had loaned him her money for the service station business that had failed so many years ago, she thought and spoke of everything they had as hers. It didn't matter to her that he had repaid her and worked all his life. As long as she saved the money, she thought of it as hers. The house in Brooklyn that they had bought with Sophie's inheritance money, she thought of as hers too.

"We should at least take a ride to South Fallsburg and take a look," Sophie said. "It doesn't cost anything to look."

***

Sophie and Harry arrived at Morris's small hotel promptly at 3:00 o'clock the next afternoon. Bertha and Morris came out to greet them. Though she was short and plump, Bertha was always meticulously groomed. Today she wore a fashionable, white pique sundress and gold high-heeled sandals. A wide-brimmed white hat atop her bleached platinum curls shaded her tanned face. "It's so good to see you." Bertha smiled, kissing Sophie and Harry.

"When did you become a blonde, Bertha?" Sophie was shocked at the sight of Bertha, who had been a brunette when she had last seen her.

"Well, with the hotel and all… I thought blonde hair would be more attractive. Everyone needs a change now and then."

"It certainly is a change," Sophie agreed.

"Come sit down." Morris led them to a white lawn table at the far end of the pool. Children splashed happily in the blue water. The smell of chlorinated water drifted in the air. Harry watched enviously as a man in a black swimsuit dove into the cool water while other guests dozed lazily on chaise lounges. He wondered what it felt like to have a vacation at a hotel with nothing to do but relax and enjoy life all day.

Bertha waved to a busboy, who promptly brought a tray of fresh fruit and tall glasses of cold lemonade.

"How are the children?" Sophie asked.

"Wonderful. There's Susan and Phyllis in the pool," she said, pointing. "And Esther's a counselor in the day camp. Did Morris tell you we have a day camp for the little children? Esther makes a lot of money in tips."

"Hotel life seems to agree with you." Harry smiled. "How do you manage it all?" Harry thought of the constant daily drudgery at the bungalow colony.

"I have a lot of help," Morris said. "What are you worried about? If you invest in this new hotel, you don't have to do anything. You just put down your money and you're a silent partner. Somebody else runs the hotel."

Sophie listened with interest. "How much do we have to invest?"

"A small investor… twenty-five thousand," Morris said. Sophie winced. "You want to make money, you have to spend some," Morris added.

"We don't have that kind of money," Harry said.

Sophie finished her lemonade, savoring the cool sweet liquid. "Show us the hotel," she said.

Sophie thought about raising twenty-five thousand dollars while Morris led them through the half-built hotel—the large ballroom and dining hall, the empty swimming pool and handball courts, and the rows of terraced guest rooms. "The builders want one big investor, but they'll settle for a few small ones," Morris explained. "I told them to count me in."

"We'll let you know," Sophie said.

"Don't wait too long. You'll miss a good opportunity."

"I think we should do it," Sophie told Harry in the car on the way home. "We could put up five thousand and borrow the rest. When the hotel opens next summer, we'll make it all back."

"What if we don't make it back, Sophie? Sometimes hotels get in over their heads and lose money."

"Did you see all the people at Morris's hotel? All the hotels in the Catskills are crowded. They're all making a fortune. Look at Morris and Bertha. That was *some* expensive dress she was wearing."

"It's a gamble. Do you want to gamble?"

"We never lost in real estate. I don't think we'll lose now." Sophie had already made her decision.

Harry puzzled over Sophie's willingness to gamble with twenty-five thousand dollars and her refusal to spend a few dollars on a movie and a night out.

The following day Sophie announced to her tenants at the bungalow colony that she was starting a day camp for the younger children. She would only charge them five dollars a child per week to have their children entertained from nine in the morning till five at night every weekday while they enjoyed a summer of leisure. Ruthie, Jeanie, Helen, and Ruthie's friend, Sheila, who was coming to spend the rest of the summer with them, would be the counselors in charge. The girls' payment would be all the tips they earned from the satisfied parents of the happy children. "The counselors depend on your tips," Sophie told the tenants. "How else would they know they're doing a good job?"

The day camp business flourished, and the girls were busy with their new charges all day. Ruthie was delighted to have Sheila with her, and Sophie no longer heard complaints about boredom. Jeanie liked being in charge of the little children. She and Helen played endless games with their group of four-, five- and six-year-olds. They organized scavenger hunts and nature walks, sing-a-longs and games of hide and seek.

Jeanie had less time to read now, something she could spend hours doing. She had taken a sudden interest in ancient cultures and visited the small library in town, taking out all the dusty books she could find on ancient Egypt, Rome, Greece and Peru. Now she had to wait until five o'clock, when day camp ended, to sit in the cool shade of the front porch and lose herself in the books. She liked to imagine herself on a dig in Egypt, excavating the ruins of an ancient tomb, discovering a jeweled chest with priceless gold, or the mummy of a lost pharaoh.

"What kind of junk are you reading now?" Helen would tease.

"It's great… It's all about archeological digs."

"What's so great about that? No one ever takes those books out of the library. They're so old, the pages are yellow."

"I'm not interested in the color. I'm only interested in the words."

Helen spent hours reading confession magazines and couldn't understand Jeanie's lack of interest in love stories. "I'm going to be a famous archaeologist someday," Jeanie announced.

"And I'm going to the moon." Helen laughed.

"I'm going to find the lost city of Atlantis."

"In a submarine or a row boat?"

"Get lost, Helen!"

Their discussions lately had been ending in arguments, and their interests had taken different paths. No one really understood her, Jeanie thought. Ruthie was too busy with her friend, Sheila, and they treated her like a baby. Harry was busy with the bungalows all day and too tired at night to listen to her. Sophie told her she spent too much time with her head in a book. And there was always the aloofness she felt with her mother, who avoided her touch as though she were a leper. Only Mitzi had understood her, and she was gone now.

***

An overstuffed envelope arrived in the mail early in August. Jeanie ran up the steps of the farmhouse, letting the screen door bang behind her as she hurried into the kitchen for breakfast. "There's a letter from Albert." She waved the envelope excitedly.

"Open it," Ruthie said, buttering a slice of toast.

Sheila, who had a crush on Albert, looked up with interest as Jeanie tore open the envelope. "Go ahead, read it," Harry said, sipping his coffee.

Jeanie pulled a playbill from the envelope. "Oh look, Albert has the lead in the August show!"

"I knew it! I knew he'd get the lead." Ruthie clapped her hands.

Sophie scrambled eggs in a cast-iron skillet. She still used the old coal stove, refusing to spend money on a new gas stove.

Jeanie read the letter aloud: *"Dear Mom, Dad, Ruthie, and Jeanie, I'm having a terrific summer. The July show was a great success. I have the lead in the August show. Wish you could all come and see me. Next week a Hollywood talent scout is coming to see the show. We got rave reviews. The local paper said I was the 'hottest new talent around.' Miss you all. Love Al."*

"Al!" Ruthie exclaimed.

"Yes, he calls himself Al," Jeanie said. "The playbill lists his name as Al Rothman." She handed the playbill to Ruthie. Sheila peered over her shoulder at Albert's new name.

"I like it," Sheila said. "Al sounds more show biz."

"Fancy, shmancy," Sophie said. "Albert's not good enough? Now he's Al." She set a plate of eggs on the table and sat down.

Harry finished his breakfast in silence. Then he picked up his toolbox and left the house, letting the screen door bang closed behind him.

Chapter 23

Harry drove into Brooklyn the following week to apply for a twenty thousand dollar loan. They would use the house in Brooklyn as collateral. By the end of the week they would add the hotel in South Fallsburg to their list of assets. Harry hoped it wouldn't turn out to be a liability.

Mrs. Goodman opened her apartment door to peek out when she heard Harry's footsteps. "How are you, Mrs. Goodman?" Harry pulled his key out of his pocket.

"I can't complain," she said, opening the door wider. "So what brings you back to Brooklyn in the hot summer?"

"Some business to take care of. Is everything all right here?"

"And if it's not all right, who is there to complain to?"

"Say hello to your husband for me." Harry unlocked his apartment door and stepped inside, impatient to escape his tenant's complaints. The apartment was hot and a dank musty odor hung in the air. Harry opened the windows and pulled off his shirt and shoes. The long drive from the Catskills had tired him and he stretched out on the bed, drifting into a light sleep.

An hour later, Harry was awakened by the rumbling of thunder. He raced to close the windows before the carpeting got wet. The short nap had refreshed him, except for a vaguely disturbing dream of Albert bowing on a Broadway stage while he watched from the balcony and then ran from the theater to escape the sound of applause. The dream tripped in and out of his consciousness as he showered and dressed for dinner.

***

It was still raining when Harry returned from the deli on Rutland Road where he had gone for a hot meal. He had an appointment at the bank the next morning. As soon as the loan was arranged, he'd be on his way back to Livingston Manor. Sophie had asked him to bring back some more blankets. August evenings could get very cold in the Catskills.

Harry opened the closet in the living room and pulled out three blankets, exposing a small carton. Pulling the carton out, Harry untied the cord and was delighted to find it filled with old photographs. He set the carton down on the floor next to his favorite chair and settled down to delve through the contents.

Harry studied a large family photo—his mother, father and brothers. His eyes settled on his oldest brother, the only one who had gone to college. If fate had made Harry the oldest, he would have been the one to go to college instead of the one who had to support his parents when Poppa's arthritis forced him to give up the tailor shop.

Harry turned the page of the picture album. There was Sophie's mother, the old bitch. All that money and she never gave Sophie a nickel. Harry turned to pictures of the children when they were small. There was a photograph of Albert and Ruthie standing over the baby carriage where Jeanie poked her head out. Jeanie was a cute one, with her peach-fuzz hair and light complexion, so different from Albert's and Ruthie's brown eyes and dark hair. He had loved holding Jeanie in his arms. Sophie's strange aloofness toward Jeanie had always puzzled him. "Don't you love this baby as much as the others?" he had asked.

"Of course I do," Sophie insisted.

"You don't act like it."

"I have three children and a house to take care of. You think I have time to play games with babies?"

Harry supposed she was right. After all, they didn't have a washing machine and a lot of the comforts they had now. Still, Sophie's detachment had continued through Jeanie's childhood, and even now he sensed a difference in her feelings for Jeanie.

Harry yawned and closed the album. A loose picture drifted out, falling on the arm of the chair. An unfamiliar handwriting on the back of the picture caught Harry's attention—*Lev Kramer, Haifa 1948*. He turned the picture over. A tall, lean fair-haired man with high cheekbones and a neatly-trimmed beard stared out at him from behind a plow. Lev Kramer. The name was familiar, but Harry couldn't recall why. He knew he had never seen the man or the photo, yet there was a strange familiarity. He certainly didn't know anyone in Israel. He'd ask Sophie about him tomorrow. He put the picture back and closed the album.

The fair-haired man in the photo moved like a troubling shadow through Harry's dreams that night. He woke early the next morning feeling vaguely disturbed.

Harry arrived at the bank at 9:00 o'clock, signed the necessary papers and the loan was assured. It was easier than Harry had thought it would be. Sophie would be pleased. In a few days they would sign the papers for the hotel investment. Then they could sit back and wait for their silent partnership to pay off.

Harry was back in Livingston Manor by 4:00 o'clock that afternoon. Sophie walked out to the driveway to meet him. "I knew we wouldn't have any trouble getting a loan," Sophie said.

"We should celebrate tonight. How about going to the Waldemere for dinner and a show?" Harry asked.

"No, the shows are never good during the week. Anyway, we can't afford to go out now. We just borrowed twenty thousand dollars."

Harry sighed as they walked up the porch steps and into the house. In the kitchen, he turned to Sophie. "Who's Lev Kramer?"

Sophie winced. The spoon she had just picked up to stir a pot of stew on the stove clattered to the floor. She regained her composure and turned to face Harry. "Why do you ask?"

"I found a picture of him with his name on the back. It was from Israel. I don't remember him. Do you?"

"He was a neighbor. I wrote you about him when you were in Panama. He moved into one of the apartments and… and his wife died." Sophie's heart raced and she reached for a dishcloth, rubbing invisible spots from the stove.

"Why did he send you a picture?"

"His brother sent it. He… He moved to Israel with his two boys and was killed in an Arab attack… Poor man." Sophie bit her lip.

"Oh," Harry said, following Sophie's erratic movements around the kitchen as she brushed crumbs off the table and swept the floor.

The family gathered in the kitchen for dinner that night. "How's Brooklyn, Dad?" Jeanie asked.

"Brooklyn is Brooklyn."

Sophie placed a steaming plate of stew in front of Harry and he ate hungrily. Ruthie and her friend, Sheila, whispered and giggled. "How are you enjoying the summer, Sheila?" Harry asked.

"It's great here, Mr. Rothman, just great!"

Harry was glad Ruthie had invited her friend for the summer. Ruthie had gained some weight and seemed happier.

Jeanie read a book about ancient Egypt from her lap. "Put the book away and eat!" Sophie scolded. Jeanie pouted and closed the book.

Harry stared at Jeanie's face now. The picture of Lev Kramer, whose fair hair and high cheekbones matched Jeanie's, flashed suddenly into his consciousness. The resemblance was uncanny. "Is something wrong, Daddy?" Jeanie asked.

"No... No, nothing. Finish your dinner."

***

Harry slept fitfully that night. Flashes of buried memories surfaced to haunt him—Sophie's pregnancy soon after he had returned from Panama, the premature arrival of the baby that Sophie had insisted was only eight months. Sophie's misery when he arrived from Panama, her apologies for being pregnant, her coldness toward the child after the birth all surfaced in his dreams now and took on a nightmarish quality. Had Sophie lied to him all these years? Harry woke early, his skin clammy with perspiration, his head aching. Sophie stirred and mumbled in a half sleep, "Harry, are you okay?"

"Go back to sleep," he said, and he dressed quickly for an early morning walk to clear his head.

***

Sophie was cooking eggs on the coal stove when Harry returned from his walk. The kitchen was silent except for the coffee pot that perked on top of the burner. "Coffee?" Sophie asked.

Harry nodded and sat down heavily on a chair. "Are you worried about the hotel?" Sophie poured the steaming brew into a mug for Harry.

"No, I'm not thinking about the hotel... Was there ever anything between you and Lev Kramer?"

Sophie set the pot on the stove with trembling hands. Why, after all these years, did Harry have to ask her this now? Damn that picture. Why had she been so careless? Why hadn't she destroyed the picture along with the letter? She turned to Harry. "Are you crazy? Lev Kramer was a neighbor, nothing more."

Harry was silent, searching out Sophie's eyes with his own, but they avoided his. "Look at me, Sophie! I want the truth! Was there anything between you and Lev Kramer?"

"He's dead."

"That's not an answer."

"Have I ever lied to you?"

"I don't know. I know that Jeanie doesn't look like you or me."

"Jeanie is your child… yours and mine. How could you even think anything else? Children don't always look like their parents. Because she resembles some neighbor who's been dead for years, you think… How could you think such a thing?"

Something in Sophie's eyes betrayed her words, yet Harry wanted to believe her. He didn't know if he could face such a truth. He finished his breakfast silently, brooding over his suspicions.

"Harry, we should go out and celebrate tonight at the Waldemere. After all, you don't go into the hotel business every day," Sophie said, breaking the strained silence that had settled over the kitchen.

"Maybe another night," Harry said, no longer in the mood to celebrate.

***

On Monday morning, the Rothmans signed the contract, giving them ten percent ownership of the newest Catskill hotel, along with the Solomons and other investors. Their hotel partnership was launched.

Chapter 24

Jeanie was not looking forward to the new school year. She felt like an alien in the hostile new world of middle class East Flatbush, where her peers had grown up together, taking their nice homes, good clothes and family vacations for granted. She longed for her old friends, most of them now living in Brighton Beach, Sheepshead Bay and other parts of Brooklyn. Sometimes she'd take the bus and visit her old friends, but as time and distance separated them, they drifted further apart.

The first Saturday after school started in September, Sophie took Jeanie and Ruthie on a shopping trip. They took the subway to Fulton Street in downtown Brooklyn. Large department stores displayed manikins dressed in the latest fall and winter fashions. Shoe stores, dress shops, bridal shops, luggage stores and lingerie shops lined the streets that were crowded now with shoppers. Traffic crawled and horns honked. Women and girls hurried across the streets, carrying boxes with bold inscriptions—A&S, Martin's, A. S. Beck, and National Shoes.

Sophie steered Ruthie and Jeanie into Mays Department Store. "Momma, can't we go to A&S or Martin's?" Jeanie pleaded.

"Those are expensive stores," Sophie said. "You'll find nice clothes in Mays for less."

"Nobody in school wears clothes from Mays."

"Can we just look in A&S?" Ruthie asked.

"Don't waste my time. I don't have all day to shop. Pick out some skirts and sweaters and try them on," Sophie ordered.

The girls looked through racks of cheap woolen skirts. Jeanie found two plaids, a navy and a tan skirt. "Put one back," Sophie demanded. "Three's enough."

"But Momma, you said…"

"You have some clothes from last year that are still good."

"But Ruthie has four skirts."

"She's older, she needs more." Sophie scowled at Jeanie.

They weaved through crowds of women and girls, picking through piles of sweaters strewn in large wooden bins. Jeanie found a powder blue sweater set and Ruthie chose a coral sweater to go with a brown wool skirt. Then Sophie waited on a long line to pay for the clothing.

They left the store and walked down Fulton Street toward the A&S department store, stopping at Nedick's for long hot dogs smothered with mustard and sauerkraut, and orange drinks with crushed ice.

Ruthie stopped in front of the A&S window to admire a manikin dressed in a gray tweed skirt and pale, yellow cashmere sweater. "Isn't that beautiful!"

"The clothes we bought in Mays are just as nice," Sophie said.

"Let's go in and look," Jeanie said.

"I have to get home," Sophie said impatiently.

"Please Momma, just for a few minutes," Ruthie begged.

The store smelled of expensive perfume and new leather. It was crowded with well-dressed shoppers. Saleswomen with manicured nails stood behind counters displaying blouses, sweaters, fine leather handbags, silk scarves, gloves and hats. Ruthie stopped to admire a brown leather handbag. She caressed the smooth leather with her fingertips. "Isn't it beautiful? I need a new bag for school." She looked pleadingly at Sophie. Sophie examined the price tag—seven dollars. She could probably get one just as good for three dollars at Mays, she thought. "Please, Momma. I'll pay you back from my allowance."

"Well, alright," Sophie agreed, remembering that Ruthie had not been interested in buying anything at all last year.

"What about me?" Jeanie asked.

"There's nothing wrong with the bag you have."

"It's old and I hate it. All the girls in school have new bags."

"No!" Sophie snapped.

Jeanie sulked, as Sophie paid for the bag and steered them toward the exit. "Hurry," Sophie said. "It's 4:00 o'clock already and Albert's coming for dinner tonight."

***

Albert arrived promptly at 6:00 o'clock that evening. The family had not seen him since June. The kitchen smelled of roast chicken and baked sweet potatoes, chicken soup and rice pudding. The door swung open. "That smells fantastic," Albert said.

"Albert!" Sophie put down the spoon she was holding and kissed him on his cheek. "You got so thin."

"Albert!" Jeanie ran into his arms, nearly throwing him off balance.

"Hey, you into football?" he joked.

"You look great, Al." Jeanie squeezed his hands affectionately.

"You look pretty good yourself." He surveyed the new curves that had replaced his little sister's once boyish figure and he whistled.

Ruthie came out of the bedroom. "Albert, we missed you so much." She hugged him.

"Ruthie!" He held his sister tight as if his embrace would protect her from the pain he still saw in her eyes. "You look terrific," he lied. Ruthie had put on some weight and she seemed happier, but she had changed. The innocence and hopefulness had vanished from her eyes. Like a wounded bird, she seemed alone, abandoned, waiting for the next predator. Albert looked away from her eyes.

"Come." Ruthie took his hand. "Tell me all about your acting career." She led him into the kitchen where Sophie bent over the open oven door, spooning gravy over a roasting chicken. The smell of garlic and herbs hung in the air. Ruthie pushed Albert playfully into a kitchen chair and sat opposite him. "Talk," she commanded. "Tell me all about your summer."

"Later. You first. Tell me about your summer."

"It was the usual boring stuff," Ruthie said. "We started a day camp."

"No kidding? Make any money?"

"A little. Sheila spent a few weeks with us, and that was nice."

"I hardly made any tips," Jeanie added, as she folded paper napkins and arranged silverware on the table. "I never saw so many cheap people in one place and so many bratty kids."

Albert laughed, mussing Jeanie's hair affectionately.

"You know, I switched to a commercial course at Tilden High School," Ruthie said.

"Why'd you do that?" Albert couldn't hide his disappointment.

"Well I… I didn't see any point in continuing with an academic course. What would I do with science and math and language anyway? It won't get me a job as a secretary."

"What about college?"

"College isn't for me. I want to graduate and get a job, meet people in the business world… It's more exciting than burying myself in school for God knows how many years."

"Ruthie, I know you want to go to college." Albert looked into her eyes, reading the disappointment there. "Don't do this. You're giving up on yourself." He touched Ruthie's arm.

"No, I'm not."

"Tell her, Albert. She won't listen to me," Jeanie pleaded.

Albert turned to Sophie. "Mom, how could you let Ruthie do this?"

"It's her decision," Sophie said. "And I think it's a good one. She'll make money, meet nice young men in the business world, and…"

"Ruthie, listen to me," Albert pleaded, turning away from Sophie in disgust. "You're making a terrible mistake. You have to change back to an academic course. Don't give up on something you really want."

"My mind is made up," Ruthie said with resignation, avoiding her brother's eyes.

The sound of quick footsteps in the hall announced Harry's approach. The front door swung open and Harry stepped inside, the smell of spicy pipe tobacco lingering about him. He smiled, holding out his work-worn leathery hand for Albert. He saw no one else in the room.

"How are you, Dad?" Albert grasped his father's hand firmly.

Harry scrutinized his son for several minutes. "You look good. You're studying hard?"

"Sure, Dad."

"Go wash up," Sophie directed. "Dinner'll be ready in a few minutes."

Albert followed Harry into the bathroom, closing the door behind him. Harry watched Albert in the mirror that hung over the sink, while he soaped his hands that seemed permanently stained. "What's on your mind?" Harry asked.

"Ruthie. How could you let her drop the academic course?"

Harry studied Albert's face in the mirror. His son's lips were set in an angry line of accusal. "I tried to talk her out of it. Believe me, I really tried. But I got nowhere."

"You didn't try hard enough!"

"I only want her to be happy. She says she wants to get a job. She pleaded with us to let her do this."

"And you believe her? You believe she'll be happy? How can you think she'll ever be happy after what happened?"

Harry turned suddenly toward his son, his hands dripping water onto the blue tile floor. "You have no right to blame me!"

"I do blame you. I blame Sophie and I blame you! As if her life weren't ruined enough. Now you'll let her throw everything away." Albert's eyes blazed.

Harry clenched his fists and the muscles in his jaw tightened. "I told you there's nothing I can do! Maybe she'll change her mind after she goes to work."

"It'll be too late then. You and Sophie have a special talent for doing everything too late."

"Enough, Albert! Did you come here to argue?" Harry's voice rose.

"Hey, what's going on in there?" Ruthie knocked on the bathroom door.

Harry dried his hands on a towel and opened the door. Albert followed him into the kitchen. The family gathered around the kitchen table. Jeanie watched her father and brother avoid each other's eyes.

"Albert, when are we going to see you in a play?" Ruthie tried to distract Albert, sensing that she had been the subject of the argument she had heard through the bathroom door.

"Maybe you'll see me in movies?"

"Are you serious?" Jeanie looked up from her plate.

"I was never more serious. Remember when I wrote you about a Hollywood talent scout coming to see the summer stock play? Well, Mr. Adler, who works for Universal Studios, is interested in me."

"Oh, Albert!" Jeanie clapped her hands.

"He wants me to fly out to Hollywood for a screen test. He already offered me a walk-on part in a new film."

Harry stopped eating his chicken and looked silently at Albert. His mouth felt suddenly dry.

"It's so exciting," Ruthie said. "My brother, a famous actor."

"I'm not famous yet… but it's a great opportunity."

"It's very flattering, but you can't believe this man. Who is he anyway? He comes out of nowhere and promises you the world, and you believe him?" Harry's voice was edged with irritation.

"He's called me a few times since the summer. He gave me his card and told me to call him as soon as I get to Hollywood."

"What about college? What about medicine?" Harry fumed.

"I don't want medicine." Albert looked into his father's eyes. "You wanted it for me. I never wanted it. I want to act more than anything. I'm going to do it," Albert said with absolute conviction.

Harry's face turned ashen. He felt a pain deep within him, as if a mortal wound had been inflicted. He had felt like this only once before in his life, when his daughter had been raped and he had held her poor bruised body in his arms. Harry pushed his plate away now and stood up. "No!" he raged. "I won't let you do this!"

Sophie dropped the cover of the pot she was holding and it clattered to the floor. She hadn't heard Harry sound so angry since their quarrel so many years ago, before he left for Newfoundland.

"Albert, how can you give up two years of college now? Listen to your father. Don't do this," Sophie pleaded.

"I'm going," Albert said with finality. "I'm leaving college and I'm going to Hollywood next week."

"You're going to be a bum! A no good bum!" Harry shouted.

"Shh." Sophie tried to silence Harry. "The neighbors will hear you."

"I don't care. The whole world should hear. I have a son who's a bum! A bum actor!"

Jeanie and Ruthie watched in silence, horrified, wanting to help Albert realize his dream and yet understanding that their father's dream had been suddenly shattered.

"I'm not a bum! Bums don't work. I worked hard for my success," Albert said.

"What success? You're nothing! You're nobody!" Harry declared.

Albert winced. "You don't care about what I want. You never did. You want me to be a doctor because that's what you wanted for yourself. I can't be anything for you!"

The truth of Albert's words stung Harry. "I'll disown you if you do this." Harry's voice shook.

The color rose in Albert's cheeks and spread to his temples. "I'll do it with or without your approval."

"If that's the way you want to end this, it's okay with me." Albert turned to Sophie. "I want the money from my Bar Mitzvah gifts now. I need it to get to Hollywood."

"No," Sophie snapped. "You won't get a cent if you leave college now."

"It's my money!" Albert's eyes stung. He clenched and unclenched his fists, feeling like a helpless child again. "Then damn you! Damn you both!" Albert sprung from the chair.

"If you go to Hollywood, you're dead! I'll tell everyone my son is dead, and I'll sit *shiva* for you!" Harry shouted after Albert who raced down the steps and out of the house.

Ruthie and Jeanie slipped out quietly, leaving Harry to be comforted by Sophie. They caught up with Albert at the street corner as he headed for the subway. "Wait, Albert!" Ruthie caught his arm, panting for breath. Jeanie stood beside him. "Can we talk? Please don't go away like this," Ruthie pleaded.

"I have no other choice."

"What will you do for money?" Jeanie asked.

"I saved a little. I'll manage."

"I have forty dollars I earned over the summer. I want you to have it," Ruthie said.

"I can give you twenty dollars," Jeanie offered. "It's all I have."

Albert hugged his sisters. A tear traced its ways down his cheek and he brushed it away quickly. "I know I can always count on you two. I'll be okay. You're going to see me in movies. Take care of yourselves. And Ruthie, remember what I told you. You mustn't give up on yourself. I'll write you." He looked longingly at his sisters as if memorizing this moment, and then he turned and walked quickly down the street, away from Brooklyn, away from his family and the life he knew.

Chapter 25

Ida zipped up the back of her dress and slipped on her sensible, brown walking shoes. She had to hurry if she wanted to meet Sophie at the train station by 11:00 o'clock. They planned to spend the day shopping for clothing for Ruthie's wedding. Ruthie would be a beautiful bride, Ida thought. She was lucky to have met a man like Alex—handsome and a good future in advertising. He would take care of Ruthie for the rest of her life.

Ida hurried out of her apartment, wondering if Alex knew the truth about Ruthie.

The sky was bright with spring sunshine, and flowers bloomed in the small gardens along the streets. Ida walked briskly down Rutland Road toward the train station, passing the four-story apartment building, which Sophie and Harry now owned. Her sister's daring and good luck amazed her. The Rothman's profits had more than doubled in the two years since their first investment in a Catskill hotel. They had invested in two other new hotels in the Catskills. They had also bought a four-family house next door to the one they occupied on East 96th Street. And now they were talking about Florida and Long Island real estate. Ida found it all overwhelming. "Take care that you don't make a mistake and lose everything," Ida had cautioned Sophie.

"I haven't lost anything yet," Sophie had said.

But you lost your son, Ida had thought. *You threw him out, left him to struggle without any money when you could have helped him. Stingy. Sophie would always be stingy no matter how much money she had.* Ida would never understand Sophie. She had so much and gave so little. She was even stingy with her affection toward her children, especially toward Jeanie. Her sister was a strange woman. Yet Ida accepted Sophie like she accepted everything else in life, as though she were powerless to change it.

Ida hurried toward Sophie, who waited near the elevated train station. There was hardly a gray hair among Sophie's dark waves or a wrinkle on her plump face. She wore a yellow cotton dress that clung to her wide hips and stretched across her sagging breasts. Her brown shoes were polished, but the heels were worn and one stocking had a run in it. She carried a large tan handbag, frayed around the edges, and a paper shopping bag with *Pioneer Savings* printed on it. Sophie smiled broadly when she saw Ida. "The next train will be here in a few minutes." She hurried Ida up the steps to the platform.

"You're not wearing a girdle, Sophie. How can you buy a dress without a girdle?" Ida scolded when they reached the train platform.

"Don't worry, it's in the shopping bag."

The train clattered into the station, and the sisters found seats together before the train jerked forward and pulled out. "Wait till you see Ruthie's gown." Sophie's voice rose above the screeching train. "It's gorgeous! She looks like a model… She bought it in A&S."

"It must have been expensive."

"Don't even ask."

"You're paying for it, Sophie?"

"Me?" Her voice rang with surprise. "She wanted to buy it herself," Sophie lied. "After all, she's a working girl."

"But she has plenty of things to buy. An apartment full of furniture…"

"Alex makes a good living. Don't forget, he's an advertising executive. And I'm paying for the wedding. They'll get plenty of gifts to help them out."

Ida wanted to tell Sophie that she should take pleasure in buying Ruthie's wedding gown after all that's happened. But instead she asked, "Where are the newlyweds going on their honeymoon?"

"Florida… Miami. For a week."

"Alex is *some* nice fella," Ida said. "Ruthie's a lucky girl."

"You're telling me," Sophie said, smiling. "She was only working for the advertising agency a few months when she met Alex. They liked each other right away. It was *bashert*! Fated."

"My girls should be so lucky someday," Ida said. She dared not ask if Alex knew the truth about Ruthie.

Sophie sighed, relieved that Ruthie would be safely married by the end of June. She didn't want anything to go wrong. She didn't want Alex to change his mind, and she had cautioned Ruthie to keep her secret. "I hope you don't think you have to tell Alex everything about yourself," Sophie had told Ruthie months before her engagement.

"What do you mean?" Ruthie had challenged her.

"You know… There are some things you don't talk about. It could spoil everything for you."

"If Alex loves me, he'll still love me if he knows the truth."

"He may love you, but he may not want you."

Ruthie's eyes filled with tears. "Didn't you ever trust anyone enough to tell the truth?"

Sophie had turned her eyes away from Ruthie's haunting gaze, affirming her daughter's insight with her silence. They spoke no more of it, and Sophie could only wonder what Alex knew.

"What do you hear from Albert?" Ida's voice rose above the screeching train.

Sophie winced. "We don't hear from him."

"The girls must hear from him."

"He writes to them. He's making a living. Not a fortune, just a living. Who knows if he's telling the truth? In the meantime, he's not famous and I haven't seen his name in lights. I hear he gets small parts once in a while."

"Isn't it time you forgave him? He'll come to his sister's wedding if he's invited. I know he will," Ida implored.

"Harry won't even let us mention his name."

"How long can Harry carry on? It's two years already," Ida reminded her.

"I'm willing to forgive him, but Harry never will."

"It'll be a terrible thing if Albert doesn't come to his sister's wedding," Ida warned. "The family will talk."

"The *yentas* will talk anyway." Sophie shrugged, feeling helpless against Harry's wrath.

The train pulled into the downtown station, and Sophie and Ida got off. Smokey dank air trapped in the underground tunnel filled their nostrils as they hurried through the turnstile and up the steps, eager to fill their lungs with clean air. The streets bustled with shoppers hurrying to make purchases in the large department stores and small shops that crowded the streets. Sophie and Ida joined the throngs of shoppers and headed toward Mays department store. "Maybe we should try one of the small dress shops," Ida urged. "They have better clothes."

"I'll find something in Mays. I don't like those high-pressure saleswomen in the small stores," Sophie insisted.

Ida followed Sophie silently into Mays, wondering why her sister continued to live beneath her means. They took the escalator to the second level, where racks of brightly colored dresses lined the floor in a dizzying array, like an army of soldiers waiting to do battle. Sophie smiled. "Did you ever see so much merchandise? If I can't find something here, I can't find it anywhere." She headed for the racks marked size sixteen to eighteen and flipped through the dresses, alert for styles that would compliment her ample figure. Ida searched the racks of smaller-size dresses and the two met in the fitting-room, where Sophie grunted and struggled into her girdle. She tried on dress after dress before settling on an aqua chiffon dress that fit snugly around the bodice and fell in soft pleats around her hips and down to her ankles.

Ida nodded approvingly. "It looks good, Sophie." She knew Sophie would look better in a more expensive dress but would never be persuaded to spend more.

"I'll take it." Sophie breathed a sigh of relief, as she stepped out of her girdle and dropped it into the shopping bag. "What about you? You didn't like any of the dresses?"

"No, I'll try another store," Ida said.

Sophie paid for the dress and they left Mays, heading for a specialty dress shop where Ida found a rose-colored, silk evening dress that flattered her slim figure. Sophie admired the dress but admonished Ida. "You don't have to spend so much. Ruthie's your niece, not your daughter."

It took another hour before the rest of their purchases were completed—shoes, bags, evening gloves. Then the two sisters headed for Junior's restaurant, where they could relax over lunch. They sat at a small table in the back of the noisy restaurant. Waiters hurried from the kitchen, carrying trays of fat sandwiches, coffee and pastries to hungry shoppers and business people from nearby offices.

Sophie had to talk above the noisy chatter and clinking dishes. "I'm glad my shopping is over." Sophie stretched her legs, which ached now from hours of walking. She ate a forkful of the creamy cheesecake she had ordered and sipped the strong hot coffee. "Now I have to go shopping with Jeanie. She's always a problem."

"My Helen has to try on a hundred dresses before she makes up her mind." Ida poured milk in her coffee.

"Jeanie makes up her mind fast enough, but it's always the most expensive thing," Sophie complained.

"Well, this is a special occasion. Jeanie wants to look good for her sister's wedding… and she's the maid of honor," Ida reminded her.

"I hope Jeanie finds time to go shopping on Saturday. When she's not studying, she's in the library or wandering around the Brooklyn Museum. She worries me with her crazy talk about digging up ruins. It's not normal."

"What's to worry? I think it's wonderful. Helen is too much with the boys. All day she's on the phone talking to boys or talking to her girlfriends about the boys," Ida said.

"I hope Jeanie meets someone as nice as Alex someday," Sophie said.

"Jeanie's a beautiful girl. She'll get married one day." Ida brushed crumbs from her lap.

"Who knows?" Sophie knitted her brow. "All she talks about is going to college, being an archaeologist, going to places with strange names."

"She's only sixteen, Sophie. When she meets the right guy, she'll settle down."

Sophie finished her coffee now. The waitress brought the check, which Sophie scrutinized. Then she opened her purse and handed Ida the exact amount for her cheesecake and coffee. Ida left a tip on the table for the waitress, but Sophie did not. They left the noisy restaurant, eager to get home after their busy shopping day.

***

Albert walked leisurely out onto his front porch, clad only in shorts. He picked up the morning paper and took the mail from the mailbox. The Anaheim house he shared with three other aspiring actors was small but comfortable. He squinted in the bright California sunshine. Boring, he thought. Too much sunshine is just plain boring. He longed nostalgically for a cool autumn day in New York when the air has a hint of frost and falling leaves snap beneath your feet. Ice skating in Central Park. Broadway. Macy's Thanksgiving Day parade. Lindy's cheesecake. Ruthie and Jeanie. Would he ever go back? Maybe one day when he was famous. He hadn't done too badly these past two years. Walk-on parts in films had kept him going. All he needed was one break, one chance. Soon. He felt it would come soon. His agent kept promising, "I'm plugging for you, Al. You've got what it takes to be great." So Albert waited, went to celebrity parties and tried to meet the right people.

Mr. Adler, the talent scout, and his promise had long ago been forgotten. After three walk-on parts in grade B films, Mr. Adler had lost interest in him. Albert shuddered now, remembering their last meeting. They had gone to a downtown Los Angeles restaurant, and Mr. Adler had sat a little too close to him at the table. He let his hand slide possessively along Albert's thigh beneath the tablecloth. Albert's face had flushed crimson, and he felt suddenly sick to his stomach. "Fame involves more than just being a good actor," Mr. Adler told him.

Albert clenched his fists now, still feeling angry at having been duped. He sat down at the kitchen table, stretched his legs on a chair and sorted through the mail. Ruthie's neat handwriting on a pale blue envelope caught his eye. He tore open the envelope, hungry for news.

'Dear Al, Alex and I sat through Elephant Walk in the movie theater twice. I looked for you in the crowd, but couldn't find you. I wanted so much for Alex to see you. I wish you could meet Alex. I know you two would like each other. We're going to be married in June. Mom and Dad are making us a wedding. I hope you can come. I know Dad wouldn't mind. If you came, he would forgive you. I love Alex and I'm very happy, but I miss you. Please say you'll come to our wedding. Love, Ruthie'

Albert pressed the letter against his face and inhaled deeply, savoring the light perfume that Ruthie used to scent her letters. He brushed a tear from his cheek with the back of his hand. It took all his willpower not to dash off a reply, telling Ruthie he would not miss her wedding for anything. He wanted to be there, to see for himself if Ruthie was truly happy. He could not believe her letter. He would have to look into her eyes to know if her wounds had healed. But he knew he could not go home with Ruthie's invitation alone. He would wait for an invitation to arrive from Sophie and Harry. They had neither spoken nor written to him since the day he had walked out. Harry's words still rang in his ears, *"You're dead! I'll tell everyone my son is dead."*

If spells can be cast with words, Harry had succeeded. Albert felt that part of him had died that day. He would carry the memory of the pain he had seen in his father's eyes, knowing that he had caused it. Yet mixed with his guilt at having disappointed Harry was raging anger for expecting him to fulfill Harry's dream. Though Albert had gone his own way, he was tormented. As for his mother, he thought he truly hated her. She had let him go without any money, refusing to give him even what was rightly his, hadn't written or spoken to him in two years, and didn't care if he lived or died. What did she care about? Surely not what normal people did. Her need for money was insanely twisted, Albert reasoned. Like an amoeba that sucks in food, divides and multiplies, Sophie sucked in money, made it multiply and had no further use for it. That was her *raison d'etre.* Money—in and of itself.

Albert sighed wearily and dropped Ruthie's letter on the table. He would write to Ruthie and try to explain why he could not come to her wedding. But first he would wait. Perhaps an invitation would arrive.

Chapter 26

Jeanie fumbled with the tiny lace-covered buttons on the back of Ruthie's wedding gown. "There must be a hundred buttons here," Jeanie complained, as nervous as if it were her own June wedding day. "Finished!" she announced at last. Ruthie turned to face her and Jeanie caught her breath at the sight of her sister dressed as a bride.

Ruthie gathered the white satin train in her arms, her head bowed and her dark silky hair tumbling softly around her face. Jeanie brushed tears from her eyes as she looked at her sister whose face shone with happiness. "I'm going to miss you." Jeanie embraced her.

"I'm not going to the other end of the world. I'm just getting married."

"But it won't ever be the same between us again." Jeanie muffled a sob.

Ruthie clasped Jeanie's hands in hers. "Of course it will be the same. And we'll be living only a few blocks away."

"But Alex will want you all to himself," Jeanie said, pouting.

"Alex loves you, Jeanie. You know that."

"Still… it won't be the same. You'll see," she said dramatically, drying her eyes.

Sophie walked into the bedroom dressed in her aqua chiffon dress and new shoes dyed to match. "Momma, you look beautiful," Ruthie exclaimed.

Jeanie whistled. "I never saw you look so great." She scrutinized the dress, which fit well over Sophie's tightly stayed breasts and girdled hips. The girls had badgered Sophie into going to the beauty salon with them that morning, and the results were better than they had expected. Sophie's dark hair was carefully coiffed in soft curls, and her nails were neatly manicured.

"Look at you!" Sophie gazed at her beautiful daughter dressed in her bridal gown. She had a fleeting feeling that this scene before her was only a dream she had dreamed again and again. Her eyes stung with sudden tears, surprising her. Did she weep for Ruthie's happiness or her own relief? She stiffened, regaining her composure, and kissed Ruthie on her cheek. Then, turning to Jeanie, she scolded, "You're not even dressed. We're leaving in half an hour… and stop crying. Is this a funeral or a wedding?"

Jeanie slipped out of the room to finish dressing and repair her makeup. Harry stood stiffly in the doorway, dressed in a black tuxedo, perspiring nervously. He stepped lightly into the bedroom, taking Ruthie's hands in his, holding her at arm's length as though she were a fragile porcelain doll. Their eyes met, and he was filled with her happiness. He could think of no one who deserved happiness more than Ruthie. He wanted to say so many things… *Ruthie, forgive me for the terrible times in your life that I'm responsible for. Be happy. Try to forget.* But he said, "You're the most beautiful bride I've ever seen," and he planted a soft kiss on his daughter's forehead.

"She certainly is." Sophie smiled.

"You look pretty handsome yourself, Daddy." Ruthie smiled approvingly at Harry, who looked more like a maitre d' in his tuxedo than the father of the bride. His hair had thinned and was threaded with gray. He had grown thinner since Albert had left, and his face was pale and gaunt. As the Rothman's business ventures grew, Harry's interest in them had diminished to an almost unnatural detachment. He showed little interest in anything since Albert had left. The only intense emotion he displayed was anger when Albert's name was mentioned. "Daddy, can Albert come to the wedding?" Ruthie had asked in April when the invitations were sent out.

Harry's head had jerked up sharply from *The Daily News* he was reading. "No!" he snapped. "Albert is dead!"

"Daddy, please. It's important to me," Ruthie had begged.

"No! You'll get married without him here." Though he rarely refused Ruthie any of her requests, he was adamantly against this. Sophie could not persuade him either.

"Harry, enough is enough," Sophie had told him. "He's our son. The wedding is a happy occasion."

"No!" Harry's voice rose and his face flushed.

"Harry, the relatives will all talk. How will I explain why Albert isn't at his sister's wedding?"

"Tell them he's dead!" Harry said with finality, throwing aside the newspaper and hurrying out of the apartment to walk off his anger and despair.

Albert's name was not mentioned again after that day, and the wedding invitation that Albert waited hopefully for in California never arrived.

***

The guests arrived at the Twin Cantors reception hall on Eastern Parkway promptly at 8:00 p.m. They picked up their table seating cards and were directed to the ballroom where a large smorgasbord table was the center of attraction. Aunts, uncles, cousins and friends, dressed in their best clothes, huddled around the smorgasbord, smiling, talking, filling plate after plate with hot and cold meats, fruits, and steaming delicacies that simmered in silver chafing dishes and were served by attentive waiters. Sophie was spending fifteen hundred dollars on this wedding, and she would never let Ruthie or Alex forget it. She left Ruthie now, in seclusion in the bridal suite, where she sat on a crimson, velvet high-backed chair. Ruthie twisted a lace handkerchief between her fingers as she waited for the ceremony to begin while her bridesmaids attended her, wishing that they were in her place.

The five-piece band that had been engaged for the evening began playing as Sophie made her entrance into the ballroom to greet the guests. She moved among aunts, uncles, cousins and friends, kissing and embracing them.

"*Mazel tov, mazel tov*!" the guests called out.

"Thank you." Sophie beamed. She felt as if the good luck wishes were for her alone, as if it were her wedding instead of her daughter's.

Harry stood in the center of the ballroom, nervously shaking hands with family members and friends eager to congratulate him. Nathan, sensing Harry's nervousness, brought him a drink. "Here," he said, thrusting a glass into Harry's hand. "A little schnapps will settle your nerves. It's better than chicken soup."

"Thanks." Harry gulped the liquor, feeling it burn as it slid smoothly down his throat. He wished the ceremony were over. He heard Sophie's raucous laughter across the ballroom and over the band music. *This is her night, her wedding*, Harry thought.

Sophie held a plate piled with steaming chicken and pineapple, which she ate hungrily and then returned to the smorgasbord table to taste other delicacies. She was determined to sample everything. She gazed at the mountain of cold chopped liver decorated with flowered radishes and plump green olives, trays of smoked salmon, whitefish and sturgeon, baskets of thinly-sliced rye and pumpernickel breads, golden *challahs*, silver trays of fresh ripe melons and pineapples, and shimmering Jell-O molds. Carving boards laden with hot pastrami, roast beef and turkey were attended by waiters who expertly sliced the meats for guests.

Sophie approached a waiter now. "I'll have a little pastrami. And while you're slicing, some roast beef and turkey too… and don't be stingy. I'm paying the bill."

The waiter handed Sophie a generous portion of meat.

"Thank you. And by the way, I'm taking home whatever is left here. It's a shame it should be thrown out, all this wonderful food."

"We don't usually do that, madam," he said.

"So you'll make an exception this time." Sophie turned and headed toward Ida, who sat at a small cocktail table next to Morris and Bertha Solomon. Sophie eyed the empty plates on the table. "Why aren't you eating?" she scolded. "The food isn't good?"

"It's delicious," Bertha praised.

"I have to leave some room for dinner and wedding cake." Morris patted his round stomach.

"This is *some* smorgasbord." Ida was truly impressed. It was what Sophie had wanted to hear. Her guests, she knew, would not soon forget this wedding. Her wedding.

"Harry! Harry!" Sophie called from across the room as she moved toward him. "Did you eat?"

"I ate!" he lied, feeling his stomach tighten at the mere suggestion of food.

"Everything's delicious," she said. "I tasted everything."

"I'll bet you did. Make sure your new dress still fits you at the end of the evening," Harry warned.

"Harry with the jokes," Sophie said, turning to Nathan.

"Let's dance, Sophie." Nathan yanked her arm, dragging her onto the dance floor, his unruly hair standing out in disarray and his black bowtie askew on his neck. Though he walked with heavy lumbering steps, Nathan danced gracefully, smoothly leading Sophie around the ballroom in time to the fast music. Sophie laughed happily and Nathan hummed to himself, unaware of Sophie or anyone else now, lost in his passion for music and dance. When Sophie at last begged off, Nathan whisked Ida onto the dance floor, then Jeanie whose powder-blue chiffon dress swished softly around her hips as she tried to keep pace with Nathan. There was no stopping Nathan now. He exhausted every willing and unwilling partner in the ballroom. Then he danced alone while the other guests circled around him, clapping in time to the music. Like a whirling dervish, Nathan's feet moved lightly, spinning him around the floor while his hair fell damply over his forehead and his face glowed in rapture. Exhausted, he finally slid into a chair, panting, loosened his tie, and unbuttoned his jacket, which was damp now from his sweat-soaked shirt.

Ida approached him. "It's a good thing I brought an extra shirt for you. Here." She thrust a clean shirt at him, which she had stowed in the checkroom. Experience had taught Ida to take two or three clean shirts for Nathan to change into whenever there was music and dancing. "You're acting like a *meshuggener* again. The night is young, and there's only one extra shirt left for you," Ida scolded.

"Who cares!" Nathan said. "Let go a little, Ida. Live a little."

"*Meshuggener*… crazy!" Ida said again and turned to talk to her relatives.

Sophie's family was the loudest and most raucous of the group. Harry's relatives were somewhat quieter, and the groom's family, which occupied a small corner of the room, was considerably more reserved. Alex towered over most of his relatives, who surrounded him now, slapping him on his back, shaking his hand, planting wet kisses on his handsome face. He fidgeted nervously with the white carnation in the lapel of his tuxedo, wishing that the ceremony were over and Ruthie were his wife. He ached to have her by his side now, cursing the tradition of not seeing his bride before the ceremony. He smiled and went through the motions of being polite to his relatives, who fawned over him and cackled inane remarks in his ear. "Such a handsome groom! Alex, every girl should be as lucky as Ruthie," his Aunt Rosie told him at least three times.

Alex watched Sophie moving toward him and he flinched. "Oh, there you are Alex." Sophie dragged a relative beside her. "What do you say about my handsome new son-in-law?" Sophie asked her squat cousin, Minna, who regarded Alex as though he were a piece of meat for sale at the butcher shop.

"I'm not your son-in-law until after the ceremony," Alex reminded her, regarding Sophie with a mixture of disgust and contempt. He towered over her, standing six feet, two inches tall. His dark wide-set eyes twinkled mischievously and he smiled through even white teeth, taking the edge off his sharp retort.

Cousin Minna smiled through thin lips and stained teeth. "Nice to meet you."

"And here's my *machetunum*… my in-laws to be." Sophie corrected herself for Alex's benefit, and drew Alex's parents into their circle to meet her cousin.

Alex looked helplessly in Jeanie's direction, signaling for rescue. Jeanie glided by. "Want to dance?"

"I'd love to." Alex whisked Jeanie onto the dance floor.

"Did anyone ever tell you that you're a terrific kid?" Alex asked.

"All the time. People just open their windows when I walk down the street and shout, *Here comes the terrific kid.*"

Alex laughed, his face lighting up with a mocking grin. He had a generous mouth and a broad smile, making his face look fuller than it actually was. He was exceedingly thin, a little too thin. The pronounced limp he was afflicted with was barely perceptible when he danced. A fractured hip in childhood had left him with one leg shorter than the other. He adored Ruthie. From the moment he set eyes on her, she had struck him as sweet, perfect, virginal. Several months later, when he had asked Ruthie to marry him, she had told him of the rape. "You don't need me. I'm stained. Tainted!" The words had choked in her throat and the pain of the burden she bore turned the innocence in her face to despair. She saw the shock in Alex's eyes and she turned to run, but Alex caught her in his arms and kissed the salty tears that fell on her cheeks.

"I love you," he whispered huskily into her ear, inhaling the clean scent of her hair. "I'll always love you." Tears welled in his eyes and sorrow overwhelmed him. Was his sorrow for Ruthie or for his shattered dream of a perfect woman? A less than perfect man, a cripple, should not expect perfection, he had thought then. They never spoke of it again and Alex repressed the truth, denying it along with other thoughts he could not or would not accept.

Jeanie looked into Alex's clear dark eyes. "You owe me, Alex. I saved you from Momma and cousin Minna," she teased. "You can't possibly understand how indebted you are to me until you spend some time with Minna, who suffers from bad breath and incurable stupidity."

"I'm sure I'll owe you a lot more before this evening's over."

Jeanie slipped out of Alex's arms now. "I'm going to check on Ruthie."

Alex watched Jeanie glide gracefully across the ballroom, her long hair catching the light from the chandelier as it fell around her bare shoulders. She had grown taller and her supple body had the sensuous curves of a mature woman. Alex admired her spirit and her beauty. He had learned to stay out of her way when her blue eyes blazed. She was the only one in the Rothman family who ever challenged Sophie. But he had never met Albert.

Harry looked at his watch now. Ten more minutes and the ceremony would begin. He felt calmer after a few drinks. Nathan sat next to him at a small cocktail table, sipping liquor. He wore a fresh shirt and seemed calmer now after his feverish dance. Uncle Bennie headed toward their table, dragging his midget-like wife, Golda, behind him.

Bennie sneaked up behind Harry as he always did and slapped him loudly on his back. "Ah ha!" Bennie laughed like a madman. "You thought I wouldn't find you?"

"You thought we wouldn't find you?" Golda echoed Bennie idiotically.

"Why isn't Albert here?" Bennie demanded.

Harry flinched. "He's in California making a movie. He couldn't get away."

Harry was relieved to escape Bennie's prying questions when the maitre d' announced that the wedding ceremony would begin. Guests filed out of the ballroom into the small chapel upstairs. The last person Harry wanted to think about tonight was Albert.

The wedding party waited anxiously outside the chapel door for the procession to begin. Jeanie fussed over Ruthie's veil and handed her the bridal bouquet of white gladiolas and baby's breath. "You look exquisite," she whispered, squeezing Ruthie's hand before the organ played *A Pretty Girl is Like a Melody*, and she moved down the aisle to meet the best man.

Ruthie waited silently for the *Wedding March* to play. Was she doing the right thing? Should she marry Alex? Should she marry at all? Did she have the right to wear a white gown? These thoughts raced through her mind, and she felt a sudden impulse to flee, but Harry held firmly to one arm and Sophie to her other.

The *Wedding March* filled Ruthie's ears. Sophie and Harry guided her down the aisle. A hush fell over the chapel and all heads turned toward the lovely bride. Murmurs of admiration rang through the chapel as guests strained their necks to see Ruthie's face beneath the veil. Sophie and Harry left her in the middle of the long aisle. As Alex walked toward her, her lips parted in the sweetest of smiles. She felt Alex's warm strong hand in hers, and they walked down the aisle together and up the steps to take their place beneath the wedding canopy.

They listened to the rabbi's words and took their vows. Then Alex placed a gold wedding ring on his bride's finger. As tradition bade him, he stepped on a glass wrapped in a linen napkin. Guests sang out, "*Mazel tov,*" at the sound of the shattering glass. Then Alex lifted the veil that covered Ruthie's face and kissed her lips. She smiled into his eyes. *I'm Mrs. Alex Hartman*, she thought. *There's no turning back now.*

Harry relaxed after the ceremony and began to enjoy himself. He waltzed with Sophie, with Jeanie, with Ida. She's safe now, Harry thought. Alex will take good care of Ruthie. He trusted Alex. He liked him.

The band played a *hora.* Everyone joined hands and circled round the bride and groom who sat on chairs in the center of the circle. They clapped and danced and sang. "*Hava Nagila*" rang through the ballroom as though the joy of the music would keep them happy for all time. The bride and groom, perched precariously on chairs, were lifted high above the dancers who sang louder and danced faster, buoyed by the music, until it mercifully ended.

Waiters served thick barley soup from giant tureens and stuffed roasted capons from silver trays. White lace over crimson linen cloths covered the tables. There were monogrammed menus and matchbooks, silver candelabras and centerpieces of pink and white chrysanthemums on the tables. Sophie was glad that all these things were included in the price. She did not want to pay extra for anything. She hoped the guests would leave by 1:00 o'clock so she would not have to pay the band more money. But no one was in a hurry to leave, and they danced on long after the wedding cake was cut and coffee was served in gold-rimmed demitasse cups. Champagne bubbled as toast after toast was offered to the bride and groom. Telegrams from well-wishers who were not able to attend the wedding were read aloud by the bandleader. "*Wishing you happiness always. Though I cannot be here, you are in my heart. Albert.*"

Albert's message rang in Harry's ears and filled him with sorrow. He wished that his son were standing next to him now, sharing the family's joy. Their happiness was somehow diminished without Albert. It was his own fault, Harry berated himself now. Why couldn't he forgive Albert? Each passing year drove Harry's dream further from his reach. Was that it? Was that what he couldn't forgive?

By 2:00 a.m. the last of the guests had departed, after pressing envelopes with money gifts into Alex's and Ruthie's hands, kissing and congratulating them. For Sophie and Harry there were more exclamations of "*Mazel tov*" and words of praise for the lavish wedding. Sophie beamed with pleasure. The guests had thought she was extravagantly generous, and Ruthie was safely married.

Chapter 27

Jeanie hurried down the steps of Boylan Hall and across the frozen campus of Brooklyn College. The March wind stung her cheeks and whipped her pleated wool skirt around her legs. The late bell rang as Jeanie raced up the steps of Ingersoll hall and slipped in through the back door of the chemistry lecture hall. She slid into a seat next to Mark Lerner while Professor Zahn scribbled illegible formulas on the chalkboard. She was relieved that the professor had not seen her come in late. "Get out!" he would have ranted in his heavy German accent. "No one comes late to my class!"

I thought you were cutting, Mark scribbled a note to Jeanie in his notebook. *I was talking to my classics professor,* Jeanie wrote in her notebook. *Meet me for lunch, 12:30. We can go to Wolfie's.* Mark scribbled again. Jeanie looked at her watch. It was only 10:10 and her stomach grumbled from hunger. She had hurried out of the house this morning without breakfast. "No breakfast again!" Sophie had called after her. "What do you live on, books?"

"I'll miss my train!" Jeanie called back as she raced out of the house. She would read late into the night, mostly Greek and Roman classics this past year, since she had enrolled in two classics classes. Last night she had reread *Oedipus* for the fourth time and the tragedy still haunted her. Now she turned her attention to Mark's notes.

"What does all this mean?" She pointed to the notes she had copied.

"I'll explain later," Mark whispered.

Jeanie had come to depend on Mark these past two years to decipher chemistry for her. Ancient history, anthropology, archeology, Greek and Roman classics were her interests. She agonized over math and chemistry.

"You will use your slide ruler to make all the necessary calculations und…" Professor Zahn's voice droned on. Jeanie's thoughts drifted back to

Oedipus and the tragedy of incest.

"Wake up!" Mark poked her. "You look like you slept through the whole lecture."

"I did." Jeanie gathered her books. "It was as stimulating as ever."

"You'll never appreciate the beauty of balanced equations. You have no taste," Mark joked.

"See you later. Thanks for the notes." Jeanie hurried to her French class.

***

An hour later, Mark waited for Jeanie in front of the library. He pulled up the collar of his parka and stamped his feet. His toes were growing numb from the cold. Jeanie was late as usual, but Mark would wait. They had met in freshman chemistry two years ago and had been constant companions ever since. They looked more like brother and sister than friends. He was about six inches taller than she. His sandy-colored hair and blue eyes matched hers. They could make beautiful children together one day, he hoped, if Jeanie would stop thinking of him as a friend. He had blown his chance, he thought now, remembering the day he had tried to turn their friendship into a serious relationship. They had been alone in Jeanie's house, studying for a chemistry exam.

"I'll never understand this, Mark. I'm going to fail the final," Jeanie had complained after two hours of studying.

"Stop worrying. The final grades are curved. You'll pass… Let's take a break." He stood up, taking her hands in his and pulling her up from the sofa. Impulsively, he pulled her against him, feeling her firm breasts against his chest. His heart quickened as his arms circled her slender waist and he kissed her on the lips in a slow sensuous kiss, inhaling the light scent of her cologne.

Jeanie pushed him away. "Mark, what on earth are you doing?"

"Studying chemistry… yours and mine." He smiled.

"Mark," she laughed, "Don't ever do that again. You'll ruin our relationship."

"I thought I just made it better."

"We're friends, just friends. And I want to keep it that way."

"We can be better friends." His eyes pleaded.

"No we can't." She shook her head. "I can't think of you as anything but a friend."

"Well, I guess I'm the one who failed chemistry," he said then. They both laughed, relieving the tension.

Jeanie didn't take him seriously because he joked around too much, Mark concluded. He never kissed her again, though he longed to. He accepted the relationship she had imposed upon them. He wanted to be near her on whatever terms she chose. Maybe one day she would take him seriously, he hoped. He was patient. He would wait.

Jeanie walked toward Mark now and his pulse quickened at the sight of her soft hair blowing carelessly about her face, her long slender legs covered in gray wool knee-socks.

"Sorry I'm late," Jeanie said breathlessly.

"I can't forgive you this time." Mark frowned. "Look," he said, pretending not to be able to move. "I have frozen fast to this spot. You'll have to get the custodian with an ice pick to chop me from this miserable piece of ground."

Jeanie crooked her arm through his and tugged him, laughing. "Let's go. My brain cells are dying from starvation."

***

Jeanie didn't get home till 6:00 o'clock that night, having gone to the library after her last class to work on a term paper. "Hi," she said, poking her head into the kitchen. Sophie stood over the stove, frying cheese blintzes in a large skillet that had long ago lost its shine.

"Hello." Harry smiled wanly, looking up from the evening newspaper spread before him on the kitchen table. Sophie was silent, a grim look on her face.

"What's wrong?" Jeanie asked. "Did something happen?"

Harry shrugged, offering no explanation. Jeanie slid into a kitchen chair opposite Harry. They ate the blintzes that Sophie set before them in an unnatural silence. The fluorescent light reflected off the white-tiled walls, bathing the kitchen in bright light. The smell of cheese and melted butter hung in the air. A stranger would have thought this was a warm and cheerful scene were it not for Sophie's dark mood.

Jeanie listened to the kitchen clock ticking, aware that it was the only sound that accompanied the frying blintzes. Sophie cooked mechanically, always preparing more than everyone could possibly eat. She did not join them at the table. She never did, preferring to eat alone after everyone was finished.

"Something terrible must have happened." Jeanie broke the silence.

"No, nothing," Sophie lied.

Harry's face was as inscrutable as Sophie's, and Jeanie didn't pry any further. She knew from past experience that Sophie behaved like this only when she lost money. Jeanie didn't pay much attention to her parents' finances, since none of it ever changed her life in any way. She knew that they had a great deal of money, though the amount was never revealed to her. Sophie kept her financial business between herself and Bernie Weinstein, the accountant she had hired to do her bookkeeping and give her advice. Even Harry didn't know what their estate was worth. He had grown used to living so modestly that he no longer thought about it. He had maintained his despondency over their business affairs since Albert had left, which was the reason why Sophie had hired Bernie Weinstein. Harry merely nodded his approval when Sophie wanted to acquire more real estate holdings. He rarely mentioned taking a vacation. Sophie always insisted that they didn't have extra cash to spend. "It's all invested. The profits are all on paper," she told Harry.

They now owned Florida and Long Island real estate, shares in shopping centers in New Jersey, Florida and Long Island, along with the Brooklyn real estate and Catskill holdings. Sophie had always had faith in real estate, but two years ago Bernie had advised buying bonds and blue chip stocks. So they had bought shares of IBM, AT&T, General Motors, and Mobil Oil. Bernie had proved to be a wise counselor and they had done well. Sophie was very excited about the fast profits she made in the stock market. "It's better than real estate. You make money fast," she told Harry.

But just a few months ago, Sophie had taken a stock tip from Morris Solomon. The accountant had warned them, "Speculative stocks are very risky."

"I think we should take our chances, Harry," Sophie had said. "Morris never steered us wrong. Didn't he get us into the hotel business? And look at all the money *he* made in the stock market. What do you think, Harry?"

"If you can stand to lose, Sophie, you can take a chance. If not, maybe Bernie's right."

"Accountants don't know everything." Her mind was made up. She bought thousands of shares of a Canadian mining company, and one month later, she lost it all. Though the loss did not affect their lives in any way and barely made a difference in the vast amount of money and real estate holdings they had accumulated, Sophie felt as though she had been unjustly robbed. She was tormented by the loss and obsessed with ideas for recovering the money. But the Canadian company was bankrupt.

Jeanie put her dinner plate in the kitchen sink now. "I'm going to visit Ruthie and Alex. I haven't seen the baby for days." She buttoned her parka.

Jeanie puzzled over Sophie's mood as she walked the four blocks to the modest apartment building where Alex and Ruthie rented a tiny one-bedroom apartment on the top floor. Alex had declined Sophie's offer of an apartment in one of their buildings after he learned that she would be charging them the same rent as the other tenants.

"What kind of mother is she, making her own child pay rent?" Alex had ranted.

"That's the way she is, Alex." Ruthie tried to explain Sophie's peculiarities.

"Well I won't live in her damned house then," Alex snapped.

***

Jeanie knocked softly on the door now. Alex opened the door, which creaked on rusty hinges. "Welcome to *Inner Sanctum*." He laughed cheerlessly, imitating the mystery program they used to listen to on the radio. Alex was barefooted, his face unshaven and his clothes rumpled.

"Did I wake you?" Jeanie asked.

"I do not sleep," Alex said. "To sleep, perchance to dream…" He did a bad imitation of *Hamlet*.

Alex looked more depressed than ever, Jeanie thought as Ruthie came out of the kitchen carrying the baby in her arms. Ruthie smiled wanly at Jeanie and dabbed at some chocolate pudding that clung to the baby's face. "Let's clean you up before we hand you over to your aunt," she told Steven, who held out his pudgy arms toward Jeanie and made excited clucking sounds. Jeanie pulled a small rubber kitten from her purse now and he reached for it, laughing.

"Happy birthday, Stevie." Jeanie kissed him.

"It's not his birthday," Ruthie said.

"Yes it is. He's eight months old today."

"You have to stop spoiling him with presents," Ruthie scolded, but she looked pleased.

"Your parents certainly don't spoil him with presents," Alex said acidly. "I can't remember anything they gave him since the carriage they bought when he was born."

"They're not demonstrative people," Ruthie said, defending them.

"No one can accuse them of that. They're downright cheap. Sophie's heartless and Harry's gutless," Alex said bitterly.

Alex had lost his job over a month ago when the ad agency he worked for lost an airline account and his head rolled along with others who were equally blameless. It was Alex's dream to start his own advertising agency. Others had made fortunes in advertising. Why not him? Before he lost his job, he had been building contacts, saving money and waiting for the day when he could launch his own business. Now he saw his dream slipping away with their bank account. They were living on Alex's unemployment benefits, which barely paid the rent. Every Saturday Alex's parents arrived with bags of groceries. But Alex refused to take money from them, knowing they had little to spare. He knew he would have to find another job and start over.

Jeanie put the baby down on the living room floor and watched him crawl across the rug toward Alex, clutching the new toy in his hand. It seemed to Jeanie that the same electrically charged atmosphere she had fled from at home had followed her here. She studied Ruthie, whose face was impassive as she sat on the living room chair looking pale and vulnerable. Only her hands moved, fidgeting with a loose thread on her skirt. "Would you like some coffee?" Ruthie broke the silence.

"I'd love some." Jeanie followed Ruthie into the kitchen, eager to escape Alex's sullen mood.

"What happened at home?" Jeanie asked. "Mom and Dad are behaving like someone died."

"They lost a lot of money—thirty thousand dollars on one stock." Ruthie kept her voice low.

"Thirty thousand dollars! No wonder Momma looked like she was going to have a stroke. How'd you find out?"

"Alex and I went over there yesterday. We asked them for a loan to start a business. We can't get a bank loan because we have no collateral. Alex can't find a job, and we're almost out of money. I'm sorry I even asked them now. Alex didn't want to, but I insisted."

"They refused?" Jeanie fumed.

"That's when Momma told me they lost money in the stock market." Ruthie's ears still rang from yesterday's argument. What had started out as a plea for help had quickly degenerated into a bitter argument. She and Alex and the baby had arrived at Sophie and Harry's apartment in the early afternoon. Sophie had opened the door.

"Come in," Sophie said, taking Steven from Alex's arms and hugging him.

"Come to Grandpa." Harry held out his arms and took his grandson from Sophie, smiling broadly at the child. "How about a big kiss for Grandpa?" Steven put his arms around Harry's neck and Harry pressed his face against his grandchild's.

They sat down in the living room, with Steven on Harry's lap. "So what's new, Alex?" Sophie asked. "Any job prospects?"

Alex glared at Sophie, trying to keep from returning a sharp retort.

"That's what we came to talk about," Ruthie began. "Alex and I want to start an advertising agency. Alex knows a lot of people and he's certain he can get accounts of his own. He just needs time."

"Lots of luck," Sophie said. "In the meantime Alex should get a job. You can't eat promises."

"We went to a few banks to ask for a business loan, but they refused because we have no collateral," Ruthie continued.

"That's too bad," Harry said.

Sophie was silent, tensing in anticipation.

"We came to ask you for a loan. Twenty-five thousand would get us started. And we'd pay it all back."

Sophie flinched. "It's out of the question. We just lost a lot of money in the stock market—thirty thousand dollars. And everything else is tied up in real estate."

"Let's go," Alex told Ruthie, rising from the sofa. "I told you what their answer would be."

"Maybe we could swing fifteen thousand," Harry offered.

"Are you crazy?" Sophie glared at Harry. "We don't even have a thousand to spare. And how do we know we'll ever get it back?" Then she turned to Ruthie and Alex and asked, "If advertising is such a terrible business, why do you want to be in it?"

"You make money when you own it, not when you work for someone else," Ruthie said.

"There's no use explaining," Alex said. "She doesn't trust us. She'd rather gamble with stock she knows nothing about than take a chance on her daughter."

"You have no right to talk to me like this," Sophie snapped. "You know I want the best for you."

"Sure. As long as it doesn't cost you any money," Alex said coldly.

"Alex, don't make things worse," Ruthie cautioned.

"Sophie, it's just a loan," Harry pleaded. "Why don't we see if we can come up with a few thousand?"

"No!" Sophie's face flushed with anger. "You haven't paid any attention to our accounts. We have nothing to spare."

Harry struggled with his inability to defy Sophie once more. He had been so detached from their business ventures and finances that he didn't know if

Sophie told the truth now. He'd talk to her later, try to persuade her.

Alex took Steven from Harry's arms. "Let's go, Ruthie. We'll make it without their help," he fumed. Then turning to Sophie, he said, "You lived up to all my expectations."

"What's that supposed to mean?" Sophie regarded Alex coldly.

"Think about it."

"You think I wouldn't give you the money if I had it?"

"Yes, that's what I think!" Alex hurried Steven and Ruthie out of the apartment.

Jeanie turned to Ruthie now. "I don't believe they don't have money to loan you. Momma's afraid she won't get it back."

"Maybe, but Alex is furious. He wants nothing to do with them," Ruthie said.

"I'm angry at Dad too," Jeanie said. "He behaves like everything belongs to Momma. And she makes all the decisions."

"You know how Dad's been since Albert left."

Jeanie frowned. "It's inexcusable."

"Dad came over later in the afternoon. He loves the baby so much. The only time he really seems happy now is when he's with Stevie. I can't take that away from him. He gave me some money before he left. It wasn't much, but…" Ruthie's voice broke off and her eyes filled with tears. She was ashamed of her parents. Though Alex never blamed her, she felt somehow responsible for their behavior. She should have known better than to ask Sophie for money, she thought now.

"Maybe I can talk some sense into them," Jeanie offered.

"No, please don't. Alex wouldn't take anything from them now."

Jeanie felt her own anger simmering. It too was born of shame.

***

Jeanie gave vent to her anger as soon as she returned home. She had always confronted and challenged her parents' actions and this time would be no exception.

Harry sat in his favorite chair in the living room. Sophie sat on the sofa, engrossed in a TV show. Jeanie threw off her coat. "How could you refuse to help Ruthie and Alex?" she accused her parents angrily.

"You don't know anything about it," Sophie said defensively.

"I know everything." Jeanie's voice rose. "Ruthie told me they asked you for money to start a business and you refused. It's despicable."

"Don't use your college words on me. It's none of your business. You don't understand," Sophie said caustically.

"We don't have all the cash they need." Harry tried to sound convincing.

"We just lost a lot of money in the stock market," Sophie said.

"Alex and Ruthie were not asking for a gift. They were asking for a loan," Jeanie said.

"How do I know I'll ever get my money back? It's Alex's responsibility to support his family, not mine," Sophie said coldly.

Red spots crept into Jeanie's cheeks. "You're turning your back on Ruthie," she exclaimed.

"We never turned our back on her," Harry protested.

"But that's exactly what you're doing now."

"She's a married woman," Sophie spat.

Jeanie looked at her mother aghast. "You mean you've absolved yourself of all responsibility for her because she's married? Your money is more important to you than your daughter. What about your grandchild? Don't you have any feelings for him? What's all your money for, if not to help your children when they need it? You behave like strangers to your own children!"

Sophie's face reddened. "You have no right to say that to me. Someday our money will be yours. It's for all of you."

"Ruthie and Alex need it now," Jeanie pressed.

"They can't have it now," Sophie said with finality, and she rose from the sofa and walked out of the room.

***

Alone in their bedroom that night, Harry tried to persuade Sophie to reconsider. "Maybe we could manage ten or fifteen thousand," Harry said feebly.

"I told you we don't have the cash. Ask the accountant if you don't believe me."

Harry knew that if he defied Sophie and made a large withdrawal from one of their bank accounts, she would know immediately. "I want to help them," Harry told Sophie firmly. "Alex has been out of work for a long time."

"There are other kinds of jobs. Maybe he should try something else," Sophie said coldly.

Harry drew a deep breath. "It wasn't his fault. That's what advertising is like."

"And you're asking me to give them fifteen or twenty-five thousand to throw away in an advertising business that has no future?"

"Owning an agency is not the same as working for someone else. It's just a loan."

"I'll never see that money again if I loan it to them."

"Don't you believe in your own children? Don't you care about their future?"

"I do. That's why I'm not loaning them the money. When the time comes, they'll have plenty of money."

"What time is that, Sophie?" Harry fumed. "When no one needs it anymore?"

"I can't take it with me," she said. "Someday they'll have more than they could possibly spend."

"We could help Ruthie and Alex now, when they need it." Harry felt like he was talking in circles, trying to persuade Sophie to reconsider.

"It's out of the question. We would have to liquidate some real estate. I won't do it. And Alex isn't my child," she said as an afterthought.

Harry was speechless. Sophie really didn't consider Alex as having any relationship to her. She felt detached and absolved from all responsibility for Ruthie since her marriage. Was this the same woman he married so long ago? Had she been like this then? Was he blind all these years? These thoughts whirled painfully in Harry's mind all through the night as he tossed restlessly in bed. He berated himself for allowing Sophie to have total control of their money. Sophie had spoken about everything they had as being hers for so long that slowly, over the years, Harry had come to believe that everything *was* hers. He felt emasculated, helpless, confused.

Sophie slept quietly in her bed, across from Harry. He was glad they had separate beds now. He did not want to touch her. He listened to Sophie's even breathing. He gazed at her calm face in the moonlight that filtered through the window and his anger hardened into hatred.

Chapter 28

Jeanie waited impatiently outside the house for the mailman on the last Saturday in May, ready to pounce on him for a long-awaited letter from the University of Pennsylvania. Brooklyn College graduation was just a month away and her future lay in the contents of that letter.

When Jeanie saw the mailman turn the corner, she raced down the street to meet him. "Any mail for Rothman?" She smiled her most charming smile.

"Rothman? Oh, you're at the other end of the block. You'll have to wait."

"Please," Jeanie begged. "I'll take all the mail for my house. Save you a trip."

"Well, awright," he said, disarmed by her smile. He rummaged through his mailbag and handed her a packet of mail. Jeanie's hands trembled as she flipped through the letters and plucked out an envelope from the University of Pennsylvania. She tore open the envelope, her heart pounding.

"Thanks," she mumbled as she read the determination. Her face broke into a dazzling smile as she ran back to the house.

"I got it!" she shouted, flinging the door open.

"Got what?" Sophie asked, as she sat at the kitchen table sipping her morning coffee.

Harry looked up from the roll he was buttering. "It must be good news," he said.

"I got the fellowship in anthropology. I can't believe it!" Jeanie twirled around the kitchen, unable to keep her feet still.

"What does this mean?" Sophie asked, as if everything Jeanie had told her over the past few months had slipped by her unheard, uncomprehended. In September Jeanie had asked Sophie and Harry if she could go to graduate school to study archeology. "I'm not supporting you anymore," Sophie had told her. "It's time you got a job and got married."

"I can't get a job in archeology without a graduate degree," Jeanie had explained.

"Then get another kind of job. I put you through Brooklyn College. That's enough."

"Brooklyn College was free," Harry reminded her.

"Well, we supported her all through college," Sophie said.

"Momma, I always worked in the summer. I paid for my books and lab fees, and my clothes," Jeanie said.

"Well, enough is enough," Sophie said. "You're going to be twenty-one years old. It's time you settled down, got married."

"She has time to get married," Harry said. "She's just a kid."

"Twenty-one isn't a kid anymore," Sophie declared, recalling her own desperate longing to get married when she was twenty-one.

"I have to go to graduate school. It's the only way I'll ever get to go on a dig. That's what I really want."

"I'm not paying for graduate school," Sophie had threatened. "Running around the world digging up old things is no life for a young woman."

"Maybe you'd like to go to medical school like your friend Mark," Harry offered again, clinging to a vain hope that perhaps his daughter would reincarnate the dream his son had buried.

Sophie glared at him. "Have you lost your mind?" What kind of thing is that for a woman to do?"

"It's a fine idea, Dad, but medicine isn't for me," Jeanie said. "But if you're willing to send me to medical school, why can't I study archeology?"

"You can't do either," Sophie snapped. "I'm not paying for anything else. You could have been a teacher or a nurse. You could meet a nice young doctor and get married."

Jeanie looked pleadingly toward Harry, who gestured helplessly with his hands. "We'll see," he said. It was what Harry always said when he had to oppose Sophie.

Jeanie knew she would not get any financial support from her mother. Harry's feeble efforts to persuade Sophie would fail as they always did once she made up her mind. Harry would give Jeanie some money when he could, but not enough to help her through graduate school.

Harry never went to the bank anymore. He had no idea how much cash there was in their accounts. Sophie and their accountant had taken complete charge of their money. He collected rents from their apartment buildings, traveled to the Catskills every now and then to see if everything was running smoothly at the hotels, and made monthly trips to Long Island to collect rent from the shops in the Levittown shopping center they now owned. He liked talking to people, but he had no interest in the money. It no longer seemed like a tangible thing to him—something he could use to change his life if he chose to.

Jeanie had determined then that she would find a way to make her dream a reality with or without their help. "I'm going to be an archaeologist," she had told her parents back in September. "I'll find a way." She waved the letter triumphantly before them now. "Here's my free ticket to graduate school."

Harry smiled. "Congratulations. I'm very proud of you."

"What will you live on?" Sophie asked. "Who will pay your living expenses? I don't want you to do this."

"I'll get a part-time job. I'll manage," Jeanie said defiantly. Then she headed for her room to telephone Mark, barely able to contain her excitement.

"Mark!" Jeanie shouted into the phone. "I got the fellowship!"

"Jeanie, that's so great. I… I'm happy for you," Mark said, feeling a sudden ache at the thought of parting from Jeanie. He was completely in love with her. Their lives would take different paths now. He would be at Cornell University, studying medicine, she at the University of Pennsylvania.

"Are you okay Mark? You sound funny."

"I'm okay. We… We'll have to go out and celebrate tonight."

"I'd like that… Mark, I'm going to miss you. You're my best friend, you know."

"I'll miss you too." Mark's voice was hoarse.

"You sure you're alright?"

He cleared his throat. "Just swallowed a frog I'm dissecting," he joked.

Jeanie laughed. "Now you sound like the Mark I know."

"I'll meet you in front of your house at 7:30," he said. "I'll be the man with the webbed feet." He hung up the phone, dreading their separation.

Still clutching the treasured acceptance letter in her hand, Jeanie left the house and walked briskly toward her sister's new apartment. The seven blocks sped by as her mind raced with plans.

Jeanie rang the bell on the door of the spacious new apartment Ruthie and Alex rented. Alex had finally started his own ad agency. It had been a long struggle over the past two years, but the apartment, new furniture and summer vacation they planned were proof of his success. And Alex had done it without any help.

Alex opened the door now, smiling broadly. Steven sat on top of his shoulders, laughing happily. "Aunt Jeanie!" Steven held out his arms to her.

Jeanie took Steven in her arms and hugged him.

"What brings you here so bright and early?" Alex asked.

"Look!" She waved the letter. "I got the fellowship!"

"No kidding!" Alex took the letter from her and read it. "Well, I'll be... You really are something." He gave her a congratulatory hug.

"What's all the excitement about?" Ruthie came into the hallway wearing a new peach-colored morning robe.

"I got the fellowship!" Jeanie had said those words so many times this morning, and yet she barely believed it.

"I'm so happy for you." Ruthie embraced her. "Does this mean we'll never see you again?"

"I'm only going to Pennsylvania."

"But soon you'll be a famous archaeologist and you'll go off to the jungles of New Guinea or to Peru?"

"That doesn't happen so fast," Jeanie said.

"Come have coffee with us and tell us your plans." Ruthie took her sister's hand and led her into the large cheerful kitchen where clay pots filled with geraniums and African violets blossomed on the windowsill. She was happy for Ruthie and Alex. They had a good marriage, and success had brought contentment to their lives.

"I haven't made any real plans yet," Jeanie began. "I'll have to go to Pennsylvania, rent an apartment and find a job."

"How will you work and study and teach at the same time?" Alex asked.

"I'll have to. Mom and Dad won't give me any money."

Alex's jaw tightened in anger. "Sounds just like them."

"Momma doesn't want you to go," Ruthie said. "She's afraid you'll never get married."

"I'm not thinking about getting married right now. Maybe I will some day, when I'm too old to do anything else."

"What about Harry?" Alex asked.

"He said, '*We'll see,*' as usual. But we all know what that means."

"Yes, I know what it means," Alex said bitterly.

"Don't worry." Ruthie squeezed Jeanie's hand. "We'll help you."

"I couldn't take any money from you. You're just getting on your feet."

"We can help a little," Alex said. "We want to."

Jeanie's eyes filled with sudden tears and she swallowed hard, gaining control. "I... I'll be alright," she said. "I have some money left from last summer's job, and Morris Solomon asked me to work in his hotel this summer. I make good tips as a waitress, and the money should get me through the first few months."

Ruthie poured coffee into white china cups. "Oh, I nearly forgot to tell you. I was so excited about your news." She set the coffee pot down on the stove. "More good news. I got a letter from Albert yesterday. He's coming to New York next week."

"Really?" Jeanie burst with excitement. It had been eight years since any of them had seen Albert.

"He really means it this time," Alex said. "He even sent us his flight number and arrival time. I may actually get to meet the famous Al Rothman."

"And he says he has a surprise for us," Ruthie said.

***

Jeanie walked home slowly, lost in her thoughts. Sophie had dampened her happiness, and Harry's cowardice had added fuel to her anger. She had not realized how much they had hurt her until Ruthie and Alex had offered their help. She could not take money from Alex and Ruthie. She was more determined than ever to make it on her own. She would do whatever it took to realize her dream. Hard work didn't frighten her. Jeanie brightened at the thought of living away from home, away from her mother's disapproval and her father's indifference. She walked up the steps of the house now wondering what surprise Albert had in store for them.

Chapter 29

Jeanie waited beside Ruthie at the arrival gate at Idlewild Airport, searching for her brother among the passengers hurrying by. She wondered if Albert had changed much after eight years. Would her father and brother forgive each other now?

"There he is!" Jeanie nudged Ruthie. "He's gorgeous!" She was astounded at how much Albert had changed. He moved with absolute confidence, as though he were walking across a stage to take bows after a fine performance. He wore his thick brown hair longer now, and his face had a rugged quality that bore an uncanny resemblance to the Harry of yesteryear. He was expensively dressed in white slacks and a smartly-tailored navy blazer. Heads turned in the crowd to admire him and the shapely blonde beauty at his side.

Jeanie pushed through the crowd and touched Albert's sleeve lightly, not quite certain that this imposing man was her brother. "Albert?" she asked.

Albert turned and his face lit up with a familiar smile. "Jeanie!" He hugged his sister so hard that she gasped for breath. Releasing her, he stared in disbelief and beamed. The child he had said goodbye to eight years ago was a strikingly beautiful woman now. It was hard to believe that time had wrought such a change. "You're beautiful! Can you act? I'm going to get you a part in a movie!"

Jeanie laughed. "You look pretty damn good yourself."

Ruthie approached while Alex and Steven kept some distance, allowing Ruthie a few moments alone with her brother. "Albert!" Ruthie ran into his arms. They embraced and looked into each other's eyes, finding no words necessary to express their happiness at seeing each other again.

Alex approached with Steven perched on his shoulders. He cleared his throat, bringing Ruthie out of her reverie. Ruthie grasped Albert's hand.

"Meet Alex and our son, Steven."

Alex held out his hand. "Hello." He smiled warmly. Steven surveyed the stranger cautiously from where he sat on his father's shoulders.

"I'm glad to finally meet you." Albert looked from husband, to son, to Ruthie, and his eyes filled with tears. Ruthie's sadness when he had seen her last had haunted him all these years. Now he saw happiness in her eyes and in the way she looked at her husband and son.

"Say hello to your uncle Albert," Ruthie told Steven. But Steven pressed his lips together, stubbornly refusing to speak to the stranger.

"Never mind. You won't be able to shut him up later," Alex said.

"I'll be right back. There's someone I want you to meet." Albert turned to look for Elizabeth, who waited quietly at the side of the terminal for the emotional family welcome to subside. Albert crooked Elizabeth's arm under his and guided her over to his family. "This is my surprise. I'd like you to meet Elizabeth... my wife."

Jeanie gasped. "Why didn't you tell us?" She took Elizabeth's cool hand in hers. "I'm happy to meet you." She stared at Elizabeth's face, a perfectly shaped oval with a flawless complexion and green eyes. She had the smallest nose Jeanie had ever seen and sensuous lips. Her fine blonde hair was tied back casually at the back of her neck with a white silk scarf.

"Welcome to the family." Ruthie smiled in disbelief at the stunning woman who was Albert's wife.

"You have excellent taste," Alex said to Albert, taking Elizabeth's hand and smiling.

"Al talks about you all the time," Elizabeth said softly. "I'm so glad to finally meet you all."

"I want to go home," Steven whined.

"Good idea," Alex said. "Get your bags and I'll bring my car around to the exit door. We'll go back to our house for a celebration."

Jeanie watched Albert and Elizabeth walk toward the baggage claim area as strangers' heads turned to admire the handsome couple.

Jeanie turned to Ruthie. "I'm speechless!"

"I like her," Ruthie said, but she knew instinctively that Elizabeth was not Jewish, and she worried about her parents' acceptance of Albert's wife.

***

"Your apartment's beautiful, Ruthie," Albert said, putting his bags down.

"Want to see my toys?" Steven tugged on Albert's sleeve. He had warmed up to Albert during the car ride from the airport.

"Sure. Nothing I like better than toys." Albert followed the child into his room.

Ruthie led Elizabeth into the living room. Elizabeth settled herself comfortably in a blue velvet chair, gracefully crossing her long legs. She took a silver cigarette case from her bag. "Would you mind if I smoke?"

"Of course not." Ruthie set a crystal ashtray on the table next to Elizabeth's chair and then sat on the sofa opposite her. "You must be tired from your trip."

"No, just from the change in time. Even a three-hour time difference can upset your equilibrium."

"I've never been to California. Albert tells me it's beautiful."

"It is. But I'm sure New York is too."

"You don't come from New York?"

"No, Chicago. I did a lot of modeling there and acting. Then I went out to California. I've been there ever since."

"So you've never been to New York?"

"This is my first time here. I know I'm going to love it. Al talks about New York endlessly. Also about you and Jeanie and the rest of his family. I can't wait to see Broadway and Fifth Avenue, Central Park, and The Plaza. Even the Bronx Zoo."

"With Albert as your guide, you'll see every inch of the city, even some things you don't expect," Ruthie said, wondering how much Albert had told Elizabeth about herself and their parents.

The apartment door opened and Alex and Jeanie carried in paper bags filled with Chinese delicacies from a nearby restaurant. Ruthie and Jeanie unpacked the bags and set the table. Drawn by the smell of ginger, garlic and oyster sauce, Albert and Elizabeth came into the kitchen. "Only Chinese food from Brooklyn could smell this good." Albert put his arm around Elizabeth's shoulders. "Doesn't this look great?"

"It does." Elizabeth smiled. "I like Brooklyn already."

"Don't just look at it. Everyone sit down," Ruthie ordered from where she stood at the stove brewing a pot of oolong tea.

"Let's not forget the wine," Alex said, opening the refrigerator and taking out a bottle of champagne.

"I'll get the glasses." Jeanie opened the kitchen cabinet.

The light conversation over dinner and the bubbling champagne put Elizabeth at ease. She liked Albert's family so far. She wondered what his parents were like and why no one spoke of them.

"A toast." Alex held up his wine glass. "To Albert and Elizabeth on their marriage." They all drank.

"A toast to Jeanie and her fellowship in anthropology," Ruthie said.

"Fellowship! Did you get a fellowship?" Albert asked.

"I did." Jeanie beamed.

"Why you devil. You've been keeping it a secret from me."

"I only just heard last week."

"What are you planning on doing in archeology?" Elizabeth was fascinated. Jeanie turned to her, elaborating on her dream to be part of an important dig one day.

Alex faced Albert now. "Are you planning on seeing your parents?"

"As a matter of fact, yes I am. It's been a long time, but it's never too late to make amends."

"Amends for what, Al?" Elizabeth asked.

"I never wanted to burden you with family problems, but I haven't spoken to my parents in eight years." Elizabeth's eyes widened. "My father never forgave me for becoming an actor," Albert explained.

"But you're so successful, such a fine actor," Elizabeth said.

"An actor isn't a doctor, and that's what my father wanted for me... No, for him."

"Maybe you should phone them, Albert," Ruthie suggested.

"I'll just go over there tomorrow with Elizabeth and surprise them."

"Tomorrow's Sunday," Elizabeth said. "Could I go to church first? I always go to church on Sunday morning."

An uncomfortable silence settled over the group. "Of course you can. There must be a church around here somewhere," Albert said, breaking the silence.

"Albert, maybe you should call Mom and Dad first. They don't like surprises," Jeanie said. Albert's homecoming was traumatic enough. Bringing home a bride who was not Jewish was potentially explosive.

Ruthie jumped up. "I almost forgot the fortune cookies." She removed a wax paper bag filled with crisp cookies, which she passed around. Elizabeth pulled out the small white paper that was tucked into her cookie and read the fortune aloud: "Life is like a magician. One surprise follows another."

***

Albert and Elizabeth planned to spend the weekend with Alex and Ruthie before going to Manhattan to look for an apartment. Albert was due to begin rehearsals for a role in *The Midnight Sun*, and they planned to stay in New York for as long as the show ran. It was Albert's first Broadway role and he was ecstatic. Elizabeth would sign up with some modeling agencies and go to auditions whenever she could. She too hoped for a part in a good play one day.

Albert phoned his parents that night. "Albert, is it really you?" Sophie's voice boomed over the phone.

"None other. I'm going to be in New York for a while. Should I… should I come over to see you?"

"Well, I'd like to see you, Albert." There was a long silence. "Hold on, let me talk to your father."

Albert heard muffled voices in the background and he knew Sophie was arguing with Harry, trying to convince him to forget the old hurts. "Come over tomorrow," she said at last. "We want to see you."

Albert hung up, surprised by sudden tears that welled in his eyes. He wanted Sophie and Harry to be proud of his success as an actor. He wanted them to meet Elizabeth. He was certain they would love her as he did.

***

The next morning Albert waited outside the church for Elizabeth. Her deep devotion to Catholicism was something Albert could not understand, yet he never questioned her faith or stood in her way. He took her arm as she left the church and they walked a few blocks to his parents' house. Elizabeth wore a green dress that matched her eyes. Her face was radiant and her blonde hair fell loosely around her shoulders. "Do you think your parents will like me?" Elizabeth asked apprehensively.

"They'll love you." Albert squeezed her hand as they climbed the steps to the apartment.

Sophie opened the door and stood transfixed, gaping at Albert as though she was seeing a ghost, unable to speak for several moments. "Albert!" she said at last. "Come in! Come in!" She took his hands, pulling him into the apartment. "And bring your friend," she said, aware now of Elizabeth standing beside him. "You're really here." Sophie's hands fluttered.

"It's me," he said. They embraced and then Albert stepped back, taking Elizabeth's hand. "This is Elizabeth," he said.

"Hello," Sophie said, not taking her eyes off Albert, who looked so much like Harry had at that age that it brought goose bumps to her arms. "Why are we standing here? Come into the living room. Sit down. Would you like a cold drink?" Sophie bustled around the room, fluffing the sofa cushions.

"No, thank you," Elizabeth said, surprised that Albert's mother was so fat, though she seemed pleasant enough.

"Your father will be right in," Sophie told Albert, hoping that Harry would indeed appear and behave civilly. He had promised he would.

"You come from California too?" Sophie asked Elizabeth.

"Yes. That's where Al and I met."

"I'll bet you're an actress. A beautiful woman like you must be an actress."

"Thank you for the compliment. Yes, I am."

"So how are things?" Albert asked. "Business is good?" He fidgeted with a button on his jacket.

"It's a living. I can't complain." Sophie's eyes rested on Albert as she shifted restlessly on the sofa.

The bedroom door opened and Albert stood up as Harry entered the living room. He was not prepared for the toll that time and unhappiness had taken on Harry. The vigorous man he had seen eight years ago was transformed into a lethargic gray-haired man who seemed to have shrunken into himself.

Albert held out his hand, swallowing hard. "How are you, Dad?"

As if in slow motion, Harry reached out and grasped Albert's hand. "I'm good… I'm good," he said, startled by the change in his son, feeling as though he were gazing at himself in a mirror from the past.

"Is something wrong?" Albert asked.

"No… nothing. You just look so different… so changed."

"We've all changed," Albert said, then turned to Elizabeth. "I'd like you to meet Elizabeth."

Harry took her hand cordially. "Nice to meet you."

Sophie sighed, relieved that all was going well so far. "How about some fruit?" she asked and hurried into the kitchen, taking refuge in food. She returned quickly with a large glass bowl filled with apples, pears, bananas and grapes. "Take some fruit. Don't be bashful," she coaxed Elizabeth.

"So what brings you to New York?" Harry asked.

"I got a part in a new show that's opening on Broadway."

"That's nice," Harry said. "I hear you're a real success."

"I suppose I am."

"We saw you on television," Sophie said. "On *Studio One*. You were wonderful. We were very proud."

"Your mother called all her relatives to make sure they didn't miss the show," Harry added.

"Ida called the next day. She couldn't get over your performance," Sophie said.

"How is Aunt Ida?" Albert asked.

"She adjusted very well after Nathan died… He just fell down dead on the street one day. A heart attack." Sophie wrung her hands, remembering the terrible day just eight months ago.

"How do you like California?" Harry asked.

"I love it there," Albert said, finally sitting back and relaxing, feeling that the bitter resentments of the past were beginning to be swept away.

"Someday I'd like to visit California," Harry said, his eyes settling on Elizabeth.

"Were you born in California?" Sophie asked Elizabeth.

"Originally I come from Chicago." Elizabeth explained how her career took her to California.

"I hope you and your friend can stay for dinner." Sophie smiled at Elizabeth. "I'm cooking stuffed cabbage, and I made chopped liver."

"I have something to tell you both." Albert took Elizabeth's hand in his. "Elizabeth is more than my friend. She's my wife."

Sophie and Harry stared at Elizabeth now, unprepared for this news. Harry stiffened in his chair, looking from Albert to Elizabeth and back to Albert again, unable to speak.

"I… we didn't expect this… We had no idea, Albert." Sophie's voice wavered.

"I'm old enough to get married and so is Elizabeth."

A leaden silence descended on the room. "Aren't you happy for us?" Albert asked.

"Of course we are." Sophie wrung her hands. "It… It's just that it's been so long since we've seen you, and now… We're just so surprised." Then she turned to Elizabeth. "Elizabeth is a Jewish name?"

Albert winced. "I'm not Jewish," Elizabeth said quietly.

"We love each other very much," Albert said, hoping his parents would understand that nothing else mattered.

Harry sat motionless in his chair, his head spinning with this new insult from Albert, and rage fomented within him. He stiffened suddenly, the muscles in his face tightening, the veins in his temples pulsating.

Sophie looked at Harry and the color drained from her face. "Harry, are you alright?"

Harry sprung from the chair suddenly. "A *shiksa*!" he shouted. "You brought home a *shiksa*!"

Albert's face, which only moments before had shone with happiness, was now filled with horror. His arm went protectively around Elizabeth's shoulder. Bewildered, Elizabeth looked from Harry, to Sophie, to Albert. Her face paled.

"It's not bad enough that you're an actor. You had to marry a *shiksa*!" Harry screamed at Albert as though Elizabeth were no longer there. "Out!" He pointed to the door. "Get out of my house. I never want to see you again! And take your *shiksa* with you!"

Albert bolted from the sofa, his head reeling from Harry's venomous words. He pulled Elizabeth up, her hands suddenly cold to his touch. His only thought was to flee. His legs felt weak and he choked back a sudden nausea. He willed himself to move toward the door, and it seemed like an eternity had elapsed before he reached it, yet it was only seconds.

"Wait! Don't go. I'll talk to your father," Sophie pleaded, her words echoing in the hallway as Albert fled down the steps with Elizabeth.

***

They walked for what seemed like miles, their footsteps reverberating against the pavement, each lost in private agonies. Time and place had lost its meaning. Only distance and flight seemed important. Albert stopped at last, aware that daylight was fading and they had walked to the entrance of Prospect Park. He led Elizabeth to a bench where they collapsed in exhaustion. Albert clasped Elizabeth in his arms and held her tight. He wanted to melt into her, to erase his father's venomous words that still stung his ears and stabbed like shards of glass in his mind, morphing into hatred.

Elizabeth wept softly into Albert's shoulder. "I'm sorry, Al. I… I'm so sorry this happened."

Albert pressed his face against hers, pained more by the unhappiness he had caused than by his own misery. "I love you. You're the most important person in my life." He kissed her eyes. "Forgive me." Any hope of reconciliation with his father was lost forever now, and Albert was overwhelmed with sadness in spite of his rage. How could he have been such a fool to think his parents would accept Elizabeth simply because he loved her?

Albert hailed a taxi. "Let's pick up our bags at Ruthie's apartment and go on to Manhattan. We're going to be happy here, I promise you." He kissed Elizabeth's lips, savoring their sweetness like a balm for his wounds.

Chapter 30

Jeanie spent the summer of 1959 waiting tables at the Concord Hotel in the Catskills. She was determined to save enough money to pay for the room she had rented near the University of Pennsylvania. She started her days at 6:30 a.m. and finished work in the dining room at 9:30 at night. On weekends she also waited tables in the nightclub till midnight. By the time Sunday evening arrived, Jeanie collapsed in exhaustion, her back aching and her feet swollen. She was grateful that Monday was her day off and she could sleep and relax at the outdoor pool.

On the last Sunday in July, there was a frantic phone call from Ruthie. "It's Daddy," Ruthie sobbed into the phone. "He had a stroke!"

Jeanie gripped the phone, her hands growing cold and her heart pounding. "Is he… is he dead?"

"He's alive, but we don't know how long. Come home… come quick!"

***

Harry was still unconscious when Jeanie arrived at Brookdale Hospital's intensive care unit the next morning. An oxygen tent covered his chalky face. Jeanie wept when she saw him, remembering the last angry confrontation they had before she left for her summer job. She had come to Albert's defense, berating her father for causing an irreparable rift. "He's your son," she had told him. "He loves you and you threw him out. Why? Because he fell in love with a woman who isn't Jewish?"

"I have no son," Harry had said coldly. "Never has anyone in this family married out of our religion. He had no right… no right to bring home that *shiksa*!"

"Can't you see how much they love each other? What's done is done. Try to accept it," Jeanie had pleaded with him.

"Albert did this to spite me. He knew it would kill me, and it will," Harry prophesied bitterly.

Remembering those words and the vacant look in Harry's eyes that day, Jeanie thought surely he would die now. She had been angry with her father then, but she had also understood his deep disappointment because Albert had not been all that Harry had hoped for. And she understood his sorrow over Albert's break with Judaism, which had been a tradition in their family for generations. Though Harry was not a religious man, it was an unspoken commandment in their family that one did not marry a gentile. Jeanie had pitied her father then for all the years of happiness he would miss and the years already lost to anger. But she loved him in spite of his flaws.

Sophie sat silently at Harry's bedside, twisting a handkerchief in her hands. There were dark shadows beneath her eyes and she sighed deeply, her large breasts rising and falling. Ruthie put her hand on her mother's shoulder to comfort her. Jeanie took Sophie's hand in hers and looked into her eyes. Was that pain she saw there? Did she love Harry, or was that fear she saw—fear of being alone? "He'll be alright, Momma." Jeanie tried to assure her. "You'll see… he'll get better. He's a fighter."

"I don't know," Sophie moaned. "Only God knows." She dabbed at her eyes with her crumpled handkerchief. "It's Albert's fault. Why did he have to bring home a *shiksa*?"

"Momma, you're upsetting yourself again." Ruthie tried to calm her.

"You can't blame Albert," Jeanie said.

"Albert doesn't care if his father dies. Ruthie telephoned him. Do you see him here?" Sophie asked, looking around blankly. "He won't even come to see his father on his deathbed."

"Dad's not going to die," Jeanie insisted, trying to convince herself as well as her mother.

"I tried to make amends," Sophie said, more to herself than to her daughters. "God knows I tried… I wrote to Albert. I told him to be patient… that Harry would forgive and forget. I even sent a wedding gift. And what did I get in return? Nothing. Not even a thank you note."

Jeanie had no words to comfort Sophie. She could not help feeling that Sophie was reaping what she had sown. She remembered her conversation with Albert on the telephone several weeks ago: "Do you know what our dear mother sent us as a wedding gift? My own money, the money I got as Bar Mitzvah gifts when I was thirteen, the money she refused to give me when I went to California and needed it." Albert had laughed sardonically. "She kept the interest on my money. That's what I call motherly love. She's about as warm and caring as a dead mackerel." Albert's bitterness was palpable.

"Albert will be here. I know he will," Ruthie said.

***

Harry remained in the intensive care unit at the hospital for ten days, and slowly he began to recover. He stayed in the hospital all through the month of August. Jeanie traveled into Brooklyn from the Catskills every Monday to visit him. Ruthie was there every day, but Albert never came.

***

Jeanie could barely contain her excitement as she packed hurriedly for her move to Pennsylvania. She threw books into cartons and clothing and shoes into suitcases, impatient to be done with the trivia and begin her studies. She had not planned on having to take all her belongings with her, but her parents' decision to move to Florida and sell the house in Brooklyn had made it impossible for her to leave anything behind.

Harry's doctor had prescribed immediate retirement for him. Though he had recovered from the stroke and there was no permanent damage, Harry was frail and despondent. Work of any kind was out of the question. "I suppose I'll get to take a permanent vacation now," Harry had said without enthusiasm.

Sophie was happy about the move to Florida. "I always wanted to live in Florida," she said, excited about the prospect of being close to a growing real estate market where they already had holdings and she could acquire more with first-hand appraisal of the market.

Two days after Labor Day, Mark arrived in his new white Rambler, which his parents had given him as a graduation present. They packed Jeanie's cartons into the trunk and piled the rest of her things on the back seat. "I feel like I'm going on an expedition," Mark told Jeanie.

"I'm so glad you're helping me move to Pennsylvania," Jeanie told Mark. "My father would have driven me, but…"

"I wouldn't have missed seeing you off for anything. I may not see you again for the rest of my life." His eyes swept over Jeanie longingly.

"We'll always be friends."

"That's what I was afraid you'd say." He opened the car door. "Get in."

Mark was unusually quiet during the drive to Pennsylvania, while Jeanie chattered about her plans. When they arrived, she showed Mark around the university campus. Then she directed him to a small rooming house two blocks away, where she had rented a tiny room on the top floor. "This is it. Home!" Jeanie smiled, opening the door to her room.

Mark helped her carry carton after carton up the four flights of narrow steps to her room. "You'll never be able to unpack all this stuff." Mark sighed in exasperation at the size of the room.

"I'll manage. I'm good at juggling things," Jeanie said.

"You'd better take some courses in magic instead of anthropology."

Jeanie laughed. "Mark, I'm going to miss you."

"Me too," he said, and took her in his arms.

Jeanie thought he was joking again, until he pulled her against him and kissed her hard on her lips. Caught off guard, Jeanie responded to the warmth of his kiss, the feel of his body against hers, the comforting strength of his arms circling her. But a moment after these fleeting thoughts and confused feelings, she pushed Mark away, fearing she would compromise their friendship.

Before Jeanie could utter a word of protest, Mark walked swiftly out of the room and shut the door. She watched from the window now as Mark got into his car, her fingers touching her lips that still tingled from his kiss. She felt suddenly abandoned as Mark's car disappeared down the street. She dwelled on the passion in Mark's kiss and how she had responded… too deeply. She vowed not to let that happen again.

Chapter 31

For the next two years Jeanie worked harder than she had ever worked in her life. She immersed herself in her studies, taking courses in anthropology, geology, botany, human paleontology, photography and history. She studied languages—Greek, Aramaic and Hebrew. She learned drafting, surveying, stratigraphy and map-making with her heart set on being a field archaeologist. She taught *Introduction to Anthropology* three times a week and worked as a waitress in a nearby coffee shop at night.

At twenty-three, Jeanie was strikingly beautiful and on her way to becoming an expert in ancient Middle Eastern cultures. She fretted over every expedition she missed. Caves along the western shores of the Dead Sea were discovered where Shimon Bar Kochba and his followers had taken refuge centuries ago after revolting against Roman rule. Jeanie longed to touch the artifacts discovered there, to feel the excitement of centuries past.

Jeanie worried about having the money to join an expedition. She barely managed to pay her expenses now. Her fellowship had been extended for another year. Albert and Ruthie sent her money regularly and generously offered more. Jeanie refused, borrowing only what she absolutely needed and vowing to pay it all back. She was too proud to ask them for the thousands of dollars she would need to travel with an expedition. Sophie adamantly refused to send Jeanie any money, angry that she had extended her studies for another year.

Harry vegetated under the Florida sun like an over-ripe grapefruit gone to seed, rarely communicating with Jeanie or anyone else in the family. He spent hours fishing in the nearby murky canals, dwelling on the past and fantasies of what could have been. He lost all interest in the family business, leaving Sophie to deal with it. Sophie had plunged into Florida real estate, investing in new developments and making extraordinary profits. As their wealth grew, it became more of an abstraction for Sophie. Figures on ledgers were as intangible as shadowy dreams. She was fifty-seven years old now and Harry was fifty-five. Sophie still entertained the idea that some day she and Harry would spend their money. That day had not yet arrived, and Sophie's greatest pleasure was still derived from tallying her assets. As for her children, one day they would share the wealth, but they would have to wait.

***

Jeanie gathered her lecture notes after the bell rang and watched her students file out of the lecture hall. She'd have to hurry if she wanted to get to her job at the coffee shop by 5:00 o'clock. She shivered as she glanced out the window at the snow flurries that had begun to fall from the gray February sky.

Philip Ardsley walked in through the back door of the lecture hall. "There you are, Jeanie. I'm glad you didn't leave yet." Philip walked toward her with a folder of papers in his hand.

As Jeanie's supervising professor in the Department of Anthropology, Philip was someone Jeanie saw every day. Thirty-five years old and good looking in a bookish sort of way, Philip knew how to charm people who could further his academic career. He's the perfect WASP, Jeanie thought as Philip approached. Thick horn-rimmed glasses didn't hide his deep blue eyes. He had a strong jaw and sensuous lips. Jeanie wondered why she had fought his advances for so long. She was probably the only virgin left in the entire university, she thought now.

"I'm still here as you can see." Jeanie flashed a smile at Philip. "But I have one foot out the door."

"I want you to review the new mid-term exam I made up and let me know what you think." He handed her a folder.

"Mid-term! The new semester's only just begun." She took the folder from him and his hand brushed lightly against hers, sending a small tingle through her fingers.

"I like to be ready for everything. How about you? Are you ready for everything?" His eyes swept over her.

"Maybe I am," she teased.

"Are you ready to share a bottle of wine with me in my apartment tonight?" Philip never tired of trying to seduce Jeanie.

"Yes, I will share some wine with you tonight," Jeanie said.

Philip's head jerked in surprise and he flashed a dazzling smile at her. "See you at nine then… my apartment."

"See you later." Jeanie glided out the door, an amused smile on her lips.

***

By the time Jeanie had finished work that night and hung up her uniform, three inches of snow had settled on the sidewalks and was still falling heavily as she pulled up her coat collar. She had rushed to the coffee shop bootless and hatless, fearing she would be late for work again and lose her job. A brisk wind blew icy crystals into her face, which caught in her long eyelashes as she hurried to Philip's apartment.

Jeanie rang the doorbell and stamped the snow off her wet shoes. She heard Philip's footsteps and had a momentary impulse to flee, but the door opened and he stood facing her, a sensuous smile playing on his lips. He took her icy hands in his and led her into the apartment. "You're soaking wet. Here, let me take your coat. And take those wet shoes off," he ordered.

"It's snowing, or haven't you noticed?" Jeanie unbuttoned her coat. She had been to Philip's apartment only once to pick up some test papers, but as she looked around, she noted that it looked the same. A massive mahogany desk held stacks of books and piles of neatly clipped papers. Shelves crammed with leather-bound volumes on every archeological subject imaginable stood behind the desk. Philip had placed a bottle of Bordeaux wine and two wine glasses on a coffee table near the sofa, and the room glowed softly from the fireplace. The room was inviting, except for the garish, African ritual masks, which Philip had brought back from an expedition to Nigeria. They hung menacingly on the wall.

Philip uncorked the wine bottle while Jeanie warmed her fingers and toes near the fireplace. Philip handed Jeanie a glass of wine and she sipped it slowly, feeling the warmth penetrate to her frozen limbs. She shivered and Philip put his arms around her shoulders. "You really are chilled." They sat on the rug in front of the fireplace. Jeanie stared at the flames licking at the heavy logs and it brought back memories of the terrible fire that she had witnessed as a child. She remembered watching from her parents' bedroom window as a neighboring house was consumed by flames. In her mind she saw the people who had stood weeping in the streets and the faces of those who had died. She shuddered and took a long drink from the wine glass.

"You're so pensive tonight," Philip said. He rubbed her cold toes in the palms of his hands. Jeanie stiffened. "Relax." He smiled disarmingly. "I'm only warming your toes. I haven't gotten to the rest of you yet."

"I have to warn you, Philip. I'm a virgin."

"Are you?" His eyes widened. "I didn't think there were any left."

Jeanie began to relax. Philip refilled her glass. The wine in her empty stomach was beginning to make her feel heady. Philip's hands moved expertly under her skirt, over her calves and up her thighs. Her body tingled and grew hot with the rush of desire. Philip's warm breath was on her neck as he unzipped her skirt and helped her out of her sweater. She moaned as his lips moved softly over her breasts and down her stomach.

"You're beautiful," Philip whispered hoarsely. He undressed quickly. Jeanie felt his hardness against her naked thigh and she wanted him desperately. Philip prided himself on doing everything well, and he made love to Jeanie with perfect finesse and practiced expertise. She laid back on the rug afterward, her body still throbbing, while Philip's fingers played in her hair. Her eyes rested on the wall where the raffia masks hung and their garishly barred teeth seemed to mock her. She wondered why she had waited so long, and what she had been saving herself for. She sighed and turned toward Philip. "You are sweet," he said, kissing her softly.

While Jeanie showered, Philip cooked cheese omelets for them. It was a dish he prepared for all the women he made love to in his apartment. When Jeanie emerged from the shower wrapped in Philip's terrycloth robe, supper was already set on the small, round kitchen table. A French bread, the half-empty bottle of wine and a bowl of fruit completed the meal. "This is delicious," Jeanie said, savoring the omelet and remembering that she hadn't eaten since lunch. "I didn't know you could cook so well."

"I'm a man of many talents." He smiled, covering her hand with his. "You'll have to sleep here tonight. It looks like a blizzard out there." Philip pointed to the kitchen window and the outside sill covered with a small mountain of snow.

"I can't do that," Jeanie protested.

"Of course you can." He grinned seductively.

Jeanie shared Philip's bed that night. It was the beginning of many nights when she would share his bed.

Chapter 32

Florida. It was not a place to stay in the summer, Harry decided as he looked out the kitchen window at the rain-drenched patio. Rain and heat. It was only June, but so hot already that steam rose from the lawn even as the rain cooled it. Only alligators and grapefruit trees could thrive in this swamp, Harry concluded, longing for New York. Two years in Florida had seemed like twenty. He missed Jeanie, Ruthie, his grandchildren. They only saw each other once or twice a year now. Sophie insisted that it was too expensive to travel to New York more often. He wondered if Sophie missed anyone. She was too involved in buying and selling Florida real estate, in making even more money.

"Sophie, why don't we spend the summer at a hotel in the Catskills?" Harry had suggested months ago.

“"Hotel life isn't for me," Sophie had said.

"But this heat in the summer is unbearable. Maybe we could rent an apartment in New York for the summer."

"The doctor wanted you out of New York and you want to go back there in the summer... the worst time to be in New York."

"The doctor doesn't live in Florida in the summer. If he did, he'd tell me to go back to New York."

The telephone rang, interrupting Harry's futile efforts to change Sophie's mind. Sophie went into the hallway to answer the phone. "Momma, it's Jeanie. How are you and Dad?"

"Getting along. And you?"

"The reason I called is to tell you that I was invited to join an expedition to Greece and... I want to go because it'll help me finish my thesis. But I need to borrow two thousand dollars from you. I'll pay you back."

Sophie was unmoved by the urgency in Jeanie's voice. "If someone invited you, they should pay for you."

"It doesn't work that way," Jeanie explained.

"I can't loan you that much money. How will you ever pay it back?"

"I will. I'll get a job soon," Jeanie promised.

"Well, get a job and then you'll be able to go anywhere you want."

"This is very important to me," Jeanie pleaded.

"What's so important about running around the world? It's time you settled down."

"I studied for years so I could go on an expedition like this one."

"No," Sophie said with finality. "I won't give you any more money."

Sophie heard a loud click. Jeanie had hung up without even saying goodbye.

Harry walked into the hallway. "Who was that on the phone?"

"Jeanie."

"She didn't want to talk to me?" Harry's eyes widened in surprise.

"No, she just wanted money... two thousand dollars to go on some crazy expedition to Greece."

"And you said no?"

"Of course I did. I'll never see that money again," Sophie bristled.

"I'm sure she'll pay it back. And even if she can't, you won't miss two thousand dollars."

"Do you want her running around some foreign country digging up old ruins? It's dangerous. She's crazy and so are you."

"It's her career. She never asked for much. I think you could show you care for once in your life."

"Don't talk to me about caring. Did you care about what you said to Albert when you drove him away?" Sophie's voice rose.

Enraged by the truth of Sophie's words, the blood rose in Harry's cheeks. "You're going to regret what you just did to Jeanie," he prophesied as he stormed out of the house.

Chapter 33

The summer flew by and Jeanie lived frugally, saving most of the money she earned from teaching summer classes at the university. She devoted her free time to research for her Masters thesis. She had hoped to obtain first-hand information from a trip to Greece and a field study of Ugarit, where earlier archeological discoveries had proved the link between Greek and Hebrew civilizations. But Sophie's refusal to help her get there made that impossible. She would have to use existing research to complete her thesis.

Mark telephoned from New York in July. He was working as a laboratory technician for the summer and was about to enter his third year of medical school at Cornell University. "I haven't seen you for two years. I've forgotten what you look like," Mark told her on the phone.

"I need to work on my thesis, but we'll see each other soon," Jeanie had promised, and she hung up the phone feeling a pang of loneliness, longing to see Mark again.

Jeanie continued teaching classes through the fall semester. By the time the last of the autumn foliage had fallen from the trees on the university campus, she had completed her thesis. Through similarities between Ugaritic, Hebrew and Greek literature and language, her research had proved a common background between Hebrew and Greek civilizations. When her thesis was accepted in December and she earned a Masters Degree in Anthropology, she told Philip, "I'm leaving the university. I can't afford the luxury of academic life any longer."

"Let me try to get you other courses to teach. You could work toward a tenured position." Philip tried to persuade her to stay.

"It's what you want, Philip."

"I'll miss you," he said, but Jeanie knew Philip already had other women in mind to warm his bed, and parting would leave no scars for either of them.

***

On a cold January day in 1961, when newspaper headlines announced John F. Kennedy's inauguration as President of the United States, Jeanie received a letter accepting her for a job as assistant curator of Egyptology at the Metropolitan Museum of Art in New York City. She was excited about returning to New York and eager to earn a salary that would eventually enable her to join an expedition.

***

Jeanie stepped off the train onto the platform of Grand Central Station, crowded with commuters hurrying to subways and taxis. Vendors sold newspapers and magazines, candy bars and hot coffee. Her eyes drank in the scene like a thirsty nomad returning to a favorite oasis. Crumpled paper wrappers and cigarette butts littered the waiting room, where people sat on cold benches waiting for trains. Muffled announcements trailed out of loudspeakers. Jeanie took a deep breath. She had missed New York—the smells, the excitement, the anticipation of something always about to happen. She fell into step with the crowd now, hurrying toward the subway that would take her to the Metropolitan Museum. She carried only a small suitcase. The rest of her things would arrive at the end of the week. She had sublet a small studio apartment on East 68th Street, and she would be able to walk to the museum from there every day.

***

Dr. Frank Richards, the curator of the Egyptian collection, was waiting for Jeanie when she arrived at the museum. They had met in October when Jeanie had come for an interview. "Welcome to Egypt." He shook her hand firmly. He was a tall confident man in his early fifties, with a year-round tan from frequent journeys to Egypt, where he arranged for artifact loans and additions to the museum's permanent collection.

"I wish it were Egypt," Jeanie said.

"You'll get there one day," he assured her. "Our collection is the next best thing."

Jeanie was familiar with the enormous Egyptian collection in the museum, but Dr. Richards took her behind the scenes now and explained her duties in detail. The laboratories and workshops where restoration and classification took place were impressive. She would be working here as well as arranging for exhibits, loans and donations.

It was 1:00 o'clock by the time Jeanie stepped out of the museum into the cold February day, her head buzzing with instructions for her new job which would start tomorrow. She walked briskly down the steps, stopping on the sidewalk to admire the museum's impressive stone façade with its Greek columns. She walked slowly along Fifth Avenue toward her apartment, munching on a warm pretzel she had bought from a street vendor, oblivious to the cold. She felt dizzily happy to be back in New York. Buses crowded with passengers crawled along Fifth Avenue, spewing exhaust fumes. Taxi drivers honked their horns as pedestrians wove through traffic to cross the streets. By the time Jeanie reached her apartment, her fingers and toes were numb from the cold. She took the elevator to the fourth floor and fumbled for the key in her purse. She considered herself lucky to have gotten the apartment from a friend of Albert's who was willing to sublet it to her. There was one big room furnished with a brown Castro convertible sofa-bed, two leather chairs that looked like discards from a dentist's office, and a glass coffee table. An old roll-top desk from a Salvation Army shop stood in a corner near dusty book shelves. A bistro table and two chairs separated the main room from the windowless alcove that served as a kitchen.

Jeanie put down her suitcase and the bag of groceries she had picked up at Gristedes on the way home. She kicked off her high-heeled shoes and hung her coat in the closet. Then she unpacked her suitcase and changed into jeans and a sweater. After cleaning the apartment and showering, she cooked spaghetti on the small two-burner stove, made a salad and opened a bottle of wine. Then, wrapped in her white terrycloth robe, she sat down at the small table and sipped the wine. A Chopin polonaise filled the room with music from a portable radio. Jeanie wrote a list of friends she had to call, many of whom she had lost touch with. Mark was number one on her list. She would call him as soon as she got settled. She breathed deeply, savoring the euphoria that enveloped her now, sensing that the most important part of her life was about to begin.

Chapter 34

Jeanie got caught up in the pace of work at the museum. She had spent the past few days in the museum workshop, reconstructing a large vase from pottery sherds that had arrived from an Egyptian dig. It was like piecing together a difficult puzzle. She felt like a detective, looking for clues that would date the vase. Several sherds had inscriptions on them, which made the piece more valuable and the tedious work more exciting.

Weekends were spent renewing old friendships. She saw Albert and Elizabeth when their busy schedules allowed. They had done well. Albert appeared in television dramas, landing one supporting role after another. It was good compensation for not being a major star. It paid for their posh apartment on Central Park West and expensive vacations abroad.

Jeanie sometimes spent Sundays with Ruthie, Alex and the children at their estate in an exclusive Great Neck community on the north shore of Long Island. Alex's advertising agency was now one of the hottest shops in Manhattan, earning millions of dollars.

***

Jeanie called Mark soon after she settled in New York, but it was months before he was able to get away from his studies for a weekend. They met at P.J. Clark's restaurant. It was early evening on the first Saturday in April when Jeanie hurried along Third Avenue to meet Mark. It was still light out and the air was balmy, good signs that spring had arrived. Jeanie had discarded her wool coat for a light trench coat, and her winter boots for brown leather pumps.

Mark was already waiting in front of the restaurant when Jeanie arrived.

His familiar face and warm blue eyes brought a smile to Jeanie's lips and a rush of happiness. She hadn't realized how much she had missed him till this moment. "Mark!" She rushed into his arms.

"Who else would leave a fresh cadaver to meet a crazy archaeologist?" He embraced Jeanie, suppressing his desire to smother her with kisses. He held her at arm's length and looked searchingly into her eyes, surprised by her new maturity.

"You look wonderful, Mark. But you're studying too hard. I can see from the dark circles under your eyes."

"But not tonight. Tonight is ours." He took her hand, leading her into the restaurant. They walked through the narrow front room where a crowd gathered around a long bar, talking and laughing. Jeanie breathed in the smell of beer and wine and salted peanuts as a hostess led them to a table in the back dining room. Red and white checked tablecloths covered the small tables, and dark wood floors glowed softly in the dim light cast from antique brass fixtures. Mark ordered London broil and a bottle of wine from a tall waiter wearing a long white apron.

"Tell me all about medical school," Jeanie said, her eyes shining.

"It's rough, but I only have one more year. And you know me, I've always been a sucker for hard work."

"Have you decided what you'll specialize in?"

"I'm leaning toward pathology. Maybe forensic medicine."

"Are you serious? You mean you're not going to be an ordinary doctor—one I can call when I have a sore throat?"

"No, that's not for me. I'm not going to have an office on Park Avenue either. Just give me a laboratory where I can feel at home, and patients who never complain. We're not so different after all. You dig up bodies and I dissect them."

Jeanie smiled. "You always did march to your own drummer. That's what I like about you."

"Is that all you like about me? What about my charm and wit? What about my body?"

Jeanie laughed. "I'm glad you're still you, Mark."

"What does that mean?"

"Oh, you know. Even though I haven't seen you for over two years, we can renew our friendship without feeling like strangers. We have a special friendship, Mark."

The waiter brought crisp green salads and warm dinner rolls.

"Does that mean I must suffer from unrequited love my whole life?"

Mark asked dramatically, concealing the truth of his words in jest.

"You should have been an actor," Jeanie said, taking a forkful of salad.

"Fill me in on the past two years," Mark said.

"Well, you know most of it from my letters."

Their dinner arrived, and the waiter uncorked a bottle of wine. Jeanie told Mark about the university and the classes she had taught. After a second glass of wine, she told him about Philip. "It was really a very shallow relationship," Jeanie said. "I'm glad it's over."

Mark was silent, brooding. He knew he had no right to resent her relationships with other men, but his love for her was undeniable and his jealousy unbearable.

Jeanie sipped the wine. Mark ordered cheesecake and coffee for them. Then he took a small envelope out of his jacket pocket and flashed two tickets in front of Jeanie's eyes. "Surprise! I got tickets for *Oedipus* at The Circle in the Square."

***

When they arrived at the theater in Greenwich Village, it was already filling up with college students—young girls with long hair and long skirts and bearded hippies in shabby clothing. Jeanie's and Mark's fashionable clothing and careful grooming set them apart from the rest of the audience. "I feel like a leper," Jeanie whispered to Mark when they took their seats.

The lights dimmed and the play began. The stage was bare, except for two plasterboard replicas of Greek columns. Jeanie became absorbed in the action of the familiar play while Mark watched her face, sensing that the theme of *Oedipus* still disturbed her.

At last the Greek chorus chanted its final, haunting message: "…While our eyes wait to see the destined final day, we must call no one happy who is of mortal race, until he hath crossed life's border free from pain."

When the lights came on, Jeanie was unusually quiet. "I should have gotten tickets for a comedy," Mark said when they were outside on the street.

"The play was wonderful," Jeanie said, but her eyes had a distant gaze.

Mark led her to a nearby coffeehouse, one of many that dotted the Greenwich Village streets. Young people and tourists crowded around small tables in the smoky, dimly-lit coffeehouse, and waiters carried trays of hot espresso and sugared pastries.

Mark ordered cappuccino for them. "It was only a play," Mark said, trying to bring Jeanie out of her somber mood.

"But incest is real. It was tragic in Sophocles's time and it still is thousands of years later." Jeanie sipped the hot cappuccino.

"How about showing me around the Metropolitan Museum tomorrow?" Mark asked.

"I'd like that."

"Good. Let's leave Oedipus in Greenwich Village." Mark paid the bill, and they took a taxi to Jeanie's apartment. Mark walked her to the door.

"It was a great evening, Mark. Thank you."

"I've missed you very much. Two years is a long time," he said.

"It is, but isn't it wonderful how our friendship survives?"

"You've changed," Mark said.

"How?"

"Nothing I can put my finger on… More mature, maybe. More beautiful, definitely."

"You're teasing me." Jeanie smiled.

Mark looked into her shining eyes, her lovely face and, spontaneously, he took her in his arms and kissed her passionately. Jeanie clung to him, responding to his kiss, not wanting it to end. Then she slipped out of his embrace and stepped back. "No," she said. "We mustn't do anything to spoil our friendship. It's very special to me."

Jeanie saw the hurt in Mark's eyes then.

"You're special to me and so is our friendship. But… I want more, and I think you do too."

"You're wrong. I just want our relationship to go on the way it was. It's beautiful and… love will destroy it."

"You're the one who's wrong. Relationships change and grow. You've got everything twisted. You refuse to recognize your own feelings. Love… physical love doesn't destroy a friendship. It feeds it, makes it grow into something even more beautiful." Mark put his hands on Jeanie's shoulders and looked into her eyes. "Tell me you didn't feel anything when I kissed you."

She tried to look away, but he wouldn't let her. "I didn't feel anything except the love I've always felt for you… love for a friend," she lied.

He took his hands off her shoulders. "In that case, I'll never bother you again." The muscles in his face tightened and he turned to go.

"Mark, don't leave like this. You're angry and…" But Mark was down the steps before she could say more.

***

Jeanie slept fitfully that night, tormented by a dream in which a shadowy figure chased her down a dark corridor leading to a door that would not open. Marks' face loomed behind the door and she tugged on the doorknob, frantically trying to reach Mark as the footsteps drew closer.

The next morning Jeanie phoned Mark, determined to set things right. She had never seen him as angry as he had been last night and it upset her. It had been a perfect evening, and then one kiss had changed it. Jeanie held the phone to her ear and counted the rings… three, four, five. Why didn't he pick up the phone? Finally, after the eighth ring, she heard his familiar voice: "Hello."

"Mark, I'm so glad you're home. It's Jeanie."

"Yes, I know." His voice was flat.

"I hope you're not still angry with me. I want to apologize if I did anything to hurt you. And I want to thank you for a wonderful evening."

"Okay."

"You're not angry then?"

"No… Let's just forget it."

"Are we still friends?"

"Yes, still friends. Always friends." His voice was tinged with sarcasm.

"I sense that you're still angry."

"Jeanie, stop dissecting me. I'm the pathologist, remember."

"Okay then, I'll change the subject. What about our museum date today?"

"I'll take a rain check. I've got some studying to do," he lied.

"I was looking forward to it. But I… I understand. Your work's important. I'll call you next week." Jeanie hung up the phone.

She had not set anything right, she thought. Mark was still angry. And now he didn't even want to see her. She would give it time. Their friendship would endure. It had been built too carefully over time to crumble now. Why had she responded so impulsively to his kiss? The question disturbed her all through the day, and she vowed never to let it happen again.

Chapter 35

It was a hot day in early August 1963 when Dr. Richards left a news clipping on Jeanie's desk at the museum. "*...Excavation will begin in October at Masada, the rock fort...*" Jeanie's heart quickened as she clutched the news announcement and hurried into Dr. Richard's office.

"They're excavating Masada!" Jeanie waved the paper in front of Dr. Richards.

He looked calmly up at her from where he was seated behind his desk and smiled. "I thought you might be interested."

"Interested! I'll be devastated if I don't go. Do you think they'll accept me? There will be thousands of applicants..."

"Calm down. A personal letter of recommendation from me will surely help."

"Do you think so? I'd be so grateful, Frank."

"You know it's only for a two-week period."

"I want... I hoped to be there for the entire excavation." Jeanie could not hide her disappointment.

"I'll see what I can do to arrange for a month or two. After all, you're a trained archaeologist, not an amateur. But we couldn't spare you from the museum for longer than that."

"Thank you, Frank." Jeanie smiled. A month or two was better than two weeks, and once she proved her usefulness, perhaps they would let her stay on. She valued her work at the museum, and the past year and a half had been challenging, even exciting at times, but she had waited what seemed like her whole life for something like this—Masada.

***

Early in September, a letter arrived accepting Jeanie's application to join the expedition. It was a form letter and only assured her of a two-week stay. It came with a long list of instructions. She was to arrive on October 24th and make her own travel arrangements. All her personal belongings would have to be kept under an army cot, which meant only necessities could be brought. Jeanie packed a duffel bag with work clothes and boots she had purchased in an Army-Navy surplus store. She packed a warm hooded windbreaker and a heavy wool sweater for the cold desert evenings, shorts and cotton shirts for the hot afternoons. Two books and a diary got tucked between her work clothes to occupy the evenings.

The day before her departure, Jeanie finished her preparations and waited for Mark to pick her up. Most of her belongings were in cartons on the living room floor, waiting to be transported to Ruthie's house on Long Island for storage. The sublease on the apartment would expire while she was away, and Jeanie hadn't looked for another apartment. She still hoped to remain in Israel for the entire two seasons of the dig. She had saved enough money for her airfare and living expenses if she wanted to stay in Jerusalem or Tel Aviv for a while. Once she got there, she had no intention of hurrying home. If necessary, she would arrange to work on a kibbutz to extend her stay. She took particular satisfaction in not having to ask Sophie for anything. Her mother's words over the telephone yesterday still irritated her now as she tossed a hairbrush, soap and toothpaste into the duffel bag. "A girl your age should be married already. Israel is a dangerous place. You'll get killed by an Arab," Sophie had said.

"I'm going no matter what you say," Jeanie told her.

"You should marry Mark. He's a nice young man. A doctor. He has *some* future…"

"Momma, I didn't ask you for anything. No money, nothing. I don't need your advice either. I just called to say goodbye."

"Goodbye. I hope you're not doing something you'll be sorry for later."

Harry picked up the phone then. "Take care of yourself. And have a good time," he said, as though she were a little girl going off to play in the sand. He had not asked her if she needed anything. He had stopped asking that long ago.

***

The doorbell rang, interrupting Jeanie's thoughts. Mark smiled at her from the doorway, a stethoscope draped around his neck. He had been able to get a few hours off from New York-Presbyterian Hospital, where he was interning, so he could help Jeanie move her things to Long Island. "Mark, this is terrific of you to help me," Jeanie said.

"It's good practice for me. In case I fail as a doctor, I can always get a job as a moving man."

Jeanie laughed. "I'm going to miss you more than anyone."

***

It was nearly an hour before they arrived in front of the imposing oak doors of Ruthie's starkly contemporary house.

"Please stay for dinner, Mark," Ruthie insisted.

"I have to get back to the hospital."

Ruthie disappeared into the kitchen, leaving Mark and Jeanie to say goodbye in private. Ruthie wondered if her sister was blind to Mark's love or merely indifferent.

Mark put his arms around Jeanie and held her close for a brief moment. "I know you'll make great discoveries," Mark predicted. Then he had a fleeting feeling of foreboding, which he dismissed as his unwillingness to let her go. "Before I forget…" Mark took a small bottle of pills from his pocket. "The medication I promised would calm your nerves on the plane. It's Valium. You'll probably need only one."

"Thanks, Mark. I don't know why I'm so nervous about flying." She took the bottle from him. Then she put her arms around him, hugged him quickly and stepped away, not giving him time to respond. "Take care of yourself, Mark. I'll write."

Mark smiled. "I'll wait for your letters," he said, stepping into his car.

Jeanie waved goodbye as she watched Mark's car disappear down the road.

***

El Al flight 767 took off on schedule early the next morning from Idlewild International Airport. Jeanie looked out through the plane window as New York grew smaller. Cars on the Belt Parkway looked like wind-up toys, speeding along make-believe roads. The bridges, the high-rise buildings, the trees all seemed like props on a Lionel train set as the plane climbed higher into the clouds. Then there was ocean. It seemed that all the world was ocean and sky.

Jeanie dozed now, exhausted from the anticipation of the past few days. Ruthie's words moved in and out of her consciousness, following her from New York. "Can't you see Mark's in love with you," Ruthie had said. Mark's familiar face, his smile, the way he looked at her mingled with thoughts of all she had left behind—her work at the museum, friends she'd miss, Broadway, bicycling in Central Park, Sundays with Mark.

Ten hours later, the plane taxied down the runway of Lod International Airport in Tel Aviv. Jeanie's legs felt stiff as she walked across the tarmac to the customs inspection station. She squinted in the bright late-afternoon sunlight. The air was warm and dry against her skin. Her duffel bag weighed heavily in her arms. She put the bag down now and waited in line in front of a customs inspector. Israelis called greetings in Hebrew to friends and relatives who had disembarked from the plane. A small boy wearing a hand-knitted skullcap clung shyly to his mother's skirt as she embraced an American relative.

Jeanie handed her passport to the customs inspector. He asked a few questions in English and stamped her passport. "*Shalom.*" He smiled. "Welcome to Israel."

Chapter 36

Jeanie woke early the next morning. Her muscles still ached from the long hours she had spent traveling the day before. After breakfast she checked out of the hotel on Zemenhoff Street and took a *sherut*, an oversized Israeli taxi, to Beersheba.

She looked out the window of the *sherut* at the landscape as they sped along bumpy roads toward Beersheba. A member of the Masada expedition was assigned to meet each new group of volunteers there. Jeanie's eyes swept over the miles of desert dotted with black goatskin tents where Bedouins lived. Thousands of years had passed and Bedouins still grazed their goats and sheep and camels the way their fathers had, moving from valley to hilltop with the seasons, unchanged by time.

The *sherut* left Jeanie off at the municipal gardens in Beersheba. An expedition bus that would take her to Masada was waiting. She climbed aboard, giving her name to the guide who checked it off on a clipboard. She sat next to an attractive, dark-haired young woman who spoke to her in French. The bus filled up quickly. When all the seats were occupied and the names of the volunteers checked, the guide put down his clipboard. "Welcome to the Masada Archeological Expedition," he said first in English, then in Hebrew. He smoothed his moustache with his fingertips and explained the day's agenda.

The bus pulled out and drove along a modern highway through the desert to S'dom. An hour later, Jeanie felt her ears pop as the road descended twelve hundred feet below sea level. "If you look to your right, you'll see the Dead Sea." The guide's voice sounded muffled and Jeanie swallowed hard to clear her clogged ears. She looked out the window at the motionless blue water of the Sea of Salt. They drove northward along the edge of the Judean desert and then turned onto a track that led inward toward the hills. The bus bumped its way slowly along the last hundred yards of rough terrain and then came to a stop. Jeanie got off the bus with the other volunteers.

"There it is." The guide pointed. "Masada!" Jeanie caught her breath. She squinted in the bright sunlight at the desolate rock that loomed above her. "Now we climb," he said, leading them to a narrow snaking path that traversed the stony slope. "It's not as hard as it looks. The army made it passable." The volunteers followed the guide slowly up the winding rocky path, which twisted sharply at each curve. Jeanie recalled Josephus's description of the snaking path, which he had written nearly nineteen hundred years ago. Those who had struggled along this path—Hebrews and Romans—had seen this very same sight. Gray and reddish rocks were twisted into strange grotesque shapes. They climbed higher and higher. It could have been the moon, Jeanie thought as she looked down below at the Dead Sea's gleaming water. She could see for miles in every direction. Beyond the sea were the mountains of Moab, turned red now by the flaming sun.

An hour and a half later, the group reached the summit. Miles of desert and rugged mountains stretched below and around them. No one spoke, mesmerized by the exquisite isolation and austere beauty. Jeanie caught her breath and trembled with excitement, sensing centuries-old secrets buried in the dust.

"I told you it wouldn't be disappointing," the guide said. He led them across the western edge of Masada to the base camp located on a flat outcropping of rock. Jeanie was assigned a tent with several other women and given ration tickets for her meals. She stored her duffel bag under her army cot. The makeshift showers were primitive, but Jeanie was grateful for the hot water that washed away the dust and sweat.

Dressed in clean khaki slacks and a white cotton shirt, Jeanie walked across the compound to the dining tent, accompanied by the French girl, who had befriended her on the bus, and a Canadian photographer.

After a dinner of roasted chicken, boiled potatoes and tomato salad, there was a documentary film about Masada's history and a short lecture. Then the volunteers filed out of the tent into the warm October evening. The moon appeared like a collage pasted on the blackened eastern sky amid millions of dazzling stars. Jeanie sat alone on the sand outside her tent, reluctant to leave the beauty of the desert sky for sleep. Her thoughts returned to the small band of Jews who had held out here against an army of 15,000 Romans nearly twenty centuries ago. She had believed the Hebrew historian, Josephus, when she had read his account. Now she would take part in uncovering the truth. She shivered, thinking of the small band of Zealots who had chosen death at their own hands rather than surrender to the Romans.

Jeanie went into the tent and undressed in the dark. Most of the women were already asleep. She stretched out on the cot and pulled the army blanket up to her chin. Within minutes she was asleep.

***

They were awakened early the next morning. After breakfast, they were divided into English and Hebrew-speaking groups for a tour of the excavation site. This being the Sabbath, there was no work on the site today. Jeanie went with the English-speaking group to the northern section of the summit, where a man in faded army khakis waited for them. She hoped to meet Professor Avi Sharett, the leader of the expedition, but that would have to wait. She would have to be content with one of his assistants for now.

David Kramer stood very still, one foot resting on a large rock while the volunteers arranged themselves around him. His gray eyes swept coolly over the group. Beneath a growth of dark stubble on his face, Jeanie could see that he was young, not more than twenty-nine or thirty. He wore heavy workboots and his khakis were streaked with rock dust. Despite the cool desert morning, David wore his shirtsleeves rolled up and his collar open at the neck, exposing tufts of dark hair. He was nearly six feet, lean and muscular. His face looked as though it had been chiseled into sharp angles that fit perfectly together. He had not shaved in four days, and his dark hair was tousled and flecked with dust from early morning work on the summit. David had no use for Sabbath idleness. He believed war had secured Israel for the Jews, and he chose to fight rather than pray.

David had served in the Israeli army for three years before studying archeology at The Hebrew University in Jerusalem, where he had become one of Sharett's prize students. Like Jeanie, he too had waited a long time for something as monumental as Masada. Now he was anxious to get on with the excavation and impatient with the new group of amateurs he would have to instruct. He disagreed with Sharett, who insisted on including the whole world in the expedition. David felt it should be the labor of Israelis to uncover their own history, but he was not going to argue with him. He acknowledged that he would not be here at all now if not for Sharett. And Sharett had put him in charge of one entire section of the excavation, an opportunity not easy to come by.

Jeanie assessed David, noting all the details of his careless grooming. He looked more like an untamed lion than an archaeologist bent on uncovering the past. She found him oddly attractive nevertheless.

"Shalom. I'm David Kramer. Call me David. I'll be your leader for the next two weeks. You'll be responsible to me… and I'll be responsible *for* you. I trained as an archaeologist with Professor Sharett," he boasted. "The work you'll be doing will be difficult, tedious and sometimes dangerous. You must *never* do anything without directions from me. We don't want any accidents. Is that understood?" He frowned at the intimidated volunteers as they nodded assent. Then he glanced at the clipboard he held in his hand, which listed the names of his new charges and descriptions of their backgrounds. "I see we have a student of archeology among us—Jeanie Rothman."

"I'm *not* a student," Jeanie announced. "I'm a field archaeologist!" Her blue eyes met his defiantly.

"My error." A mocking smile played at the corners of David's mouth, and his eyes swept over Jeanie. She would not like dust in her clean hair that shone in the sunlight now and fell softly around her shoulders. Nor would she like dirt under her fingernails or perspiration stains on her clothing, despite the trouble she had taken to dress casually. American women liked soft beds and private baths. They wanted to share the excitement of discoveries but not the hard work. She would have to prove herself just like everyone else. David had been alerted by Sharett to watch Jeanie carefully. If she proved useful, she would be invited to stay on with the expedition. Jeanie Rothman looked too refined and delicate to withstand the desert heat and grueling work.

Jeanie out-stared David now. His handsomeness was little compensation for his arrogance. Even his smile was mocking. She felt naked beneath his piercing eyes, but she stood her ground, challenging his insulting gaze.

David turned his attention back to the group, relating the history of the site. "The Roman king, Herod, built his remarkable palaces and fortress on this rock one hundred years before the Great Revolt." He pointed to three hanging tiers etched out of the side of the cliff and covered now with rubble—a remarkable work of engineering, even in modern terms. "We hope to find out what Herod intended these buildings to be." David read part of a description of the palace from passages in Josephus's account: "In A.D. 66, the Jews revolted against Roman rule in Judea, now known as Israel. They held the Romans off for many years but finally lost. In the wilderness, a small band of Jews known as the Zealots still held out. There were approximately one thousand of them, and they held out here in the palaces that Herod had abandoned. For seven months, from the autumn of A.D. 72 to the spring of

A.D. 73, the Zealots withstood a Roman army of 15,000 men led by General Silva." David pointed to the ramp the Romans had built and the outline of Silva's camp that was still visible.

"You all know the end of the story," David continued. "We hope to find proof. Did the Zealots choose suicide when faced with Roman slavery? If so, they would have destroyed most of their possessions rather than let them fall into Roman hands. We'll be looking for things they buried behind walls and beneath floors, especially bits of parchment and scrolls. Professor Sharett's theory is that the Zealots brought their holy books with them and they are still buried here because sacred Hebrew writing would not have been destroyed."

"Now we'll see the site," David said. The volunteers followed him, climbing to the northernmost point of Masada on iron steps that army engineers had recently installed to connect three terraces jutting out of the rock. Some of the rubble had already been cleared, and the group could only guess at the real function of the structure that was visible now.

"Step carefully," David cautioned, as he led his charges south to a cluster of buildings thought to be Herod's storerooms. Covered by mountains of debris now, it was hard to tell what they were. The volunteers followed David around the ruins of several other buildings, including a Byzantine sanctuary from the fifth century A.D.

The day grew warmer as the sun rose higher in the desert sky. Jeanie pulled her sweater off, tied it around her hips, and rolled up her shirtsleeves. In spite of her thick boots, the soles of her feet ached from climbing over sharp stones. They walked around the perimeter of Masada, inspecting rows of stone piles. David stopped here. "We'll begin digging here tomorrow," he announced. Some of the volunteers looked disappointed, hoping they would be assigned to a ruin that looked like something more than rubble. "Aerial photographs indicate that the casemate wall is here," David told them.

Jeanie wiped the perspiration from her forehead with the back of her hand. Her throat was parched from hours of trekking through the dusty ruins. She longed for a drink of cool water, but thirst and discomfort did not diminish her eagerness to begin work here. She could taste the excitement along with the dust in her mouth.

"Assignments and instructions will be given out tomorrow morning. Gook luck," David said as he led the group back to the base camp.

"Mr. Kramer!" Jeanie called out as David walked away.

He turned to look at her, his gray eyes sweeping over her body. "Call me David."

"David, can I examine the aerial photographs of the casemate wall?"

"They're in the administration tent."

Jeanie walked beside David to one of the larger tents. Maps of the site hung inside the tent, and rows of metal file cabinets were arranged behind a long table. A man in his mid-forties sat at one end of the table, examining sketches. He was clean-shaven except for a well-trimmed mustache. He looked up when David and Jeanie walked in.

"Professor Sharett, this is Jeanie Rothman, one of the archaeologist volunteers from the United States."

Sharett took the pipe out of his mouth and smiled at Jeanie. "Dr. Richards wrote to me about you. He expects great things from you."

"It's good to meet you, Professor Sharett. I hope I won't disappoint Dr. Richards or you," Jeanie said.

"Jeanie would like to see the aerial photographs of the casemate wall," David said.

"Of course," Sharett said.

David opened a file cabinet and pulled out a large folder. Jeanie sat down at the table and studied the photographs. Her well-trained eyes picked out the outlines of a double wall foundation. "The Zealots probably lived within these double walls," she announced.

"We suspect as much." Sharett was impressed with her interpretation.

"Thank you for letting me see these." Jeanie closed the folder.

"Welcome to our expedition," he said. "And good luck."

Jeanie felt David's eyes on her as she walked briskly out of the tent, eager to escape his arrogance for the solitude of her own thoughts.

Chapter 37

It was still dark outside when Jeanie and her tent mates were awakened the next morning. Jeanie slipped her underwear on under the blankets, which provided the only warmth and privacy in the tent. After splashing cold water on her face and hurriedly brushing her teeth, she pulled a heavy sweater over her head and laced her boots. She tightened the belt on her slacks, noting that she must have lost weight during the past week.

An Israeli volunteer dished out scrambled eggs, cereal and thick slices of dark bread at a counter in the mess tent. Jeanie helped herself to a mug of strong hot coffee, placing it on the tray next to a plate of scrambled eggs. She sat at an empty table where earlier risers had left coffee stains and breadcrumbs. David sat at a table to her left. Had she noticed him before, she would have sat at the other end of the tent. She felt David's eyes on her now, and she looked up at him. He nodded, raising his coffee mug to his lips, his gray eyes still on her.

Dawn was breaking when Jeanie left the mess tent and joined the volunteers who had gathered around David. When everyone was accounted for, they began to climb the steep ramp built by the Romans nineteen centuries ago. They reached the top where the rubble-encased wall stretched along the very edge of a vertical slope. David gave out assignments. "You'll work in groups of two and three to a small section. Every stone, every grain of sand is to be examined." He explained the use of the many tools laid out for the volunteers. He demonstrated the use of the pickaxes, sieves, trowels, paring knives and brushes. Wheelbarrows, baskets, buckets and sacks were assembled to carry away the rubble and any small objects that were found.

Jeanie worked with Rachel, the Canadian photographer who shared her tent, and Eric, a young man from England. First they cleared the larger stones from their assigned section of wall. For three hours, Jeanie lifted rocks and heaved them into wheelbarrows. Her back ached and her arms felt heavy and sore. She pulled off her sweater and threw it on a nearby rock. Another hour of grueling work uncovered nothing but more rubble. Finally, when she thought she could not bend over and pick up one more stone, David called: "Lunch break!"

They sat on the rocks, eating cold sandwiches. Jeanie washed down the sandwich and the dust in her throat with some cool water. They went back to work, pushing and heaving rocks and chopping stubborn stones with pickaxes. Jeanie was alert for any sign that might indicate they were reaching the stratum where Zealots may have lived. But hours of tedious clearing of debris dragged on as the sun climbed higher in the desert sky. Jeanie's shirt clung damply to her body. She rolled up her shirtsleeves and the legs of her pants. She pulled her long hair back and secured it with a rubber band she had in her pocket. Her throat was parched and her eyes gritty with dust. She put down her pickaxe to get a drink of cool water. When she had filled her cup from the water barrel, she looked up to see David walking toward her. He was checking on his groups and surveying the progress. "Finished for the day already, Miss Rothman?" he asked.

Jeanie's cheeks flushed crimson. "Even horses stop for water, Mr. Kramer!" She turned quickly and walked away from him, returning to her section of the wall where she picked up an axe and began chopping with renewed energy. David watched her silently for a few moments, admiring her spirit and her bare legs.

Work stopped at sundown and the volunteers returned to camp. After washing away the day's dust and grime in the shower and drinking what seemed like gallons of water, Jeanie collapsed on her cot and fell into an exhausted sleep, passing up dinner for the welcomed rest.

***

On the way up the ramp the next morning, David fell into step beside Jeanie. "I didn't see you in the mess tent last night," he said. "We can't have our volunteers missing meals. You won't last three days in this desert heat without food, much less two weeks."

"I intend to last two seasons here, Mr. Kramer. And I don't need your advice on nutrition."

"You can call me David. I suppose you don't need my advice. You look like you've done a pretty good job taking care of yourself."

Why did he infuriate her so? Jeanie thought now, her body tensing as he walked beside her.

They reached the casemate wall just above the ramp and stopped to examine the grapefruit-sized, Roman rock missiles that had been uncovered the day before. Remnants of the final assault on Masada. Jeanie picked up the tools she needed and walked to her digging site with Rachel and Eric. Rachel had tired of taking pictures of the rubble. She hoped something substantial would be uncovered before her two-week stint was up.

By the end of the second day, they had begun to find sherds in the sieve. Rachel and Eric were very excited and wanted to call David over immediately. "We'll probably find hundreds of pieces of broken pottery," Jeanie explained. "Unless it has writing on it, or it can be pieced together with other sherds to form a vessel, it's not that important." Rachel and Eric looked disappointed. "But it probably means that we're getting close to something. And it may help us date the stratum," Jeanie consoled them.

Jeanie was right. They had uncovered hundreds of sherds that day, which they loaded into buckets and tagged. They would be washed in the camp watersheds and some of them would be pieced together to form jugs, jars, bowls and cooking pots.

All through the rest of that first week, they scraped and sifted, sweated and swallowed dust. On Friday afternoon, there was a great commotion near the site of the storerooms. Everyone laid their tools down and hurried to the spot. A storeroom that was intact had been uncovered. Jars that had once stored food, some with Hebrew inscriptions, were plainly visible, intact and untouched by time. Date and olive pits, and bronze coins lay in the dust on the floor. Other storerooms where food and vessels had been deliberately destroyed gave testimony of the Zealots' last acts against the Romans. They did not want their conquerors to enjoy their stores of food, but neither did they want them to think that they died from famine. The untouched rooms were the enduring proof of the choice they had deliberately made.

Rachel took dozens of pictures. The excitement was contagious. Soon they all returned to their assigned sites with renewed energy, digging until nearly sundown. Work stopped earlier today in observance of the Sabbath.

Jeanie was grateful for a day of rest. Her body ached with fatigue, and her arms and legs were scorched from the sun. David had cautioned her to stay covered in the sun, but she had stubbornly defied him. Now she realized he had been right and she would have to be more careful. She worried now that she would not be asked to stay on at the end of the following week unless she got lucky and discovered something of importance. One thing they had more than an abundance of on this expedition was archaeologists.

***

By the time digging began again on Sunday morning, Jeanie approached it with renewed determination. David had kept his distance, and Jeanie's anger had cooled along with her sunburn.

Jeanie and her group were finally approaching floor level in what looked like a dwelling chamber. They used whisk brooms and soft brushes now. By noon, Jeanie had uncovered only a sooty kitchen floor. But by the end of the day, they had unearthed a clay cooking stove and a bronze oil lamp. Rachel and Eric were ecstatic. Jeanie was pleased but hoped for something far more important. David came by to inspect their site. Smudges of soot covered Jeanie's face and arms. Her hair was flecked with dust. "Good work," David said, surveying Jeanie along with the discoveries. "Now you look more like an archaeologist," he told her and walked off.

"I think he likes you," Rachel told Jeanie after David left.

"Don't' be ridiculous." Jeanie blushed. "He's arrogant, conceited and egotistical."

"Still, I wouldn't mind if he were interested in me," Rachel said.

***

As the end of the week approached, it looked as if Jeanie and her team would make no further discoveries in the chamber. Then, as Jeanie brushed away a pile of dust in one corner, there appeared what seemed like a heap of ashes. "Rachel, Eric! Over here! Get the soft brushes. Careful now, there may be something here."

On their knees, the three cautiously brushed away the dust and uncovered a small pile of ashes. In the ashes lay the pathetic remains of a Zealot family. A pair of leather sandals, a bit of wooden comb, a box of eye paint, several clay pots, cooking utensils and bits of cloth that had once been clothing. It was a touching sight.

Rachel ran to get David. Other volunteers nearby stopped digging and crowded inside the chamber. It was not the first time remains like these had been found. Other chambers had revealed the same. But each time, it brought tears to the eyes of those who beheld these humble remains. It confirmed what Josephus had described on that final tragic day.

David entered the chamber. He stood beside Jeanie, looking at the heap of objects that lay strewn among the ashes. Silently he observed a tear that coursed down Jeanie's cheek. She was overwhelmed by the piteous site of the last moments of this family's life when they had collected their belongings and set them on fire. It was no longer a story that she had read in a history book. The truth lay in the ashes at her feet.

The expedition photographer arrived and took numerous pictures before anything could be removed from the ashes. Sharett arrived to inspect the find and congratulated Jeanie and the rest of her team. When the excitement subsided and the crowd dispersed, David knelt down beside Jeanie and they carefully removed the objects from the ashes, placing them in a container for cleaning and examination later.

"You've had good training," David told Jeanie when they had finished.

"Does that surprise you? Or do you consider only Israelis worthy of digging here?"

"As a matter of fact, I do. But I don't make those decisions."

"Thank goodness you don't," Jeanie said, brushing dust from her hands and walking abruptly away from David.

***

Late that evening, David went to Sharett's tent. "Jeanie Rothman is a good archaeologist. I think she should be invited to join the expedition," he told the Professor.

Chapter 38

Jeanie remained on the dig during the entire first season. She attributed her good fortune to her talents as an archaeologist and to Sharett's kindness. She considered David a hostile enemy who sought to trip her up and terminate her stay on the dig, and she avoided him as much as possible. Sharett had given Jeanie her own section of the wall to excavate and her own team of volunteers every two weeks to manage as she saw fit.

Jeanie had adjusted to the hot days and cold nights in the desert, but she was not prepared for the first sandstorm she encountered. It happened early one evening in late January as she walked toward the mess tent for dinner. The wind rose suddenly and whipped across the compound, carrying every loose object in its path. Baskets and buckets flew through the air, and great gusts of wind pulled down the smaller tents. Sand caught in Jeanie's hair and lashed against her face. Her eyes felt gritty, and she closed them instinctively and pulled her sweater in front of her face. She turned her back to the wind and was quickly disoriented. She listened for shouted orders but heard only muffled cries through the wind-swept sand. Another great gust threw her off balance and she fell to the ground, coughing. Her heart pounded and she panicked, imagining herself buried in an avalanche of cold sand. Then she felt strong arms encircling her, pulling her from the ground, dragging her through the wind and sand, and finally reaching shelter inside a tent. He set her down on her feet. "Are you alright?" he asked anxiously.

"Yes… Yes, I think so," Jeanie coughed, seeing David through a blur of sand in her eyes as he disappeared into the storm again to salvage who and what he could.

It was an hour before the wind calmed enough to venture out of the tent. Jeanie walked to the mess tent for some hot coffee, still shaken by the sudden storm. Others were already gathered here, and the tent buzzed with animated conversation. Jeanie filled a mug with steaming coffee and looked around for an empty seat. She saw David sitting alone at the far end of the tent. His face looked drawn and his eyes red-rimmed and tired. Jeanie walked toward him. "Thank you for helping me," she said.

David looked up. "I would have done it for anyone."

"I'm sure you would have! A dog. A camel. Maybe even an Arab!" Jeanie snapped, and she turned away from him abruptly.

"That's not what I meant," David said quickly. "Please sit down."

Jeanie wheeled around and faced him, still holding her coffee mug. This was the first time she had heard David say, "please." She hesitated for a moment, then sat on the bench across from him.

"I didn't know that was you out there… But I'm glad it was," David said, his eyes burning into her.

Jeanie's face flushed. "I suppose you're used to storms like this. I've never seen anything like it."

"You never get used to sandstorms. You just learn to cope with them."

"I imagine living in Israel all your life gave you a lot of experience."

"I didn't live here all my life. My father brought me here when I was three years old. I was born in America."

"Then you're an American," Jeanie said, surprised.

"No, I'm Israeli. I don't consider myself an American. I served in the Israeli army. My father died for Israel."

"I'm sorry."

"Almost everyone in Israel has had someone close to them die for Israel. It's a way of life. We all take it for granted."

"What about your mother?"

"My mother died in America. From pneumonia. I don't remember her."

"It sounds like you haven't had an easy life."

"I'm not complaining." David lifted the coffee mug to his lips. "What about you?"

"You'd probably think my life was dull."

"Nothing about you is dull." David's eyes locked on hers.

"I grew up in Brooklyn and lived there most of my life. Even went to college there."

"I lived there too," David said. "Before I came to Israel. My father told me we lived in an apartment in Brownsville and, after my mother died, an American lady was very kind to me. I don't remember the lady or Brownsville." David pulled a leather wallet from his back pocket. He took out a worn picture and handed it to Jeanie. "This was my father, Lev Kramer."

Jeanie looked into the gray eyes of a fair-haired bearded man who bore no resemblance to David. "He looks like a very sensitive man." Jeanie studied the picture. Had it not been for Lev's beard, perhaps David would have noticed that Jeanie bore a striking resemblance to him. "You must look like your mother," Jeanie said.

"So I'm told. And who do you look like?"

"I don't look like either of my parents. When I was a child, I sometimes thought I was adopted… But I know that couldn't be. My mother's not that generous."

"You mean she's stingy."

"Let's not talk about my mother. Anyway I think I'd better get some sleep." Jeanie rose to leave.

"I'll walk you to your tent."

"I can find my way. The storm's over. Good night."

David watched her leave the tent, his arrogance slipping away from him unnoticed, like a snake shedding old useless skin.

***

Much of the work at Masada during the next two months was routine—endless scraping and sifting. Jeanie continued to dig in sections of the casemate wall. David worked with a small group on a northwestern section of the wall whose structure was different and seemed to indicate that it had been special in some way. Part of it was rectangular, and it extended into the summit. Removal of the first layer of debris had revealed a stone bench circling around a large hall. Further digging uncovered four benches, each beneath the other. They seemed to be seating tiers, and they faced five broken columns that rose from the floor. The columns had been taken from Herod's palace and brought here for something special. The structure faced Jerusalem. Sharett's theory was that this structure was a synagogue. David agreed. If definite proof was found, it would be the earliest known synagogue in existence. David kept digging, determined to find proof.

Jeanie was beginning to feel that she was destined to find only ordinary objects—stone cups, pottery, cooking utensils, copper coins, fragments of cloth and leather. She would have liked to work on the impressive building in the west, which was undoubtedly a palace. A fine mosaic floor that Jeanie admired had been unearthed. Beautifully executed olive branches, pomegranates and fig leaves were part of the central design, and intricate geometric patterns formed an exquisite border.

Late one afternoon, hot and exhausted from a day of fruitless digging, Jeanie sat on the chamber floor, her back against the stone wall. She wiped her damp forehead with the back of her hand, smudging it with dirt. Her throat was dry and her head ached from the heat. She was too tired even to go to the water barrel for a drink. Days of endless digging and nothing to show for it but dirt and stones, she thought. She idly picked up a trowel next to her leg and banged it against the wall. A hollow sound echoed back. Jeanie turned and tapped the stones again, listening to the sound. Her fingers groped along the wall, discovering some loose stones. On her hands and knees now, Jeanie worked with feverish newfound energy, pulling away loose stones.

A hoard of silver shekels gleamed out of its dusty hiding place in the wall. Jeanie screamed, "Silver! Silver!"

Word of the rare find spread quickly and volunteers swarmed to the chamber from all over the site. David was among them. "Jeanie, this could be really important," David told her. Together they removed the hoard of coins, placing them in a cloth bag. "I'll take them into camp right now and have them examined," David said.

"I'm coming with you to the laboratory," Jeanie said, too excited to go on digging.

Jeanie paced back and forth inside the tent that served as a laboratory, until Avrum, a coin expert, announced, "Three of the coins were struck in the year five."

Only six such coins were known to exist in the world. Jeanie's hands trembled now as she held a coin in the palm of her hand. On one side was a chalice with the inscription, *'Shekel of Israel'* in archaic Hebrew. She turned the coin over where there was an olive branch with three flowers and the words, *'Jerusalem the Holy.'* She looked at it through a blur of tears, feeling deeply grateful that she had been somehow chosen to make this discovery.

This was the first time in the history of an excavation that so many coins were discovered at one site. And they were found in a stratum that could be dated to the Jewish War against the Romans. Jeanie felt at that moment that if she accomplished nothing else in her lifetime, this would be enough.

The discovery of the coins also won Jeanie quick admiration among the other archaeologists on the expedition. They met each night in the administration tent to discuss strategies, theories, discoveries. When Jeanie voiced an opinion now, everyone listened. She was no longer the American princess here for some excitement as David had earlier had them believe.

She had asked for no special treatment. She had endured the desert heat, cold nights, sandstorms and grueling work. And her discovery could not be attributed entirely to luck. It was good judgment and an eye for what was important that had uncovered the coins.

David's thoughts dwelled more and more on Jeanie. She was beautiful, talented and intelligent. A rare find, especially for an American woman. And he wanted her. David had never experienced rejection from a woman, but Jeanie consistently avoided him, except for their short conversation during the night of the sandstorm. David knew it was his earlier arrogance that had gotten him into trouble, but most women were willing to put up with it. Not Jeanie. She had not even noticed that he had changed. She avoided him in the mess tent, during evening briefings and on the dig. Though his eyes followed her, she seemed not to notice.

Chapter 39

Harry waited near the mailbox, impatient for the mailman to arrive. The sun beat down on his head and beads of perspiration formed on his neck and face. What else was there to do in Florida except wait for the morning mail? Harry thought. His only enjoyment was hearing exciting news about other people. Why had he allowed Sophie and that incompetent doctor in New York to talk him into moving here? "Florida's the land of sunshine," Sophie had said. "You'll love it." Well, Sophie was wrong. She left out the part about the rain, relentless heat and boredom. Florida was a mosquito-infested swamp where people came to die, and Harry hated it.

Harry mopped his face with a handkerchief and waved to the mailman as he approached in his mail truck. "Morning, Harry," the mailman said, pulling up next to the mailbox.

"How're you today, Bob? Any mail for us?"

"Here it is." He handed Harry a packet of mail. "Looks like you got an airmail letter."

"Must be from my daughter. She's in Israel… An archaeologist," Harry boasted.

"No kidding? Well, I hope it's good news. You have a nice day now."

"You too." Harry hurried to the house with his packet of letters.

Sophie sat outside on the patio, sipping coffee, absorbed in reading a local newspaper article. Harry stepped out onto the patio and waved Jeanie's letter in his hand. "It's a letter from Jeanie," he said, tearing it open and reading it aloud:

'Dear Mom and Dad,

The excavation is going very well at Masada. This is the most exciting thing I've ever done in my entire life. Yesterday I made the most wonderful discovery. I unearthed some silver coins. Three of them were struck in the year five. It's very important because they were found in a stratum that can be dated to the Jewish War against the Romans. It's exactly the kind of proof we're looking for. I don't know if you understand all I'm writing, but this is more than I ever dreamed would happen. I'll explain it all when I see you. I'll write again soon. Please take care of yourselves.

Love Jeanie'

"Isn't that exciting!" Harry said. "My little girl making big discoveries."

"She's not a little girl," Sophie said. "She's a grown woman and she's not leading a normal life."

"Living in Florida is normal?" Harry asked. "Maybe if you're a grapefruit."

"That's not funny, Harry. Maybe if you took an interest in some of the things going on around town, you'd be happy here."

"Nothing happens here except when there's a hurricane," Harry said, walking out of the patio.

"Where are you going?"

"To get my fishing pole. I'm going fishing. The fish are more exciting than the people."

Sophie sighed, feeling helpless in dealing with Harry's despondency. He had not been the same since his stroke… since the final break with Albert. Why was he so unforgiving, so destructive to himself? Well, at least he showed interest in Jeanie. Life was full of ironies. Her daughter—Lev's daughter—was in Israel, the very place she herself had refused to go with Lev. How different her life might have been if she had left Harry and run off with Lev. She would have lived on a kibbutz and never had her own home. She would have had to share things with others. What an unappealing idea, Sophie grimaced, sipping the last of her coffee. And then when Lev was killed, she would have been burdened with his two boys. She had her own children to care for. She didn't need anyone else's children. And what about all her real estate and money? She'd never have had all that in Israel. She may even have been killed by an Arab… Yet there was something exciting about Lev Kramer, even now as she remembered him after all these years.

Sophie watched Harry walk down the path, his fishing pole and tackle box in his hand, and she called after him. "Harry, don't stay out in the sun too long. And wear your hat."

Sophie rose from the patio chair, her coffee cup in her hand. She must dress and be ready in half an hour. Her real estate agent was picking her up to show her some nearby property where a new shopping center was planned. Sophie loved the idea of a new venture with the prospect of more money to be made.

Chapter 40

Rain was a rare occurrence in the desert. But when it fell, it could happen without warning. The Masada volunteers had been cautioned about sudden torrential rainstorms. With the sun blazing overhead late one April day, rain was the furthest thing from Jeanie's thoughts as she worked on a section of the casemate wall. Then ominous dark clouds filled the desert sky and the wind rose, whipping Jeanie's hair around her face.

Jeanie retreated inside the chamber. She heard David's voice outside, shouting orders. "Everyone back to the compound now!" He loves to give orders, she thought, and decided to ignore him and stay in the chamber until the storm passed.

Within minutes the digging site was empty, except for Jeanie, who now began to doubt the wisdom of her choice. Then the rain came—an avalanche of water pouring from a sky transformed into a raging sea. Like a sinking boat, the chamber filled with water. What had been dust at her feet only moments before was now a rapidly rising river of muddy water, swirling above her ankles. She couldn't stay here. The walls were dangerously close to the edge of the slope and the weight of the mud could easily collapse them, sending them careening down the steep sides to the depths below. And she would go with them.

Jeanie groped her way out of the chamber. Her boots were filled with water. The rain washed over her, soaking her face, her hair, her clothing. She put her arm up to shield her eyes as she walked toward the ramp. Slick with mud, the ramp had become as dangerous as a ski slope glazed with ice. She would have to traverse it as best she could to reach the shelter of the camp below. Her first steps sent her sliding. She flung her arms out to stop her fall. There were only rocks and mud to cling to. An involuntary scream escaped from her throat as she slid several yards down the slope on her stomach. Her hands, cut by the sharp stones, were bleeding now, and her ribs were bruised. She stopped sliding finally and clung precariously to the mud-slicked rocks as rain washed over her relentlessly.

***

David checked the tents in the compound to make sure everyone was safe. Though he was no longer responsible for Jeanie, he instinctively checked her tent. He began to worry when no one had reported seeing her. David checked again—Jeanie's tent, the mess tent, the laboratory. He went out into the storm, running toward the ramp where he saw a huddled figure a few yards below the casemate wall.

Cautiously, David climbed the steep ramp, sliding backwards again and again in the slick mud. Rain lashed against him, but he kept his eyes on Jeanie, determined to reach her. Climbing sideways like a skilled skier traversing a treacherous slope, David summoned all his strength until he reached Jeanie. He lay down next to her in the mud, placing his arm across her back. "Can you move, or are you hurt?"

Jeanie turned her face toward David. A look of surprise and relief mingled with fear in her eyes. The rain pounded against her with such vengeance that she had not even heard David climbing the ramp. "I'm alright. Just scared."

"Take my hand. I'm going to help you back up the ramp. We're closer to the top than the bottom."

Jeanie felt David's strong grip close around her hand. She willed her body to get up and follow David. He held firmly to her, half dragging her up the few yards to the top of the slope. They took shelter in Herod's palace, collapsing on the floor of an empty room while the storm raged outside.

Catching his breath, David turned to Jeanie. "Are you sure you're alright?" His gray eyes looked worried as they swept over her.

"I'm okay," Jeanie said, panting. "I'm sorry… You could have been hurt because of me."

David took her hands in his. "You've bruised your hands." He bent his head and pressed his lips into the palms of her hands, sending exquisite sensations of pleasure through her. She looked down at the floor, unwilling to respond to this new feeling. David lifted her chin gently and looked into her eyes. He saw desire there, and he covered her lips with his. It was a long sweet kiss, filled with all the promise of a first kiss.

The rain stopped as suddenly as it had started, and the desert sun blazed overhead once more. David stood up, pulling Jeanie with him, holding her against him. Her wet clothes clung to her as David's hands slid across her back, down her thighs, over her breasts. "David, we mustn't," Jeanie whispered.

"Why not? I want to make love to you here in Herod's palace."

"Everyone will be looking for us. We must go back to camp." Jeanie pulled away from him.

They walked out of the palace ruins and Jeanie squinted in the bright sunlight. The mud was already beginning to dry. People hurried about in the camp below, cleaning up after the storm. Some were already climbing the ramp to assess the damage to the digging site.

***

Jeanie and David spent every evening together after that day in the storm—every evening till the first season of the dig ended in May. They were together, but never alone. There was no place to be alone in the close living quarters of the compound. "Stay with me in Jerusalem," David said to Jeanie on their last night at Masada. It was both a plea and a command.

"David, I thought a lot about what happened on the day of the storm. I don't want any more to happen. We have our careers to think of. Let's not spoil it."

"The second digging season doesn't begin until October. Let me show you Jerusalem. Five months is a long time to be alone in Israel."

"No, David. Something inside me says no."

"What are you afraid of?"

She did not answer. The look in David's eyes told her she had hurt him.

"You American women are all frigid… all afraid to feel."

"I'm not frigid!" Jeanie said defensively.

"Oh, then you're not a virgin? I thought maybe you were afraid because you're a virgin."

Jeanie's face grew hot with anger. David had not changed, she thought now. It was all an act to get her into bed so he could claim her as one of his conquests.

"Think whatever you like! I'm not staying with you in Jerusalem."

***

The next morning, Jeanie boarded the bus for Tel Aviv. David returned to his apartment in Jerusalem. They never said goodbye.

Chapter 41

There was a letter from Mark waiting for Jeanie at the American Express office in Tel Aviv. She tore open the envelope, picturing Mark's face and hearing his voice as she read his words: *'I miss you, Jeanie. When are you coming home? New York is not the same without you, especially long walks in Central Park…'*

Mark had finished his internship and was working as a medical researcher at New York Hospital's Pathology Department. It was what he wanted, and Jeanie was happy for him. She missed Mark and longed to see him… to touch him. She folded Mark's letter and dismissed her thoughts as sentimentality. She was not ready to go home. Not until she saw all she wanted to see. Not until the Masada expedition was over.

Jeanie walked out of the crowded American Express office onto the streets of Tel Aviv. The morning sun blazed overhead, promising a hot summer day as she set out to explore the city. Buses screeched and people jammed the sidewalks. When Jeanie reached Magen David Square, she found herself in the middle of an open-air market where vendors sold everything from kitchenware to clothing, fresh vegetables and fruits. People bargained in Hebrew, English, French, Yiddish and Arabic. She watched shopkeepers measure dried beans, nuts and spices from large canvas sacks, and she took dozens of pictures.

Wandering down narrow streets that led into the Yemenite Quarter, Jeanie soon got lost in a tangle of alleyways with squat houses and tiny stalls crammed with wares. It was noon before she found her way back to Dizengoff Street. She stopped to buy falafel-stuffed pita at an outdoor stall and walked on, munching the warm pita. The streets were beginning to empty during the mid-day heat. Jeanie stopped at a small outdoor café, where she sat at a table in the shade and ordered cold coffee. She sipped the coffee and thought about the jumble of languages she had heard. The sound of Yiddish brought back memories of her childhood in the Brooklyn marketplace. Then thoughts of David intruded—his face, his gray eyes, the feel of his lips on hers. She paid for the coffee and hurried back to her hotel.

Jeanie was still thinking about David when she reached the Hotel Europa. She showered, lay down on the bed and fell into an exhausted sleep, with David's face drifting in and out of her dreams. It was dark when she finally awakened. As she dressed for dinner, she vowed not to think about David again.

***

Israel was an archaeologist's dream. There were primitive Stone Age tools, Canaanite, Israelite, Philistine, Greek, Roman, Crusader, Arab and Turkish remains. Jeanie spent the month of June traveling along the coast to Ashkelon, Caesarea and Acre. In July, she explored Safad, Nazareth, the Jordan Valley and Tiberias. And she thought of David again and again, and deliberately avoided Jerusalem.

On a hot day in August, Jeanie took a bus from Tel Aviv to Eilat, traveling through the Negev. A flat tire stopped the bus midway through the desert. Jeanie stepped off the bus into the thick dusty heat with the other passengers while the driver changed the tire. It brought back memories of Masada and the dig. The heat had seemed tolerable at Masada. Now it pressed in on her like a fiery wall, sucking the oxygen from her lungs. She leaned against a boulder near the roadside, and her eyes swept over mounds of sandstone and dunes strewn with black volcanic rock. The world seemed suspended in this barren stillness. A sudden loneliness swept over Jeanie, and she longed to see David.

By the time the driver changed the tire and they reached the port city, Jeanie had pushed thoughts of David out of her head. She went on a boat cruise into the bay where she saw mountains of coral through a glass-bottom boat and hundreds of exquisite rainbow-colored fish.

The following day, Jeanie moved on to explore Haifa. Then she took a *sherut* back to Tel Aviv and thought about the city she had avoided—Jerusalem. And David.

Chapter 42

Jerusalem was David's city. King David had built its fortifications, planned its temple and made it the capital of Israel. Jeanie could understand why King David had chosen Jerusalem as she gazed through the window of the speeding *sherut.* They climbed higher along the road that curved and swooped upward into terraced hills where old olive trees and cypresses grew. Jeanie's heart quickened at the sight of pale pink buildings, church spires, domes, minarets and the battlements of the Old City. Though its name meant *city of peace,* Jerusalem had fallen into the hands of one conqueror after another over the centuries, each leaving his mark on Jerusalem.

The driver pulled up in front of the hotel on Jaffa Road. Jeanie paid the driver, picked up her bag and walked into the small hotel. Vaulted ceilings, large gilded mirrors and potted palms lent an aged elegance to the interior.

"I have a reservation," Jeanie told the concierge at the reception desk. The plump middle-aged woman showed Jeanie to her room on the second floor, at the top of a winding staircase.

"*Shalom.* Enjoy your stay in Jerusalem," the concierge said before closing the door.

Jeanie looked around the room. The heavily-carved dresser, a bed with a gleaming brass headboard and a colorful Oriental rug appealed to her senses. For as long as she could afford it, this was going to be home. Though it was not expensive, she worried that her money would not last another month until October, when she could return to Masada for the second season of the dig. She wouldn't borrow money from Ruthie or Albert, but she could stay on a kibbutz and work for her keep if necessary. She pushed her worries out of her mind now and unpacked her bag.

By the time Jeanie left the hotel, it was 6:00 p.m. and she was eager to explore the city. She walked along Jaffa Road, down King George Avenue, past the oddly Victorian King David Hotel. Buses, taxis, and *sheruts* made a tangle of traffic as people hurried home from work and gathered in restaurants and cafés. On Ben Yehuda Street, Jeanie watched a tall dark-haired man step off a bus. She caught her breath. She was about to cry out, "David," when the man turned and she saw that he was a stranger. Disappointed, Jeanie wandered aimlessly for awhile. The air had grown cool and she shivered now, berating herself for forgetting her sweater.

A sign over a small restaurant read, *Ta-ami.* Jeanie peeked through the window at the tables crowded with diners and read the menu on the window that advertised low prices. She went inside and waited for a table, her stomach growling with hunger as she inhaled the smell of roasted meat and baked eggplant. Laughter and loud conversations in Hebrew echoed through the restaurant. When Jeanie was finally ushered to a small table, she ordered stuffed *koosa*, a savory hot zucchini dish, which satisfied her hunger. She finished her dinner and paid the bill, eager to escape the cigarette smoke swirling in the warm air.

Outside on the street, Jeanie breathed deeply, filling her lungs with the cool night air. She walked slowly back to the hotel, feeling a mixture of peace and excitement. The secrets of Jerusalem lay before her.

***

Early the next morning, Jeanie sat in the hotel dining room, sipping coffee as she gazed out the front window at Zion Square. Shopkeepers opened their shutters for business and people ran for buses as Jerusalem awakened for a new day. Jeanie loaded her camera with a fresh roll of film, walked out of the hotel and boarded a bus for Hebrew University and the Givat Ram campus.

***

The university was a large complex of modern buildings surrounded by rolling hills. Jeanie found her way to the administration building where a group of tourists had already queued up for a 9:00 a.m. tour of the university. She joined the group and followed the guide through the landscaped grounds. "The physics building is to your right. The library..." The guide's voice droned on. Jeanie's mind wandered as she trailed behind the group, her eyes searching the faces of passersby for David.

When the tour ended, Jeanie went to the library where she browsed through anthropology books and read some journals. Chiding herself for thinking she would see David, she left the library and headed for the cafeteria.

The cafeteria was beginning to fill up when Jeanie walked through the door. The clatter of dishes and noisy conversation brought back memories of Brooklyn College and the University of Pennsylvania. Jeanie picked up a tray and joined the food line. Someone touched her elbow from behind. She wheeled around and found herself staring into David's gray eyes. For several moments she was speechless, her hands tightening around the empty tray. "David. I… never expected to see you here." She felt stupid after the words left her mouth. Why else had she come here?

"Jeanie, where have you been hiding all these months?" David did not give her a chance to answer. "Come with me." He took the tray from her and led her to an empty table. "Sit down. I'm not letting you get away from me again."

Jeanie sat down, her heart thumping, still looking into David's eyes. He seemed taller than she had remembered. Leaner. More muscular. "I was traveling," she said.

"Why didn't you call me?"

"I didn't know where to find you?"

"I'm in the phone book. Where are you staying?"

"The Dan Hotel."

"Stuffy old place," David said.

"I like it. It has character."

"What have you seen in Jerusalem?"

"I just arrived yesterday."

"Wonderful! Then I'll show you my city."

Jeanie was so happy to have found David, she did not protest. After lunch, David showed her the university's archeology department and museum, and the laboratories where he worked on restorations. He talked and she listened. The sound of his voice filled her ears, and she did not want to leave his side even to return to the hotel to change her clothes for dinner. When David left her at the bus stop, she promised to meet him at 8:00 o'clock.

***

David was already waiting in front of the restaurant when Jeanie arrived on Luntz Street. He smiled as he watched her walk toward him, her slim hips swaying beneath the folds of a blue skirt, her soft hair framing her face.

"*Shalom*, David. Did I keep you waiting? The bus was slow."

"I thought maybe you ran away again."

The restaurant was large and crowded. People waved to David as they walked toward a table. They stopped several times and David introduced Jeanie to friends from the university. When they finally sat down, David ordered roast lamb and eggplant for them. The waiter brought a carafe of wine, and David filled their glasses. "*L'cha-yim*," he said.

"To life," Jeanie echoed, her eyes never leaving his face as she lifted the glass to her lips.

A bearded young man in army khakis approached their table. "*Shalom*, David. Who's the beautiful stranger?" he asked.

"Meet Jeanie Rothman," David said.

"Oh, an American," he said.

Jeanie spoke to him in Hebrew, and he left when the waiter arrived with their dinner.

"How did he know I'm American?" Jeanie asked David.

"You look like an American."

"What does that mean? I think I look like everybody else here."

"Your clothes, your hair, everything about you is American."

"You make it sound like a liability."

"No. I like your hair and your clothes and everything else about you. So did my friend. That's why he came over to annoy me." He reached for Jeanie's hand across the table. "I'm sorry I brought you here. I should have taken you to a quiet restaurant. Tomorrow I'll take you to Shemesh."

They finished their dinner, and David poured more wine for Jeanie. She barely tasted the food. She was aware only of David's eyes on her. Desire had replaced his former arrogance.

David paid the bill, and they rose to leave. Friends called to David, inviting them to join their group. "Not tonight," David answered, taking Jeanie's hand and hurrying her out of the restaurant. She drew in a deep breath when they got outside, feeling heady from the wine. "I'd better get back to my hotel and get some sleep," she said.

"I want to show you where I live," David said.

"Maybe another day."

"Just for a little while. You'll be back in your hotel within the hour."

They took a *sherut* to David's apartment. It was a modern, two-story cement-block building. David had a small apartment on the second floor. He opened the door and they stepped into a plainly furnished living room. Bookshelves crammed with books lined one wall, and stacks of papers were heaped on a coffee table. A small kitchen was visible through a half-open door on one side of the room. Another door led to the bedroom. David closed the door softly behind them. "What do you think?"

"It's definitely your apartment, David."

"What does that mean?"

"You have no interest in interior decorating, but I like it."

David opened the terrace doors, and they stepped out onto a small square of concrete. The ledge was lined with potted plants. The night air was cool against Jeanie's bare arms. She looked up into the star-filled sky and shivered slightly. David stood behind her. He put his hands on her shoulders and gently turned her around to face him. Then he held her against him. She could feel his heart beating. Or was it hers? She felt the tautness of his muscles, like an over-wound spring. As his lips brushed her face, her lips, her neck, her hunger for David mounted.

Jeanie didn't remember if she had walked or David had carried her into the bedroom. Had she undressed or had he undressed her? It hardly mattered now that their naked bodies touched. David kissed her. "Jeanie, Jeanie." David's voice was muffled in her ear. He buried his head in her neck. She moaned and then reality slipped away. Their arms and legs intertwined and Jeanie lost all sense of where her limbs ended and David's began. David and their lovemaking were all that mattered. The world sped by. Nothing would ever be the same again.

They lay back on the damp sheets afterwards, still touching. David's fingers played in the soft tangles of Jeanie's hair. "Stay here tonight," he said.

"I can't," she protested, but David's kiss silenced her. She knew she could not leave him. Her hands moved over David's body, feeling his taut smooth muscles, the soft hair on his chest. Her fingers stopped on a small scar that creased his thigh. "How did you get that?"

"The Sinai War," David said indifferently. "A bullet wound. It's nothing."

"You could have been killed." The truth of her words suddenly terrified her. David would always fight for Israel. He lived in constant danger. She could not bear to think of losing him now.

David looked at Jeanie in the dim moonlight that filtered through the window and saw the fear in her eyes. He folded her in his arms again. "You mustn't worry about me. I'm indestructible." She felt him grow hard against her and desire dispelled her fear. Never had she felt such urgency. Nor had she ever dreamed that love could be like this. Fleetingly, she thought of her affair with Philip and how little emotion had been attached to it. She knew she could never part from David unscarred. She already cared too much.

Chapter 43

The next morning Jeanie moved into David's apartment. By noon, she had unpacked and was ready to tour Jerusalem with David as her guide. When they arrived at Mount Zion, the sacred site of King David's tomb, David donned a skullcap and Jeanie tied a scarf around her head. They entered the medieval building that led to the tomb.

Flickering candles cast eerie shadows on the damp stone walls surrounding the tomb. Brocade hangings and silver Torah crowns adorned the walls. The air was dank and heavy with the smell of melted candles. Jeanie watched men in long black coats and wide-brimmed hats chanting rhythmic prayers in muffled tones, their long earlocks bobbing as their bodies swayed. "The tomb's a fraud," David whispered in Jeanie's ear. "King David is buried with the other kings of Judea on the Ophel where the temple stood."

"I think you're right." Jeanie nodded in agreement.

David led Jeanie to Yemin Moshe, where they strolled through the artists' quarter, stopping at small shops to admire the paintings. An hour later, David said, "Enough sightseeing. Let's eat."

It was late afternoon when they arrived at the King David Hotel and were seated at a small table in the outdoor patio. David ordered omelets, potato pancakes, coffee and cream-filled pastries. Jeanie inhaled the sweet smell of new blossoms from the garden, and listened to the peal of church bells and the cry of a muezzin from a distant minaret. David covered Jeanie's hands with his. "Tonight I'll cook dinner for you. A feast," David said. But when they got back to David's apartment, they forgot all about dinner, so absorbed were they in their lovemaking.

***

September sped by, filled with the sights, sounds and smells of Jerusalem. David took Jeanie to Ein Kerem, Abu Ghosh, the Sanhedriya Tombs. They spent days exploring the Alfasi grotto where a necropolis had been uncovered dating from the Maccabean era.

Jeanie asked David to show her Mea Shearim, the religious quarter of Jerusalem where the Hasidic religious sect lived. "Why do you want to see those *meshugeners*?" David frowned.

"I want to see everything in Jerusalem."

"The Hasids don't even recognize the State of Israel," David said impatiently. "They're waiting for the messiah to arrive and give it to them officially. They'd all be killed by Arabs if we didn't protect them."

"They're entitled to their beliefs."

"Anyone who's not willing to fight for Israel doesn't belong here."

Jeanie persisted, and they took a bus the next day to Mea Shearim, where they wandered through winding cobbled alleys. It was like an old European ghetto transplanted from Russia or Poland to modern Israel. Bearded men with bobbing side curls, long black coats and beaver-trimmed black hats trudged the streets, their faces pale from long hours of studying the Torah. In spite of the midday heat, women hid their arms beneath long-sleeved dresses and covered their legs with heavy stockings and long skirts. Married women covered their heads with wigs and kerchiefs. Small boys with pale faces and long curling *payot* wore yarmulkes over closely shaven skulls.

Jeanie was glad she had worn a long-sleeved shirt and the longest skirt she had, which fell just below her knees. A warning sign in the marketplace in English, Hebrew and Yiddish proclaimed: *Jewish Daughter—the Torah obligates you to dress with modesty. We do not tolerate people passing through our streets immodestly dressed. Committee for Guarding Modesty.*

Jeanie looked down at her bare legs and naked sandaled feet and felt as if she had committed sacrilege. David had advised her to leave her camera in the apartment but Jeanie had taken it, hoping to take a few pictures. Now the camera provoked angry comments in Yiddish from passersby. David took the camera from Jeanie and answered the comments defiantly. "David, don't provoke them," Jeanie pleaded.

"Have you seen enough of this?" David asked impatiently.

"Not yet," Jeanie said, and David followed her down a narrow street where dozens of small shops sold religious ornaments. Clotheslines were strung between buildings and wash hung precariously there to dry. It brought back memories of Jeanie's childhood on Prospect Place, where Sophie had hung the wash on a line outside the kitchen window. Brooklyn and her childhood seemed long ago and far away, but the past seemed to hang suspended here.

Jeanie stopped at a small shop to buy a *mezuzah*. She opened the ornament and peaked at the sacred parchment scroll inside, but it was too small to read. "Why are you buying that?" David asked.

"It's a gift for my sister, Ruthie. She asked me to buy a *mezuzah* for her."

"It's nonsense," David said.

"But Jews all over the world still hang *mezuzahs* on their entrance doors for good luck." Jeanie paid the shopkeeper for the *mezuzah*.

They walked to the edge of Mea Shearim and stopped at the Mandelbaum Gate. A sign read: *Israel Police Force. Frontier Post.* Whitewashed barrels with black bands barred the road leading to the eastern sector of Jerusalem, under Jordanian control. "We can't go any further," David said bitterly. "But one day Jerusalem will be united."

David was unusually quiet as they rode the bus back to the apartment, preoccupied by his dream for Jerusalem and Israel.

***

David had avoided taking Jeanie to Yad Vashem, but as the last days of September fled by, he knew she must see it, however painful. So they went early one morning when the air was sweet and clear.

Jeanie squinted in the bright sunlight at the massive rectangular building. The memorial to six million Jews murdered by the Nazis stood silent and mournful at the top of a hill. They walked through the entrance gate with its twisted steel façade that formed strange patterns with jagged edges that exuded despair. An eerie stillness filled the vast stone interior. Dim eternal flames flickered in the center, casting shadows across floor plaques etched with the names of death camps. Dachau, Bergen Belsen, Auschwitz… The names cried out in the nightmarish silence. Jeanie bowed her head and murmured the *kaddish* prayer for the dead whose presence she felt so strongly, while David stood silently beside her.

They walked out into the sunlight and David led Jeanie to a nearby building filled with photographs of unspeakable horrors. "David, I don't want to see any more," Jeanie protested. But David led her through the building. Jeanie closed her eyes. "I'm going to be sick," she said.

"Look!" David ordered. "I want you to see everything so you'll understand how I feel, why I'll always fight for Israel."

Jeanie looked at torturous photographs. Children with vacant eyes stared out of starved cadaverous faces. Mass graves with tiny skeletons heaped upon each other. Gas chambers. Crematoriums. Always eyes stared—vacant, pleading. Jeanie brushed tears from her face, and finally David led her out of the building.

On the last day of September, David took Jeanie to Ramat Rahel, the kibbutz where he had grown up. In the southernmost part of Israeli-occupied Jerusalem, the kibbutz had been the scene of bitter fighting in the 1948 war. David's father, Lev, had died here in that terrible struggle. Each time David stepped onto the grounds of Ramat Rahel, his memories carried him back to the last night he had spent with his father.

Lev had taken David to the small synagogue on the kibbutz grounds and together they had chanted ancient Hebrew prayers. Lev's eyes had shone with pride as he listened to his son's well-learned prayers. After the service, Lev had given him a small silver *Star of David* on a silver chain. "It belonged to your mother, David. She would have wanted you to have it for learning your Hebrew prayers so well."

David had worn the *Star* proudly. But the next day, his father's eyes were closed forever when he was struck down by an Arab's bullet. David buried the silver *Star* with his father's body, and he no longer went to the small synagogue to pray.

A powerfully-built man of medium height walked toward David and Jeanie now. At his side was a tall willowy woman dressed in overalls and workboots. Wisps of dark hair curled around her forehead from beneath a paisley kerchief.

David took Jeanie's hand, and they hurried along the path. The brothers embraced. Then David kissed the smiling woman. "You stayed away too long," the woman scolded.

"I want you to meet Jeanie Rothman," David said. "Jeanie, this is my brother, Joel, and my sister-in-law, Leah."

Joel held out a tanned work-worn hand. "I'm always happy to meet David's friends."

Leah smiled at Jeanie, the corners of her eyes crinkling. She looked younger than her forty-two years. Joel's and Leah's four children suddenly appeared and David picked up the youngest girl, Rebecca, who was only five, and whirled her around. The children bombarded David with questions about Masada. Ari, the oldest son, who was now fifteen, smiled shyly at Jeanie. "Can I go with you to Masada?" Ari asked David.

"Maybe next year," David promised.

"Ari wants to be an archaeologist like his uncle," Leah told Jeanie.

"I don't blame him," Joel said. "It's more exciting than farming."

Joel and Leah showed Jeanie around the kibbutz. They were proud of their library and school. Lunch was a community affair in the communal dining hall that buzzed with animated conversations. Dishes clattered as homegrown vegetables, bowls of sour cream, steamed potatoes, fresh bread and platters of cheese and fruit were passed around. A parade of people came to their table to greet David and meet Jeanie.

Before they left, Joel took David aside. "She's more than a friend, this American girl?"

"Yes, she's more than a friend. I love her."

When they were ready to leave, Leah told David, "Come back soon. And bring Jeanie. We like her."

"We'll be back when the expedition is over," David promised.

***

"I like your family," Jeanie told David on the bus back to the apartment.

"They like you too. I could tell," David said.

"Is that important to you?"

"I'm glad they do. But I would love you anyway."

Jeanie was silent, turning the word love over in her mind. Did he mean he really loved her or was he using the word casually?

When they returned to the apartment, they made love as though it were for the last time. They would not be alone again until the Masada expedition was over. "I love you," David whispered. "I'll always love you."

Chapter 44

It was a bright October morning when Jeanie and David arrived at Masada for the second season of the dig. Jeanie's heart quickened as she looked up at the awesome rock fort. She could almost smell the dust of the excavation, feel the cold steel of the trowel as she chipped away rubble to uncover the final truth. David grasped Jeanie's hand, and they began the steep climb to the campsite, their duffel bags slung over their shoulders.

Members of the expedition arrived throughout the week. There was much preliminary work and planning to be done before the first group of volunteers arrived in November. Maps were studied, finds were reevaluated, strategies were planned. Jeanie was assigned to continue digging along the casemate wall. David would work on the section where Sharett suspected a synagogue was buried.

The digging was as grueling during the second season as it had been during the first. They had to be more careful now as they approached the lowest stratum where more and more artifacts were uncovered. Jeanie used small spades and whisk brooms as she got closer to the Zealot level. Among the hundreds of sherds she uncovered were a small gold ring, a leather sandal and bits of clothing.

One afternoon Jeanie found a brittle leather pouch with bronze coins. In one of the chambers, next to a small clay oven, she uncovered a delicate breastplate of beaten gold, blackened with dust and debris. Using a soft paintbrush and puffers, she brushed away the dust and found lovely jewels set in the breastplate. Each time Jeanie made a discovery, her stomach fluttered with the thrill. In spite of the relentless sun burning her skin, the frigid nights and the desert winds that blew grit into her eyes, Jeanie was never happier. This was everything she had dreamed of. And she had David too. She knew without a doubt that she loved him.

***

A most dramatic find one January day sent everyone running to the steps of Herod's private bathhouse. There, leading to the cold water pool, lay the skeletons of a man, woman and child. A silver scale of armor and remnants of a Jewish prayer shawl lay next to the skeletons and, most important, an ostracon—a broken bit of pottery with a Hebrew inscription. This was more concrete evidence that the Zealots had lived and died here.

David continued digging in the northwestern section of the casemate wall. The strange columns they found had been transported from the palace-villa at the summit and brought to this spot for something special. When David's team finally reached floor level, David discovered a hole filled with small stones and dirt. He dug carefully. An opening had been deliberately cut into the floor. David scooped the dirt out with his hands and reached into the hollow floor, where his fingers curled around a brittle piece of parchment. He lifted it out with extreme care, his hands trembling, yet he knew he could not open the scroll. He sent for Sharett and word of a major discovery spread through the camp. The scroll was immediately removed to a laboratory in Jerusalem where it would be opened, smoothed and photographed by infrared process.

Days later they all learned how important the find was. The scroll was the last two chapters of the *Old Testament Book of Deuteronomy*. David became a hero overnight. Sharett gave orders to excavate the entire floor. Another pit was uncovered containing another scroll—*The Book of Ezekiel*. Here at last were Biblical documents that proved this was indeed the synagogue of Masada.

By the end of the second season of the dig, fourteen scrolls had been found—*Genesis, Leviticus, Psalms* and apocryphal books. One was found in the palace-villa on the summit and several had been buried inside the casemate wall. Jeanie and her team uncovered *The Book of Jubilees* in its original Hebrew text in a wall tower. And in a large square building next to a storeroom, a ritual bath—a *mikvah*—was unearthed.

By April, the expedition drew to a close. Mounting evidence pointed to the presence of the Zealots and corroborated Josephus's account. But where was the proof that the Zealot leader, Ben Ya'ir, and his men had cast lots for the selection of ten who would carry out his final gruesome plan? It seemed as though they would never find such proof.

After each day's dig, sherds and other items found were put in pails, tagged and returned to the campsite where they were routinely examined. It was at the end of one such ordinary day that eleven ostraca dug out of the casemate wall were found in one of the pails. Each bore a Hebrew name inscribed in the same hand. One sherd bore the name Ben Ya'ir.

Jeanie stood beside David, staring at the sherds that lay scattered on the table in the administration tent. She caught her breath, overwhelmed by the evidence. Nine hundred and sixty men, women and children had chosen death at their own hands rather than slavery. That fatal day had marked the end of Jewish independence until the State of Israel was proclaimed in 1948. Jeanie reached for David's hand and squeezed it. She finally understood why he would always fight for Israel.

***

Jeanie pulled on a heavy wool sweater and slipped quietly out of her tent. It was a cold April evening much like other evenings in the desert. Moonlight cast grotesque shadows across the sand and a myriad of dazzling stars dotted the sky. David was already waiting behind the administration tent. Jeanie hurried toward him, and he caught her in his arms. "What took you so long?"

"I had to wait till the others were asleep."

"I don't care if anyone knows I love you." David kissed her. His hand slid under her sweater, over her breasts.

"David, not here!" Jeanie pulled away.

"Next week then. We'll go back to Jerusalem when the expedition is over. You'll stay with me."

"David, I can't go on living with you. I have to go home."

He held her so tight then that it took her breath away. "Marry me."

Jeanie was stunned into silence. She didn't expect David to make such a commitment.

"Answer me."

"David, I… don't know what to say."

"You don't love me then."

"I do love you. I've never loved anyone the way I love you."

"Then marry me."

"It's not that simple. I'm American and you're Israeli. Are you asking me to give up my country?"

"This is your country too. You're a Jew."

"But you want me to live in Israel with you."

"Yes, always." His arms circled her and he kissed her lips, her face, her neck.

"Yes. Yes, I'll marry you," Jeanie said, unable to imagine her life without David.

Chapter 45

Soon after El Al flight 467 took off for New York City, Jeanie began to feel uneasy. Flying alone had always unnerved her, but now her anxiety mounted over the choices she had to make. She rummaged through her shoulder bag for the bottle of Valium pills Mark had given her when she had left New York. Mark had pressed the bottle of pills into her hand before he said goodbye. "Take one when you get on the plane. It'll calm you. There are thirty pills, but I don't think you'll be taking thirty trips," Mark had said. Jeanie had not opened the bottle again since that day, but now she took a pill from the bottle and swallowed it with a cup of water the stewardess had brought.

Mark had been so good to her, Jeanie thought now with a pang of anguish. She had not told him about David in her letters. She would have to tell him now. She knew it would hurt him. She had never encouraged Mark, so why did she feel so guilty? Mark would understand at last that she never meant their friendship to develop into anything more. It was time he started thinking about finding a woman he wanted to settle down with… start a family and live a normal life instead of waiting around for her to fall in love with him. Still, the image of his face loomed before her now, and she dreaded their meeting. Once she had even thought that maybe she had deeper feelings for Mark than she cared to admit, but that was before she met David. It was only hours since David had left her at the airport and she missed him already.

The stewardess moved down the narrow aisle pushing a lunch cart. She handed Jeanie a tray with plastic-looking food. "Coffee?" she asked.

"Yes, please," Jeanie said.

Jeanie sipped the strong black coffee. Sophie would undoubtedly be planning a grand meal for her homecoming. Food and money—that was

Sophie's life. Jeanie wondered how her parents would look after all this time. They hadn't said much in their letters except that Florida was like paradise. Although Sophie had written that Harry was not feeling well, she was vague about his symptoms. They were in New York now for their annual visit. They drove in once a year, the trunk of their car loaded with Florida grapefruits, oranges, mangoes and watermelons, which they brought as gifts for the family. After spending two weeks at Ruthie's house on Long Island, they moved on to Ida's apartment in Brooklyn where they waited for Jeanie.

No one knew about David or about Jeanie's plans to marry and live in Israel. Jeanie wondered how they would all take the news. Sophie would no doubt be ecstatic, having written her off as an old maid. But how would they feel about her leaving the States for good? Well, they would have to accept it. David was in Israel and so was all the antiquity she could ever hope to dig up. It was more than she ever dreamed could happen for her. Her family could visit. Ruthie and Albert would visit, she knew. Sophie, who could not even part with the price of an airmail stamp, would never come to Israel. But that was okay. Nothing her mother could do would hurt her again. She had everything she wanted now.

"Can I take your tray?" The stewardess interrupted Jeanie's thoughts.

Jeanie handed her the tray of uneaten food. Her eyes felt heavy, and she leaned back against the seat, gazing out the window into a sea of clouds. Then her eyes closed and she dreamed… *Clouds floated in the sky above Mt. Scopus, where David had taken her on their last day together in Jerusalem. She could feel his closeness, his strong arms around her shoulders as they stood on the summit looking at the breathtaking view. The wilderness of Judah and the Dead Sea to the east, the mountains of Moab across the Jordan, and Jerusalem to the west. David pointed to the Old Walled City. "One day, Jerusalem will be united. I want to be here when that day comes," David said. Jeanie shivered, seized by a sudden chill. David held her closer, but not even the warmth of his body could shake an icy grip of foreboding.*

Jeanie awoke with a start, her heart pounding and beads of cold perspiration on her brow. "David!" she called out.

"Are you alright?" The stewardess was at her side.

The sound of the plane's engines and the sight of the blue sky outside the window brought Jeanie back to reality. "Could I have some water, please?"

She sipped the cool water the stewardess brought and tried to pull her thoughts away from the disturbing dream.

***

It was 9:00 p.m. when Jeanie finally walked through the customs gate of the international arrival building at the airport. "Jeanie!" Ruthie waved as she stood next to Alex in the waiting crowd. Jeanie ran into her sister's arms and they embraced, tears of happiness mingling with their smiles. "I missed you so much," Ruthie said.

Alex kissed Jeanie. "We're glad you're home, stranger."

"You got so thin. Don't they eat in Israel? You look gorgeous," Ruthie said.

"One question at a time." Jeanie laughed, brushing away tears of happiness.

"Let's get out of here. I hate crowded airports." Alex took Jeanie's bag, and they walked to the parking lot.

Alex unlocked the door of his new 1965 white Cadillac. Jeanie whistled. "Is this yours or did you rent it to welcome me home?"

"It's ours." Alex grinned, opening the back door for Jeanie. She stepped onto thick carpeting and sank into plush leather seats.

"Business must be good, Alex," Jeanie said.

"We got a few new accounts. I can't complain."

"I wish he'd retire," Ruthie said. "Then maybe we'd get to enjoy some of our money. We might even get to see each other for more than ten minutes a day."

Alex started the car and headed toward the Belt Parkway. "Tell us about Israel before we get to Ida's apartment and Sophie starts talking," Alex said.

"There's so much to tell. I loved every minute of it… I'm going back soon."

"Going back?" Ruthie asked. "You just got home!"

"I'm going back to be married."

Ruthie gasped. "Married? Who? I don't believe it!"

"Don't tell me you're marrying an Arab," Alex said.

"No, David is Israeli."

"He must be an archaeologist," Alex said.

"He is. He's also handsome and wonderful… And I love him."

"Why didn't you bring him with you?" Ruthie asked. "When do we get to meet him? How could you keep such a secret?"

"We just decided to get married last week."

"Momma's going to be so happy. She'll want to make you a big wedding."

"David and I are going to be married in a few weeks when I return to Israel. We're just having a simple ceremony on a kibbutz where David's family lives."

"We're not going to be invited to the wedding?" Ruthie asked.

"You're invited if you want to come to Israel."

"Oh, Alex." Ruthie squeezed Alex's arm. "Israel! Can we go? It'll be so exciting. I've never been anywhere except Florida."

"Of course we'll go. I wouldn't miss Jeanie's wedding for anything."

"Wait till Albert and Elizabeth hear. I know they'll want to come too. They're in California for a few weeks," Ruthie said.

"How are things between Albert and Dad?" Jeanie asked.

"The same… still not talking. It hurts me so much. I tried, but…"

"You can't talk to a wall," Alex said. "Harry's a stone wall."

Jeanie sighed and looked out the car window at the familiar landscape as they sped along the Belt Parkway. She wished David were with her now.

"Don't expect Sophie and Harry to come to Israel for your wedding," Alex said.

"I don't," Jeanie said.

"Of course they'll come," Ruthie said.

"Your sister knows them better than you do," Alex told Ruthie.

"They'll come to their own daughter's wedding," Ruthie insisted.

"Not if it costs money," Alex said.

"I don't believe that," Ruthie said.

"It's not important to me," Jeanie said.

"You're better off without them," Alex said. "They'll do something to embarrass you."

"That's not fair," Ruthie said.

"What's fair, Ruthie?" Alex's voice rose. "Is it fair that Sophie sold your wedding gown to some stranger without asking you?"

"Alex, please don't talk about that now," Ruthie pleaded.

"Did you hear that?" Alex shouted to Jeanie. "Sold her daughter's wedding gown for a few shekels. Ruthie left her gown in their apartment in Brooklyn and when they moved to Florida, Sophie sold everything. She figured everything was hers, including the wedding gown. Then Ruthie remembered the gown was there and when she asked, Sophie's memory suddenly failed her. But we found out. Harry finally told us."

"Why do you have to talk about this now?" Ruthie admonished.

"Why not? Who are you trying to protect, Jeanie or them?"

Jeanie sighed. She was silent, overwhelmed suddenly with an impulse to flee back to Israel, back to David. Why had she come home at all? Why hadn't she just telegrammed that she was getting married?

"You've upset Jeanie," Ruthie told Alex.

"Sorry," Alex apologized, as he parked the car in front of Ida's apartment house. They stepped out of the car. Jeanie looked at the four-family brick houses along the familiar tree-lined street. Nothing seemed to have changed. They walked up the narrow stairway to Ida's apartment. Alex knocked on the door.

"They're here already," Sophie's voice echoed from behind the door.

Sophie opened the door. "Jeanie! Is it really you?" She embraced Jeanie, kissing her on her cheek. Sophie had grown so fat, Jeanie could barely get her arms around her. Her unbound breasts met the rise of her belly, which protruded out of a chartreuse polyester pantsuit.

"Hello," Harry said, standing behind Sophie in the dimly lit foyer. He was dressed in a blue and yellow Floridian print shirt and checkered pants.

"Daddy!" Jeanie kissed him, trying to conceal her shock at how frail he looked.

"Jeanie!" Ida's shrill voice overpowered the others. She hugged Jeanie affectionately and then scrutinized her as though she were examining sale merchandise for damage. "Sophie, look how thin she got." Ida shook her head in disapproval.

"How can I see in the dark?" Sophie asked. "Come inside! Come!" She led them into the living room, where they all fired questions at Jeanie.

"So tell me, you had a good time?" Sophie asked.

"They didn't feed you?" Ida asked. She hurried into the kitchen and returned with a bowl of fruit and a can of peanuts.

"We heard you made wonderful discoveries," Harry said. "Maybe we'll go visit Masada. I'd like to see for myself. What do you say, Sophie?"

"Someday." Sophie silenced Harry with her usual noncommittal response. "So what will you do now?" she asked Jeanie.

"Take a fruit!" Ida commanded Jeanie.

"Jeanie has a surprise for you," Ruthie said.

"Yes, I'm going to be married," Jeanie announced.

"Oh!" Ida clapped her hands. "*Mazel tov, mazel tov*!" She rose from the sofa and planted a kiss on Jeanie's cheek.

"That's *some* surprise," Sophie said. "All of a sudden! Who are you marrying? He's Jewish?"

"Yes, David is Jewish."

"Thank God. He has a good job?"

"He's an archaeologist, like me."

Sophie frowned. "Does he make a living?"

"I'm moving to Israel," Jeanie said.

"Why?" Harry asked. "Can't you get married and live here?"

"David is Israeli."

"So he can come to America," Ida said.

"Don't mix in, Ida," Sophie scolded.

"We'll never see you if you move to Israel," Harry said.

"You can come to Israel and visit," Jeanie said.

"She's right." Alex glared at Sophie again. "You can see another place in the world besides Florida and Brooklyn."

"Aren't you happy that Jeanie is getting married?" Ruthie asked.

"It's wonderful," Sophie said. "We want to meet David and his family. We want to make you a wedding, just like we did for Ruthie."

"I don't want a wedding."

"She'll take the money instead," Alex said, smiling.

"David can't come here right now. He's too busy. We'll be married when I return to Israel."

"You just got home and you're going back already?" Harry asked.

"I'll stay for a few weeks."

"She looks tired, Sophie," Ida said, as if Jeanie were in another room.

"We're tired too." Alex rose from the sofa. "Let's go Ruthie. Tomorrow's a work day for me."

Ruthie kissed her sister goodnight. "We'll see you tomorrow. I'll pick you up at 3:00."

"I'll make coffee," Ida said.

***

They sat around the kitchen table. Jeanie listened to the buzz of the fluorescent light and the ticking of the old teapot-shaped clock on the wall. The brown and yellow linoleum floor gleamed with polish, and the old stove shone from Ida's relentless scrubbing. Sophie set coffee cups on the table and folded paper napkins.

Harry and Jeanie studied each other silently across the table. Harry struggled to cling to the memory of the little girl he must let go of now because she had grown into a beautiful woman.

Jeanie looked into her father's vacant eyes. His cheeks were sunken and his face a map of wrinkles—rivers of disappointment. Where was the spark that once lit his eyes?

Ida set a plate of sliced sponge cake on the table and poured hot coffee into their cups. "Take a piece of cake," Ida ordered.

Sophie put a slice of cake on Jeanie's plate and then helped herself to two. "Sophie, you should lose some weight." Ida looked disapprovingly at the cake on Sophie's plate.

"They're small pieces," Sophie protested, putting a forkful of cake in her mouth.

"I told you some day you'd have *nachas,* good luck, from Jeanie," Ida told Sophie and Harry.

"I never thought I'd live to see this day," Sophie said, smiling.

"I wish we could meet David," Harry said. "He's a nice boy?"

"He's not a boy, Dad. He's a man."

"More coffee?" Ida asked.

"Not for me. I'm going to bed." Harry rose and kissed Jeanie goodnight. "I'm happy for you."

"Leave the dishes, Ida. I'll do them," Sophie ordered. "You can go to bed."

"Good night then," Ida said.

Sophie and Jeanie faced each other now. "Are you sure you're doing the right thing?" Sophie asked.

"I love David."

"But Israel… it's so far away. It's a different life."

"My life is with David."

"There are plenty of nice American men."

"I want to live in Israel. My work is there too."

Sophie took Jeanie's hands in hers. "I want you to be happy. When you're not happy, love flies out the window."

"I'm happy when I'm with David. And I'm going to bed now because I'm exhausted."

***

Sophie washed the dishes at the kitchen sink. She was relieved that Jeanie was finally getting married, but she couldn't help feeling uneasy about Israel. She remembered how Lev Kramer had pleaded with her to go to Israel with him. And now her daughter, Lev's daughter, was going willingly where she had refused to go. Life sometimes plays tricks on you, Sophie thought as she turned off the light in the kitchen.

Chapter 46

When Jeanie came in for breakfast, Sophie was sitting at Ida's kitchen table, buttering a fresh roll. "You're up early."

"I have a lot of things to do," Jeanie said

"I'll make you some eggs." Sophie rose.

"I can get my own breakfast." Jeanie poured coffee into a cup and sat down across from Sophie. "Where is everybody?"

"Dad drove Ida to the grocery. Do you have a picture of the man you're going to marry? You didn't tell us his family name."

"Kramer, David Kramer." Jeanie brought her handbag into the kitchen, rummaged through it, and pulled out some photographs. "Here's my handsome David." Jeanie handed Sophie a photo of David standing in front of the Damascus Gate.

Sophie brushed the crumbs off her fingers and held the picture under the light. "So this is David Kramer. Very handsome." David's gray eyes stared out at her from the photo. Something in David's eyes made Sophie uneasy. The familiar name made her heart quicken. These were the eyes of the little boy she had cared for—Lev's son, the child who had sat on her lap, craving comfort after his mother died. Sophie's face paled and her hands trembled as she dropped the picture onto the table.

"What's the matter, Momma? Don't you feel well?"

"Are... are David's parents alive?" Sophie tried to compose herself.

"No, his mother died in America. Pneumonia, I think. And his father died in Israel in 1948. Why?"

"And... and do you know his father's name?" Sophie prayed silently that she would not hear the dreaded name.

"Lev. David's father's name was Lev Kramer."

Sophie gasped and rose from the chair. Then she stumbled back into the chair.

"Momma, what's wrong?" Jeanie was beside her. "You look sick. I'll call a doctor."

"No… I'll be all right. Listen to me." She grasped Jeanie's shoulders. "You can't marry David." Sophie covered her face with her hands. If God had to find the worst punishment for her, He had found it now. Why? Why? Hadn't she suffered enough with her sin all these years? Did Jeanie have to suffer now too?

Jeanie pulled her mother's hands away from her face and saw that it was streaked with tears. "What are you talking about? Why can't I marry David?"

"Don't ask me to tell you why. Just this once in your life, do as I ask," Sophie sobbed.

"Tell me why! I never loved any man the way I love David. I'm marrying him. I can't live without him."

"You can't! He… he's your brother."

"What?" Jeanie's knees suddenly felt weak, and she sank onto the floor. "Tell me!" She reached out and shook her mother.

"David's father… Lev Kramer and I… We… He lived in our building and…"

"And what?"

"I was lonely. Harry was away. And Lev was lonely. His wife had died… It just happened. Lev Kramer is your… your father," Sophie sobbed.

"What are you saying?" Jeanie's stomach churned, and she swallowed hard to keep from vomiting. "How could you do this to me?" she wailed, tears coursing down her cheeks. "And David. Oh God, how can I ever tell him? What have you done to us?"

"Jeanie, there was no way for me to know."

"You lied to me. You lied to Dad. You lied to all of us."

"I never meant to hurt you."

"You hurt me my whole life. You never wanted me or loved me. You never stopped punishing me for being alive. I remind you of your sin every day and you can't forgive me for that. But now I can't forgive you. My life is over. It's as if you held a gun to my head and pulled the trigger," she screamed.

"Please don't say that. You're young. You'll forget."

"Never! You can't understand that I'll always love David because you never loved anyone." Jeanie spat the words.

"I do love you."

"No more lies, Momma. You always pushed me away. You never cared about my achievements, my disappointments. I never asked for much. But when I asked, you always said no."

The truth stunned Sophie, and tears streamed down her face.

Jeanie rose from the floor now as if propelled by an alien force. She stumbled as dizziness and nausea pressed in on her. David—her brother. Her lover and her brother. Sophie was talking, crying. What was she saying? Jeanie couldn't hear. *Brother* was the only word echoing in her ears, reverberating in her brain, shattering her mind into thousands of fragments like slivers of glass hopelessly broken. Run. She must run. She fled from the apartment, down the stairs, out the front door.

Sophie ran to the door. "I'm sorry," she cried out. "Come back… You didn't marry him. It's not so bad. Come back, Jeanie!"

***

Jeanie didn't remember boarding the train. But there she was, sitting in the train. Where was it going? She must get control of herself, she thought. Her eyes darted frantically around the train. Lights seemed to flash everywhere. Why were the lights so bright? They hurt her eyes, and she pressed them closed. The sound of the train clattering along the tracks grew louder in her ears until it was deafening. She covered her ears with her hands.

"Are you okay, Miss?" a man sitting next to her asked.

Jeanie stared blankly at him, not hearing his words, not answering.

The train screeched into the Fiftieth Street station. Jeanie jumped up from the seat, the sound of her heart thumping in her ears. Cold perspiration stained her blouse. She pounded on the train door with her fists. She had to get out. The lights were blinding, the noise unbearable. The train doors opened and she fled from the train and up the steps, pushing through the crowd to escape the subway.

Out on the street, she breathed deeply. Run. An inner voice propelled her as she ran through throngs of early morning crowds hurrying to work. She raced across streets where cars and buses sped. Exhaust fumes filled her lungs, and she gagged and coughed. A speeding taxi honked its horn, but Jeanie didn't care. She ran because when she stopped, she heard her mother's words again: "*Brother. Your brother. David is your brother.*"

It was afternoon by the time Jeanie stopped running and sank onto a bench overlooking the East River. She looked at the murky water. Suddenly everything seemed clear, and calmness settled over her. She knew what she had to do. She could never tell David. She loved him too much. David would get over her eventually. Even Sophie could die with her secret if she chose. She was overwhelmed with hatred for her mother. She reached into her handbag now, and her fingers closed around the plastic bottle of Valium. She rose from the bench and walked with determination away from the river. She knew where she was going.

***

It was 5:30 p.m. when Jeanie checked into the Biltmore Hotel. "Any luggage, Miss?" the bellman asked.

"My bags will arrive later," she answered tonelessly.

Jeanie took the elevator to the fourth floor and unlocked the door to room 407. She dropped the key on the dresser and drew the heavy brocade drapes. Then she filled a pitcher that stood on a small round table with tap water from the bathroom. She took a glass from the bathroom sink and set it down next to the pitcher. Then she kicked off her shoes and sat on the bed. She pulled the bottle of Valium out of her handbag. She'd be free soon. Free from pain. Free from thoughts. David… No, she mustn't think about David… what she had done. The unthinkable, the unforgivable. She could never have what she wanted most… David.

She swallowed the first pill. Another. Another. Hurry. Swallow all of them quickly and then be free. Ten, fifteen, twenty—she counted the pills silently like the last steps on a road to nowhere. Twenty-three. She put the bottle down on the night table and lay back on the pillow. Her senses dulled. She felt intoxicated, her mind hazy, her eyes blurry. David's face drifted in and out of her thoughts. Then Mark's face—her dear friend. Suddenly she had an overwhelming need to hear Mark's voice.

Jeanie struggled to sit up. Mark's phone number must be in her handbag. With great effort, she emptied the contents of her bag onto the bed and grasped a small book of phone numbers. Here it is—the laboratory where he works at New York Hospital. Her vision blurred as she strained to read the number. Her hands felt heavy, and her fingers moved with excruciating slowness as she dialed the number. She breathed heavily into the phone and listened to the rings in her ears. Three, four, five. Didn't anyone answer the phone there? She was so tired. She'd call back later, after she slept, she thought. Then a voice in her ear, "Hello, Pathology."

"Can I speak to Mark?" She heard her own voice as if from a distance.

"Mark who?"

"Um... Doctor... Doctor Mark Lerner."

"I'll see if he's in. Hold on."

Her eyes closed and the receiver dropped from her hand.

"Hello." Mark's familiar voice reached Jeanie's ears. Where was it coming from? She tried to focus. The phone. Yes, the phone. She willed herself to pick it up and reached with numb fingers for the dangling receiver.

"Hello, Mark," she said, her words slurring.

"Who is this?" he asked.

"It's Jeanie. I wanted to say hello. Hello... and goodbye."

"Jeanie! You sound strange. Far away. Where are you?"

"Where am I? Let me see... Um... the Biltmore Hotel, I think."

"What's wrong? You sound terrible."

"Have to go now. Really tired... sawright... I'm like Oedipus."

"What are you talking about?" There was a chilling silence. "Jeanie! Jeanie, answer me!"

Jeanie no longer heard Mark's voice. She was almost free. She dreamed. It was a dream that haunted her from her childhood. A faceless stranger pursued her down a dark corridor toward a door that would not open. She pulled and pulled on the heavy door as the stranger's steps grew louder, closer. She gasped and tugged frantically on the door. It opened just as the stranger reached his ugly hand out toward her. But she was free now.

***

Mark raced across the carpeted lobby of the Biltmore Hotel toward the registration desk. "I'm looking for a young woman named Jeanie Rothman. She's a guest here."

"I'll check." The clerk scanned the register. "No one by that name here."

"There must be," Mark insisted. "She just called me. What about the first name?"

The clerk looked again. "There's a Jeanie Kramer."

"Can I have the room number?"

"I have to call the room, sir. Can't give out that information."

"Call the room!"

The clerk returned in a few minutes. "Sorry, no answer in the room."

"Look, I have to get into the room. I'm a doctor. She's my patient and she may be very sick."

"How do I know you're telling the truth?"

Mark took his hospital identification card from his back pocket. "Now do you believe me?"

The clerk motioned for a bellman. "Open the door to 407." He handed him a key.

***

Mark found Jeanie sprawled limply across the bed, her hair tangled in the phone wire. "Jeanie! Jeanie!" Mark shook her. His fingers felt expertly for the pulse on her neck, and he pressed his face close to her lips. She was barely breathing. Her pulse was slow, weak. Mark reached for the phone and dialed the emergency number at New York Hospital. His hands trembled as he lifted the empty bottle of Valium that had his name on it. "This is Dr. Lerner. Send an ambulance to the Biltmore Hotel. Room 407. It's an OD, Valium. Hurry!"

***

It was hours before Jeanie regained consciousness. The room was spinning—white, splashes of black, lights and muffled voices. Pain in her throat. Her head throbbed. Her stomach ached. She struggled to keep her eyelids open. Someone was holding her hand, talking to her. She turned her head painfully toward the voice. "Jeanie. Jeanie, why?" Mark pressed his lips into the palm of her hand.

Jeanie turned her head away. She could not stand the pain in Mark's eyes. She watched the fluid in an IV bag drip down a tube into her arm. Go away, she thought. Please, please go away and let me die.

Mark stayed by Jeanie's side all through the night. Slowly she told him about David. She told him why. Mark was grateful that Jeanie could not see his face in the darkened room. Her words fell like an axe. Silently he wept for Jeanie's pain and for his own vanished hope.

Chapter 47

Sophie was silent, her face pale, her fingers twisting a dishtowel that lay in her lap. She sat across the table from Harry in Ida's kitchen. Her eyes darted from the polished stove to the table and back to Harry, who glared at her. "Tell me why Jeanie was happy and in love yesterday and then tried to kill herself?" Harry demanded.

"I don't know. Something must have happened between her and David."

"Tell me! I have a right to know. She's my daughter."

"It wouldn't change anything."

"I want the truth!"

Sophie turned to face Harry and began. "When you were in Panama years ago, a man named Lev Kramer moved into the apartment next to ours. His wife died, and he had two young boys. One of his children was David—Jeanie's David. They moved to Israel. Before they left, Lev and I… We… It just happened."

"What happened? You and Lev… What?" Harry's voice trembled.

"You left me for a long time, Harry. I was lonely. I thought you were never coming back. What happened wasn't intentional. Jeanie is Lev's child. David and Jeanie…" Sophie's voice faded to a whisper, and she covered her face with her hands.

Harry's face twisted with rage, his hands clenched and unclenched. "Not my child… Jeanie's not my child? All these years you lied to me! You betrayed me!"

"What good would it have done if I told you then. Jeanie *is* your child. You love her and you brought her up. What happened in the past doesn't matter anymore."

Harry grasped Sophie's shoulders and shook her violently. "How can you say that? Look what your lies have done to us! My God, Sophie, you almost killed Jeanie."

"I didn't mean to hurt anyone. What happened was long ago. Jeanie will get over it."

"You've gone too far, hurt us too much. I can't stand the sight of you!"

Sophie winced. "I'll make it up to you." Tears streamed down her face. "We can go away… maybe on a cruise."

"I don't want to go anywhere with you. Can't you see what you've done to me? I lost my son, and now I lost my daughter. I lost her and she never belonged to me. I love her and she's not mine. You did this! You loved another man, had a child with him and pretended she was my child. I'll never forgive you!"

"I never loved Lev. I love you, Harry."

"You're incapable of loving anyone."

"What about you, Harry? You can't tell me you were faithful to me all the years you were away in Panama, then Newfoundland. I know you weren't."

"How do you know?"

"I know you better than you think. What makes it right for you and wrong for me?"

"I didn't have a child. I didn't lie and deceive you. I didn't destroy Jeanie's life. You did." Harry turned and stormed out of the kitchen. There were no more words to express his horror, his rage, his despair.

Sophie followed him. She heard the lock on the bedroom door click. She knocked softly. "Harry, I'm sorry. Forgive me. We'll be happy again. You'll see, things will be different. If you loved me once, you can love me again, can't you? Harry, answer me."

***

Jeanie left the hospital two weeks later, promising the psychiatrist she would contact one of the doctors on a list he gave her. "You need help getting over your trauma. Acute depression and anxiety…" his voice droned in her ears, falling into the vacuum of her mind. She had written to David, telling him why she couldn't marry him, something she could not have done if she had not felt paralyzed, insensible.

Ruthie came to the hospital for her. As they drove to Ruthie's house on Long Island, Jeanie gazed vacantly out of the car window. They sped along the Long Island Expressway—Lefrak City, Alexanders's Department Store, rows of cars jammed into parking lots as far as the eye could see. The gray landscape changed to green as they approached suburbia.

"You'll stay with us as long as you like." Ruthie's voice was cheerful in spite of the worry in her eyes. "The children are very excited. They can't wait to show you our new swimming pool. It'll be relaxing for you."

"It must be nice," Jeanie answered tonelessly.

"Mom and Dad went back to Florida last week."

"That's nice."

"Albert and Elizabeth will be in New York in a few days."

"That's nice."

Ruthie looked at her sister anxiously. The hollowness in Jeanie's voice disturbed her more than the pallor in her cheeks and the dark shadows beneath her eyes. She reached over and squeezed Jeanie's arm.

Jeanie was silent. She wished she could feel something. All her senses were dulled—food had no taste, voices were muffled, no warmth came from the touch of her sister's hand.

Ruthie pulled into the circular driveway in front of her house. Steven and Jodi ran out to the car to greet them. "Aunt Jeanie!" Steven hugged her.

Jodi tugged at her skirt. "I made a picture for you." She pushed a crayoned drawing into Jeanie's hand.

"Thank you." Jeanie took the drawing from Jodi and forced a smile.

Alex came out to the car and kissed Jeanie. "Welcome home."

What day was it? What month? Jeanie couldn't remember. She followed Ruthie into the house. It was cool, spacious, orderly.

"Want to play *Monopoly*?" Steven asked Jeanie.

"Later," Ruthie told him. "Aunt Jeanie has to rest now."

Jeanie followed Ruthie up the carpeted steps to a large sunny bedroom overlooking the garden.

"What's wrong with Jeanie? She talks funny." Steven's words drifted through the hallway to Jeanie's ears.

"What day is it?" Jeanie asked Ruthie.

"Sunday."

"What month?"

"It's May. Don't you remember? I'll bring you today's paper."

Jeanie tried to orient herself in time and place. It's May. It's Sunday, she repeated over and over in her mind as though it were vitally important that she remember this.

"Unpack your things and lie down for a while. I'll make some sandwiches, and we can have lunch near the pool." Ruthie closed the door softly behind her and walked down the steps, brushing away tears with her fingertips.

Chapter 48

David opened his mailbox and took out a packet of letters. He thumbed through them quickly and pulled out one with Jeanie's familiar handwriting. His heart quickened as he raced up the steps to his apartment and unlocked the door, clutching Jeanie's letter. She had left only two weeks ago, and he ached for her—her smile, her voice, her touch.

David tore open the envelope and read. He drew in a breath, struggling to drag air into his lungs, refusing to comprehend Jeanie's words. It was madness. Lies. All lies. David read the letter again and again. Then he crumpled the pages into a ball, crushing the words that plunged him into the depths of despair.

"No! No!" David flung a crystal ashtray against the wall. Then one by one, he picked up each object that sat on the coffee table and heaved it against the wall. A book, an empty cup, a photograph album, a handful of coins—all made hollow sounds as they struck the wall. When there was nothing left to throw, David sank onto the floor and wailed like a wounded animal left at the side of a road to die. He had not cried since the day his father had died and he had buried his silver *Star of David* in his father's grave.

"God… God! There is no God. How could He let such a thing happen?" David shuddered. His Jeanie, his love. Their union could never be. It never should have been. Yet David knew he would not stop loving her. Why? Why? How could something so twisted, so insane, have happened? There were no answers. Only questions and guilt.

David berated himself for pursuing Jeanie. He remembered her words at Masada when he had first asked her to come with him to Jerusalem and she had refused. *"No, David. We both have our careers to think of…"* Why hadn't he listened?

David spent the next few days wandering aimlessly through the streets of Jerusalem, entombed in a shroud of pain and guilt. He retraced his steps through the places he had taken Jeanie—Mea Shearim, Yemin Moshe, Ein Kerem. Everywhere he saw Jeanie's face, felt her touch, longed to hold her in his arms. He walked for miles every day, but there was no escape from the grief and despair that haunted him.

There was only one thing David loved as much as Jeanie—Israel. Several weeks later, David marched into army headquarter in Jerusalem.

"Shalom, David." The sergeant on duty recognized him.

"I'm here to sign up for border guard duty."

The sergeant raised his eyebrows. "You've served your time. There's no need… "

"It's what I want."

"You know if fighting breaks out, you could be the first…"

"I want to be the first."

"Report back here Monday morning." The sergeant handed David his orders.

Chapter 49

Sophie stood at the stove in the kitchen of her Florida home, scrambling eggs in a cast iron skillet. Harry had risen early this June morning, as he did every morning, though he had nowhere to go and nothing in particular to do. Sophie always rose early to prepare Harry's breakfast. It was just habit, she thought now, because Harry never asked her to. In fact, since they had returned to Florida only a few short weeks ago, Harry didn't care if he ate breakfast, lunch, or dinner.

Sophie's brow creased with worry as she put two slices of bread in the toaster. Harry had been so despondent since Jeanie's attempted suicide that Sophie wondered if he would ever recover or forgive her. She agonized over the whole affair. Harry's depression was a constant reminder of her guilt, yet she was able to rationalize it and get on with her life. To Sophie, it was a terrible mistake she made a long time ago. A crazy act of fate had brought her transgression back to haunt her. If Jeanie had not had such wild dreams and had not gone to Israel to dig up old ruins, she wouldn't have uncovered the past. She never would have met David and none of this would have happened. Harry and Jeanie wouldn't hate her now. Maybe they would appreciate all she had done for them instead. Didn't they realize how much money she had amassed for them? Ungrateful—that's what they were. And Jeanie had caused all their problems from the moment she was conceived.

For a fleeting moment, Sophie recalled the day she had thrown herself down a flight of stairs when she was pregnant, attempting to abort Jeanie. *I've been punished too much*, Sophie thought now as she dished out eggs. Then she went into the living room to get Harry. "Harry, breakfast is ready."

Harry sat listlessly on an overstuffed armchair, staring into space. "I'm not hungry."

"You have to eat. Do you want to die? You'll die if you don't eat."

Harry didn't answer. He rose and shuffled into the kitchen, where he sat down at the table, picked up a fork and pushed the eggs around on his plate.

Sophie poured coffee for them. "Maybe we should go on a trip, Harry. Would you like to go on a cruise?"

"Not now. Maybe next year." His voice was flat.

"Harry, you always like to travel. It would be nice."

"I'll let you know. I'm going fishing today."

"You go fishing every day. Why don't you come with me today? I'm going to look at some property for sale in Tampa."

"I'd rather go fishing." Harry rose from the chair, leaving his breakfast half eaten.

Harry took his fishing pole and a bucket and walked out of the house without saying another word to Sophie. He walked down the road to the canal where his small motorboat was tied to the dock. He got into the boat methodically, started the engine and steered the boat into the canal. After anchoring the boat, Harry cast his fishing line and stared aimlessly at the water, tortured by his thoughts.

Why hadn't he taken the children and left Sophie a long time ago? Harry blamed himself now for the tragedies that could have been avoided. Ruthie never would have been raped if he had taken them away from that terrible neighborhood long ago. He would never forgive himself or Sophie for that. Maybe if they had lived in a better place, Albert wouldn't have had such wild ideas about acting. Albert's wish to act was probably a need to escape to a better place. And Jeanie—perhaps she chose the career she did for the very same reason as Albert—escape.

But the overwhelming sense of loss was what tormented Harry the most. He had no hope left. Albert and Jeanie were lost forever. Yet he loved them and his sweet Ruthie, and he always would. He should have forgiven Albert long ago. His anger and bitterness had driven Albert away for good. Now he could never regain his son's love. All he could look forward to was spending the rest of his days with Sophie, who had deceived him his whole life.

Harry stared at the murky canal water. He pulled in his empty fishing line as the mid-day sun beat down on his head. He had stayed out in the sun too long and was beginning to feel light-headed. Harry started the engine and headed for home. He was so tired, so very tired. He just wanted to sleep.

Chapter 50

Ruthie kept Jeanie busy, filling her days with tennis, swimming, concerts and museums. Jeanie pretended to be cheerful, said the right things, but felt as though she were watching herself from a great distance. At the end of each day, she couldn't wait to return to the quiet of her bedroom, where she collapsed on the big brass bed and slept as though she were drugged.

Albert and his wife, Elizabeth, came to visit one evening early in June. It was a warm night, and the smell of new grass and rose blossoms drifted into the living room through the open windows. "I missed you, Jeanie." Albert embraced her. They sat on the white leather sofa, and Jeanie stared blankly at a vase filled with yellow roses. Albert was stunned by the change in Jeanie. When he had last seen her, she had been vibrant and beautiful. Her eyes had shone with excitement about her trip to Israel. Now it pained him to see the sadness in her face and the dullness in her eyes. Albert had always hoped that Jeanie would somehow escape Sophie's selfishness and stupidity. It was enough that he and Ruthie had been Sophie's victims. Now it seemed to him that Jeanie had suffered the most.

Albert took Jeanie's limp hand in his. "We want you to come to California next month and stay with us for a while."

"For as long as you want," Elizabeth added.

"Maybe." Jeanie's voice was flat.

"You'll meet new people. LA is a fun place." Albert squeezed Jeanie's hand.

"We'll show you San Francisco," Elizabeth said. "And we can take a trip to the wine country. You'll love it."

"I'll let you know," Jeanie said wearily.

Soon Albert and Elizabeth rose from the sofa and kissed Jeanie goodbye. Jeanie wondered why Albert's eyes looked misty. She tried to remember what they had talked about for the past hour, but it was a great effort to think.

***

"I want you to call a doctor. You can't go on like this. You've been here for a month and you're not getting any better," Ruthie said the following day.

"I will. Soon," Jeanie said dully.

"Today. I promised Mark I'd get you to see a doctor."

"Tomorrow. I promise."

"Not tomorrow. Now." Ruthie thrust a paper with a list of doctors' names into Jeanie's hand. Jeanie went to the phone in the hallway and called the first doctor on the list. She made an appointment for the next day to appease Ruthie and Mark.

***

Jeanie never kept her appointment with the doctor. Sophie called early the next morning. "Your father… He's gone. Gone."

"Momma, what's wrong?" Ruthie's heart leaped.

"Your father is dead!" Sophie sobbed into the phone. "Dead… He's gone."

"What happened?" Ruthie's hands trembled and she could barely hold the phone.

"He died in his sleep. The doctor said it was a stroke, but I know he didn't want to live anymore. He left me," Sophie sobbed.

"It wasn't your fault." Ruthie tried to console her mother, struggling with her own emotions as Jeanie stood silently beside her.

"I'm bringing your father home. I want him buried in our family plot."

Ruthie put the phone down and turned to Jeanie, her face twisted with grief. "Daddy's dead." Tears coursed down her cheeks, and she shook with great heaving sobs.

Jeanie embraced her sister, wanting to comfort her, feeling nothing but compassion for Ruthie.

***

Sophie arrived in New York with Harry's coffin the following morning on an Eastern Airlines flight. A hearse picked up Harry. Albert took Sophie to his apartment. Ruthie thought it best to keep Sophie and Jeanie apart.

The funeral was held the following day. Alex drove Ruthie and Jeanie to the funeral chapel on Long Island. When they entered the dimly-lit, wood-paneled room where Sophie sat next to Harry's coffin, there was a hushed silence. Sophie sobbed when she saw her daughters. Ruthie embraced her mother, but Jeanie didn't touch her. "I lost my best friend," Sophie wept.

Ida arrived and there was renewed crying. "Stop it, Sophie," Ida commanded, taking charge. "That's life. We all have to go some day. We're just here for a short visit and then we must go." Ida offered her philosophy of life and death at every family funeral, and Harry's was no exception. There was renewed weeping with the arrival of each family member and friend.

Jeanie watched the scene unfold before her as though she were viewing the last act of a tragic play. Not even Harry's coffin moved her to tears. She felt detached from her body.

The service began in the chapel. A rabbi who had never known Harry delivered a meaningless eulogy. Jeanie fidgeted with the buttons on her suit and her stomach tightened. She wanted to stand up and shout, "That's not Harry you're talking about. You never knew him. You never knew what he lived for, what his dreams were, why he died."

"He was a good man. A devoted husband, father, grandfather..." the rabbi's voice rang with false emotion. Jeanie wondered how he could muster so much emotion over a man he never knew, while she still felt nothing.

They drove to the cemetery in a black limousine. Sophie continued weeping. Ruthie and Albert sat next to her, holding her hands. Jeanie sat near the window, gazing vacantly out at the summer landscape. She did not speak to Sophie or look at her.

A fine drizzle was falling when they arrived at the cemetery. Family members and friends huddled together around the open grave, their faces a blur to Jeanie. She was dimly aware of Mark standing next to her. He took her hand, pressed it gently as the rabbi intoned the prayers. Harry's coffin was lowered into the grave. Jeanie was handed a shovelful of dirt. She let it fall slowly onto the coffin, listening to the hollow sound it made. She bent over Harry's coffin then. "Shalom," she whispered. Then she turned to Mark, buried her head in his shoulder and finally cried.

The mourners walked back to their waiting cars, their waiting lives. Harry's journey was over. It was the most expensive trip Sophie ever gave him.

Chapter 51

Harry's death jolted Jeanie back to reality. Her eyes were red and swollen, her tears endless. Then slowly, she began to feel alive again. Mark helped her find an apartment on East 89th Street in Manhattan. And she returned to her old job at the Metropolitan Museum. While New York steamed in summer's heat, Jeanie lost herself in her work inside the cool corridors of the museum. She began to renew old friendships, pulling herself out of the depths of despair. She was a survivor. And Mark was always there for her to lean on. He waited, always in the shadows of her life. She counted on him, needed him, without realizing that she did. He was her dearest friend. He had seen her at her worst and her best.

Sophie returned to her home in Florida. She too was a survivor. She had survived loneliness early in her marriage when Harry had left her. She had survived a love affair and an illegitimate child, and now she would survive the tragedy her lies and deceit had caused. She would survive Harry's death. She would go on with her life. She would make amends. Money—that was the answer. She would finally give her children what she had promised, what she thought they wanted. She would give them more money than they dreamed possible.

Sophie phoned her accountant late in August. "Bernie, I want you to sell all my securities. I have to raise one million dollars immediately."

"Sophie, have you gone mad?" Bernie asked.

"No. There's a new land development going up on the west coast of Florida and I'm investing in it. I'll triple my money in two years."

"Sophie, listen to me. That's all you've got. It's not like you to put all your eggs in one basket… And what do you know about this developer? He could go bankrupt and you'll lose everything."

"I never lost in real estate."

"What about all the money you lost a few years back in the Tampa development?"

"That won't happen this time."

"This isn't a time to take chances. You're distraught over Harry's death. I understand, but don't do anything rash now."

"If you don't do what I ask, you don't have to be my accountant."

"Okay, Sophie. But at least talk to Albert. Talk to Ruthie."

"It's my money, Bernie. I don't need anyone's permission."

Sophie did not have to wait two years for her investment to pay off. Soon after completion of the development, the homes and condominiums were nearly sold out. By the time merry-makers were ringing in the new year of 1966, the Morgan Lee Randolph Land Development Company had made Sophie a multimillionaire.

Sophie did not tell her children what she had done. She was waiting for the right moment, the perfect time to tell them they were all going to be millionaires. Even Jeanie would forgive her when she had enough money to go on expeditions all over the world.

***

Time moved slowly for Jeanie. The summer of 1966 passed uneventfully into autumn. She tried not to think of David, but world events were an ever-present reminder. Though they had agreed not to contact each other again, Jeanie phoned David in October when news reached her of Syrian terrorist attacks on the outskirts of Jerusalem. There was no answer at David's apartment. She called Joel and Leah at Ramat Rahel. "Hello, hello, it's Jeanie. How are you and the children?"

"Jeanie, it's good to hear from you. We're all okay," Joel's familiar voice boomed.

"I tried to reach David, but there's no answer in his apartment."

"Didn't he tell you? He's in the army again."

The color drained from Jeanie's face. "No, he didn't. Is he okay?"

"He's fine. Don't worry about David. He can take care of himself."

"I'm worried about all of you."

"We're used to dealing with terrorists here."

"The news reports sound worse than ever."

"I'll keep you informed. Jeanie, you don't have to worry about us."

Jeanie hung up the phone and a sick feeling spread through her stomach.

Now David was in danger and she felt responsible. David's last words still haunted her. *"I'll love you till I die,"* he had written in his last letter over a year ago. She shared his torment, and she prayed he would make a life for himself, find someone else to love. She never expected him to rejoin the army, and now she feared for his life.

Jeanie worried endlessly as she followed the news events. In the first ten days of May, there were eleven terrorist attacks by Syrian Fatah raiders. On May 14, the Egyptian army mobilized for war while Israel celebrated its Independence Day. Events worsened with each passing day. On May 22, a radio broadcast announced Egyptian President Nassar's decision to the world: *"The Israeli flag will no longer pass the Gulf of Aquaba..."* Jeanie shuddered. She knew war was inevitable now but hoped the UN would somehow intervene. As the Security Council debated in New York, war broke out in the Middle East on June 5th.

Jeanie listened to endless news reports as the war raged. She could do little else but pray for David's safety. The war was short, only six days. But in those six days, Israel drove the Egyptian army from the Gaza Strip and the Sinai Peninsula, and took the Golan Heights and the Jordanian sector of Jerusalem. The Temple area in the Old City of Jerusalem was again in Israeli hands after two thousand years. Soldiers wept and prayed at the Wailing Wall, and Jeanie prayed that David was among them. She had tried in vain to reach him and Joel by phone. Now she could only wait and hope.

Five days after the war ended, a letter arrived from Joel. Jeanie's hands trembled as she opened the envelope, and her legs felt suddenly weak.

15 June 1967

My Dearest Sister,

There is no easy way for me to tell you that our David is gone. He was among the bravest who fought along the Jordanian front. I was with him in the hospital before he died. I brought him news of our occupation of the Old City. He wanted to be there, to touch the wall of the Old Temple, but he was at peace knowing that at last Jerusalem was united and he had lived to see that day. He had no regrets. He said he had everything he wanted in his life and much more than some. He said, "Tell Jeanie I love her." For us, and I know for you, David will always live in our hearts.

Love, Joel

Jeanie was inconsolable. What was left for her now if she could not even hope that David would be happy again? The finality of David's death brought with it such pain and emptiness that she envied David's peace. The anguish she had caused him tormented her. Her memories carried her back to the last day they had spent together in Jerusalem, and she shuddered at the terrible irony. They had stood on a hill overlooking the Old Walled City. *"Someday Jerusalem will be united again,"* David had prophesied.

What a price we pay for our dreams, Jeanie thought as she wept for David, for herself, for hope lost.

Chapter 52

Bright sunshine poured into Jeanie's bedroom through the half-closed blinds, waking her early on this cold December morning. She pulled the blanket up to her chin, huddling in the warmth of the bed. It was Saturday and she was going to pamper herself today. She hadn't treated herself well in months. Maybe it was the sunshine that made her feel good, or maybe she was done with grieving.

It seemed like her grief would never end, suffocating her, drowning her in a sea of tears. And then slowly, like a curtain descending on the final act of a tragedy, it was over. Jeanie knew that deep inside her was a wound with a permanent scar. But now she clung to a kernel of hope that had taken root.

Jeanie stretched, threw back the blankets, and stepped onto the carpeted bedroom floor. She wrapped herself in a warm fleece robe and went into the bathroom to wash her face. As she looked at her reflection in the mirror that hung over the sink, she considered herself fortunate. Most people didn't love their work as much as she did. She had made important discoveries at Masada. And she had accomplished all this in spite of Sophie's opposition and disinterest… and Harry's apathy. She didn't blame them, but she didn't credit them with ever helping her either. Even though she understood, finally, why Sophie had always resented her, she couldn't comprehend why Sophie showed no love for anyone. At least she wasn't like her mother, she concluded as she walked into the tiny kitchen and filled the coffee pot with cold water. Sophie could no longer touch her. She would build a good life for herself with her work and those who loved her… like Mark.

What would she have done without Mark to lean on? He was always there for her when she needed him. He had saved her life, watched over her like a worried parent as she slowly recovered. He was beside her at Harry's funeral. Jeanie smiled and decided it was time to show her gratitude to Mark. She put down the bowl of eggs she was mixing and reached for the phone. She would invite Mark for dinner tonight.

Jeanie listened as Mark's phone rang five times and wondered where he could be so early on a Saturday morning. She knew he had the day off today. Finally, after the eighth ring, she heard, "Hello." It was a woman's voice.

"Hello. I… I must have the wrong number," Jeanie said.

"Who are you calling?" the woman asked.

"Mark Lerner."

"Hold on. I'll get him."

Jeanie was so surprised to hear a female voice in Mark's apartment that she could barely answer when Mark came to the phone.

"Hello."

"It's Jeanie. I'm sorry I called so early. I… I didn't know you had company."

"Yes, my friend, Ellen… Ellen Sandler. She's a resident in cardiology at the hospital. I… I invited her for breakfast."

There was an awkward silence and Jeanie said, "I'm sorry if I disturbed you. I was calling to invite you for dinner this evening, but if you're busy…"

"I've already made plans to take Ellen to the theater. But I'll take a rain check."

"It was thoughtless of me to call you at the last minute and expect you to be free. Enjoy the theater and… I'm sorry if I interrupted your breakfast."

"No problem. I'll be in touch." Mark hung up.

Jeanie held the phone to her ear for a few moments, dazed, listening to the dial tone. Then she replaced the receiver. She stared at the bowl of eggs near the stove and then poured them into the sink. She was no longer hungry. The beautiful day suddenly lost its luster, and the feeling of euphoria that had lifted her spirits just moments ago was replaced by a whole range of emotions that she was not prepared to face.

Jeanie poured hot coffee into a mug and sat down at the kitchen table. A flood of feelings overwhelmed her as she sipped the coffee and tried to deal with the thoughts racing through her head. "I invited Ellen for breakfast," Mark had said. Did he think she was a naïve fool? Breakfast comes after dinner… after sex. Ellen had slept there… in his apartment. Well, why not? It was time Mark found someone he cared for. Isn't that what she had told him to do and wished for him? Then why did she feel like this now when it had finally happened? Was she jealous? No, that was ridiculous. She was just very dependent on Mark and used to having him available as a sounding board whenever she called. Lately, they had been spending more and more time together, and he had never mentioned Ellen. That's why she was so surprised, Jeanie concluded. After all, she reasoned, he's a grown man and he can sleep with whomever he likes. She had no right to expect him to be there for her all the time. They were just good friends and she must stop thinking about this now. It was childish.

Jeanie put her empty coffee mug in the sink and hurried to dress. What she needed was a brisk walk in Central Park to clear her head. Then a shopping spree at Bloomingdale's, followed by dinner and a movie with friends. It sounded like a perfect day. But when she walked through Central Park, huddled inside her hooded parka, she couldn't shake one persistent feeling… jealousy.

Chapter 53

All through the following week, Jeanie struggled with her jealousy and waited for Mark to phone. When he finally called Sunday evening, her heart leaped at the sound of his voice. "Jeanie, I'm so glad you're home. Are you busy for dinner tomorrow night? I know it's short notice, but..."

"Dinner sounds wonderful." Jeanie couldn't conceal the eagerness in her voice. It was foolish of her to have been jealous, she thought.

"I want you to meet Ellen."

There was an awkward silence. Jeanie swallowed hard. "I'd love to meet Ellen," she lied.

"Great. P.J.'s at 7:30 tomorrow. See you then."

"Goodbye." Jeanie hung up the phone. Her hand ached from gripping the receiver when Mark spoke that woman's name—Ellen. Jeanie didn't want to meet her. She dreaded facing the woman who was obviously taking Mark away from her. She knew she had no claim on him, but there was no denying her feelings went beyond friendship.

Jeanie brushed a strand of hair away from her eyes. Ellen was obviously more than a casual friend at the hospital if Mark wanted them to meet. She worried about how serious the relationship was. Well, it couldn't be too serious if Mark never talked about Ellen until recently, she rationalized.

Jeanie walked into the bedroom now and picked up her hairbrush. She looked in the mirror and began brushing her hair vigorously. *I'm being childish,* she thought. *But if Ellen thinks she has any claim on Mark, she's wrong. I've been a fool, but I won't be a fool any longer. I must mean more to Mark than Ellen. And... and I love him. He can't be serious about this woman. How could Mark have asked her to meet them at P. J.'s? That was where she and Mark had spent so many evenings together. How could he be so insensitive?* She slammed the hairbrush down on the dresser and brushed angry tears from her eyes.

Jeanie's thoughts tormented her all through the night. When she woke the next morning, she was exhausted and emotionally depleted. She showered, dressed and had a hasty breakfast. Then she hurried to work.

Jeanie stayed at the museum until nearly 7:00 o'clock, absorbed in setting up a new exhibit and determined to push Ellen and their impending meeting out of her thoughts. But now it was time to go.

In spite of the cold night, Jeanie walked from the museum to P.J.'s on Third Avenue. She wanted to clear her head. By the time she opened the front door of P.J.'s and stepped into the warm friendly restaurant, she had vowed that she would fight for Mark. Ellen wasn't going to have him. He belonged to her.

Jeanie walked past the long bar, where a lively after-work crowd mingled, to the restaurant in the rear. Mark saw her at once and waved from a table near the window. It was only a short distance to the table, but it seemed to Jeanie that she approached in slow motion.

"Jeanie." Mark took her icy hands in his. "I'd like you to meet Ellen Sandler… Dr. Ellen Sandler."

"Hello." Jeanie forced a smile and sat down stiffly as Mark held the chair for her.

Ellen offered her cool hand. "It's nice to meet you. Mark's told me about you and what interesting things you've done."

Jeanie wondered how much Mark had told her as she assessed Ellen. She was certainly a beautiful woman, with dark hair tied back in a chic knot and subtle eye shadow accenting her hazel eyes. She was dressed very smartly in a white cashmere sweater and gray wool skirt. An exquisite strand of creamy pearls hung around her neck, glowing in the soft light. Jeanie suddenly felt that she looked shabby in comparison. She had been so distracted that she hadn't given much thought to her dress or makeup today. "What has Mark told you?" Jeanie asked.

"That you're an archaeologist and you've been excavating at Masada. I'd love to hear about it."

Jeanie talked for a while about Masada, but her mind was not on Masada.

The waiter arrived with their dinners, and Mark ordered a bottle of wine.

Jeanie turned to Ellen. "Mark tells me you're doing your residency in cardiology."

"Yes. My father's a cardiologist in Los Angeles. I suppose it's what I've always wanted."

"Will you be joining your father's practice?"

"I'm not sure yet," Ellen said, her eyes resting on Mark.

"She'll be a great cardiologist no matter where she practices." Mark smiled at Ellen as he refilled her wine glass.

"I know Mark will love living in Los Angeles," Ellen said. "It's such a lovely city, and much less of a hassle than New York.

Jeanie suddenly found the food in her mouth dry and tasteless. "I love New York," she told Ellen. Then she turned to Mark. "I didn't know you were planning on moving to Los Angeles."

"It's a possibility." Mark reached across the table and took Ellen's hand in his. "Ellen and I are planning on marrying soon. That's why I wanted you two to meet."

Jeanie dropped the fork she was holding onto the table and her eyes widened in surprise. They both looked at her, waiting for a response. It seemed to Jeanie that endless time passed before she could answer, but it was only seconds. "How wonderful." Jeanie faked enthusiasm, but the words sounded hollow in her ears.

"I'm so glad you two like each other," Mark said.

A barely visible smile crossed Ellen's tight lips. Jeanie winced and then lifted her wine glass to toast them. "To a long and happy marriage. And may you have many beautiful and bright children."

"Thank you." Mark grinned.

"Children aren't in our plans," Ellen said. "These days people have to choose between children and their careers. There isn't time for both."

Mark's eyes widened in surprise. "Children are in *my* plans."

"You'll change your mind, darling. Wait till you're settled in LA and set up in a wonderful practice. It'll be more than enough for you."

Jeanie watched Mark smiling at Ellen, and she wondered when he had changed and how it had escaped her notice. She knew that Mark wanted children in his life and he wanted to continue in research. He certainly didn't want to go into private practice. But Ellen appeared to have planned the rest of their lives. Was Mark so in love with her that he would allow this? Ellen was cold and calculating, Jeanie concluded. And she hated her. But Ellen was also beautiful and strong willed, and maybe that's what Mark needed. Jeanie had come here tonight prepared to fight for Mark and win him back, but now she thought she had lost the battle.

Jeanie struggled through dessert and coffee and then said, "I'm sorry I can't stay and chat longer, but I have to be up very early tomorrow to work on a new exhibit at the museum. Thanks for sharing your wonderful news with me." She looked into Mark's eyes and saw that he was happy.

"I'm glad we met," Ellen said.

Jeanie hurried out of the restaurant, eager to escape Ellen's scrutiny, the closeness of the man she loved, and the devastation of losing him.

Chapter 54

Christmas was only a week away, and Jeanie hoped that the holiday mood would lift her spirits. But the dazzling lights, the elaborately-decorated shop windows, and the lively crowds only served as a bitter contrast to her unhappiness.

Two weeks had passed since she had met Ellen. Anger, jealousy, resentment and overwhelming feelings of loss finally settled into resignation. Jeanie concluded that she had no right to expect Mark to be there for her, waiting his whole life for her to realize she loved him and wanted him. She knew he wanted a wife and family. She could have been his wife if she hadn't denied her love for him all these years. If she hadn't been so blind and stubborn and stupid, she could have avoided the tragedy in her life. Now it was too late. Her life would go on, but it would never be the same without Mark. Jeanie couldn't help feeling that she had no control over her destiny. Perhaps her life was fated from the very first moment she had been conceived in sin.

Mark phoned a few days before Christmas. "Jeanie, why haven't I heard from you? Are you alright?"

"I'm fine," she lied. "I've been busy. What about you… and Ellen?"

"Ellen's finishing her residency in a few weeks. Then she's taking some time off to arrange our wedding."

"I didn't know you were planning a wedding. It'll be beautiful, I'm sure. Ellen seems very organized."

"She has every detail planned already. By the way, the wedding will be in Los Angeles. Ellen's family lives there and it'll be easier. I hope you'll come."

"I… I wouldn't want to miss your wedding." Jeanie swallowed, choking back tears.

"You sound funny. You sure you're okay?"

"I'm okay."

"I'm driving to Florida after the first of the year. There's a medical symposium in Ft. Lauderdale, all about viruses. You know how I love virology."

"Sounds great. Is Ellen joining you?"

"No, she's flying to LA to make the wedding arrangements."

Impulsively, Jeanie said, "Florida sounds wonderful. I haven't had a vacation for ages. Would you mind if I hitched a ride with you? And I haven't seen my mother for a long time. I should visit her."

"I'd love your company on the drive down."

"Are you sure? Do you think Ellen will mind?"

"Of course not. She knows we're just friends."

"I'm glad you called, Mark. I'm looking forward to a few days away in the sun, and I probably wouldn't have thought of going on my own."

"You're working too hard. Sounds like you need a rest. We'll leave on January 2nd. I'll be in touch and let you know what time I'll pick you up."

After she hung up the phone, Jeanie felt unexpectedly elated. In spite of the fact that Ellen was going off to arrange the wedding, she was going to spend a few precious days with Mark. Though she held out no hope, she was happy with the prospect of being alone with Mark, even if it would be for the last time.

***

It was a long drive to Ft. Lauderdale, but Jeanie didn't mind. She lost all sense of time as she watched the changing landscape through the car window and lost herself in easy conversation with Mark. His quiet laughter was contagious. She forgot all else except that she was happy, and only the time they shared together now was important. She wanted to store these moments in her memory to draw strength from later like a starving animal that feeds on a cache of food.

They reached Ft. Lauderdale in two days and checked into a luxurious beachfront hotel where Mark had reserved a room months ago. The symposium would be held in the hotel's convention center. Mark had tried to reserve a room for Jeanie when she had decided to go at the last minute, but all the rooms were booked. As they pulled up in front of the hotel, Mark said, "I didn't tell you because I thought you'd change your mind about coming along, but you're going to have to share my room. Every room was reserved."

"I could stay at another hotel. I don't want you to be inconvenienced."

"The room has a sitting room with a sofa bed. I can sleep on that, and you can have the bedroom. Anyway, this is the best hotel here and you'll get a good rest."

Jeanie hesitated. She didn't know how she would handle her feelings if she stayed in the same room with Mark for three days.

"Please say yes, Jeanie. It's only for three days, and I promise I won't get in your way."

"I'm not worried about you getting in my way."

"Then it's settled." Mark opened the car door for her, and a bellman took their luggage out of the trunk.

Mark was busy attending meetings during the next two days. He rose early and left before Jeanie even opened her eyes. She spent two days relaxing, with nothing to do but lay on the beach, swim and read. Mark spent late afternoons with her. They played tennis, walked on the beach and swam in the hotel pool before dressing for dinner. Jeanie couldn't remember when she had felt happier or more relaxed.

As they waited for their dinner to be served in the hotel restaurant on the second night, Mark turned to Jeanie. "I have to tell you that the National Institutes of Health offered me a grant to do viral research at their headquarters in Bethesda, Maryland."

"How exciting! How could you keep such a secret?"

"Well, I have mixed feelings about it."

"It's what you always wanted. You've talked about doing research for the NIH for years. And now it's happening. This is wonderful news!"

Jeanie's excitement was contagious, and Mark couldn't help remembering Ellen's disinterest when he had told her. He was silent now, and Jeanie sensed that something was wrong.

"You *are* going to accept the grant?"

"I'm not sure. Ellen doesn't think it's a good idea. She thinks doctors get lost in research and just scratch out a living. And she wants us to move to LA so she can join her father's practice. She says I can do research out there or teach at a university… even go into practice."

"How do you feel about that?" Jeanie probed, understanding for the first time that Mark would have to change his whole life for Ellen… even give up his dream.

"You know how I feel about research. I won't get rich doing it, but without it, there's no progress in medicine. I love research… but I don't want to lose Ellen. She's a wonderful woman."

"Surely you two can compromise."

"Ellen's not compromising."

Mark's words only fueled Jeanie's feeling that Ellen was wrong for him.

The waiter arrived with two large platters of steamed lobsters. Mark ordered a bottle of champagne. "You know you're spoiling me with all this good food and wine. I don't know if I can face going home to spaghetti dinners," Jeanie said, smiling.

"We could stay here and keep eating lobster and drinking champagne every night."

"It's been a wonderful vacation for me. Thank you for letting me tag along."

"I'm glad you're here. I've enjoyed your company. I always have." Mark reached across the table, covering her hand with his. Jeanie didn't draw her hand away. She didn't know what to do or say, so she remained silent, relishing the warmth of his hand on hers.

They lingered over coffee, listening to a three-piece band play familiar melodies. In the center of the lavishly-decorated restaurant was a small dance floor, surrounded by huge potted plants, where several couples danced. "Would you like to dance?" Mark asked as the band played *Moon River*.

"I'd love to." Jeanie rose from her chair.

They walked to the dance floor and Mark held Jeanie close as they danced. She tried not to concentrate on his body pressed against hers, and it took all her control to keep from stroking his face and telling him how much she loved being in his arms.

When the music ended, Jeanie no longer trusted her impulses. "I think I'd better get to bed early tonight," she said. "I'm going to visit my mother tomorrow. It's a long drive, and I need to get an early start."

Mark signed the bill and they took the elevator up to their room. Once inside the room, Jeanie kicked off her high-heeled shoes. Mark turned on the TV. "Look, an old Judy Garland film... *Meet Me In St. Louis*."

"That's a great oldie. I think I'll watch for a while." Jeanie sat next to Mark on the sofa.

They were silent, absorbed in the film for half an hour, unconsciously aware that they were only inches apart. Mark loosened his tie and took off his jacket. As he reached across the sofa to toss his jacket on a chair, his hand brushed against Jeanie's bare arm. She turned to look into his eyes and he saw something in hers that he had never seen before—desire. Impulsively, his hand moved to her cheek, touching it tentatively, as though discovering something new. Jeanie barely moved or breathed, his touch sending exquisite shocks through her. She turned her face up to his. He bent to kiss her lips, and suddenly she was in his arms and there was no longer any hesitation in his touch. They kissed and kissed again. He stroked her hair and buried his face in her neck. Neither of them could stop now. Their bodies moved as one. Their feelings, suppressed for so long, were set free, carrying them far from reality. Their lovemaking was all that existed now. Jeanie gasped as waves of pleasure swept over her.

When it was over and they lay in each other's arms, Jeanie wondered if it had all been a dream, something she had unconsciously fantasized about, longed for. But when Mark covered her face with soft kisses, she knew it was not a dream. He was real and he was beside her now, holding her in his arms. A deep fulfilling peace enveloped her. She wished this moment would go on forever. Jeanie had believed she would never love again after David. And this was an incredible unexpected gift. It had happened so naturally that it had taken them both by surprise.

After a long while, Jeanie slipped out of Mark's arms. She sat up and looked into his eyes. "I love you. I… I'm sorry this happened. I haven't any right to…"

Mark pressed his finger to her lips to silence her. "Not now. Let's not talk now."

"But we have to. You're engaged to Ellen. You're going to be married in a few weeks. And I have no right to you. But I love you. I was too stupid to realize it before. I know you love Ellen and she's beautiful and bright…"

"Do you think Ellen or any other woman could ever have made me stop loving you? I've always loved you." Mark took her hand, pressing his lips into the palm.

"But you're going to marry Ellen."

"All these years, Jeanie, I waited for you… hoping. I finally gave up because I thought it was futile. Now everything's a mess." Mark sighed deeply.

"What do you want to do?"

"I don't know. I don't want to hurt Ellen." Mark looked pained.

They talked long into the night, deciding nothing, and then finally, exhausted, they slept in each other's arms. They had agreed that Jeanie would visit Sophie in the morning, leaving Mark alone for the day to think.

Chapter 55

Jeanie rose early the next morning, borrowed Mark's car and set out for Sophie's house on the west coast of Florida. She hadn't phoned ahead to tell Sophie she was coming. She didn't know what she would say to her mother after all this time, but something propelled her—a nagging question still forming in her mind and weighing heavily on her heart.

***

Several hours later, Jeanie pulled up in front of Sophie's gray weathered house. She stepped out of the car onto a broken concrete path. A leafless tree leaned menacingly against one side of the house, and a lone tiger lily bloomed in the weed-choked lawn. The flower stood out starkly like the only sign of life in a surrealistic painting.

Jeanie walked along the path to the front door and knocked hesitantly, her hand trembling slightly. She heard slow shuffling footsteps behind the door—an old woman's footsteps. The door creaked on rusty hinges as Sophie opened it. She stood in the doorway—large and shapeless, clad in a faded green housedress and frayed brown slippers. Strands of gray threaded her once dark hair. Purple shadows rimmed her eyes, and small creases lined her mouth.

Sophie looked at Jeanie as though a ghost stood before her, and her eyes filled with sudden tears. Then silently, she held out her arms to embrace her daughter. "Jeanie." Tears spilled down her cheeks and she held Jeanie in a tight embrace.

"Momma," Jeanie murmured softly, her face buried in her mother's shoulder, the anger she had felt for so long turned to pity now.

Sophie led her daughter into the shabbily-furnished living room. They sat facing each other on the threadbare brown sofa, not knowing what to say after all the time and pain and sorrow.

"You look wonderful," Sophie said. "What a surprise. You should have told me you were coming. I would have…"

"It was a last-minute plan. I can only stay for a few minutes." Jeanie's eyes rested on the dusty coffee table and the worn carpeting.

"A few minutes? But I haven't seen you for so long. What can I say in a few minutes?" She could tell her daughter now, Sophie thought. Now was the time. Jeanie had forgiven her. Why else was she here? "I want you to know that everything that happened in the past was not meant to hurt you. How could I have known?"

"I didn't come here to talk about the past."

"I'm glad you came." Sophie's eyes watered. "I didn't think you ever wanted to see me again. I'm going to make it up to you."

"You can't."

"Just listen. Two years ago, I invested in a real estate development in Florida. I made millions. I was keeping it a secret so I could surprise you and Albert and Ruthie. But it's time you knew because the money is for all of you. Someday it will all be yours and Ruthie's and Albert's." Sophie smiled broadly.

Jeanie was silent, searching her mother's eyes for something she had come here to learn.

"Didn't you hear what I said? You're a millionaire."

Jeanie didn't answer. She understood, finally, what she was searching for, why she had come here today. It was a truth she had never been able to face. There was no need to ask her mother if she ever loved anyone. Money was love to Sophie. It was as simple as that.

Jeanie rose from the sofa. "I'm going now."

"But you just got here. I wanted you to know about all the money. It's a dream come true." Sophie took Jeanie's hands in hers. "It's all for you. I did it for *all* of you."

"No, you did it for yourself. It's your dream."

"That's not true," Sophie protested.

"It's alright. I understand. And it's not important anymore. Goodbye, Momma." Jeanie embraced her and walked quickly to the door.

"Come back and visit again soon. Don't be a stranger," Sophie called from the open doorway as Jeanie hurried to the car. Sophie smiled and waved goodbye, happy that her daughter had forgiven her. She wondered why Jeanie hadn't seemed interested in the money. And what a strange thing she had said,

"It's your dream." All that money isn't a dream. It's reality, Sophie thought as she closed the front door and puzzled over why Jeanie seemed so ungrateful for the unbelievable wealth that would one day be hers.

***

Jeanie drove back to Ft. Lauderdale, back to Mark. As she sped along the highway, she thought about the past. Masada, David, and her mother's deception unraveled like a film in her mind. She had been a victim of Sophie's twisted love for money. But that part of her life was over now. She could love even though her mother was incapable of love. Sophie could never hurt her again. Jeanie brushed tears from her eyes now. She knew with certainty that she loved Mark and she was going to fight for him.

A roadside sign read 50 miles to Ft. Lauderdale. Jeanie had been driving for three hours, but she pressed down harder on the accelerator now, impatient to reach the hotel. She would tell Mark that he mustn't marry Ellen. Ellen was wrong for him, and he had to break off his engagement to her. As Jeanie got closer to Ft. Lauderdale, she prayed that Mark had arrived at the same decision.

***

It was dusk by the time Jeanie arrived at the hotel. She parked the car and hurried to the room. When she opened the door to the room, it was dark. She switched on the light and called, "Mark." There was no answer. He must have gone for a swim, Jeanie thought, kicking off her shoes. But when she opened the closet in search of her sandals, she saw that Mark's clothes were gone. She went to the dresser and opened the drawers where Mark had stored the rest of his clothing. They were empty.

Jeanie raced out of the room, slamming the door behind her. She took the elevator to the lobby and hurried to the front desk. "Has Dr. Mark Lerner checked out today?"

The clerk checked his registration book. "Yes, he did. Left a note for you." He handed Jeanie an envelope. She tore open the envelope and read a hastily-scribbled message from Mark.

Jeanie,

Sorry I had to leave before you got back. I had to fly out to LA to be with Ellen. Please drive my car back to New York for me. I'll explain when I see you.

Mark

Jeanie was stunned. She crumpled the note and threw it in a nearby trash basket. Then she turned to the clerk. "Please have my bill ready in the morning. I'm checking out."

"The bill's been taken care of by Dr. Lerner."

Jeanie walked back to the elevator, her face flushed with anger. There was only one explanation for Mark's hasty retreat. He couldn't face telling her that he was going to marry Ellen in spite of last night. She had lost. That was obvious. But Mark's cowardice angered her. And the way he had left, in such a hurry, without an adequate explanation, infuriated her.

Chapter 56

Jeanie started out for New York before dawn the next day. She was so incensed over Mark's behavior that she had hardly slept. Asking her to drive his car back to New York while he took off to visit his fiancée was insulting. Jeanie gave vent to her anger all through the first day of the long drive. By evening, she was so emotionally exhausted that she checked into a roadside motel and fell asleep immediately, giving no thought to dinner.

She woke the next morning with renewed energy, ravenously hungry, her anger subdued. After breakfasting on French toast and coffee at the motel coffee shop, she started on her way again.

All through the day and into the evening, Jeanie drove steadily. Slowly her anger turned to resignation. She reviewed everything in her mind over and over again, finally concluding that it was Ellen who Mark loved, not her. She had given him time to think things over, and his absence when she returned was proof of his decision. Why else did he rush off to be with Ellen before she had even returned? He couldn't face her and tell the truth—not after their night of lovemaking. They never should have made love, but she did not regret it. She simply misinterpreted the depth of Mark's feelings, or perhaps she had projected her own feelings.

Jeanie opened the car window, but not even the breeze that swept over her could temper the thoughts that tormented her. She shouldn't have come to Florida with Mark. Maybe she unconsciously wanted all this to happen. Now she'd ruined a long and special friendship. Mark will marry Ellen, Jeanie decided with conviction. Only a little over a day ago, she was determined to fight for Mark. Now she must tell him their lovemaking was a mistake. She didn't want him to feel guilty about her. She would apologize, let him off the hook… tell him that he and Ellen belonged together.

By 2:00 a.m. the next morning, Jeanie pulled up in front of her apartment building in Manhattan. She took her suitcase out of the car, walked into the building and took the elevator to her apartment. Relieved to be home at last, she threw the car keys on the kitchen table, deciding that tomorrow, after a good night's sleep, she would return Mark's car and tell him everything she had planned to say.

***

The next day was Sunday. In spite of everything on her mind, Jeanie slept late. Two days of driving and the emotional energy she had spent trying to resolve things in her mind had exhausted her. Now she felt depleted as she dressed slowly, trying to delay her inevitable meeting with Mark.

***

It was 1:00 o'clock in the afternoon by the time Jeanie rang Mark's doorbell. He opened the door and stood before her, dressed in faded jeans and a white sweater, tanned, looking irresistibly handsome. "Ah, the woman I've been waiting for." He smiled warmly. "What took you so long?"

Jeanie stepped into the apartment, disarmed by Mark's smile. "I brought your car back. It's parked around the corner." Her voice was flat as she handed him the car keys.

"What kind of greeting is this?" Mark searched her eyes, a puzzled look on his face. "What's wrong?"

"Nothing... nothing at all," she stammered, forgetting her planned speech now. "How's Ellen?"

"Ellen's okay. I stayed for the funeral and then came right back to..."

"What funeral? Who died?"

"I didn't have time to explain in my note. While you were visiting your mother, I got a frantic call from Ellen in LA. Her father died suddenly of a cerebral hemorrhage... All those doctors around and no one could save him. There was only one flight out of Ft. Lauderdale to LA that day and I barely had time to pack."

"I'm sorry about Ellen's father," Jeanie said. "She must be very upset."

"She is. The whole family is. Ellen stayed in LA with her mother and..."

"I suppose you'll be getting married soon."

"I expect to."

"I... hope you'll be very happy. I really have to go now." Jeanie turned to leave, desperate to escape before tears spilled down her cheeks.

Mark was behind her now, his hands on her shoulders, stopping her at the door. He spun her around, his eyes flashing. "When we made love, you told me you loved me. Do you say that to everyone you make love to?"

Jeanie's hand swung out in anger, but Mark caught it in midair and held tight. "Tell me the truth, Jeanie. No more long dialogues about what great friends we are and how sex will spoil it. Did making love spoil everything for you? You sure fooled me the other night. You should have been an actress instead of an archaeologist."

All the pent up emotions that had consumed Jeanie for days came rushing out in a flood of tears. Mark still held tight to her arm. "Tell me how you really feel!" Mark demanded.

"I love you, and you belong to someone else." Her words spilled out in broken sobs.

Mark took her in his arms, burying his face in her hair. "It seems like I've waited all my life to hear you say you love me." He stroked her hair and Jeanie looked into his eyes, bewildered. "But you're going to marry Ellen."

"You didn't give me a chance to explain. You came here with your mind made up. Ellen and I broke our engagement. It was a mutual decision. She wanted to stay in LA and take over her father's practice, and she wanted me to stay there with her. Ellen had my whole life planned and I had no part in the planning. I also decided to accept the research grant with the NIH, and Ellen wouldn't hear of it."

"And if Ellen had agreed to everything you wanted?" Jeanie asked.

"What do you think?"

"I don't know anymore."

"I love you. I always have. That's the real reason I couldn't marry Ellen. I knew it would never work."

Jeanie put her arms around Mark. Then she kissed him. It was a long sensuous kiss. "I'm going to tell you I love you every day for the rest of my life."

"Is that a promise?"

"It is."

"Then stop crying." Mark brushed the tears from her face. "You're not supposed to cry when you're happy."

ELAINE BOSSIK had three careers: as magazine editor, medical writer and teacher in the New York City school system. She is now a staff columnist for Scriptologist.com, writing how-to articles for aspiring screenwriters under the name of Elaine Radford.

While her professional experience helped shape her writing, her fascination with people—their motivations and the everyday dramas they create—is the inspiration for her fiction. She believes that really great stories begin and end with provocative characters.

Growing up in Brooklyn, NY and as a young adult traveling in Israel, she found the rich details for the events that take place in this novel.

Visit Elaine Bossik's Web site at www.elainebossik.com

Visit the publisher, Portable Shopper, LLC, at www.scriptologist.com

CPSIA information can be obtained
at www.ICGtesting.com
Printed in the USA
LVOW13s0717290318
571589LV00033B/505/P